the game
of giants

the game

of giants

a novel

marion douglas

Freehand Books gratefully acknowledges the financial support for its publishing program provided by the Canada Council for the Arts and the Alberta Media Fund, and by the Government of Canada through the Canada Book Fund.

This book is available in print and Global Certified Accessible™ EPUB formats.

Freehand Books is located in Moh'kinsstis, Calgary, Alberta, within Treaty 7 territory and Métis Nation of Alberta Region 3, and on the traditional territories of the Siksika, the Kainai, and the Piikani, as well as the Iyarhe Nakoda and Tsuut'ina nations.

FREEHAND BOOKS
freehand-books.com

Library and Archives Canada Cataloguing in Publication
Title: The game of giants : a novel / Marion Douglas.
Names: Douglas, Marion K. (Marion Kay), 1952– author.
Identifiers:
  Canadiana (print) 20240286316
  Canadiana (ebook) 20240286324
  ISBN 9781990601644 (softcover)
  ISBN 9781990601651 (EPUB)
  ISBN 9781990601668 (PDF)
Subjects: ISBN: Novels.
Classification: LCC PS8557.O812 G36 2024 | DDC C813/.54–dc23

Edited by Naomi K. Lewis
Design by Natalie Olsen
Author photo by Monica Bennington
Printed and bound in Canada

SECOND PRINTING

Canada Canada Council for the Arts Conseil des Arts du Canada Alberta Government

Dedicated to the memory of Anna M. Ellis

the game

of giants

one

MY PARENTS HAD joined a choir, the Mesmer Voice Capades, and were suddenly out in the evening. As a result, during the fall and winter of 1964, a middle-aged woman named Constance Tandy babysat my brother Adrian and me. Constance had been a teacher and still did some supply work, and this, in my eyes, gave her authority. Also, I liked her voice; it was low and unhurried, a lozengy drone from a face I recall up closer to mine than most, in fact any, others had been.

She liked to tell Adrian and me about her sightings of ghosts, an outline of a great aunt she had seen by the pump on their farm, on a foggy night, or a gesture from a shape by a misty pond. "Looked a lot like my grandmother," she said, "couldn't have been a coincidence." As if the similarity were what was remarkable, not the spectre in the dark. But because Constance never seemed to get a crystal-clear view of her figures, I was skeptical, even at the age of eight, and it fell to me to reassure Adrian, who was fourteen months younger and scared. I must have been unconvincing, because to this day he still believes in spirits and haunted places but not necessarily souls, unlike my girlfriend Lucy who believes in life or something after death and is never afraid of what might be there in the dark or the void.

Constance was fired. After Mom and Dad left the choir (Mom having been diagnosed with bladder cancer, and survived, to be fitted with, as she has said so many times, an unacceptable bladder bag), both parents said that they should have "let Constance go" at the start of all that ridiculous talk, not just because the topic was ghosts, but also because she was a kleptomaniac. I will never forget hearing that word for the first time: a something maniac. Immediately, I thought of a twirling creature, a baton on legs. "What's that?" I asked Mom.

She said, "A person who can't help but take things." This was even better. I pictured hands under a higher power. *I can't help but take this thing.*

"But how do you know?" I asked. "How do you know she's a kleptomaniac?"

"It's common knowledge," said Dad.

This was also the first I had heard of common knowledge, another gripping discovery. Everybody knows the common knowledge.

At the time, I had a coin collection in a flimsy narrow cardboard box without even a lid. One of the corners had come partially unglued. I had a few fifty-cent pieces and older dimes, pennies, and nickels I thought had some significance and future value, and one silver dollar from 1956, the year I was born. For security reasons, I suppose, I kept the box in the living room, on a bookshelf where I rarely checked on it, jammed as it was behind two childrearing guides, Dr. Spock and another book called *Up the Years from One to Six*, which I assumed no one ever bothered to read. Upon learning of Constance's klepto-mania, I thought of my coins but did not check on them immediately. How would Constance have known the whereabouts of my collection, unless *she* had decided to consult Dr. Spock, which she would never have done, would she? I wanted the suspense and the real and pos-sible horror, which took on a *shape* like a quivery pair of white fabric gloves, to be mine alone. I waited three days, until Mother was out at a doctor's appointment, Dad was working (he had his dental practice in the front room and insulated sunporch), and Adrian was outside, in the yard, in his snowsuit.

I guess it was after school hours. I looked at Adrian through the kitchen window; the snow was Ontario slush, and he was as wet as someone who had walked into a lake and returned to shore, and yet he would not likely come inside until I called him. Ideal conditions for a spine-rattling discovery. I went to the living room and withdrew the childrearing books, and there it was, empty space, nothing. My collection was gone, and I felt a shadowy affiliation with Constance: I may have loved her. I returned the books, walked to the kitchen, and looked again at Adrian. A gust of wind brought a silhouette, an out-line, of snow and condensation down upon him. He looked up, and I knew that had he known a kleptomaniac or a ghost had taken my coins, he may have screamed the way Roger, my son, has been known to, out of excitement and anxiety. But he had no idea, and I didn't tell him, or anyone, my collection was gone, and no one but me missed it. I wanted the kleptomania all to myself, which goes to show there was a high-ish percentile rank level of emotional hoarding there from early on. I can't blame my *self*, or my occasional Roger-ambivalence, on my parents.

In the parking lot of the Children's Hospital, for instance, after Roger's developmental assessment, I wanted to make a run for it.

"We might have something more empirical by this afternoon." That's what the pediatrician, Dr. Von Daniken, the first to see Roger, had said, as if he would be handing us a hospital clipboard with encouraging pie charts. I had high hopes. Then later, at the conference with the assessment team, Von Daniken had asked, "Do you understand the meaning of percentile ranks?"

"Yes, yes, I do," I said, with obvious irritation.

"It's not the same as a percentage."

"Yes, yes, I know that." Saying yes twice, twice.

"Imagine there are one hundred rungs on a ladder and Roger is at the third."

I said, "I *know* what a percentile rank is. So does Lucy. We have both taken a statistics course or two" — although Lucy later told me she hadn't, and that the explanation had been helpful. We'll take the reports and be on our way, I wanted to say, but you can't walk out on the medical profession, and we stayed until we had heard all the discouraging numbers.

On an April afternoon in Calgary, before the clocks had changed, the sun was getting low, but everyone else in the parking lot knew spring was here to stay. You could tell by the way cars were reversing out of spots with assuredness, while my restless legs wanted to run, and I think I could have gone some distance, to the foothills, loping along Highway 1. But I didn't run, and Roger chose that moment to begin to tell time. He loved watches, they were his hobby, he was wearing two on his left wrist, and as Lucy was looking for her pack of cigarettes, from the backseat Roger said, "Four o'clock," clear as a bell. Lucy made a big fuss, getting out of the car and unbuckling

Roger and telling him he was at the top percentile rank. I was glad, but I must confess I thought it was nothing more than a lucky guess. He was not yet three and had moments before heard me say it was almost four. I was smiling but angry, a trick I have.

"Roger's life is his life," I said to Lucy, when she was back in the driver's seat. "I won't let it be clubbed into dank submission by those people, thank you Charles Bukowski for that thought. Or *my* life either. We won't be clubbed by the pediatrician and the so-called support so-called team."

"They really didn't seem like they wanted to club us," Lucy said, "into submission," she added. Cigarette in hand, she was waiting for the lighter. "They wanted to be helpful."

"Well, I *feel* clubbed, so therefore I am." I was whispering, of course, so Roger would not hear. "I feel sick. I feel empty. I think I've lost the guts I used to have because they've been clubbed out of me."

The lighter popped out. Lucy lit up and exhaled. "No you haven't," she said, as she put the car into reverse. "You still have all your guts." She smiled at me, then at Roger in the rearview mirror.

Later that day, that night, with Roger in bed and me in the bathroom, staring into the mirror, searching for causes in my eyes and the shape of my mouth and the palm of my hand, I remembered Constance and kleptomania and thought, I have it! Or something very similar, a secret cache of bagged goods that if slashed open would look like a load of wet and unwashed snowsuits pulled from the storm drain when the system backed up. Oh, that's nothing, I would say, gathering up my warm and fungal worries, not a coin collection, that's for sure. Go ahead and cringe.

I didn't run down the highway, I didn't run out of the house on 6th Street (that day), I stayed for a long time in the bathroom with the many misty shapes of things to come and tried as I have so many times since to arrange the cause with the effect and failed. Returning to the living room, I was like a hive of insects, some with stingers, others just ready to buzz, and I said to Lucy, "Even if there is a Dennis, a brother of George, I'm pretty sure Roger gets a lot of it, a lot of the third percentile, from me. When I look in the mirror, I see a low-grade type of maniac."

Lucy sighed, rather unsupportively.

two

WHEN GRANDMA DRURY died, Dad shut down his dentistry practice for five days plus Sunday, and he and Adrian and I drove to Fort William, which is now half of Thunder Bay. Mom was going to come but changed her mind at the last minute, a tactic she employed so often we were incredulous when she did join us. "Oh, Mom," Adrian said.

"Suit yourself," said Dad, neither angry nor sad. I wonder if Mom wanted us to plead with her, or if she really didn't want to come, or if she wanted to be alone, with all of us out of her field of vision. She made us sandwiches, and very early in the morning we left with a cooler.

We would be staying in a motel somewhere and arriving for the second day of visitation, which Dad explained to us would mean looking at Grandma in her coffin. Immediately and in his adamant fashion, Adrian said, "I can't do that," but I knew I would have to, and that I could. Grandma Drury was my best relative, and there weren't many from which to choose. Along with dead parents, Mom also had no siblings. For years, I did not entirely believe this and thought she had a concealed family of brothers and sisters. I looked at houses for signs of them, the Lowes. (Lorna Lowe was Mom's maiden name; you should be a movie star with that name, her friends from Owen Sound, whom we never met, used to tell her.) Dad's family was far away and hardly counted, except for Grandma, who wrote unforgettable messages in her cards, like, *keep smiling cutie* and *wear this brooch and think of your old grandma*, things I said to myself in times of sorrow and yearning. Hearing from Dad I would have to look at my grandmother, dead, in a coffin, had brought me to a halt and then a divide. I was one part carrying on, drinking water, eating toast, and one part waiting to be electrocuted. So that when I finally did see her, I felt relief: all I had to do was look. I had worried myself into thinking there would be more, I would have to lie next to her, or thank her, make a coffin speech, I'm not sure. I looked, and then I turned away. She was not breathing, that was certain.

Seconds later, Dad flopped to his knees and sobbed. In my peripheral vision, I saw his sudden and bulky movement, his *shape*, and for a moment thought Grandma had risen from the dead. Very briefly I was joyous, then I knew better. The immediate problem became, no one went to Dad. His three brothers, even Uncle Angus who had a reputation for being jittery and always looking for distractions, things to fix or arrange or break, all stood motionless in the receiving line.

Already, Adrian was outside with his cousins; he was carefree. Taking a glance at eternity and Grandma, unrisen, I said, "Dad, it's okay. She's in heaven, I'm pretty sure." On his knees, he cried more noisily, like a kindergartener, and I deduced that he had been Grandma's favourite, he had become a dentist, after all, while the others standing there doing nothing to provide solace had stayed in the area and become an insurance agent and a grocery-store owner and a con artist. I would have liked some reassurance from Grandpa that this was the case, but by then he had such severe dementia he wasn't allowed at the funeral. Everyone said it would have just confused him. I patted Dad's shoulder and said, "It'll be okay."

"No, no it won't," said Dad, meaning what, exactly, I did not care to know.

"Just stand up," I whispered, in a type of harried Jesus imitation. "It's okay, everything's okay." And at last Dad stood. (Eight years later, when his heart gave out, I thought maybe at the funeral, he'd been having a telltale cardiac spell of some sort.) But that day, at age eleven, after I had taken one more spellbound look at Grandma's face, I suspected that *okay* was not a word you would find on a list of recommended coffin-side guarantees.

If it is possible to faint and continue walking, to turn your consciousness dial to potato, that is how I survived the next two-and-a-half days. My cousins were all boys and at every key moment disappeared with Adrian. I began to wish I had a cold-, flu-, or lockjaw-type of excuse to escape and even called the train station from Grandma's house where we were staying to find out about schedules and fares; back then you could take the train right to Flax. But I had no money, and I couldn't leave Dad, and he promised me we would leave the day after the burial and the reception at the church. "What day will that be?" I asked. He didn't know for sure, something depended on Grandpa, then Dad had to answer the door for a neighbour with a cake.

Once the dream of the train ride home was abandoned, I floated on the surface of events to the graveyard and the interment, Dad having defined the word, me asking, "Does that have to be the plan?" This was early August; the sun was hot. I had not had enough to drink, and as a curious happiness began to rise from my feet to my face, I recalled the school trip I had taken to the Huron Village at Midland, and the story of the Huron tradition of digging up the dead and taking them along with each move. I vowed to Grandma, in a whisper behind my right hand, I would dig her up when I had a house of my own and move her to a graveyard nearby, a place where the holes weren't so deep. Then I fell into the pile of dirt. I finally did faint. This time Uncle Angus made a move and picked me up and took me to his car. "I'm parked in the shade," I heard his deep voice vibrate into the bones behind my ear. In the backseat, he had some *mix* and gave me a drink, I'm pretty sure it was lemon gin with lemon lime, and I told him he was nice. I think that was the first time I paid an adult a genuine compliment and became aware of wanting compliments in return. Angus just said, "Thanks, honey." We sat and drank the mystery liquid until it was time to head to the church. "Let's go get ourselves some sandwiches and date squares," he said, gesturing out the window to Dad that he would drive me. Again, presumably drunk on mix, I told Angus he was nice, to which he sniffed outward loudly through nostrils I observed closely, waiting for more, as if they might take a stab at speaking, nasally I supposed, *you're pretty nice yourself there, Rosie.*

After the funeral, on the long ride home to Flax, I invented coatex. I was nowhere near puberty and did not even know the function of Kotex, other than to understand it was a private product having to do with women, Mom. Coatex was its parallel product, I decided. It was an internal coat, inside me, a warm wrapping at my very centre, not including my heart necessarily, which was off to the left. Coatex warmed my shuddery bright interior, as if I had a car light in a coat in the dark centre of myself. I never told my friend Anastasia or anyone about coatex, but by the time I returned to Flax, my vital signs were enveloped. I've never been well equipped. Some are, others are not. I've seen this even among the parents at Roger's pre-kindergarten: you can pick out the trembling ones. A close-up look at death, and my father falls to his knees. I faint. I expect an uncle to speak through his nose, I coat myself with coatex. I dig in below the third percentile rank. I carry on. Along the way, little bits of damage may have occurred, events may have snapped a thread of DNA or frayed a fragment of the more unknowable RNA.

SEPTEMBER 1971, I missed the first two days of Grade 11, the Tuesday and Wednesday after Labour Day, because of an ear infection. On Wednesday night, feeling better from the antibiotics Dad found for me in a drawer, I biked to my best friend Anastasia's. Upstairs, Anastasia's room was cool and dark as always, with the shade down and the window open. There was no breeze, and I could smell the dog, King, who lifted his head from the bed where he lay next to Anastasia.

"Hi, King," I said.

"Sorry about your ear," said Anastasia, lying on her back, staring at the ceiling. "Although it's hard to be *that* sorry, because I've never had an ear infection, so I don't know what it's like."

"Well, it hurts, or it did."

"But it's all in your head."

"Yes, har har, I guess so." I kissed King's forehead and sat in Anastasia's desk chair.

"I'm in love with Mr. Beebe," she said. "We're in the same class, by the way, thanks for asking. 11B. It's nearly all girls for some reason. You, me, Ruby, Lorraine, Audrey, and etcetera and etcetera. Maybe that's why I fell in love with Mr. Beebe in the first five minutes of geography class. He started talking about his personal life, about how he's not interested in buying a big new car every other year, in fact he has the oldest, most beat-up car in the teachers' lot, that the rear window got smashed and he's fixed it up himself by removing the broken bits of glass and he might just leave it that way. So, I went out into the teachers' lot at noon the first day of school to look around, and there it was. I stood right behind it, and I could smell HIM wafting out from the interior of the car, and I started to fall in love more." Anastasia played with King's floppy left ear. "I'm going to put some underwear in his desk," she said.

"Why don't you put it in his car?"

"His wife or kids might find it, that's why. So I'll need you to do the actual drawer work. Ha ha. Drawer work, if that's okay. It'll be new, back-to-school underwear, stainless, I mean. Will you do it? I won't let you get caught."

"Yes," I said. "Sure. Why not?" Anastasia never ruffled my surface, I didn't allow it, and so, hence, ergo, I usually wound up doing as she told me, despite having been called once, by Anastasia herself, a patsy. "Is this the new Latin book?" I asked, lifting a heavy beige text titled *Latin for Canadian Schools*.

With Anastasia's assistance, King nodded his large head. And this is how I came to spend an entire night in the nurse's room at the Mesmer and District High School, and to see death again, and to have my central nervous system jangled.

Mr. Beebe discovered the pale yellow underwear, still creased from its packaging, in his drawer less than thirty minutes after it had been placed there, *secreted* Anastasia liked to say, by me, early one sunny September morning. Judging from his first-day-of-school soliloquy on the topic of indifference to social standing, it may be that he was a little depressed, throwing up his hands, because rather than go to the principal with the underwear he taped it to his blackboard with the chalk question, "Did anyone lose these? Please claim at your earliest convenience." Abby, Anastasia's sister, perhaps because she was in the ninth grade, perhaps because her mother still dressed her (she was a child teen), allegedly raised her hand and said, "Those belong to my sister. I'll take them for her."

Abby can't have known, but she was skilled at guessing the truth and sneaking around undetected, which created the impression she was clairvoyant. Back then there were not that many varieties of girls' underwear available, and they tended to be homogeneous in everything but size and a few pastel variations in colour; Abby would at least have known this. Anastasia was horrified but would never betray such a blunt emotion. She told people her sister had some psychological problems, and that she, Anastasia, did not own any pale, yellow panties: the truth, as she had given her only pair to Mr. Beebe.

To me, she said, "You need to help me out. We need a diversionary tactic. I can't have Mr. Beebe or anyone thinking or even suspecting or even half-thinking, having a subconscious thought, that I did this, so I want you to go into Mr. Beebe's room and write on the black-board at the back of the room in big block letters. I want you to write, 'Anastasia Van Epp may be a slut, but the panties are mine. Signed, Anon.' That way I am no longer a suspect. Obviously, I would never write that about myself. And because it will take some time to write the message, because I want big letters, filled in, not empty, I want chalk-filled letters, you might have to stay in the school until Drake" — the janitor — "leaves, then write the message, then," and Anastasia paused because now she knew she was about to ask too much, "maybe even sleep in the nurse's room, because I think the doors are set so an alarm goes off if you leave after a certain time. But that would be easy. All you would have to do is get up early and stay in the girls' bathroom for a while, then emerge. You can tell your parents you're at my place, that we have a geography project, which it is kind of."

Looking directly into Anastasia's eyes for maybe five seconds, I said, "I'm not worried about sleeping over in the nurse's room." What I wanted to say was, you actually want me to write *slut*, a word I have never spoken, or possibly even thought?

This was the cost of having a best friend two or three years ahead of her time. And so, I continued, saying I had no reservations and the thought of sneaking around in the empty school until Drake left, and sleeping in the nurse's room, filled me with elation. I was already thinking of the little flashlight I would bring and the food I could likely steal from the cafeteria. "This is something no one else on the planet has ever done," I said to Anastasia in my firmest tone of voice.

"Well, maybe." Anastasia did not, as a rule, encourage.

We wasted no time, as Anastasia was very eager to *clear* her name. Monday morning, I informed my mother I would be staying at the Van Epps' overnight to get started on a project, something pertaining to population growth. I had located the little flashlight on the weekend, checked its batteries by shining it around my room, savouring the promise of stealth, then shoved a change of clothing into my round overnight bag with its imitation silk lining and pockets for lipsticks and intimate female items requiring a designated pouch.

Of course, I had to keep the overnight bag in my locker, where it would fit only on the diagonal after some hard and deforming pushes. The day went by. With the anticipation of rescuing Anastasia's repu- tation, I probably had a touch of early onset mania, klepto or other. We spoke very little, and Anastasia along with everyone else left the school at 3:24, because clubs had not yet started. I began my furtive skittering in the girls' washroom, which was conveniently next door to the nurse's room, my intended base camp. Back and forth I went, sometimes standing on a toilet in a locked cubicle while Drake was mopping the floor ("crazy fucking girls" he said, pushed on the door and left), sometimes hiding behind the filing cabinet in the nurse's room. For a reckless ten or more minutes, I sat on the bed, listening to Drake vacuuming nearby. I imagined what I would think the vacuum cleaner was if I did not know it was an electrically powered device for suctioning dirt, what a worried girl from Puritan times might think. The devil, I presumed, the growling approaching voice of Satan.

I looked into the hallway and, with Drake's back to me, slid in my knee socks to the stairwell and down to the band room. Rumour had it Drake did not enter the band room because the band teacher did not trust him around the instruments with the vacuum, and already there were papers on the floor and a wrapped piece of Juicy Fruit, which I fell upon before settling in amongst the clarinets. If Drake did come in, I would say I was practising, had forgotten everything over the summer, which was true, although I was no longer in band; I had quit. Everyone signed up for band thinking it would be fun. "Band!" And then it turned out to be discordant drudgery, once so extreme I had actually fallen from my chair laughing, the type of laughter that feels at the time as if you may never recover, but you do, and there is Mr. Hofsteder, staring and waiting for you to get back on the chair with the clarinet.

I lay down for a while on the risers and fell asleep until six-thirty! The Juicy Fruit must have been drugged, though much of the previous night I had been awake with excitement, the madness, so maybe I was tired. By that time, I was pretty sure Drake was gone, but to be certain I would wait until seven, killing time by looking in Hofsteder's desk drawers. A pitch pipe. Another pitch pipe. Chalk galore to fit into his five-line staff-making device, the very sight of which made everyone ache for sleep while marvelling ever so remotely about this device for chalk and clefs. Who invented it? Who? Think of the asymmetry without it. Never minding the time, I went upstairs. I needed to forage.

The cafeteria would be dark, so I got the flashlight, leaving the overnight bag in my locker, slamming the locker door shut with an echoing bash of fearlessness. No one. In the cafeteria, a dim light shone from the kitchen, and I stood for a moment thinking Drake might be in there, making a sandwich, guzzling milk, but he wasn't. I made my way into the food preparation area, turned off the flashlight and gazed out into the empty and lifeless cafeteria. The room smelled like high school hair and luncheon meats. In the walk-in cooler, I found bread, apples, and a large jar of Cheez Whiz. Deeper inside, where I feared to go, were the meats, I assumed. I made myself two sandwiches, took two apples and poured a large glass of chocolate milk, washed the knife and put it away, took a tray, and carried my meal to the nurse's room. I turned on the desk lamp and ate. I was happy to be there. Although the building was not exactly saying *make yourself at home* to me, it was saying something.

One of my most memorable and tasty meals! I pushed the tray under the bed and went to get my overnight bag. The hall was dusky now, with light entering at regular intervals from the open doors of the classrooms. My locker was near the end of that main hallway, mere feet from Mr. Beebe's room, so I slammed my locker door shut again and decided now would be the best time to write the message. With still enough outdoor light and the wood-slat Venetian blinds down, no one would see me, whereas the flashlight would most certainly draw suspicion.

There stood the desks. The tops were hinged, and I lifted the one closest to Mr. Beebe's desk, thinking I might find a valuable, a jewel or a chocolate bar, a note — I was the ghost of Constance, apparently, unable not to want to take something — but it was empty and disappointing, so I got to work. Using the side of a half-length of white chalk and filling one entire section of blackboard, I wrote in capital letters: ANASTASIA VAN EPP IS A SLUT BUT THOSE ARE MY PANTIES (illustrated with an arrow indicating the underwear still taped to the wall behind Beebe's desk), signed, Anonymous. My heart was beating fast as I returned to the comfort of the nurse's room with my bag. There was a radio on the desk, so I turned it on and found the Windsor Motown channel, CKLW, and danced with Martha and the Vandellas, then sat down, buzzing. I had a fleeting urge to defile small objects, and I kicked over the nurse's trash can, then set it upright and realized I should report in to Anastasia on the nurse's clean phone. She picked up, and like an astronaut, I shouted, "Mission accomplished."

"Shhhh! That's fantastic!" Anastasia whispered. "You've got more guts than I thought you had." A compliment!

"Can anybody hear you? Or me?"

"No, they're all doing things. They're Van Epps. Did you forget?"

"Oh, okay. Well, I made a very delish sandwich from the walk-in fridge, and now I'm going to relax and do a bit of homework and go to bed. I brought a little travel alarm clock so I can wake up early."

"Thanks, Rose. I really, really appreciate it. Abby's threatening to start blabbing to my parents. I had to give her five dollars. You've for sure got more guts than I thought. You must have an extra pancreas or something."

"You sound a bit like you have laryngitis."

"Well I don't. We can't just blab in our normal voices."

"Okay," I whispered, "tomorrow it will all be taken care of. The new suspect will be Anonymous."

"Here comes Mom. I better go. See you."

Instead of homework, I began reading brochures from the nurse's desk drawer. One was titled Teens and Worry. Some studies suggested worry in teens could be caused by a lack of intimate support. The school nurse could in some situations provide this intimate support. Intimate support made me think of a Kotex belt, and then I remembered coatex. I put the brochure away. Had anyone ever stayed the night in the nurse's room of Mesmer and District High School? Until that date, most unlikely. I tried to close the blinds on the nurse's room window, but they did not respond to the lever; when I pulled the cord to lower them to the sill, they rose and stuck halfway up the frame. I looked out at the nighttime and the yard, remembering I had more guts than Anastasia had thought, and turned out the light.

In the night, I awoke to a very dark room and was frightened by myself, that is, of myself. My watch said three-fifteen, and I actually thought of calling Constance, she might have been awake, and I was likely the only person in Mesmer, in Flax and all of the surrounding towns, occupying such a large building alone. I imagined arenas and churches I knew of, but they were not in the same category, and besides, they would be empty as a public building should be at this hour. There were factories, but they would be humming with machinery and employ at least one security guard and two nighttime maintenance men sharing many megawatts of light, talking on walkie-talkies, knowing at all times where the others were, meeting for a smoke at a designated time and place. I could easily picture them and wished they were here. For a minute or two, I shuddered.

If I walked the hallways with the flashlight to hurry up time, surely the police would come. I simply had to accept the unlikelihood of any other building of Mesmer High School's dimensions housing a sole occupant in the dark. *Be that as it may*, Mom sometimes said, out of the blue. "Be that as it may," I said aloud. That is when I saw, or thought I saw, a shape, a face, momentarily appear and disappear outside the nurse's room window. I made a sound (a squeak from Roger's repertoire) and stood on the bed so as to hang a blanket from the curtain rod, a heavy but effective drape. It was likely just my imagination or someone up early, hunting or fishing, maybe a drifter, but regardless, no one with a key to Mesmer DHS, I assured myself. Cold and yet some comfort. I shook like King in the winter when he was sick, then I stopped. I was also hungry. Anastasia had better remember to bring me a butter tart. She had better say something more about my guts, how many I had, or offer up another type of compliment, that I should at the very least be on the basketball team. I turned on the overhead light and closed the door, and there were the desk and its drawers again, and the locked file cabinet. With the metallic indifference of things before me, I stood and turned off the light. Once my eyes had adjusted to the darkness, I pushed aside the blanket curtain and looked outside. Nothing and nobody, only the two maples and the long stretch of sidewalk to the street. My panic ebbed away.

I woke up before six. From the hallway came a very pale trace of the new day, the first percentile rank of morning. At six I would go outside. I didn't care if an alarm went off. I would run, and who would possibly be around to catch me? The principal, Mr. Warren, was at least fifty pounds overweight. I would also, thinking about my guts and Anastasia, take myself to the cafeteria with the wise and cautious use of my flashlight. Just keep it away from the windows, and low, toward the inside of the corridor. I would get myself another large glass of chocolate milk and two more Cheez Whiz sandwiches, then go outside.

Without incident, I travelled the hallways and entered the cafeteria and was soon ready to go with my glass of milk and sandwiches. Morning! I put on my jacket and waited, and the alarm was on my mind, at the back, then the front. I tried to deduce logically when it would be turned off, if it in fact existed, but morning was here, enough was enough. I went to an easterly facing window to view the conditions and was able to see a bit of uncluttered horizon, pink and red, in stripes, the colours of Abby Van Epp's favourite party dress, her clown gown, Anastasia called it.

I knew then where I wanted to go. Out the east door and across the street and down a slope was a no-man's land people called the selvage and through the selvage ran a path, created by high school students, to the trees and the railroad tracks where I planned to eat. With my glass of milk in my left hand and the sandwiches in my jacket pockets, I walked the long corridor and pushed open the door. My body wanted to teeter, but it did not. No alarm! Only birds who had been up for hours, no doubt, why had I not thought of them? I should have gone out earlier. The space around me was now a little brighter than the crows flying by, and there was the selvage, visible with its inviting pathway, grey against the dark, wet grass. In the lowest section, ground mist hovered, and I knew I was on my own, and this was fine. I ran across the street, trying for a smooth gait, and down the slope without tripping; this was a good way to run, actually, this could be a new event for the track and field day: the chocolate milk two-hundred-metre slap dash. Why slap? No reason. I disappeared into the trees and followed the path to the tracks, where I sat down. They were cold, but with my shaking hands I drank the milk. Leaning the empty glass against a notable tree, I decided to have the sandwiches farther down the line. The brightness to the east was climbing higher in the sky and onto and within the trees, whose trunks remained very black and independent while the crowns touched, I noticed. This was Dad's idea of heaven, trees, or so he had said when I asked him when Mom was in the hospital.

At first, I thought I smelled bacon, but it was just wood smoke, not the fresh kind thrown off by a merry fire, a *jub-u-lant* (to use Abby Van Epp's mispronunciation) fire, it was the final throes of a blaze from the previous night. I carried along the tracks toward the scent, looking for a place to sit and eat, when I spotted a delicate plume of smoke within the trees, thirty or forty paces from where I stood. Maybe someone was here with me. A crow cawed twice and fell silent. Thinking of guts, I walked toward the smoke, cracking a branch loudly, and was able to see a *shape* on the ground. Of course, I thought of the figure in the window, but there had been no reports of killers in the area, there never were, so I came closer and stopped. It was a boy, and although I was standing close enough to touch him, he didn't move. He was lying beneath a blanket, his head resting on cedar branches. I cleared my throat, and again, he didn't move, in a way that seemed at odds with early morning. My feet, standing there, so close to the boy's chest appeared disrespectful, so I knelt down and said, hello, quietly, then once more, louder. The crow cawed again, and the sun at that moment came fully up, just like that, rushing between the trees, and I could see that the boy's face was not right. I thought of Anastasia and touched his cheek. It was cold like a book that had been left outside overnight. Setting one of the sandwiches down for him, then the other, I stood up and left, taking the path to the edge of the selvage, where I stopped and waited, just within the trees. I knew I needed to wait for more than a while, because the school library didn't open until 7:45. I had to walk back and forth, within the trees, back and forth, on cold feet; I had to keep moving, but for short intervals I rested behind a specific tree and pictured the cold boy. My hands were no longer shaking, but I worried my breastbone might crack in half from a nervous desire to leave the scene.

At 7:46 by my watch, I entered the school through the front door. The secretary was there, and I could see the library was mercifully open. I went to my locker, found my history book, sat in a carrel, stared at the cover. I carried on; but at noon I told the secretary I was sick, my earache was back, and I called Mom to come and get me. I never told anyone about the person at the window and the boy I found and the dying fire and the sandwiches I left. How would I have explained my presence? And as for Anastasia, she would have blabbed to people just like her sister, eventually, making up a story for why I was there that morning that had nothing to do with her underwear. He, Lance Feldskov, was found later that day by two Grade 12 students who'd gone for a walk. I heard it all from Anastasia, who called that evening.

"They found a dead guy!" she screeched. "Did you hear? By the tracks, past the selvage. They had the cops and a coroner, and an ambulance had to drive across the selvage. It looked so strange. I don't think I'll ever forget that sight, the ambulance lumbering over the selvage. I think I might draw it for an art project."

Anastasia had not mentioned the sandwiches, which I worried might have implicated me via the dusting for fingerprints, and I stayed home the next day as well.

"By the way," Anastasia said when she called after school on Wednesday, "thanks again for taking care of the Mr. Beebe situation. Everybody thinks it was Ruth Ann Cole now. Mainly because she's saying it was. She just wants attention from him. Everybody does, apparently. Are they sheep, or what?"

"I don't know. Some are, I guess."

"You don't sound right. Is your eardrum broken?"

"No, but it's still hurting some."

"Well the story's all going to be in the papers tomorrow, the Mesmer paper and the Flax so-called paper. I already heard he was diabetic, and he didn't eat his sandwiches. If he'd eaten them he would still be doing whatever it was he was doing, running away from Kitchener. Did you see his friend on the news?"

I had not.

"His friend David. He kind of looked like a duck, his teeth or some-thing. Anyway, he said this Lance guy had some problems at school and at home, and he talked about running away, and he guessed he finally did it. Except he should have taken his insulin. He knew what that was like, because he has diabetes, too. Then he said, diabetes, type one, also, is what I meant. Then he kind of giggled. I had to respect the duck for that. He didn't put on a big show."

"I'll watch the news tonight," I said.

"Are you still in the hammock?"

"No. I was just in the hammock yesterday afternoon."

"Has your mom ceded the couch to you?"

"She's usually only there for some of the afternoon. She's actually doing the dishes now." I didn't like Anastasia to speak of my mother in this way. "I'm just going to help Adrian with his English. I don't want the couch."

The next day students in droves ran downtown at lunch to get a copy of the *Mesmer Times*. I stayed at school. Anastasia had a dentist appointment, with my dad. By the time I had my study spare at 2:15, there were several copies of the paper in the library, abandoned but emitting a warmth from living hands and the room, which was as hot and unusually humid as the day outside. There, on the front page, was a large school photo of Lance Feldskov. He looked like he was about to be interrupted in a daydream by the flash, he looked prepared to be startled.

Lance Feldskov had very dark hair and his skin seemed pale, but the photo was black and white, so, hard to tell. He did not wear glasses, and his eyebrows were scant; I wondered if he pulled them out. Occasionally a person did that, idly, while listening in class. He made me think of something I might find inside a box. I didn't mind that I had touched him. In the article, his dad was quoted as saying, "I was hoping he would go to university and become a lawyer." His mother was not quoted, or pictured. There was a picture of the friend, David, whose top teeth did protrude a bit, and a science teacher at his desk who said, "Lance got off on the wrong foot," meaning this school year. I wondered how, exactly.

Although the face in the paper caused a chill to pass through me, like a quick breath from the cafeteria walk-in freezer, I knew I would not likely faint. However, to be safe, I sat in a remote carrel and bent forward, put my head between my knees, and looked up my own skirt.

It was a pleated creation, navy blue. On Thursday and Friday we had to wear skirts, part of a phasing-in or phasing-out process from mandatory skirts and dresses to jeans or cords. The previous year we'd had to wear skirts on Wednesday, Thursday, and Friday.

I believed in the impossibility of fainting with one's head between one's knees. For some time, I assumed this prophylactic position, regarding the greyish gusset of my underwear and considering the landscape behind it. We had learned in biology, the female baby is born with its full complement of eggs, which meant when my mother was born Lorna Lowe, half of me was within her, meaning also that maybe half of me spent at least some brief time within my grandmother, as my mother gestated. Grandmother Lowe of the car accident. The same could be said of half of Lance Feldskov, and I wondered if his grandmothers were both alive and if I should someday call one or both of them. I still think that from time to time, but what would a phone call achieve?

I couldn't look at the paper again. Maintaining my first aid anti-fainting position, and using my hands like little trained animals on the surface of the carrel, I folded the paper together, then in half so the pictures would be hidden, and sat up until my equilibrium was restored. I turned my chair away from the wall and decided to take a look at the stacks.

NOW I'M WONDERING, was there some damage to an ovum or two, back then, when I came across Lance Feldskov? I missed my next period, and that had never happened before and has not happened since, except for when I was pregnant with Roger. Not one other time. I picture the ovum that was to be Roger staying rather than going, and then, eight years later, setting sail, a little worse for wear. I suppose that's a terrible thought. I don't share it. I love Roger, I'd give up my life for him, but I'm always wondering.

AND THEN THERE'S my mother.

The spring of 1974 I was in Grade 13, Ontario's extra year of high school. Anastasia had gone to the University of Guelph for early admission and had changed. When I called, she sounded as if another person were growing inside her, speaking through her larynx. She wanted to talk about *psychopathy*, she was interested in Charles Manson, she said she might never return to Flax, she wanted to be urbane. "Oh, okay," I said. "Interesting." This was a new Anastasia, but I missed her, she was still my only real friend, and I had split up with my boyfriend in March.

For the May 24 weekend, I decided I would hitchhike to Guelph; in those days, hitchhiking was common among teenagers. I asked Mom to drive me to an intersection of Highway 9 and a busy county road; from there I could get to Elora and then to Highway 6 and Guelph. She agreed. We drove the fifteen miles to the intersection, where she pulled into a gas station lot, and we sat for a moment with the engine idling. I didn't want to get out of the car. I think I wanted to have a coffee with her, but would not have said so. The landscape was grey, and the sky was low and threatening, and, with no warning, I began to cry. I sobbed, and I don't recall ever having sobbed before except once when I was four or five and got sawdust in my eyes, but never like this, for no reason and in the company of my mother.

She did not respond. She looked out the driver's side window as if to spare me the embarrassment of being a bladder bag of tears, and I stopped crying as suddenly as I had begun. I probably blew my nose, I had an army surplus bag like many young people had back then, and I likely did some rummaging in there, delaying, and Mom said, "I guess you should get going." I had to agree.

"Yes," I said, "I guess I should. Thanks for the ride." And I thought of the Alice Munro story. I left the car and headed to the side of the highway. I didn't wave, I didn't think anything of it, I didn't think that was strange, that was sad, why did I cry, why did my mother not say something or at least pat my hand, maybe I shouldn't go after all. I stuck out my thumb and got a ride all the way to Guelph with a man who was Baha'i. He gave me a book of scripture pertaining to his faith, and I took it, thinking Anastasia might be impressed, but at the bottom of the Gordon Street hill, within walking distance of the university, I dropped it in a garbage can. Then I decided I couldn't see Anastasia, and I reversed directions and hitchhiked homeward, but to Lake Huron. The route took me past my parents' house. Adrian was living in Port Elgin at that time, he had quit school soon after he turned sixteen and was already working for Bruce Nuclear or Douglas Point as it was called then, so I stayed with him. I was there by the time the sun went down, and as he opened the door to his bacon-infused apartment, my despair lifted.

Mom wasn't consistently like that, though, she wasn't, she had her ways of conveying connection. The Christmas before the hitch-hiking incident, I was still in a relationship with a boy in my grade known as JJ, short for John Jacob. In November, I decided I would make a gift for him, a scarf. Mom eagerly embraced this idea. She had been completely cancer-free for eight years and was prepared to be enthusi-astic. The scarf was black and green stripes in an endless garter stitch, a behemoth. I made errors and Mom did repairs. She was patient and kind. Completed, it was more like a man-shawl than a scarf, but Mom seemed to think it was quite an accomplishment; she wanted me very much to be a girl who made scarves for a boyfriend.

On our last date prior to the holidays, I presented the scarf to John Jacob. He was going skiing with his parents, so we would be apart for two weeks. He opened the package and wound the scarf around his neck, and it stood erect like a tube he could withdraw his entire head inside. I laughed, but he didn't, he said thanks, it's great, but he didn't have my gift yet. Two or three days before Christmas,

JJ must have dropped a package off on the front porch, because Mom found it and brought it inside and handed it to me in the kitchen, where I was sitting eating a shortbread cookie and drinking tea. The gift was small and cylindrical, about the height of a can of nuts but smaller in circumference. I would have taken it upstairs, but Mom said, "Aren't you going to open it?" She was excited, almost dancing, shifting her weight from one foot to the other. I had never seen her like that. I think she thought it was going to be jewelry, maybe even an engagement ring.

"I guess I will," I said. I was happy about making her happy and the likelihood my gift would please her. We had never had a similar type of moment, female like that, festive or promising. I can still see her upper body moving back and forth with glee, as if we were friends at a party. I opened the gift, and it was probably, in all the history of human courtship and its public display, one of the lowest points. I didn't ever tell Anastasia. The gift was a can of a type of aerosol spray, maybe Glade, but JJ had removed the wrapper and, in its place, taped a cartoon from a magazine or newspaper, the gist of which had something to do with human odours. I didn't read the entire text, but the message appeared to be that I stank or the air around me did, although I don't *think* that's what JJ meant. He thought he had a *quirky* sense of humour and most likely that this would be hilarious, not having come up with any better gift idea and being too cheap to buy something. But with my mother being there, with our shared anticipation — it was the most intimate moment I had ever had with her — we were both crestfallen. Once she had taken a look at the gift, and stopped moving of course, she was silent. I said, "I guess it's sup- posed to be a joke gift." I knew she felt a little sick about me feeling humiliated, and I felt I had disappointed her, and there was nothing for either of us to say about the tastelessness of a joke gift about odours for a girlfriend at Christmas, so when Mom wasn't looking, I took the gift up to my room so it would be out of sight. Then that night I put it in the trash outside, concealed inside two paper bags. We didn't say any more about it. I don't know if she told Dad or Adrian; I keep intending to ask if he ever heard about it.

"Never give a joke gift," my mother has said to me more than once, and I think she has forgotten why she says it. For the first several months of Roger's life, I think she may have categorized him as a joke gift, I don't know how else to put it, someone I could return for exchange. Did I? Did I think that?

three

I MET GEORGE, Roger's father, in the summer of 1975, in Fort Smith, in the Northwest Territories, while working as a volunteer after my first year of university, part of a summer exchange program meant to bring together people of different backgrounds and ethnicities. We were building an A-frame youth drop-in centre with a group of local people who were mostly the same age as we out-of-towners, that is, young, except for our supervisor and one man who left.

There were twelve of us who flew in from various spots in southern Canada, and we were housed in little apartments we called suites, with one double bed and a foldout couch. For some reason, there was no effort made to sort us out by gender, the arrangement was supposed to transcend such socially engineered nonsense. In my suite were George and Ruby and me. Ruby and I shared the bed, and George had the foldout couch.

Ruby was the youngest of us all, and she was homesick. She spent one entire night in our bed, crying, with her head on my shoulder. At first I felt sorry for her, then I began to worry about building an A-frame the next day on no hours of sleep. It's a little bit interesting (to me): my mother's number one emotion is to feel sorry for others (she hardly knows), and I have limited patience for the weeping of acquaintances. Mom would have done well with Ruby, whereas I became tired of her mucous on my T-shirt.

After three days, Ruby went home. Then the oldest, a tall, bald man named Stanley who must have been at least in his fifties set up a kind of shrine in the hallway late at night with candles, knocked on our doors, and invited us to pray. He was naked. The rule of law was breaking down, but nobody was in charge, certainly not our foreman, Gerry, who had arrived from Windsor with his large bag of pot. Luckily, Nancy from PEI, who had organized the cooking schedule, called the cops. Next day, Stanley was gone. And for some reason, the night of Stanley's shrine, with Ruby out of the picture, George, in our now two-person suite, lit a couple of candles himself and moved into the bed with me. For this, he had a communist's rationale, explaining that in a few years, society would collapse, and we'd all be living in suites, paired up with someone, working for nothing, peeling logs for community centres in northern Canada. Sometimes he seemed to be joking and sometimes not, which was a problem we all had with George. Who was he really? I learned later the communist talk was unserious, he was a psychological libertarian, he said, and rarely voted. But at the time he moved into my bed, I didn't think it really mattered who George was, as I had concluded we were living in an eight-week sociology experiment after which I would return home to my parents, both of whom would still be alive and living in Flax, and onward to my second year of university.

However, I fell under the spell of George, and when it was time to leave, he talked me into going to his parents' ranch. They had just gone away for six weeks, he said, to Europe, to Italy, and I agreed to go because I wasn't that wild about returning to university, and I liked the sound of the word *ranch*. (I have always been drawn to individual words and a person's manner of speaking, one of the many reasons I like and love Lucy, and to a certain extent Asa, with whom I had a brief, *emotional only*, affair.) George introduced the idea as we were lifting off from the Fort Smith airport. This was the end of August, and all the spruce trees were as green as they would always be, massed together around the town like a placid horde, waiting for the houses to crumble. The river was neatly confined to its trough, a little low, with rocks breaking the surface near the townsite. Those rocks reminded me of a type of date George and I had been on. One Sunday morning he'd said, "I found a nice spot by the river. Do you want to go take a look? I'll make some sandwiches with your wonder bread." (I baked all the bread, and it was so good, my fellow suite-dwellers called it won-der bread) "We can have a picnic," he said. "I love picnics. I don't think I've been on a picnic since I was maybe seven or eight, with my mother and sister." George often used the same word three or four times in one spoken paragraph. He delighted in repetition for emphasis.

"Sure, George, that sounds nice."

We walked from our brown six-plex to the river's edge and hop-scotched over the large rocks as far as we could into the river's body where the rapids were still tame. The Slave River was a place from elementary school textbooks, a place I had thought about long ago, and then there I was. I told this to George, who sat in his white T-shirt and jeans, unwrapping the sandwiches. He had brown hair and brown eyes, and the back of his head was flat, a feature which made him seem in need of help. Dimples appeared when he smiled, and because of these, everyone trusted him, except Nancy.

George had said, "Alberta is just down there," indicating south with a nod of his head. "Not that far at all." A point he made again, repeatedly, as we took off in the little twin-engine plane. "Within a few minutes, we'll be flying over Alberta. I'm pretty sure those trees are relatives of Alberta trees; I think we can see some Alberta buffalo already, I bet they've got Alberta buffalo licenses. They have to, they're in Wood Buffalo Park, it's a government-run place."

As we climbed into the northern blue sky, George looked out the window and shrugged his shoulders. "You should stay for a while, stay at my parents' ranch. They have a little cabin. You could stay there. They're going away for six weeks, they're already gone, so you wouldn't have to spend any time with them. Not that they're ogres or anything, but we could be there, we could camp out on the land, we could set our souls free." He turned and smiled his dimples into place.

By the time we landed in Edmonton, I had said, okay, sure. George said, "You'd better call your parents so they don't come to Toronto to meet you tonight," then gave me a pile of quarters so I wouldn't have to reverse the charges. "Nobody likes reversed charges," he said.

I listened to the coins bing into place, very aware of being a person who was going to a ranch.

Dad answered and I said, "Hi! I'm not coming home just yet, so I hope you and Mom haven't left for the airport yet."

"No, we're still here as is evident by the fact I am able to answer the phone. How are you?"

"I'm fine. I just don't have much time to talk. I'm going to stay on at a friend's ranch near Calgary for a while. I'm putting off university for a year or six months."

"Are you sure that's a good idea? They say . . ."

"Yes, I'm positive it's a good idea. I have to go. They're going to want more quarters. I'll call when I get to the ranch." I enjoyed saying ranch, I was infected with George's tic for repetition. "Say hi to Mom for me."

"Okay, bye, then. If you're sure."

And as it turned out, *if you're sure* were the last words Dad said to me, and *say hi to Mom for me* were the last words I said to him.

After the short flight to Calgary, George's friend Brian picked us up in a pineapple-scented car and drove us south on Highway 22, closer to the Rockies than I had ever been and very close to the bewitching foothills, which do cast a geographical spell.

Brian had to get back to Calgary, so he left us in the forlorn dusk. I had thought we would spend at least one night in the parents' big house, to luxuriate in its space and amenities, having been in the crowded and minimally windowed six-plex for two months, but George walked right by it with our bags, saying the cabin's this way. We crossed a stream on a wobbly foot bridge, strode across the farm-yard, which was still, silent, and devoid of life, onto a trail that took us southwest away from all other buildings, and into an open field of short grass. The sun was well behind the mountains, but behind them the sky was orange. The foothills, dark and rounded, looked as if they might one day become edible buns for the mountains.

The cabin sat maybe half a kilometre from the ranch house, unsheltered by trees and wholly utilitarian, with a front porch and chimney. It resembled the beginning of an incomplete project, a Western-look village for tourists or a high school construction assign-ment. The front door scraped open. George flicked on the overhead light and smiled at me with pride. His cheeks were pink. "Isn't it great? I'll make a fire in the stove and get some food from my parents' place. They've got more fridges than most people. I mean it. They pile up food for this very reason, the possibility that people will want to stay with them for a while. And here we are: those people. You can unpack."

"I'm thinking I might take a bath."

"There's a tub," he half-shouted directly into my left ear. "Take a look at the bathroom," he said, guiding me from behind by the shoulders. "Just let the water run for a bit. Are you happy to be here?"

"Yes, I am. I'm very happy."

He kissed me on the neck and said, "I'll get eggs and bread and coffee and fruit. Anything you'd like from the Petrie larder?"

"Some tea and maybe some carrots and a chocolate bar. Anything we tended not to eat in Fort Smith."

Rusty old water gurgled into the tub and drained, followed by clear and presumably spring-fed water, far from industry and foaming cleansers. The six-plexes had only had showers, no tubs; this would be luxurious. I didn't think I had experienced luxurious prior to this moment, and I said so to George when he returned. He had a cardboard box filled with food, and brought it into the bathroom to display each item for my approval as I lay in the tub. "See," he said. "Eggs, bread, butter, jam, carrots like you said, a chocolate bar like you said, ginger ale, cheese, red peppers only a little shrivelled, which we not once had in Fort Smith, matches, and a *Calgary Herald* from last week."

"Did your parents leave a note?"

"No, the Petries do not leave notes. Anyway, I'm going to start cooking now, I'm going to fry some eggs because..."

"Because?"

"Because a frying egg is a what?"

"Oh right, a frying egg is a happy egg."

"That's right. Don't forget that!"

EARLY THE NEXT MORNING, I put on a T-shirt and shorts, and looked out the west-facing window. The sun was just up, and the colour of the light on the fields was new to me, yellower than is normally seen in nature except in the yolks of eggs from the young hens at Van Epps'. I wished for Anastasia. She was at the University of Toronto now, we hadn't seen one another since last Christmas.

I had to get outside to watch the mountains light up, and that was when I first found the combination lock on the inside latch of the front and only door. Thinking there must be a security reason, I returned to the bedroom.

"Why's there a lock on the door? I can't get out. What's the combination?"

"I just thought it was wise. We're all alone here. I'll open it."

"No, just tell me the combination. I'll open it. You can stay in bed."

"No, I'll get it, I'll get it," said George, with his playful, martyred sigh.

"I want to see the sky. The light is so beautiful."

George stood there naked, twirling the dial on the lock, opened the scraping door, returned to the bedroom to put on sweatpants and a sweatshirt, and sat on the porch while I admired everything in sight.

"Well, that's what morning in the foothills looks like pretty much every day," he said.

"Why didn't you tell me the combination?" I asked, from several paces, with my back to George. Then, taking a deep breath of Alberta air, I turned to look at him.

He shrugged and said, "It's my old high school lock. I have a thing about nobody else knowing the combination. I have dreams about it, people knowing my combination."

"If you have that kind of worry, I think I'd rather stay in the big house until your parents get back. Why don't we do that?" I asked him. He was sitting on the one wicker chair.

"No, I don't like their house. I don't really like *them* that much. They aren't what you would call nice people, and they're not what you would call horrible either. They're people you would just rather not call, period. So I prefer the cabin."

"But I feel confined if you're going to lock the door and not tell me the combination. I don't like being confined. I can't stand it, actually. I won't tell anybody from your old high school," I said, "your combination, I mean. 31-7-17. 36-5-21. I'll give them a fake one."

George was impervious. "You're not being confined. If you want out, I'll unlock the door. And it's only at night," he said, then added, "I'm not proud of my locking you in. I just feel better that way."

At this, I regarded George in a new light and experienced a rational type of panic, alone in the foothills with a man who was ashamed of his locking me in.

"Okay," I said. "Let's go find a newspaper somewhere."

George had said we could use his parents' truck.

"I don't have much money. Do you?"

"No," George answered, obviously relieved and refreshed by the change in focus, "but my parents have money. Let's go up to the house and I'll find us some cash."

We drove to a convenience store in Pincher Creek and bought a paper and coffee to go. In the next six weeks, we went to Pincher Creek several times, to the convenience store early in the morning for newspapers and to the grocery store in the afternoons. I wondered why I didn't decide to stay in Pincher, as it was called, refuse to return to the cabin, go to the RCMP, but what would I have said? Even to myself, I had no credibility, despite the fact George was now keeping the lock locked during the day when we were in the cabin, cooking, eating, or lying on the bed beneath the big and heavy quilt. And, curiously, when I was beneath the heavy quilt in the dimly lit bedroom, I experienced euphoria. When George and I went for walks in the vicinity of the Livingston Gap, I experienced euphoria. The warm wind rushed at us like loving birds and George said, "Some people think this was where the first people in America walked, this was their route, from Siberia, across diagonally and through the Gap. It was possibly an ice-free corridor for the first occupants of North America. Think of it. And now we're here."

"And that's a limber pine," he said, another time. "A limber pine is a what?"

"I don't feel like playing that game," I said, and George stopped talking until we were back in the cabin, and I was cooking. George loved to watch me cooking. He sat in the one armchair and kept the woodstove fire going and smoked and listened to the radio, sometimes making comments. This was now September of 1975.

"So, Bill Davis is back in in Ontario," George said. "Only as a minority, but that's better than the alternatives, don't you think?"

This observation was meant to goad me, probably because I had not cooperated with his sentence completions or driven into Pincher Creek to buy him a cake. I did not respond. "Oh right, you like the NDP, don't you? I forgot there for a moment." At times like this, he said my name. "Rose. I can tell when you keep peeling and don't say anything that you don't agree with me."

"True enough," I said.

"True *enough?* Not more than enough true? Just true enough?"

Sometimes I thought about where I would be buried in the event George killed me, or his parents never returned and we stayed forever, finding currency in the big house. Other times I thought, many would envy me this lifestyle, lifestyle being a relatively new concept, along with concept. I thought of buying a sewing machine with George's parents' money and sewing long skirts for myself. I knew I only had to mention it, and George would take me shopping for the machine, fabric, and thread and settle in to watch me sewing with a double-seamed devotion.

But, one day, there they were, the parents, pounding on the cabin door, saying "George! George! We're back!" We were dressed, it was late afternoon, the lock was on, and I was making a stew. George twirled away at the combination, and on the porch were a red-haired woman, very trim, well-dressed, and a bit leathery of skin and next to her a bald man with a hawkish nose, who asked George immediately and gruffly, "Who's your friend?"

"This is Rose. Rose," said George, placing his hand on my back, "this is Meredith and Hank." I shook Meredith's brown and ring-laden hand, then Hank's. They were *beat*, but we could come up to the house for a coffee if we wanted, which is when I asked if I could use their phone to make a collect call home, George could hardly intervene under the circumstances, and found out my father had been dead for more than a week.

I made arrangements with Air Canada, and the next morning Hank took me to the airport. George did not want to come, he had a backache, a headache, and an earache and stayed under the heavy quilt as I packed. He was still under it when I said goodbye. I had the ticket home from the summer, I could use it, I had been told, I said to Hank, worrying about all the money we had siphoned from their supply. Hank asked if George had said much about his background.

"Not a lot," I said.

"He's not ours," said Hank. "He's a foster child. Not a child anymore, obviously, but he's been with us since he was thirteen."

"Oh."

"He shows no inclination to leave," added Hank, looking at me, seeming to imply, you've been sleeping with a hoax.

Now I was uncomfortable with Hank and fearful and disbelieving of going to a home without Dad. My forehead was heating up, and I was glad I had not made any long skirts, but was wearing worn-out jeans and an army surplus jacket.

"It's a beautiful little cabin that you have," I said.

"Mind if I turn on the radio?" Hank replied.

"Not at all."

Music, Paul Simon, "Take Me to the Mardi Gras." I felt that Paul Simon understood me then and always had.

At the airport departures level, Hank got out of the car, pulled my bag from the trunk and without actually looking at me said, "Safe travels."

"Thanks," I said, in a cheery voice, and that was it. Dad being dead seemed highly improbable.

PEOPLE IN FLAX, needless to say, wondered where I'd been. Someone with a mild case of dementia had written in the Flax Funeral Home guest book, "Where's Rose?" My mother had done a half-hearted job of explaining. "I can't get in touch with her. She's in the outback of Alberta. It's not unlike her to disappear like this," she had said to Mrs. Van Epp, or words to that effect, even though I had no history of unexplained absences.

I called Anastasia in Toronto, and she screamed into the phone, "Where were you? What kind of daughter misses her own dad's funeral?"

I told a range of lies, all on the same continuum. *I was staying at a ranch, and it was hard to get to a phone. I was a long way from the ranch house; you have to understand distance is not the same as it is here. It was even hard to get to a store to buy a newspaper.*

"You didn't think of calling your mother once in six weeks?"

"Yes, I did think of it, but the one time I was near a pay phone in Pincher Creek, it was out of service. And I didn't want to rack up a bunch of long-distance charges on the ranch house phone. I didn't expect Dad to fall over from a heart attack."

"Okay, okay," Anastasia said, "but you've certainly entered the annals of Flax history. Twenty years from now when the historical society is writing up the sesquicentennial history of Flax, there will be a picture of Rose Drury and the caption, *where was she?*

"Ha ha," I said, pleased and comforted to be the object of Anastasia's attention within the context of social malfeasance. And, of course, I was still expecting Dad to show up.

Three days after my return, Adrian and I spent a Saturday evening on the empty beach in Kincardine, drinking a bottle of Donini. The waves were small and fell in tired thumps. The wind had died to nothing. I created a picture of me in a cabin far from all amenities and close to the gap where, the story was, Indigenous people had broken through the mountains on their way from Russia to the Americas; Adrian accepted this scenario as a good reason for my absence. We talked about Mom, who was not one to cry or even blow her nose and speculated about her experience of grief. Was she in denial about her sorrow, or did she have none? And if so, why or why not?

"Part of me thinks she's happy to finally have the house to herself, except for you being back," said Adrian. "She's always wanted peace and quiet. *Is it too much to ask for a little peace and quiet?* The drilling from Dad's chair got on her nerves, I don't blame her for that. All that bone smell. But we were never very noisy. I think the most noise I ever made was when I pulled my dresser over that time by opening up the top drawer as far as it would go and making a display of all my cars and tractors. *What on earth?* Mom comes tearing into my room. *Good heavens, I thought I was going to have a heart attack.* Meanwhile, Dad doesn't even flinch at his drill. I don't think he ever flinched, probably not even when he had the heart attack. Flinch and Flinchless: that should be their names."

"I'll never understand them," I said, "especially Mom. I might understand Dad better, in retrospect. Maybe we'll discover some notes or drawings he left behind in a journal."

"Yeah, right. Dad kept a little locked diary."

"Maybe he'll come back as one of Constance Tandy's ghostly shapes and reveal what he was thinking while he was freezing all those faces. Did you ever think maybe he was taking drugs? Dental drugs of some sort? Remember when he fell to his knees and cried at Grandma's casket? Maybe the result of one too many sedatives."

"No. I don't remember Dad anywhere near Grandma's casket, let alone crying. I never saw him cry."

"You don't? How can you not remember that? He fell to his knees and sobbed."

"I was playing with the cousins, likely. Somebody had pockets full of cap guns and pop guns, and they sent us outside."

"Mom would *never* fall to her knees and sob."

"She might if there was an overpowering racket that would not stop, or if a whole bunch of things went wrong at the same time, like fuses blowing and branches breaking off trees and landing on the roof, a pipe busting in the basement, and the Gables not shovelling their sidewalk in the dead of winter for two weeks. And a big crack in the windshield of the Buick."

Impressed with this inventory of Mother's irritants, I laughed and said, "I'm saying I don't see her sobbing next to my casket. Yours maybe, but not mine." Against the vast inertia beneath their surface, the waves almost seemed to want to stop.

"Mine? That's a joke. She'd be having a big garage sale of all my old stuff. She wouldn't be sobbing." Adrian drank the final dregs of wine straight from the bottle.

"Oh, I think she would. She's always at least liked you. She felt sorry for you because of your reading problems. She always thought I was picking on you."

"No, no, no."

"Yes, yes, yes," I shouted half-drunkenly. "Every time I read out loud, she'd accuse me of showing off. Are you trying to make your brother feel bad? Meanwhile, showering you with hockey equipment and fancy swimsuits for your competitions. You winning competitions apparently wouldn't make your sister feel bad."

"Well, it didn't, did it?"

"No."

"She'd cry at your casket, I'm pretty sure."

For a moment, the water roused itself into audible waves, maybe the worn-out wake of a freighter somewhere out on the horizon. "You're lucky to live here. Good old Lake Huron. It's more my idea of heaven than trees. I'd like to just float on its surface in a little boat."

"For eternity? I think you'd get sick of it," said Adrian, poking at the sand with a stick.

"I guess. Eventually I'd scramble onto land. Then I'd go to your house."

"Let's not talk about eternity. The word makes me feel sick. I can't believe I even said it. Some form of Dad has to be out there somewhere. If there isn't any life after death *anywhere*, just kill me now." And at that pronouncement, Adrian stood, and brushing sand from his jeans, added, "Let's go to my house and drink some more cheap wine."

Two weeks later, like a phantasm, George appeared. He had hitchhiked across the country to Flax and asked at the Two Star diner where I lived. It didn't take a detective, as he said. There was George in the doorway. I heard him before I saw him. My mother was on her feet, so she answered, thinking it would be the Avon lady with her moisture cream. I was sitting in Dad's armchair, wondering how long it would continue to smell like him, when I heard the following exchange.

George's voice: "You must be Mrs. Drury. I'm George. Is Rose in?"

Mom: "Yes, she's right here. Come in."

By then I was up and at the door. This was now early November, and the front yard was covered in oak and maple leaves. As George stepped inside, a zephyr whipped up a whirling devil of dust and leaves, indicating, I thought at the time, George's loose affiliation with hell.

"Hello, George," I said, "this is a surprise." When I am not, I can't make my voice sound surprised, although I don't think I sounded unsurprised; doleful, a language expert might have said.

"A good one, I hope," he said.

I nodded. He had with him a very large backpack.

"I might as well just ask outright. Do you mind if I stay for a couple of days? I came to the conclusion I should see a bit of the country."

In her preference for people she hardly knew, my mother was like George, and I felt she wanted me to embrace some, any, romantic life, which might expedite my departure from Flax. She liked her solitude, she may have been enjoying Dadlessness, I had to think. Mom said, "You're welcome to stay in Adrian's room as long as you don't object to a layer of dust on everything."

"I love dust," George answered. "Adrian's room and I will get along famously, as they say. Isn't that what they say, Rose?"

"They say getting along famously, but not usually in reference to dust," I said, reluctant to enter into his language games so soon.

We were having tea and Fig Newtons in the living room, when George said to my mother, "I don't mean to pry, but is Mr. Drury buried in Flax? I'm assuming Flax has a cemetery."

"Oh, yes. He is. The cemetery's right on the edge of town."

"I'm very sorry for your loss." This was the sort of utterance George could produce with sincerity. "I hope it doesn't seem presumptuous, but I bought a little wreath on my way here." It was in an opaque plastic bag he'd been holding when he showed up at the door. "If it's all right, I'd like to take it to the cemetery."

"We could walk," I said, instantly leery of being in any enclosed place with a key and lock mechanism, even if it was a car, and I was at the wheel. The wreath was not large, about the size of a dinner plate with metal legs, Rest In Peace its message, a relief to me as I feared, knowing George's contagion for intimacy, it might say Dad, it might bear miniature golf clubs.

"You two go," Mom said. "I'll work on the crossword."

Less than two hours after his arrival, George was walking with me to the Flax Cemetery, cutting through side streets to avoid the busyness of Main Street. "I hope I'm not intruding at a time of family grief," he said.

"You're not."

"Your mom looks sad."

"She tends to look that way some of the time."

"How are you feeling?"

"I'm feeling okay. I miss him, obviously. It all seems very strange. I think it would seem more real if I'd been here when he died."

"I hope you don't blame me."

"No, no, of course not." Although I did.

"It's good you and your mom have had some time together."

"Yes, I suppose so, although after I'd been home for a day, Mom said, 'You know he was fooling around with Loretta Decker for a while. Maybe more than a while.' I said, 'I didn't know that.' 'Well he wasn't the great saint everyone thought he was,' she said. 'I didn't know people thought he was a great saint,' I said. She could see I was getting mad, so she went to her couch to lie down, which is what she does, by way of concluding a conversation."

"Who's Loretta Decker?"

"Never mind. She's not around anymore."

At the graveyard, the sod on Dad's plot, greener and lusher than the surrounding autumnal turf, had obviously been faithfully watered by the maintenance man. The peg legs of George's wreath sank with too little resistance into this surface, and I shuddered.

"Are you glad to see me?" George wanted to know.

"Of course," I said — I was glad to see him, partly — and he put his arms around me and hugged me tight on the flabby sod. I was not then thinking in percentile ranks, but I knew the story of George and me, so far, was not sheltered within the lump of low, medium, or high average; it may have huddled *below* the third percentile.

"You've never noticed that I have a smell about me, have you?" I asked, JJ's joke gift, for no reason I could think of, rearing its head among the headstones.

George laughed. "What do you mean?"

"Like B.O. as my mother would say, or something?"

"No. Do *I* have a bad smell?"

"No, you smell good." He did, like skin and soap.

Later on, after dinner, in George's presence, Mom said to me, "You know, if I hadn't actually seen him dead in the casket, I would have had a sneaking suspicion he'd run off to B.C. to look for Loretta."

I said, "Mom, do you have to say that again?"

"I just had to get that off my chest."

"How many chests do you have?"

Mom said pffft, then laughed a bit. George offered to do some dusting. Mom laughed again, small titters, nothing uproarious.

I went up to my room and listened to Stevie Wonder, *Innervisions*, on my turntable. A couple of times I opened the door and stood in the hallway, listening. Mom and George were talking and talking in the living room. They were getting along, like a what? Like a what? Like a house on fire.

I WROTE A LETTER to Nancy, who was still living in the north. I thought of phoning, there was an upstairs extension where privacy was possible but improbable, given George's near constant presence and my mother's reluctance to leave the house. Even if they didn't overhear, there would be the phone bill: What's this call to Hay River, NWT, with George amplifying mother's alarm. Why would you call Nancy? Did you call her before I got here or after? May I please look at the bill, Mrs. Drury? I always felt that Nancy didn't care for me. I'm pretty sure Nancy liked you, I would have to protest. Remember the time she said, without your muscles we would never have got the car unstuck, that time we rented one, and got stuck, off-road around Pine Point?

That's not really the same thing as liking me, George would say. If I said, without Rose's brown hair the top of her head would be sunburned. Would that mean I liked you? And so on.

In my letter to Nancy, I did not mention the padlock in the foothills. I said, *Hi Nancy, I hope you get this. I'm assuming you are still in Hay River. I'm back home now, working part-time at the local diner. It's ironically named the Two Star, but despite this it gets a lot of business. Fortunately for me, one of my former classmates works there, too. Bonnie Edwards. She's really good at impersonating people, so she makes me laugh a lot. Of course, we can only do this in the kitchen or out front in the presence of one or two extreme regulars. And only if the impersonatee is from out of town.*

Anywho, I took a little side trip before heading home. I stayed for six weeks with George at his parents' place south of Calgary. I decided to take a pass on university for this year. George's parents were away in Europe, his foster parents as it turns out. Then they returned and George's dad drove me to the airport, which is when I found out about the foster status. George shows no inclination to leave, he said, the foster dad.

But he was wrong about that. Two weeks after my arrival home, George showed up on the doorstep with an extra-large backpack, asking if he could stay for a couple of days. Fifteen days later, and he's talking about joining the Flax volunteer fire department. He has cleaned the eavestroughs and is talking about painting the walls in my dad's dentistry waiting room. By the way, my dad died; I probably shouldn't say by the way. I should have mentioned that earlier. He died while I was at George's parents' place, and once I found out, I came straight home. I'm sad obviously but have hardly had time to think about it or let it sink in, mainly because of George. The entire cascade of events seems unreal.

My mother loves George. You are likely the only person on earth who would immediately understand this. As does already a portion of Flax, love George, I mean. A very nice fellow, they all say. He comes to the Two Star when I'm at work and orders pie and complains about the service. Hardy har har! You can picture this, I am sure.

I like George, but I find it strange — and also not — that he just appeared like that and shows no inclination to leave, to quote the person I thought was Mr. Petrie. I like him, as I just said, but I would prefer him to go away soon. The one time I asked him if he could maybe tell me what his short- and long-term plans were, his face took on that crushed look. You know that look. You saw it that time we were all out at Wood Buffalo, and you asked him why he was so much more talkative with people he hardly knew, e.g., the park ranger who was guiding us around. Maybe that crushed face is just a way to make people feel sorry for him; I do feel sorry for him, now that I know about the foster parents, in a limited way. I don't know why he has foster parents, though. I don't want to ask, because I don't want to feel any sorrier for him.

I don't know what to do. I can so easily see George settling in with my mother and the Flax opinion makers while I do what? Move into an apartment with Bonnie Edwards?

I'm pretty sure this will not come as a surprise. George brought a wreath with him, and his first order of business was to put it on Dad's grave. What can I say? Okay, bye for now. XO Rose Drury

I AM NINETY-NINE-POINT-NINE percent positive George intercepted Nancy's response to me. Easy to do, as he was now in the habit of picking up the mail at least a couple days a week when I was at work and Mother was not feeling up to it. Despite her lassitude, she did enjoy going to the post office some days, and so did I, but not as much as George; there was a bit of competition to get there with the key. Going with someone else ruined the experience. Going with two other people had the potential to ruin the day. Opening the post office box was an act best performed alone; it afforded a glimpse into an inviting other world most people wanted to enter. As George said, if there were a postmaster for a day contest in Flax, everyone would enter. Who would enter? Everyone.

I came home from work, and Nancy's response was there, on the counter. I have never seen an envelope that has been steamed open and resealed, but this one had a tremulous look to it, as if it were nervous. And there was George's indifference. The return address was clear, and he had picked up the mail, although *when* the letter had arrived, I had no way of knowing. I simply pictured George tucking the letter away, steaming it open in the middle of the night, reading it a dozen times, maybe even recording key phrases in a notebook, resealing it with clear glue, carrying it in his pocket to the post office, and returning with it so as to place it on the counter with mentally and maybe even physically rehearsed insouciance.

Nancy said, *I'm so sorry to hear about your dad. That must have been a terrible shock. I can't imagine. My condolences.* (Here she had drawn a red heart, like a cinnamon candy.) *I'm doing well. Frank and I have moved in together, and I'm working at the school for now doing secretarial work while the regular secretary is on a leave for some reason nobody wants to talk about. Speaking of nobody wants to talk about: George. It's too bad he has foster parents, but he's twenty years old, so it's irrelevant to the situation and the topic of mooching, which I see as the central issue here. Would you show up at someone's house and expect to be taken in indefinitely? No. Apply your own standards for yourself to George, and you will begin to see the problem clearly. I know you like him, and I like you, and sometimes like comes in the form of a kick in the ass from a frozen boot. Nuff said. It's cold here already, and the daylight hours are becoming brief, so you have to make the most of whatever sunshine there is. Frank says hi, and he is sorry about your dad too. Write again soon. Love, Nancy*

Of course, George did not use the word mooch immediately. He waited a few days before announcing, "I guess I'd better find some kind of work. Wait a minute, I've already been offered a job at the creamery. The last thing I want to be is some kind of mooch." And a few days after that, apropos of nothing, he opined, "It's important to expect others to live up to the standards you set for yourself." And eventually, regarding the quality of a store-bought pie he was eating, "It's better than a kick in the ass from a frozen boot."

"Where'd you hear that expression?" I asked.

"Nancy used to say it. Didn't you ever hear Nancy say that? She said it all the time. Well, not all the time; nobody says anything all the time, but frequently." His creamery job started the next day.

IN THE EVENINGS, Mom and George were talking more and more. I sat in Dad's old chair, George sat in the other and rarely used swivel armchair, and Mom lay on the couch. We didn't watch TV much, we listened to George.

George liked to talk about his childhood years in Lethbridge. One evening, he said he and his friends used to get pieces of cardboard and go skating on Henderson Lake on windy days. The cardboard became a sail, and they could fly across the lake. Sometimes the wind gusts would be fifty miles an hour or more. They really thought they might fly. At this, my mom smiled. Lethbridge had the perfect conditions for cardboard-sail-skating, George said. Hardly any snow, wind, and a big lake in the centre of town. Sometimes there'd be dozens of us down there, sailing around, crashing into each other. It's the kind of thing Cornelius Krieghoff would have painted if he'd been living in Lethbridge at the time, in the late fifties. Mom laughed a little. There'd be Christmas cards now. People would say, why I think that's George Petrie. Where? There! Get out the magnifying glass.

Then we were all quiet for a moment. "Tell some more stories, George," Mom said.

"My dad and I used to go fly-fishing in Montana," he said. "The Missouri River is really wide in some spots, but not too deep. There was a place we used to go to somewhere not too far from Helena, maybe. I'd stand on the shore, and he'd walk out. Once there was a deer in the water, upstream from Dad. I left my rod on the shore and went out to see it. I waded out and the deer just stood there. As I got closer, the current got stronger, and I thought maybe it was afraid of the current, like I should have been. I got about an arm's length from it, and we looked at each other. It had such brown eyes, and I remember wondering what I looked like to it. As in," George turned to me and asked, "What kind of animal would be wearing a plaid shirt?"

"A Canadian animal?" I suggested.

"One from a ranch," said George, seeming to be pleased with my response. "And *then*," he continued, lighting up one of his five daily smokes, inhaling, exhaling dramatically, "I thought maybe it was hoping I had something for it to eat, so I staggered back to the shore and staggered out again with an apple. I held it out, and the deer just stared, so I took a bite and spat it into my hand and came closer with the bite of apple in the palm of my hand, and it ate it."

"Oh," said Mom, "that's quite a thing to have happen."

"I gave it several bites," George went on, "the whole apple except the core, which I threw in the water and watched as it floated away towards my dad who had his back to me. I thought the core might attract a bunch of fish, and as they sailed past Dad he'd see the core, catch a giant fish, and then turn to me and say, 'That was a pretty smart thing to do, George.' But no.

"I waded back to shore and sat there. I didn't even bother pretending to fish. The deer finally took a few steps, at least it didn't have any broken legs, I thought, and that's pretty much the end of that story."

I had been wondering this, and finally decided to ask. "So why did you wind up with the foster parents?"

"My dad had a violent temper. One day he hit my sister. We were in the backyard, and she fell and hit her head on the concrete that supported the clothesline, and she was injured, she had a brain injury. Dad wanted us all to say it was an accident, but one day I drove my bike to the police station and told them. I said I wouldn't live there anymore. In the end, he didn't get convicted of anything, it was considered an accident, but I never went back. The province found a place for me to live. Alberta stepped in, I like to say."

My mother said good heavens. I wondered how likely this was to be true.

George never did provide, to my mind, irrefutable evidence of his surname. He was a Petrie, he said, like the people who owned the cabin. They were all Petries. Had he changed his name? No. Were they relatives? No. Well yes, distant cousins.

Picture the village of Flax being shaken in long waves, like a town-sized blanket. We, or primarily I, were figurines lifted and settled into matrimony by this action. Flax loved George, George loved Flax, but because he could not marry the incorporated village, he chose a representative, me. And because, I suppose because I am related to my mother, and I could not marry all of the kingdom of Sadsack, I chose George. George Petrie.

We could live in Guelph, I could finish my degree, and he could get a job. I said okay, fine. My best friend was elsewhere, my mother was thinking of having an auction of Dad's dental equipment, my brother was working at the nuclear power plant, and I felt I had to make a move. We married on March 21, 1976. It was a civil ceremony with Bonnie Edwards, my colleague from the Two Star Diner, and Mom and Adrian and his girlfriend Susan, now wife, in attendance. My mother made us a nice dinner — that's what George wanted. "All I want is a nice dinner," he said. I did not tell Anastasia until sometime that summer.

We moved to Guelph, and George got work as a firefighter. I had three more years to complete my degree. He paid my tuition, paid for my books, paid the rent, everything for these years. He did not lock me in or out of the apartment. However, in the summer of 1979, after I had finished my third year and was taking one independent study course called childhood pathologies, while we were sitting on the couch eating rice pudding I had made at George's request, he pulled a Polaroid picture of an erect penis out of his wallet and asked, "How do you like the look of that?"

I said, "What do you mean?"

And he said, "I mean, do you like it?" It was clearly not his penis.

I said, "It's hard, I mean difficult ha ha, to like a picture of a single body part."

This was his way of introducing me to the idea of an open marriage. He'd been looking into it, there was a group of swingers in

Guelph, and he wanted to join us up. He could not be monogamous for one more day. Or, more accurately, he said, he didn't want me to be monogamous. I asked, how is this congruent with locking a person in a cabin? He said, I didn't lock *a person* in a cabin, I wanted *you* to stay with me, just like now.

"You want me to stay with you via the insurance of a swingers' group?" I wasn't hysterical or even upset. I was wondering like an anthropologist how far from the norms he and I might be. The unfortunate thing is, I gave it a try. I gave it a try. In my mind, I imagine I saw headlines from magazines on how important it was to work on your marriage, and to save it. But truthfully, when I look back, I was an out-of-body person, then. I was about a yardstick away from myself at all times. It's how I was. Somewhere along the way, apparently, I had moved out.

The swingers were all older, at least twenty years older, and there was one couple that offered what George wanted. He had a very specific preference. He wanted a specific husband to have sex with me while he and the husband's wife watched. George told me they, Irene and Larry, could come over at *any* time, their kids were older, they didn't need a babysitter, all I had to do was agree, which I could not do, not at first, not for that summer, but George stopped wanting sex with me, so eventually I said okay, and this made him happy, no, overjoyed was the word he used. He asked me to bake him a chocolate layer cake from scratch, and while I watched, except for my one piece, he ate the whole thing.

October 13: I remember the date of the swinger sex. Close to the Speed River, I sat outside in a lawn chair and contemplated catching a bus to anywhere in Guelph or beyond. Leaves fell and were a comfort to me, though, because they had the weight and carelessness of thoughts I had had prior to October 13, and because of them, the leaves I guess, I had the strength to return with the lightweight lawn chair half an hour before the appointment. "You're back!" George said, with glistening eyes, I think he had been crying.

"For Christ's sake," I said. Let's get this over with, I thought. And the doorbell rang because Irene and Larry were early. In her raspy voice, without any introduction, Irene said, "You're in for a treat." I laughed when she said this, and my face likely turned red. Other than that, not much was said, and I have tried to forget what they looked like. George got two chairs from the kitchen so he and Irene could sit and watch, and Larry and I got undressed and we did it. He did have kind of a biggish dick. We couldn't be under the sheets *for the show*. I thought, once they were gone, George would be interested in me again, that he would be turned on by this display of swinger-ism, but he seemed less interested. That very night he fell asleep on the couch and stayed there all night and the next and the next. I didn't know what to do. I felt stupid and dirty, and in the middle of the fourth or fifth night I called a friend I had, a gay man named Andrew, and asked if I could stay with him for a few days. I can very clearly remember walking to his apartment in the middle of a perfect October night, with my books and the little overnight bag I had jammed into my high school locker years ago. I was experiencing a mood cocktail, happy with the evening and the leaves, feeling like Dad might be in the trees, awake and alive, embedded within the weather, and I was glad to be away from George, but also sorry to be leaving him. Andrew asked some questions I didn't answer honestly and told me I could sleep on his couch. Once in the past, after a statistics class, he had told me, out of the blue, maybe I should be a lesbian. I looked at myself more closely in the mirror for a bit after that. As it turns out, I guess he was somewhat right.

When I went home the next afternoon to get my typewriter and think, George was still there, watching TV. He hadn't gone to work. When he saw me, he said, don't leave me, Rose, and started to cry.

And I pictured him standing all night in the doorway of his junior high, like he said he had (in the vein of Lance Feldskov, maybe) because his dad was in a rage, and I thought of the supposedly brain-injured sister and his foster parents, his ambiguous surname, and decided to stay. After that we got along like siblings, we slept in bed like siblings, like Adrian and I used to do, talking and laughing and singing. George would ask me to sing a song, and I would, something like "Wichita Lineman." I droned through my final year, and George encouraged me to apply to grad school, wherever I wanted. I thought that was kind of odd.

A week after my graduation, he told me he was planning to move in with someone named Candy, but that he would continue to *help me out*. My mother and I were his closest family, after all. I wondered if he might change his name to Drury. In August 1980, we had conjugal relations one last time, because we were still married, and I was obviously leaving, packing my things into boxes for George to send later, when I had an address. I moved to Calgary, and four months later knew for certain I was pregnant. Roger the ovum had met Roger the sperm. Poor little Roger. What a start. When I think back, I can't help myself, a shuddering wave of remorse passes through me like inchworms.

four

I TOOK THE TRAIN to Calgary, leaving in late August with two suit-cases and the nascent Roger. I was already nauseous, and that may have affected my farewell to George. Nausea makes the present go off, as if the moment were pre-treated with bad memories. As well, he had wasted no time moving half in with Candy, whose very name embroidered bright colours on the hems of my biliousness. But he had come to see me off; he wouldn't have felt right if he hadn't.

You know I like to feel right, Rose? I had more saliva than usual and wanted to open my mouth and drool onto the hot pavement. The train was late, of course, but George insisted on staying and waiting. I directed my eyes at a soggy cardboard box by the tracks and felt myself absorb its absence of structure, then shake it off.

"George," I said, "I'm pretty sure I might be pregnant. I'm very sickly, and we didn't use a condom that last time."

George became pale, his blood rushing inward, hiding, I could tell. He said, "I've been thinking of joining the armed forces."

I said, "What? Did you hear what I just said?"

"Yes, I heard," answered George, not defensively, more like a person in an audiology booth, listening for beeps. Then, "Here comes your train. I can hear it, too. I hear the train a'comin'! Can you sing a Johnny Cash song for me before you go?" He spoke slowly, not rushed at all despite his obvious desire to see me leave.

"No," I said. I wanted to push him in the chest. "You should go now. Just go. Get lost." I had stopped being polite to him in May, when he started *seeing* Candy within the context of our open marriage, but he continued to wait with me. The train arrived with all of its silver cars and the settled faces on board. George hugged me, and the porter helped stow my bags. I sat and waved and, with my nausea and my uncertainty, saw George as nothing more than a marbled cut of meat, then as an income, then, despite everything, as a friend in need. Andrew-who-said-I-should-be-a-lesbian appeared and waved goodbye from the platform, and this brought tears to my eyes. I chugged out of Guelph. I was leaving. I did not feel unfettered or even alive, but later, by around Sudbury, I did.

I had a berth; George had insisted on paying for one. "I insist," he said, "you know I will always insist." The guilt of Candy equalled train fare with berth plus ten thousand dollars in a certified cheque for tuition, books, housing, and so on. I had never been so rich. Between

Sault Ste. Marie and whatever stop came next, I lay beneath my heavy CN blanket as the train rocked and rolled. The moon was full, and the trees ran by in somber crowds. I thought of Dad. He got a hammock for Mom when she came home from the hospital and strung it between two of his backyard trees, but of course he was the one who used it most; Mom didn't want a hammock. And I thought of Mom and gifts and the ignominy of receiving a wrapped package you'd later place double-wrapped in the garbage. Then I remembered my promise to Grandma Drury, to dig up her bones and bring her with me whenever I moved. In the window, I could picture her narrow face and her thin lips, her hazel eyes, and her solid white hair, always short and in a bob. I would have been glad to have her bones there with me; I would have tucked them under the scratchy blanket, just for the smoothness of them. I would have. And then a hard-moving sorrow overcame me, and I cried for several clacks of the train's progress, then fell asleep but was up and ready for breakfast by the time we arrived at what we now call Thunder Bay, Grandma's old stomping grounds.

In Winnipeg, we stopped for an hour, and people got out and strode with purpose to a store with thoughts of Coca-Cola or extra-large bags of potato chips. By then I was tired, pregnant tired, but had convinced myself my symptoms were all psychological, my body was relaxing after almost four years of completing George's senten-ces, making him layer cakes, and singing him songs, not to mention the months when I had been wondering what he was doing with other women, specifically Candy. I wondered if he had chosen her, knowing her name would fill me with bile and saliva, even at a distance of two thousand kilometres.

Eighteen hours and countless prairie vistas later, I was in Calgary. I was back in the West. My malaise had lifted, and I felt my period was imminent. Standing outside the train station, knowing no one in a dry and dusty climate, was exhilarating. There were the mountains again, grey monuments to the earth's inner life, its mind. I asked a cab driver what he would recommend for a cheap but decent hotel, and he took me to the Ambassador Inn on 16th Avenue; a friend of his ran the kitchen there. With the nausea gone and the air so washed, the sunlight whiter, the sky bluer, I was a person in a creation story, arriving at a smoky black and white motel.

The Ambassador Inn was on a direct bus route to the university, so all nearby neighbourhoods were potential homes. The next day I went looking for an apartment. I called a number I had found on a typewritten ad at the Co-op grocery store and met Carmen, who worked for a map-making company. She had short dark hair and was wearing a short-sleeved dress with coloured blotches that looked like zinnias. When I mentioned I was staying at the Ambassador on the recommendation of my cab driver, she laughed uproariously. The upstairs of her house had been converted into a one-bedroom apartment, accessible by a trembling set of wooden stairs that clung to the exterior of the north wall. I loved this feature, and Carmen seemed to like me. I could move in the next day, because the place was semi-furnished with a bed, a new mattress, a table, two chairs and one armchair. The walls were white and sloped in the bedroom and living room. Carmen told me the house had been built in 1913, as had the nearby school, Peter Lougheed Elementary, recently renamed, having previously been known as Renforth School. I wondered why she had mentioned the school and if I looked pregnant. I couldn't, could I? One never knew what people saw.

At the foot of my outdoor staircase was a driveway called an easement nobody used for parking, because Carmen did not have a car, and the neighbour, Lucy, whose nickname was Lucky, Carmen told me, parked her pigmobile, as she called it, on the street. Lucy and Carmen had created a flowerbed at the end of the easement, where two metal gates opened into their yards.

"We gave ourselves a prize last summer for best easement flower-bed in Renforth," Carmen said, and laughed again. Renforth was the neighbourhood.

Then Carmen told me I could use her phone to call home collect, and at the sound of Mom's voice, mine became unsteady with nerves and sorrow. Pregnant and distressed? I visualized the ads I had seen for something, the Catholic church, planned parenthood, an abortion clinic? Mom wanted to know right away if I missed George. She did not know he was living with Candy, because I hadn't told her. In her mind, I had left George, probably temporarily, to go to school for two years at a program available only in Calgary. She revered George, because he called her often, helped her with repairs, addressed her as Mrs. Mom Drury, and even offered to pick her up and drive her to malls or concerts she had no interest in. When we visited, she always made pancakes for him and would continue to do so after I was gone, when he visited alone, without Candy.

"Are you going to call Adrian? He's been asking about you."

"Yes, I will. Once I get my own phone hooked up. How are you? Are you doing things?"

"What do you mean?" She resented the question, I could easily tell.

"Going out. Doing things."

"I go to the post office, the grocery store. Are you asking if I have some sort of fear of doing things?"

"No. Just. Do you ever think about getting a job?" Why had I broached this subject? Maybe I did think she was a bit unhinged, now that I was half a country away. Or lazy; she had been living off the avails of Dad's life insurance since he died. Of course, look at me.

"Once in a while," she said, "I wouldn't mind working in a store."

"That would be all right, wouldn't it?" My period seemed to be starting, I could feel the menstrual pressure.

"I suppose so," Mom said. Her voice was trailing off, a sign she was not enjoying the topic.

"I had better go. This is collect after all."

"Bye, then. Call when you have a number."

"I will. I will."

My first night in my new apartment, I sat in the brown corduroy-upholstered armchair I would eventually buy from Carmen and move with my suitcases of belongings and the boxes George would dutifully send, to Lucy's place. We would call the chair my dowry. I looked out my west-facing window, which also overlooked the street, 6th Street. Being on the second floor was cosmopolitan, I believed. I went to the bathroom, no blood, and returned to my chair. I was in the West, facing west. I would buy a tape player and radio combination tomorrow, the day I met Lucy.

LUCY! MY NEW NEIGHBOUR! I liked her immediately, and I think so did the multi-celled Roger. Because her last name was Strike, she was nicknamed Lucky, *and* she smoked, as it seemed was her pre-destiny. You would have thought her parents would have known better than to name her Lucille. Could they not have foreseen, within ten minutes of entering the first grade in Lexington, Kentucky, she would be free-associated with an international tobacco conglomerate? I think in certain circumstances she even signed her name Lucky; a letter from a bank mistakenly delivered to my mailbox was addressed to Miss Lucky Strike.

She said, "I've never really been what you might think of as a Lucille, so I'll answer to Lucky. It's a dog, you know, a mutt, running at top speed with its long floppy ears moving, flopping I guess, to be repetitive. I did use my more conventional middle name of Abigail for the period of time I was employed as a kind of meteorologist with KEGA out of Lexington." We were in the easement.

"You're a meteorologist? That's . . ." I wanted to say fabulous, a word I never use or actually used once, when Anastasia told me to. (*Say it's fabulous*, she barked at me, in reference to her rabbit-collar coat.) Lucy didn't wait for me to complete my sentence.

"Well, they were desperate times for KEGA, the Keg 88.8," she said. "I only had a bachelor's degree from the program at University of Western Kentucky, truthfully, and all I did was read the weather forecast in front of a big map. The place was . . ." and she stopped as she often did in mid-sentence, without moving but searching, then continued, "like a very threadbare garment about to give way at any moment. Not even rip. The fabric of KEGA did not have sufficient integrity to rip. A manifest example of the end point, dust, as in dust unto. I quit or was released after seven months. The manager was a drunk. I didn't know this, I was too naïve, that the drunken station manager is a kind of inglorious tradition. I don't mean train stations. Your father isn't by any chance a station manager?" Lucy asked, regarding me with her expression of distant concern, as if she had just brought me into focus with her binoculars from about two blocks away.

"No, there are no station managers in my family tree. Plus, my dad is deceased."

"Oh, I'm sorry." She gave her half-smile, half-nod combination reply, which was a form of punctuation, I eventually learned, ending one topic, preparing a path for the next. "To be honest, what I think happened is they found out I was queer as a three-dollar bill. I had a girlfriend at Transylvania U — yes, it exists — she was a prof there, and I ended the relationship, and as it turns out, she was a friend of a friend of the station manager."

Again, she smiled her point-five smile, as if she were looking into a bright light, remembering something nice about me already: being from Kentucky, she may have attended charm school. She liked to wear black jeans and a white shirt with a bright blue or pink undershirt she had dyed; her hair was black and usually held back by a broad black elastic fabric band. She had a widow's peak, at which I liked to glance. She told me about the girlfriend the day we met; and then she warned me about the big and crotchety poplar in her yard. "Once in a while a big branch tears itself off in the wind, so don't stand beneath it in a storm. Poplars are a menace. They have the same life expectancy as humans, after eighty they start to fall to pieces. They're living examples of what people think they will do when they're broken-hearted."

"So you think it might be a broken-hearted poplar?"

"No, it's just old," she said, adjusting the hairband, "a fragile old tree."

She was in Calgary taking care of her elderly mother who lived in her own house, in a *better* neighbourhood, Lucy said, all financed by a stepfather who had been an oil executive and died almost two years ago. Lucy was also working as a receptionist in an optometry clinic. "Cottonwood Optometry," she said, in the voice of one answering the phone for payment. "I'm currently lacking in ambition," she added, "but that doesn't mean I'm shiftless, a condition of which I have been accused, by my mother, weekly. She forgets a lot, which insults she's used, that kind of thing, and somehow shiftless is always fresh in her mind."

Now it was my turn to smile. Overhead, the sky was still western blue. "Is it because there's less humidity here," I asked Lucy, "is that why the sky is so blue?"

"That makes sense," she said, "from a weatherwoman's point of view."

"I like it," I said. "It's a better colour than back east. No Great Lakes breathing into it, fogging it up."

Lucy nodded. "It's practically a desert here, frankly, compared to Kentucky, which is fine with me."

The very next day, a Saturday, Lucy came to my door and asked if I wanted to go for a walk, to take a look at the points of interest, as she put it, in the neighbourhood. And that, as it turns out, was the first day I ever laid eyes on Joe, tent-dwelling Joe, although Lucy and I did not ever tell him we stumbled across him in his lot, as we later called it, wanting to protect him from that knowledge, and I don't know why. I did, however, later, when he was staying with me, tell Joe that for a course on perception I had read a study which suggested that the categorizing of nearly all people took place automatically and semi-consciously upon first sight, except for homeless people: they were unassignable to a tribe or position or class or . . . home. The point being, the professor had said, we don't look away from homeless people because we don't want to see them, we look away because we can't sort them into a group they belong to when they are not before our eyes. I told this to Joe, but not that I had seen him in his tent on the edge of the golf course. The mind knows what it is doing, I suppose. Joe made no response. He wasn't much of a responder.

The day Lucy took me on my inaugural walk, she steered me towards the strip of land adjoining the golf course, which served mainly as an off-leash dog park and secondarily as a place for walking, as it was untended, with tall weeds and, according to Lucy, crocuses early in the spring. "You'll see," Lucy said, "wolf willow and other forms of shrubbery such as sage, which I used last Thanksgiving, last American Thanksgiving. Actual sage just plucked off the land," she said. She called the entire sloping piece of terrain *the verge*. She said, "It's a good thing there hasn't been much rain. The paths are dry. When they're not, the mud is clayish, and it sticks to your shoes in clods. I call that clod hopping." In fact, small stirrings of dust arose if I stomped or dragged a foot.

The path took us into a treed space, where Lucy came to a stop and said, "This is the notorious copse, as I call it, a stand of poplar and willows with a steepish path descending into its secret heart. Unless you take that path, you cannot see into the workings of the copse. Women I have met on the path, with their dogs, have warned me about drug deals and syringes; 'Don't go down there,' they've said. Naturally, I wanted to get a closer look." In the manner of a tour guide, Lucy called out, "Follow me if you're interested in the copse!" Of course, I and no one else followed her, and that is when we saw Joe; his tent abruptly became visible, a blue affair too small to stand in but a pleasing sight nonetheless, someone's bright and nylon home amidst the dark shrubbery.

Joe was standing with his back to us, peering through the trees toward the golf course as if looking out a window at the scenery. He was wearing jeans and running shoes, a black windbreaker and a bright, like a western bluebird, blue cap, a colour Roger would one day love above all others, causing me, many times, to question the effect of Joe on the developing fetus. Outside of the tent were no signs of domesticity, no fireplace, no ashes or cans or coolers. The wind came up, rattling the leaves, and I worried he might reflexively look around and see us. I whispered, "I think we should go," not because Joe seemed dangerous, but because we were trespassing on what was someone's open air, open house, and with his back to us, with his attention focused on a passing dog and its owner, I felt like a gawker.

Back on the main path, Lucy said, "He didn't look very dangerous. Maybe I should invite him to stay at my place. I feel guilty already having a two-bedroom place to myself while all I'm doing is taking care of a mother who doesn't really need taking care of. He looked like somebody's little brother." I did not surprise myself with my instant jealousy, because I was sometimes jealous for no traceable reason. On that day, in that copse, I was jealous of someone whose back I had seen potentially becoming friendly with a woman I had known for fewer than forty-eight hours.

"We didn't see his face," I said. "Don't be silly. We don't even know if he's young. He could be fifty. He could be ninety. He could have a frightening face, you don't know."

"What?" Lucy asked. "Like a . . . like a . . . wraith?"

"No, it's not funny. Like ten miles of rough road."

"I know, I know. I'm not serious about inviting him to live with me. I'm only serious about my guilt," said Lucy as we continued along the path, in an off and on again single file.

I told her about the perception-of-homeless-people study, about the mind not knowing how to categorize, and Lucy said, "But he had a tent, so I would categorize him as a camper."

"But that's not a campsite, and he's clearly hiding, which puts him into the possible category of fugitive, which is not the same as homeless, entirely."

"Well, I would say it is. And how do you know he's hiding? But if he is, and he is a fugitive, you might as well be homeless, because you can't go home, and you don't want anybody to know where you are, be it in a house or a tent."

"Be it in a house or a tent," I said. That was the first time I imitated her, not mockingly, just trying to replicate her wider vowel sounds. She didn't notice, I don't think.

"Well, that's life in the copse, as I call it," said Lucy.

Next, we were at the tree where Lucy had dumped her cat's ashes.

"I drive her up here from the U.S. of A., which was hell, Pringle having meowing fits in her carry case, and five months later, she dies. The vet gave me her ashes in a white cardboard box, that was the cheapest option, the kind of box an order of French fries might come in, wrapped in a drawstring, purple velvet bag. I didn't know what to do with these ashes; I wasn't even sure they were my cat's remains. It was hard for me to believe each cat was cremated separately, and the ashes lovingly scooped into a discrete pile.

"After a few days, I took them from my bookshelf to this very spot and dumped them at the base of this child-sized conifer," she said, patting the little spruce consolingly. "Now," she went on, "I expect to see some sign of my cat in that tree, just her outline or a denser than usual shadow of a black cat, my old Pringle."

"An ambiguous shape, you mean?" I asked, some memory of Constance Tandy, I think, making itself known via the rustling of word branches.

"Yes, that."

"So does that mean you don't really believe dead is dead," I asked, "like my little brother, who is one year and two months younger than I am, and believes in ghosts wholeheartedly? He can't not believe in them, he says. He'd be suicidal without his belief, or so he claims."

"And his sister?" Lucy asked.

"No. Not ghosts. Or anything."

"You never know," said Lucy. "It's a big and impenetrable universe, and I will continue to look for signs of Pringle in the tree." She walked a few paces, then turned to look at me, to say, "Seriously, I believe in the soul. Because when my grandmother died, my grandmother Fairfax, her soul gave my soul a little tap."

"What was the tap? How does a soul tap a soul?" I wanted to know.

"A light appeared on my bedroom wall, around the time they think she died, a kind of," Lucy waggled the fingers of one hand, "filigree on the wall, very bright."

"I wish mine would have given me a tap," I said. "I didn't get any messages, but I did faint in the mud, so maybe that was her swishing too close to my capillaries in a rush to get away."

"That could be," Lucy said. I did not normally like this sort of talk, but with Lucy that day it was different, because I liked her looks, there really was no other reason I could provide.

We headed back along the lower path, close to the golf course fence and past the east side of the copse, where Joe was still watching from his tree-branch window frame. He saw us, he told Lucy and me, later, in November. He said, "I think I saw you two walking in the park near the golf course. I heard you laughing," he said to Lucy. And it was true. She had laughed at her own observation, describing the time she had gone golfing with her mother and stepfather and a friend of theirs. "It was the outfit I disliked most," she said. "The shorts, the special shirt with the collar and cuffs. I mean, you would think I'd like it, it's quintessentially dykey, but I just don't grasp why there must be a golfing uniform. I told mother I was going to buy myself a UPS outfit for our next game, so they didn't ask me again. Then my stepfather had his infarct. Infarct is a funny word, don't you think? I don't mean to be disrespectful, and my stepfather actually said this once before his own infarct, but it sounds like a fatty mass in a drain," and she laughed out loud the laugh that Joe and I remembered.

AS I RODE the bus to the university, hoping not to be pregnant, wishing against Roger, taking an interior seam ripper to his connecting proteins, I admit, I often thought in the dialect of Lucy. Passing a *copse*, I'd think, as we dieselled past a grove of trees, or, *verge* ahead, although I was somewhat unclear about verges. Were they margins, were they borders? Presumably, they were everywhere, and yet few were as explicit as the wild space near the golf course. I took note of easements.

My period was late, and I was queasy much of the time but did not vomit, because my symptoms were mild and housed in my mind more than my viscera. In fact, I would think a word such as *viscera* and grope mentally to replace it with a neutral word such as *hallway*. Some mornings, while at school, an entire avalanche of distasteful words and sensations bore down on my limbic system, and I walked long *hallways* to distant bathroom stalls in which to sit and hide for a while. Why was I enrolled in this master's degree program in educational psychology? What if it were true and I was pregnant? I would imagine a 128-celled presence like a honeycomb, then I would picture a George the dimensions of a paperclip. The sensation would pass, and I would return to class, feeling as if I had been singled out for a discrete trial of punishment, as they said in the learning theory course.

I had told Lucy my period was late, and I had a type of nausea, paranausea, I said it was. I waited until the end of September to tell her, by which time I was more than a month late and had passed through the initial alienation of a new university, one hundred introductions, indifferent receptionists, syllabus changes, and library orientation. She appraised me, that's all I can say, with a look. Then I began lying, a type of lying, paralying, not right then, but later, as a matter of course, as they say.

One Friday in early October when my classmates were planning to go a pub for a drink, I said no, I had better not. Then I said to Peggy, who was friendly and said fuck a lot, even in class, "I think I might be pregnant."

"Oh," she said. Something about Peggy made me want to confess; she was cut out for psychology, apparently.

"Yes," I went on, "George, my husband is in Ontario. I think we're getting divorced, truth be told. He's ..." I trailed off.

Peggy said, "Well, divorced or not, you don't want the kid to have fetal alcohol syndrome."

"That's true," I said, as if considering this advice for the first time. "Anyway, I've got a bus to catch," I told Peggy and said goodbye. A week earlier, I had told my advisor, Dr. Chan, I was married, and my husband, Jeff, was at SAIT studying culinary arts. None of this mattered, did it? A little pack, no, not a pack, a *packet* of lies was apparently what I needed to add to my orientation to Calgary, to the

West, to U of C and my botched lower body (that's how I thought of it); my spirits rose, and I looked forward to riding the bus. I hoped Lucy would be home; I knew she could be, Fridays she was off at three. As I walked across the campus, I was filled with optimism. The day was sunny and warm and the leaves, mostly yellow I noticed, fell and rose in the breeze in cheerful conflict. They smelled the way they were, dry and done with life, incapable of reproduction and mess. I wasn't the type to get pregnant.

As it came to pass, by Thanksgiving weekend, all day of every day I lived next door to Lucy, I was infused with joy. I was enjoying my classes, the nausea was gone, I had an idea for a thesis topic, I was still waiting for my period, but likely this was an adjustment from moving west: my ovaries couldn't locate the moon. Never before had I been infused with joy. Some of my joy, or at least enjoyment, I can't speak to joy, was shared with Lucy. She liked to have me around. She often stood in the easement, smoking, where I could see her from the window of my upstairs apartment. If the window was open, and she could see me gaping down at her, she would yell up to me to take a break, there's a lot going on in the easement, she would say, and no, I would say, I should keep working, because I did not want to appear to be an utter minion, and I enjoyed watching her pace around and smoke and pull at the weeds in the perennial patch. Some days when the weather was cooler, she wore a black hat with earflaps. From the window, I told her my brother used to call them earlugs, I wasn't sure if this was common parlance or idiosyncratic of southern Ontario or my brother.

One day, "Easement talk!" she shouted from below, tapping her watch. "It's time for Easement Talk." I descended my dangerous stairs. "I'm thinking of calling the CBC," she said, "and asking them to find a slot for us. Nothing big, maybe fifteen minutes late at night."

"A slot for what?"

"Easement Talk!" she said, placing her hands on my ears and giving my head a shake, causing me to inflate with pleasure: little Roger must have got a shot of yellow, happy-faced neurotransmitters. "We'll have seasons. It would start slowly, but eventually we would find our audience."

"If it were you, yes, people like to look at you."

"This would be *radio*. And thanks for the compliment, you're such a complimentarian. I love you for that." She said she loved me! "But people like to look at you, too, which is neither here nor there, because it would be easement radio." She was speaking in her meteorologist's loose-limbed way. "The first season would be called One Thing. Each segment would begin with one thing you don't know about me. For example, one thing you don't know about me is that I spent a few summers on my grandparents' dairy farm. I haven't mentioned that, have I? The Fairfax grandparents, that is."

This was still October, later in the month, late in the afternoon, before daylight savings time had ended. The leaves on the choke-cherry tree were a deep dark purple and they were falling in groups.

"No," I said, "you haven't told me that."

"I told you about when Grandma Fairfax died, and the light pattern on the wall?"

"Yes."

"Did I tell you she liked to say 'for crying in the shithouse' instead of for crying out loud?"

"No, you didn't tell me that."

"Oh, for crying in the shithouse," Lucy said, then laughed. "Anyway, the cows. The cows were outside, of course, because it was summer, and my job was to go and round them up for the evening milking. Not the morning, I was sleeping for that — as I'm sure our listeners may have surmised," and she looked at me and went on. "Usually they would be as far away as possible, there were some trees in the farthest corner of the field, and that is where they liked to roost, so to speak."

I smiled.

"But once they heard me, c'mon Bossy, co-Boss, they'd start to murmur and get organized for the trip, psychologically at least, or so it seemed to me."

"Should I ask questions?"

"Fire away!"

"I don't have any, at the moment."

"Well, there were paths they had created. They didn't just walk like a bunch of kids, they walked in a line the way teachers would prefer kids to walk, and I loved how they never hurried. I remember kind of worrying about their udders, but usually I looked at their legs and their hooves. They were black and white. What they thought about was a complete mystery, because they weren't in any way playful like dogs or cats, although if I just stood in the middle of the field, they, at first one or two, then all of them, would come and look at me and sniff and exhale up close in a kindly way. It was as if little huffs were the closest they could come to making an observation.

"Well, the oldest cow, one summer, the last summer I went, the oldest one was also the slowest and the last one in the lineup, and when she walked, I don't know if it was an ankle bone or a problem with a rear hoof, but she made a clicking sound, a slightly elongated click, like something in her leg or hoof was stretching and releasing. It was a sound I could have listened to forever. I wanted to be able to make that sound, walking in the hallway of my school. It was the sound of I will never hurry for you. Because she was slowest and oldest, she got the end stall, and I liked to stand and comb her with the comb, the currycomb it was called. Sometimes I wished I could pick her up.

"She didn't have a name. I told my grandfather she had told me she didn't want one. He laughed. And then that Christmas, I guess in the fall she died, or had to be slaughtered, maybe her legs gave out, but my grandpa kept her hide for me, had it tanned and sent it for Christmas. 'This is from your friend without a name.' It was all folded up neatly but heavy, and when I touched it, it felt exactly like her, only cool. I still have it, but I don't take it out very often. I don't need to, to remember the hoof click and the slow walk. I've thought of giving her a name, posthumously, but she defies the label. She was the originator of that term."

Lucy lit a new cigarette. "Was that about ten minutes?"

"I don't think quite. But didn't it bother you? The hide of your favourite cow?"

"No, not at all. I keep it in the bottom drawer, because it's heavy."

"I once had a heavy quilt that I wish I still had."

"Where is it?"

"Not here."

"Is it in a place where we can go and get it?" Lucy asked, smiling.

"No. Never mind the quilt. I'll tell you one thing about me. One thing about me is I think I might be pregnant." Everything twirled when I said this, then became still.

Lucy raised her eyebrows.

"I was saving it for Easement Talk," I said. "The news. So, I'm glad you invented it. George is the father, the one who is supporting me financially, my ex-husband. We're not fully divorced yet, but we will be soon, because he's living with another woman and wants to marry her. I think I married George to make my mother happy, because she loved him and missed my dad, she still does, both those things I think, whereas I felt sorry for him, George, that is. Flax also liked him, the town of Flax where I grew up. I met him when I was volunteering with a youth group multicultural-Canadian-relationship-building summer project thing, and when we left, he invited me to his parents' ranch not far from Calgary, south and west of here in the foothills. We stayed in a cabin there, that's where the quilt is. There was no phone. In the cabin. His parents, well, they were foster parents or something like that, came home, and I called home from their house and my dad was dead. So, I went home, and two weeks later, there was George. He stayed and stayed and asked me to marry him. We could live in Guelph, I could finish my degree, and he could get a job. I said okay. My mother made us a nice dinner when we got married – that's what George wanted. 'All I want is a nice dinner,' he said. Anyway, this all leads to the one thing – maybe I'm pregnant. We were separated because he was seeing another woman named Candy, but we mistakenly had sex one last time. I haven't had my period yet, and that was the beginning of August, well August 11. I'm just waiting and hoping it's because of the move, my system is off-kilter."

Very dark clouds were riding in from the northwest. The weather always seemed to come from that corner of the sky. Lucy nodded and said, "People do lots of funny things in their twenties." She was thirty-three. "It's almost as if you're stupider in your twenties than in your teens. How old were you when you married him?"

"Just turned twenty."

"Aha. Exactly. The worst year of them all. I turned twenty in 1967. My parents split up, and I rolled a car. I swerved to miss a dog. The dog was okay, I was okay, too, miraculously. Then Grandma Fairfax died. Well, come on inside for a cup of tea. I'll show you my cowhide. We're shutting down Easement Talk for today. And tomorrow you have to call a doctor."

"ONE THING ABOUT shopping at Co-op," said Lucy a couple days later, "is the clerk named Liz. I like to get to know clerks, so I usually go to the same store regardless of specials or coupons. And I like to walk, so I never buy much, just what I can carry. I'm very European that way. Where's the camera? Oh right, there is no camera. This is radio.

I wanted to look intently, no, challengingly, into the camera when I say very European. Let them laugh at my affectations, my eyes would say."

"Your voice more or less says that," I said.

"I can't be sure."

"Well, you are kind of European. You speak French fluently, unlike me, the Canadian."

"But I want to be laughing at my affectation before they are, the audience." We were in the easement again, leaves were flying off trees horizontally and landing in foreign yards.

"So, anyway. Liz?"

"Do you know who I mean? She's short and has a round face, and on top of that round face is a round haircut. You know who I mean?"

"I do."

"Her hair is like a monk-do," Lucy said, and I laughed. "Liz complains in intimate detail when you ask how are you or how's your day, which you have to ask, because she asks *you* and then looks at you with a kind of beseeching and commanding eye contact until you say fine, and how's your day? Then she's off to the races. It's always something like, *it's been a hard week,* or more specifically, *since Tuesday, things have been pretty bad,*" and here Lucy sounded like Liz with her flat enunciation, the enunciation one might attribute to a tea towel or any weary piece of fabric. "*My cousin has a bone in her left foot that they had to do a biopsy on. We're all waiting for the results, but it doesn't look good. Her mom, that's my dad's sister, had bone cancer. I was so worried last night, I couldn't sleep plus, I got my menstrual,* she said, then, in the next breath, these cherries are eight dollars and twenty cents, do you still want them? There were other people in the line when she said *my menstrual,* just like that, although I suppose maybe we should all be more open about it, that might be a question we could ask the listening audience, but I said, yes, I want the cherries, and she said, *I took two Midol, and that helped a lot.*"

"So there is one person in the world who takes Midol," I said.

"For her menstrual," Lucy said.

I had a feeling we were advancing toward a conversational hairpin.

"So?" Lucy asked, catching an oak leaf as it hurried by.

"Nothing," I said, "no need for Midol. I don't know what's happening. No morning sickness or anything like that; I feel fine."

"Why have you not considered going to a doctor?"

"I've considered it, but I don't have one. Plus, it takes three months to move your healthcare from one province to another."

"That's irrelevant. I'm an American émigré, and even I know that. Alberta would just bill Ontario. Carmen said her doctor is taking on new patients, if you want a woman. Mine's a man, and he's taking patients too, I think."

The sun was ready to slide behind the mountains. A beam found its way through the rooftops and tree branches and lit up our easement. I stared westward hoping to slip away, to become a shape, a gestalt of transcendental motes. In the same way Anastasia used to hold King's old head, with her bare hands, and manipulate it into thoughtful nodding, Lucy moved my head down, then up. "Yes, I will call a doctor," she said.

Placing my hands over hers, I said, "Okay." We held hands for a moment, and I headed up my outdoor stairs.

"NOVEMBER 18. One thing that happened," I began, "was that I saw the homeless guy today. Remember? The one in the tent down by the golf course with the bluebird-coloured hat?"

"Of course."

"I was walking through the little park on my way to the 7-Eleven to buy milk, and he was sitting on a bench. I didn't look at him or recognize him until he asked, while I was walking by, 'Do you date derelicts?' So I had to laugh and look right at him, and there he was in his blue cap. I saw his face. He looked kind of funny, or possibly dysmorphic to use a word with which I am familiar because I learned it in my abnormal psychology class, like his forehead was too big and his eyes were too far apart with too much white around the irises, but the overall effect was vulnerable and lost, so I felt I had to respond. I said, it depends, I guess, and sat down next to him, because I had nowhere to go in a hurry. I didn't tell him I'd seen him before. I just asked, 'What makes you a derelict?' and he answered, 'No home, no job, six dollars in change, my name is Joe. Even my name suits the derelict lifestyle.'

"'Do you not have any place to stay?' I asked.

"He said, 'The Drop-In Centre at night. During the day, I can stay anywhere that's not specifically owned by anyone. Most places are owned or rented by someone, you start to notice, when you're a derelict.' Then he said, 'I'm not trying to make you feel sorry for me.'

"I asked him if he was from around here, and he said New Brunswick. He said he left there in June and hitchhiked out here, that he thought he'd get a job in construction, but he doesn't have any experience or skills, plus, he said, there's a bunch of other guys just like me who look more normal than me. I couldn't believe he said that; my heart kind of ached.

"So, I asked, what about something else like a store, a grocery store? And he said 'I don't know about a store hiring me. Plus, it's all very tricky when you don't have a phone number or address.' Which is when I told him he could use my phone number and my address, and he could come for dinner tomorrow night. And you can come, too, Lucy, so there are two of us assessing him. He seems very innocent. He has rosy cheeks, and his teeth seemed normal. There was black hair springing out from beneath his bluebird cap, so he's not bald." I was talking faster than usual, going on too much, because for the first time, Lucy seemed unhappy and a little bored with my easement offering.

"I asked him, do your parents know you're in Calgary, and he said, 'My parents don't even know where they are,' and he explained that his mother doesn't know where his dad is because he took off ten years ago or more, and nobody looked very hard for him, and his mom doesn't always know where she is herself, because she drinks too much. He said, 'I called her collect when I got here, and she did accept the charges, so she's good that way. I told her I'd call again when I got settled.' So I said he could call her from my place if you want."

"You haven't left a whole lot for me to do for him," Lucy said. "I like to do good deeds, too." I think she wished she had found Joe first, she sounded miffed, so I asked.

"Are you *miffed?*"

"Maybe," she said. "I just might be," and she smiled but looked away.

Then I hastened to add, "I got Carmen's doctor's name and number from her."

"Well, that's one thing, I guess," Lucy said before disappearing inside her house. "One other one thing," she said from the doorway.

When Joe came for dinner, he introduced himself to me and Lucy as Joe Travolta. "Really?" I asked, and he said, no, it was an alias, but not for any bad reason, just to make a splash, he said. Splash struck me as an endearing and old-fashioned word, also a bit feminine. The guys at the Drop-In Centre called him Fever.

I had one drink, one beer, which I didn't finish, I barely started; after five or six sips, Lucy took it and poured it down the drain, whereas she and Joe had three each: I counted. Still, I talked too much, more than usual, because I sensed Lucy's unhappiness. I think she wanted Joe and me to be at her house, for the dinner to be served on her table, for the situation to be under her aegis.

I talked about my coursework, about the course called the history of the unconscious, and about the disappointing qualities of many of my classmates. In discussions regarding the origins of childhood delays or problems, they often brought up socio-economic status or SES as they called it in shorthand, as an indisputable cause. Sometimes they spoke of poor people as if it were a given their children would be problematic. I said to Joe and Lucy, "These people are going to be psychologists. Shouldn't they be more understanding and less biased? If *they're* not going to be, who will be?" Joe answered, sincerely, that he did not know. Lucy went outside for a smoke after we had finished the main course, and she didn't come back for the dessert of fried bananas with whipped cream. I went outside to look for her, and, realizing she had gone home, I returned and sat with Joe eating the bananas and saying I didn't know why she left like that without saying good-bye, she'd never done that. I felt bereft. Joe said I'm sorry at least five times, it was likely his fault. I told him not to worry, then he told me the Drop-In Centre closed its doors at eight, and he wouldn't be able to get inside, and this is why he stayed at my place. I had two quilts from the Goodwill he used as a mattress and a sleeping bag he slept in that night and, as it turned out, the following few (twenty-four) nights.

The very next evening, after Joe had returned from his day of seeking employment, and Lucy had no doubt seen him climb my wobbly stairs, I knocked on her door to explain. "It's open," she called from the bathroom, it turned out, from the tub, and I went inside, where, from the hallway, with no ado whatsoever, half-shouting, I told Lucy I wanted to do a case study on Joe, as a paper for my course on deviance. Lucy splashed around a bit and asked if Joe had to *stay* with me, and was that how a psychologist conducted research, was that a respected methodology? Shuffling along the dark little hallway, I stopped one arm's length from the bathroom door frame and said, "Not the staying with me, but the case study would be considered qualitative research." She said, "Dear god, you are reminding me of my girlfriend from Transylvania U."

"How so?" I asked. She laughed her half laugh and said the tub was full, and she didn't want to waste the hot water and get out now to explain her ex-girlfriend's research paradigm, as she called it. Then there was silence for thirty seconds, and she said you might as well come into the bathroom and talk to me, if you can leave Fever Travolta on his own for a minute. That is when I worriedly entered the bathroom, passed by the tub, and sat on the toilet, facing Lucy, assuring myself I had seen a naked woman before, notably, myself and Anastasia Van Epp.

Lucy was not entirely submerged, her hair was piled on top of her head and, as the water was bubble-less, her breasts were entirely visible. They were the most desirable breasts I had ever seen, or imagined, desirable in that I wished I had the same breasts. If one were to take two average-sized saucers and place them on one's, or Lucy's, chest wall and inscribe circles around them, then place medium-sized brown erect nipples in the centres of the saucer circumferences, then add a mere modicum of perfectly symmetrically placed breast tissue, you would have had her breasts. I thought of a boy becoming a girl. Lucy's breasts contributed to my idealization of her, which is apparently the wrong way to fall in love.

Lucy said, "If you're not comfortable on the toilet, wheel in my desk chair," which I did, grateful to be able to move to another vantage point, mostly behind her. Lucy said, "I put half a cup of muscle-relaxing salts in the water, so I may never be able to get out. Ha ha. Cause of infirmity: overdose of therapeutic salts. Now she's nothing but a talking head in a tub."

I rolled back and forth a bit in the chair, planning not to look at Lucy's breasts again unless her head was covered in blinding shampoo.

"I know that time we saw Joe," Lucy said, "I said I wanted to invite him to stay with me, I meant it at that moment, but the idea really arose from one of those surges of empathy you get when you see the dog with its ribs visible in the SPCA brochure. I'm sure there are some people analogies, I just don't want to sound judgmental, but the surge of empathy usually comes before you know the person has an alias."

"So now *you* think he's scary. By the way, we call it the Humane Society here. Anyway, I think he just has it for fun. Who would seriously pick Travolta for an alias, if they were in trouble with the law? Besides he's just going to stay for a while, until I've got the information I need for my paper."

"And then you will summarily throw him out?"

"No."

There was a silence, a splash when Lucy knocked a bar of soap into the water with her foot. "I would argue that Travolta is the perfect alias for that very reason. No one would suspect it's an alias, and it's distracting. Here we are talking about it. Did he use your phone to call his alleged mother?"

"No, not to my knowledge."

"What, you think it's possible he got up in the middle of the night and called secretly?"

"I suppose so. He's in a sleeping bag on some quilts in the living room near the phone," I said. "Just to make it clear. Where he's sleeping."

"You didn't go and get that quilt you want, did you, for him?"

"No, of course not. How would I do that without a car, and why?"

"Because you like him?"

"I would drive to Pincher Creek and get a used quilt from a locked cabin? Immediately? For Joe Travolta?"

"I'm just being silly," Lucy said. "I don't care what quilt he's sleeping on." She slipped below the water and reemerged, her hair knot tipping a little to the left. I sighed through my nostrils, using my feet to push myself back and forth in the chair, behind Lucy's neck and shoulders.

"He's a lost soul," I said.

"We don't know if he's a lost soul. We don't even know if he has a soul. Does he ever take off that hat?" Lucy's voice was brisk and matter of fact, as if she were taking information for an optometric referral.

"Well, you're the soul expert, but my guess is he has one, because he washed the dishes after dinner last night and tonight. And I imagine he takes off the hat when he goes to bed, but I have not seen him without it. I wonder if he's got some kind of head injury or malformation. Like a big dent."

Wrenching around to regard me with her skeptical face, corners of her mouth turned down a half notch, Lucy said, "An alias and a possible dent? That's his resume?"

"No, that's not his resume. He worked for a landscaper in New Brunswick somewhere.

"And why is he not now working for a landscaper, I ask?" said Lucy.

"It's November. He's looking."

Lucy turned away and leaned forward, reaching for a soft plastic rectangular brush near the faucet. Holding the brush, propping her right elbow on her right knee, she asked, "What about the baby? Our baby?" And I suppose because I had been feeling so transplanted and alone, so separate from the province and city where I now lived (it's all one country but you can't be fooled by that), so apart from my classmates and Dr. Chan, my grad school seminars, presentations, public speaking, my absence of interest in a thesis, my fear of mountains, my extinct dad, I warmed at once to the pronoun *our*, I warmed and weakened in every joint.

"I don't know yet if it's a baby, if it's our baby," I made myself say, "or if it's a fatty mass, to use your term."

"Fatty mass or baby, I'll help you out with it," Lucy said, sloshing water as her legs extended.

"Thank you," I said.

"You shouldn't drink booze, you know."

"I know. I know."

Passing the brush backwards to me, Lucy asked, "Would you mind washing my back with this? I feel like there's a lot of dead skin I never get to."

"The bones are still here," I said. "The relaxing salts haven't melted them away."

"Mmmm," said Lucy, wrapping her arms around her knees and resting her forehead on them. "Thank you so much. This is luxury living at its finest as they say in the real estate ads."

"You're not planning to move, are you?"

"No. Of course not."

ASSUMING ROGER WAS conceived on August 11, when George and I had our final sexual encounter, he was in his second trimester of development when Joe came to stay with me. The second trimester is critical, of course, they all are, and in my foolhardy way and in my ignorance, I spent hours consorting with Carmen's new kitten, Mimi. Both of these creatures, Joe and Mimi, may have put Roger at risk. There are viruses, it goes without saying, on people and in cat feces, toxoplasmosis one might breathe in while scooping around in the litter box, raising a dust storm of contagion. I couldn't recall being near the litter box, but I had held and mauled Mimi countless times and may have accidentally rubbed my face against her asshole, she was so adorable, I may have. I may have caused poisons to rain down upon Roger's little central nervous system as I sat, many times, with Joe, breathing deeply of his homeless smell. Not to mention the second trimester frustration and at times rage engendered by Joe's single-sentence replies to my open-ended questions.

"Tell me about your elementary school years."

"Well, I was pretty much a dud from the start."

"What do you mean?"

"Just that, I was a dud."

"What made you decide to quit school?"

"I wanted to earn some money so I could get some braces and fix my teeth. I got tired of putting elastic bands on them at night. It didn't work."

"Your teeth look fine to me."

"No, they're too crooked. I'm kind of tired of talking about myself. Do you mind if I have some peanut butter and toast?"

"Yes, have all you want," I said to Joe one evening, angry and guilty because Lucy had again *strongly recommended*, as she put it, that I see a doctor.

"I thought you had Carmen's doctor's number?" Lucy had said, using the sentence structure of a veiled command.

"Yes, I do," I had said, then, "I plan to call. Very soon."

I look back on those weeks before I *knew* as a period of fetal roughhousing. Poor little cartilage-boned Roger, the size of a dollhouse doll, with lungs the size of beans, maybe, or even smaller and a heart like a lentil. Even nestled within all the blood and bones of my lower body, it's hard to imagine my cortical and endocrine threshing did not leave a mark. When Joe left without warning in December, I was relieved. One Wednesday he got up at dawn with the urge for going, I assume, and I smelled the toast and instant coffee he liked, then I heard the usual bathroom sounds and the door closing, the outdoor stairs moving against the wall, and when I got up, there was a note. "Hi, Rose. I guess I am moving on today. Not sure where to go but either west or north. Thanks for everything. I will pay you back when I get a full-time job. Joe T."

That evening, when Lucy arrived home from work, and I met her in the easement with the note, she said, "That's too bad. Not really. Oh, sorry, I shouldn't be insensitive." I studied her face for all the meanings being so rapidly conveyed and was unsure. *Our baby* had not been mentioned again, and I had not seen her naked or in the bath since that day. "Actually, do you want to come with me and meet my mom, was what I meant to say. I've been wanting to ask you but she's not always easy to be around. Since she had the stroke, she has what they call disinhibition, which means she'll say whatever pops into her head, especially if it's rude. Maybe that's what I have, come to think of it." Lucy smiled, and the streetlights came on. "I am rude sometimes. I'm sorry. I really didn't want Joe around, that's the truth of it. Do you forgive me?"

I couldn't recall ever having been overtly asked for forgiveness.

"Yes," I said, "and I would like to meet your mother. Will she tell me my eyebrows need plucking or something like that?"

"It's hard to predict. Your eyebrows are fine, so it won't be that. If she says something disinhibited, I'll give you a signal, like this," Lucy said, fluttering her right hand close to her thigh. "That could be construed as a nervous gesture, but for you and me, it will be the signal."

We ate some of the leftover chili I had made for Joe and took off in the old Oldsmobile Delta 88, the pigmobile. Lucy's mother lived in a more expensive area, and she had the look of wealth, short dyed black hair, pearls, and a beige sweater with a calf-length black skirt. Her legs and feet were bare. I noticed her feet were youthful and free of bunions and large purple veins; they could have been the feet of a teenager. I wanted to compliment her on her feet, but that seemed disinhibited, and I worried it might trigger a cascade of disinhibited retorts and maybe insults. Although at first glance, she looked healthy, and I wondered if she were faking her illness to have Lucy nearby.

"I wanted you to meet my friend Rose," Lucy said. "Rose, this is my mother, Caroline."

"What do you mean by *wanted*?" Caroline asked, as if this simple verb might be suspect.

"I mean this is my friend Rose, and I *want* you to meet her," Lucy answered, teacherly.

"Oh, I don't know why, but it sounds a bit ominous when you say wanted, as if you wanted me to meet her before I died next week."

"That's not what I meant, Mom. I'm pretty sure you know that."

"You haven't brought any other friends around, so why did you want me to meet Rose?"

Lucy's hand fluttered briefly. She said, "I don't actually have that many friends in Calgary, so I thought it would be nice for you to meet Rose, so that, in the event I mention her, you'll know who I'm talking about. Rose lives next door, in the upstairs of the house next door, and her landlady lives in the downstairs, and she used to have what? Do you remember?"

Caroline lowered herself slowly into an armchair, beige like the sweater. "I can't remember anymore today."

"A standard poodle!" Lucy said, as if announcing a prize in a draw.

"Oh, right. What's its name again?"

"Ringo. He's black. He was black, but he died, and now she has a little orange kitten named Mimi. Remember? I told you that."

I stood uncomfortably in the beige and light brown and darker brown living room, watching Caroline rise from her chair already with effort and some exaggerated huffing to announce she would get it. Lucy raised her eyebrows and opened her right palm to signal *it* was the unknown.

Caroline went off somewhere and returned with a photo album. "Sit down," she instructed, pointing in the direction of the dining room table and chairs. "I put this album together not long ago. I got tired of the photos being chronological, and so I put some of them into themes, like this one, the theme of dogs, if you can call dogs a theme. I'll have to ask my neighbour, she used to be an English teacher, didn't she, Lucy?"

No reply from Lucy in the kitchen. We sat.

"She ignores me," said Caroline, opening the album to the first page, "to hell with her. Anyway, this was Beulah, she was a beagle, we had her for thirteen years, in Lexington of course, when Lucy was young. Come and look, Lucy. *Lucy!*"

"No thanks, Mom," came the voice of Lucy from around a corner, rattling cutlery, "I want to get things done here. You show Rose. She likes dogs."

"Do you?" Caroline asked, seeming to be worried she might be boring me.

"Yes," I assured her, I *was* interested in dogs and very eager to see images of the childhood Lucy. My heart was in fact speeding up and thumping with anticipation. After several pages of Beulah and shots of Lucy in shorts and halter tops, in cowboy boots, in a riding out-fit, at a beach, with her dad, all of which I regarded with ardour and sustained delight, I had to say, "She's so adorable," meaning Lucy, of course, but Caroline understood me to mean Beulah. "She could be a terror at times. You know hounds. They'll chase a scent." Then, at a much higher decibel, "What was it Beulah went after that time, Lucy?"

Wearing blue rubber gloves, Lucy appeared in the dining room. "What, Mom, what, for pity's sake?"

"Where did Beulah go that time she got lost?"

"We don't know, Mom. Nobody knows. Only God knows, the god of beagles."

"You don't need to be smart."

"I'm not being smart. Nobody knows where Beulah was. Likely she went after a muskrat or some water-loving creature, because she took off along the creek."

Lucy disappeared, and Caroline carried on, placidly. "There aren't a lot of pictures of Howard, because he was at the boarding school, for the deaf, you likely know."

"Yes, Lucy told me she has a brother named Howard." And that he was deaf, I didn't add.

"It doesn't seem right that I have more pictures of dogs than him, but," she said, turning a page in the album, "regardless, this is the black standard poodle, Stanley. It was when I had Stanley I got rid of my husband, or he got rid of me, and Stanley and Lucy moved with me to this house," and with her bent, very white index finger, Caroline tapped a photo of a brick bungalow. "We stayed there for five years. Lucy was in high school, then, in the drama club, and see here she is dressed up at home as Cleopatra for Halloween. She liked to dress up. Stanley didn't like it, though. He'd get kind of scared."

"Stanley died from a stomach problem, but he lived a good life, ten years. Then I met Harry, and I moved up here, and we got another poodle, a female, and we named her Poppy. Lucy didn't really get to know Poppy much, because she didn't visit that often, I don't know why, she and Harry hit it off better than we do, in some ways, I mean she and I, not you. He just passed away not too long ago, well, two years or more. Same with Poppy. Well, I don't know, time gets mixed up for me. You seem like the quiet type. Are you the quiet type?"

"Maybe, yes, that might be accurate."

Lucy was rushing around now, getting the vacuum going. Caroline went upstairs to find another album, the one she had on the theme of Lucy and her dad. "You would probably like to see that one," she said, and she was clairvoyantly correct, but did not return for several minutes while I sat, and Lucy moved furniture and yanked the vacuum cleaner forward. Caroline eventually returned empty-handed and disappeared into the kitchen. "I was looking for the Howard album," I heard her say to no one. Disinhibition didn't seem that bad to me. On the way home, I told Lucy her mom seemed okay, her speech was fine, she remembered all the dogs.

Lucy said, "She is far from okay. I think she's maybe having little strokes all the time. She loses track of what day it is, and if it's morning or afternoon, and sometimes I wonder if she can actually still tell time, which is not that big a deal as long as she doesn't leave the house at night, which she doesn't generally do, at least I don't think she does. And she writes down her appointments and has a digital alarm clock. Fortunately," Lucy went on, rolling down the window so she could light a cigarette, "she likes watching TV and reading, and her friend Lorraine comes by pretty often. She doesn't want me living with her. She's made that clear by saying anything that comes into her mind, not that I want to live with her. Thanks for coming with me. It helps to have one other person know. The last time we were at the doctor's office in the waiting room, she said, 'I smell dirty feet.' And a large woman came out of one of the examining rooms, and Mom said, 'There's a real fatty.' Every time she says something like that in public I think I might have a rigour, as my grandma Fairfax used to say. Really. I get a very funny feeling inside my head like it's thinking it might have a stroke, too, then it goes away. Just for a second or two. What do you think that is, psychologist?" And Lucy jabbed in the lighter as if it might deserve to suffer.

"It's nothing, I'm sure. Just exasperation causing blood vessels to swell or constrict, and the vestibular system, in our ears, it's very mysterious — it's easy to get dizzy feelings."

"Maybe. I hope so."

"Which dog did you like best when you were a kid?"

Fully ignoring my question, Lucy said, "Speaking of clinics, I'm taking you to a walk-in clinic right now. The one by Market Mall. It's open until eleven, I think."

Experiencing a lightning-fast gush of panic, then sadness, I said, "I don't know if there's really much point. It's not as if my stomach is sticking out."

"What? You're not nuts, are you?" Lucy asked, at a red light. "Please tell me you are of sound mind, mens sana, you know," she was imploring, she was thinking, I think, I might throw off a sticky mask and be revealed as something else entirely. "You need to find out, Rose. You can't be one of those women who never knew she was pregnant until one day she has a baby on the airplane and then says, but my stomach wasn't really sticking out."

I nodded my head like a bobble-head dog on a car dashboard. "No, I'm not going to be the woman on the airplane. It's just that if I am pregnant, it's not a disease, and I only had those sips of beer that night Joe came, and since then, I've been following all the rules. What's the doctor going to tell me I don't already know?"

"He or she will tell you if you're pregnant or not, and if you're not, what's going on, if you have a growth."

"A growth? That's a nice word."

"Well?"

"Well, I might feel disinhibited in the waiting room, if we have to wait a long time." But we didn't. In the clinic, there was only one other patient, and I was soon in to see the doctor, a woman who said I could call her Helen. Lucy came with me. I wonder if she thought I would lie to her. *It's nothing, just a cyst, a small growth.* Then I told Helen I wanted Lucy there, even during the internal exam, which indicated I was likely pregnant. I had to leave a urine sample. Two days later the lab called and asked me to come in. Lucy insisted on coming with me, she managed to leave work early, and we drove in silence. My mind was empty, and my womb was probably full of creature cells. The results were positive, and Lucy was thrilled. Thrilled! On the way home, she assured me she would be the baby's dad, that she had been waiting her entire adult life to be a dad, and this was her lucky day. Wasn't I happy?

I guessed I was.

I WAS GOING to tell Mom but decided to wait, then just as I decided to wait a little longer, I called her. She had joined the choir again, back to the Mesmer Voice Capades; they had been rehearsing and caroling and drinking hot chocolate.

"Oh," I said. "Adrian told me you were thinking of signing up again."

"Yes," she said. "It's true. I thought I had better do *something*."

"Well, sounds like you're having fun. Are you doing a Christmas concert?"

"Three, yes. Three different churches. We're in demand. It's a serious choir, you know. If you miss three rehearsals, you're out. I don't mind since I doubt I'll miss any. Alma Torrance and I go together. She doesn't think it's right you get kicked out if you miss the three practices. I told her stick with me, and you won't be kicked to the curb. We sometimes stop in at the Two Star on the way home for a piece of stale pie, if they're still open."

"That sounds nice, Mom. I'm glad you're doing that." There was a silence. "I'm working at thinking up a thesis topic."

"What is a thesis?" she asked. "I don't even really know what a thesis is."

"It's just a big essay on a topic you choose, and then you have to do some research and collect some data and try to make some kind of point, statistically. It's not that interesting, really. It's mostly drudgery, I imagine."

"What's your topic going to be?"

"I'm not sure yet, maybe something to do with depression in children. What are the characteristics? It's different in children than adults."

"When I was in high school, in Grade 11, a girl jumped into the river in winter or maybe late fall, because it wasn't frozen over, and it's not that deep, but somehow she drowned, or maybe the cold killed her.

They said she was pregnant, but nobody knew. She always seemed pretty sad faced to me, pregnant or not."

"Was that in Owen Sound then?"

"Yes. So, I guess you talked to Adrian, did you? He said you called. Speaking of sad faced, George was here for the weekend. He and that new wife of his, Candy, they've split up. You likely knew that. He helped me get a few things done. Painted the storm window frames before we put them up."

"I didn't know they split up. That didn't last long. I'm glad he helped you out, Mom. Did he want you to complete any of his sentences?"

"What was that?"

"You know how he likes to say something and leave the last word or two off, and then he wants you to fill in the blanks. Like a clean towel is a happy towel. That kind of thing."

"No, he never talks like that to me." The way she said it, I might have been referring to dirty jokes. She told me George might come back next weekend and I told her my landlady had a kitten. There were pauses when I thought of saying, I have some big news or, I don't know what you will think of this, but . . . ironically, I could have used George's help. Just get on the other line and finish what I am about to say. By the way, what became of the armed forces plan?

I said goodbye and lay down, I needed to rest my 1.015 bodies. Lucy would be over in the evening and would ask: Did you tell her? Do you want me to? With the corners of her mouth turned down in her sad serious and faux serious manner. No and no.

five

LUCY AND I had not yet had what one would call a full-on sexual interaction; we had held hands and kissed, that's it. As part of my disinhibition program, Lucy and I went to a gay Christmas dance in a community hall, close to Renforth, down some wooden stairs to the neighbourhood of Bridgeland. As we approached the building, why I do not know, my legs were shaking, although, if I were to examine my heart closely, I would say it was because I expected five or six overpowering women to rush toward me, hug me, kiss me, and exclaim, "You're here! We thought you might be. Andrew called from Guelph." Outside the door, I could hear the music and the voices. I shuddered, but Lucy didn't notice. Inside, people smoked in groups, and not one individual appeared glad to see me. The hall was nothing but a large and dimly lit room with a stage, some Christmas lights, and a makeshift bar. I visualized bonspiels past, even though this was not an arena.

In Calgary, Lucy knew two gay men and two lesbians she could call friends. The men, Rob and Charles, were not there, but the lesbians, Iris and Barb, were present and had saved two chairs for us at a long, plywood-topped table. Ever so briefly, on a micro-neurological plane, I swooned as I took my seat. We all sat on the same side, in a row, Barb, Iris, Lucy, me, across from three men and one empty chair facing me, a pleasing configuration as I was freed from what I imagined might be sexually tinged social obligations. Lucy sat with her arm around me and talked to Iris while I worried a little that someone who did not like lesbians would enter the hall and shoot me, a nonplussed symbol. At the same time, I felt reassuringly normal with an arm around me. Listening in on Iris and Lucy's conversation, I smiled as if I were at ease with a room of homos, as Anastasia called them in high school, in 1975, but not now, I was certain, not in the dying days of 1980. Now she would likely say *gays*, and she would apologize for having said homos when we were teenagers. Interior conversations with Anastasia occasionally caused a muscle in my left thigh to flutter, and I poked at my leg with an index finger until it calmed itself.

Lucy got drinks, I said I'll just wait and get something, but she returned with a ginger ale for me, which I didn't really want because it seemed syrupy. After two songs, I told Lucy I wanted a club soda and left the table for the bar, where I was told I needed a ticket from the ticket table. By following the lineup, I found the ticket table, paid for two tickets, returned to the bar, and was told I had a drink ticket, not a pop or mix ticket, so I returned to the lineup, wanting to tell someone I was new to the laws of the lineup, smiling, feeling acutely out of place, hoping a social convener might come my way. I inched along, and this was when the Roger within me, I think, stepped forward with his see-through feet to help me withstand the alienation of the situation. Everyone avoided my eyes, or so I thought. When I finally had the club soda gripped in my hand, I made a quiet toast, to it, the fetus, and I began to like Roger. By then, Lucy was talking with the DJ, asking for some of the music she liked, Fleetwood Mac, John Cougar Mellencamp, even Willie Nelson, in response to which the DJ suggested ABBA, how about Donna Summer or Elton John? "Never mind," Lucy said dismissively. "Let's sit down," she said to me. Then seconds later, at the first few bars of David Bowie's "Heroes": "Let's dance."

We *moved on to the dance floor*. Moving on to the dance floor is almost as bad as I imagine public nakedness to be, then it passes, especially if you have had several drinks, which most of the others had, or a charming companion, which I had. We danced. I felt clumsy and ridiculous, and Lucy jumped up and down some, then grabbed onto me and kissed one cheek, then the other. A warmth penetrated my chest, like a druggy type of cough medicine. I wanted to go home but didn't think I should say so.

Back at the table, we resumed our previous seating arrangement with me at the end near the wall, watching. I noticed Iris was wearing a calf-length skirt with a white shirt, and I had to admit she looked, I have never really liked the word sexy, so, I would say, compelling. She was friendly, so was Barb, they took an interest, I wanted to leave. I tried to think other thoughts I should think while resisting the desire to put my head on the table and rest awhile. Then I went to the bathroom, where someone pounded on the stall door, and I said nothing.

Bending over, the pounder glanced at my feet, I saw her curly hair, her glasses, and then she left. At eleven o'clock, I said I wanted to go home, I think I'm pregnant, and Lucy smiled and whispered "Let's go then" into my left ear and her voice, so close to my temporal lobe, I think it moved in somehow and formed a shelter in my solid, closed head.

Outside, stinging pellets of snow were blowing at an angle; the wind was the kind that moves branches choppily and sends small cardboard boxes skittering along the street. For the second time that evening, I entered into communion with the parcel that would become Roger, the denser part of my abdomen I felt I should protect with my hand or the long coat I happened to be wearing. We had to climb the stairs. "Do you think the baby minds? The jarring effect of the stairs?" I asked Lucy. The baby known as me, I thought of adding.

"We can take a cab," she said. "Let's take a cab."

"No, no, we just live up there on the hill. It's fine. I just wondered. Let's walk without talking. The wind goes in my mouth. My hands are cold. Waah, waah, waah."

"Put them in your pockets," Lucy said, then she hooked her arm through mine, and we climbed the stairs to the parking lot of the Greek Orthodox church. Despite the cold and wind, we stopped at the top and turned to look at Calgary, lit up and lively and festive except for the Bow River, which would be darkly slowing with fetal fragments of its own, thin, thin ice. "Let's run a bit," I said, and Lucy said, "Maybe just a fast walk. Did you like the dance okay?" she asked. "I feel a little responsible for it."

"I liked it," I said. "To be honest, it made me feel a little lonely at times. Maybe that's why I've been thinking about the life form within," I paused, "me. Within me."

Lucy nodded in her way. She usually understood without a checklist of questions.

I STAYED IN CALGARY for Christmas 1980 and on January 1, 1981, moved across the easement and into Lucy's apartment. By then we had done *it*. She told me now I *had* to tell George and Mom about the pregnancy, and I said, yes, yes, I will. Although she had volunteered to be the dad in our arrangement, I felt my affable and yet noncommittal self was the more masculine. The fluttering presence that would become Roger did not seem like a gestalt or a shape or an outline able to outlive birth. Not that I pictured a stillbirth; no, I failed to picture any events beyond my belly and its slight girth. Pleased I was not showing much, I felt my size to be a sign of health and perhaps, yes, virtue. Well, how are you supposed to imagine another person growing inside you, I asked Lucy? This seemed like a feat to me. Writers of fiction admitted they had difficulty inventing characters out of thin air. How was the expectant mother to dream up a face, a personality, traits, names, hairstyles, a prophetic vision? Lucy didn't know, but she had a picture in her mind of someone who looked like Linus.

"Not Lucy?"

"Nope."

I wanted to ask my advisor, Dr. Chan, who had two teenage children and *was* my advisor. She was warm and approving, and sometimes asked my opinion on unexpected topics such as why do you think my fourteen-year-old girl won't wear a dress or a skirt? One afternoon in February, while in her office discussing levels of statistical significance, I told her I was pregnant. With a pleased expression, she said, "Oh. Your husband will be able to make gourmet baby foods!" I had almost forgotten about Jeff and SAIT.

And I said, "Yes, he's looking forward to that." I felt certain Dr. Chan would not care to supervise a single parent. Not that she would have thrown me out of her office and terminated our relationship, but the intimacy would have been interrupted. Intimacy interruptus, I thought, to keep myself going. I said, "Yes, my husband is really enjoying SAIT, learning lots about cuisinery," I said, hoping to eke a chuckle out of her.

She began to glimpse downward, looking for a ring, I am certain, as I tucked my left hand beneath my thigh. We continued to talk. "Have you been feeling well?" Dr. Chan asked.

"I've been fine except for the smell of meat, and the look of it," I answered.

Onward she glimpsed, glimpsing can never be concealed, but I was ahead of her, holding papers, then a binder, then a book, then my bag, finally withdrawing my left hand, as if it were cold or shy, into my sleeve. At the first opportunity, I fled Dr. Chan's office and the campus, catching the bus along 16th Avenue, feeling unreasonably fantastic, maybe because I had successfully strengthened my story to my supervisor, maybe because a chinook had blown in and the streets were slushy and the temperature high, plus twelve, people were saying. As we passed SAIT, I saw a skateboarder in shorts and watched intently, thinking it could be Jeff and wishing Lucy could be with me to laugh. And then because the bus was crowded and noisy, I got off at 10th Street and walked.

Just east of 8th Street I saw a pawn shop on the north side of the street and crossed over. I was thinking of buying a ring. The shop was called Don's Pawn. Inside, it smelled like smoky upholstery and singed coffee. Don had long red hair, almost in ringlets, and wore thick sunglasses. I told him I was looking for a wedding band in my size, and he rattled around with a key and pulled out a velvety stand holding half a dozen bands, all very plain and reminiscent of my mother.

One of the rings fit perfectly and was two hundred dollars. I paid for it with my student interest credit card and walked home with my coat open and my scarf in my briefcase. Lucy was already there!

She had got off work at four. I was so happy to see her, to be with her in her house; with no hesitation, I got the ring out of my pocket, like a man about to propose, and said, "I bought this for myself today. If you're going to be the baby's dad, I want to be married to you." I didn't mention Dr. Chan, who now seemed irrelevant.

Lucy seemed very affected by my ring. Holding it in her palm, her eyes filled with tears, something I had not yet known them to be capable of, and her usually assured mouth was not sure what to do with itself: corners up or corners down?

She said, "I love you, Rose, but are you sure you really want this? A girlfriend and not a boyfriend? You straight girls often drift in this direction."

I said, "Yes, I love you and this is not a drift." Although I preferred the oral sex with Lucy to oral sex with George, I was unenthusiastic about all forms of what I called, to myself, lower deck love. "Yes," I repeated. I undoubtedly loved Lucy and the kissing, the touching, the sleeping together. Then I told her my friend Andrew from the University of Guelph had told me he thought I should be a lesbian.

"Okay, but what do you think?" she wanted to know.

"I agree with him," I said, forcefully, manfully.

"This is the sort of risk I told myself I wouldn't take ever again, but I want to put that ring on your finger, so let's do it."

"Yes, let's do it, and let's hope neither of us has a rigour," I said, and a composite image of Dr. Chan, my mother, Lucy's mother, George and Anastasia, even Andrew, their faces organized to fit a type of poster, elbowed aside all other content in my mind, only briefly.

"With this ring I thee love," Lucy said.

"I thee love, too."

"I guess we all are Quakers now."

"I love when you say *we all*."

ON VALENTINE'S DAY, I called Mom. Lucy was still at work when I
arrived home from classes at three-thirty. At noon, I had told myself
this was the day, and since then had been moving toward the telephone. I sat in one of the booths in the library, holding the receiver,
trying to imagine what Mom would say, pretending to have made a
call. Successive approximations, this was called, and it helped. I got off
the bus and walked a bit, then entered the phone booth at 16th Avenue
and the Esso station, closing the door and enjoying a respite from the
wind and traffic. Closing a phone booth door makes a person want to
lie down, but if there is one place where that is not possible . . . I didn't
pick up the receiver, just stood with my back to the street. I should be
thankful; I *was* thankful but sometimes moments of melancholy and
phone booths and contemplating calling Mom about pregnancy weakened my bladder, so I had to get going. Ten minutes and I was home,
relieving myself, and this gave me strength; I was ready. Mom would
be home. Maybe frying herself a few potatoes to have with ketchup
and a celery stick.

"Hello?"

"Hi, Mom."

"I thought it might be you."

"Good, because I have some news for you. I'm pregnant. George is
the father. I was pregnant when I left Guelph. That's it, that's the news."

Silence. "Well, that is big news. Well. Congratulations. Are you
coming back?"

"No. I have to finish the degree, and besides, I'm not married to
George anymore."

"But he's already divorced or at least separated from that Candy."

"I know, but I can work things out here."

Silence.

"Are you frying potatoes?"

"No, not yet."

"I thought you might be, that's what I pictured you doing."

"I do do other things besides fry potatoes."

"Yes, I am aware of that, Mom." And I wondered if Phone Conversations with Mom was an essay I might write for my course on the history of the unconscious. "Anyway, the baby's due in May which works out, because my courses for this year are finished in April."

"Well, I can come out for a while."

"Okay. That would be good, that would be great. My friend Lucy is helping me. We're sharing a place now, but if you came out here that would be good. I can't really believe it's happening."

"Have you told Adrian?"

"No. You can tell him if you want."

"Do you feel okay?"

"Yes, I feel fine. At first, I felt kind of blah, but not now; now I feel good."

"That'll be three grandchildren, then. I'm building up quite a herd." She sounded suddenly almost joyful, but I thought it best to check.

"Are you glad to be building up a herd?"

"Yes. Of course I am! Do I seem like someone who doesn't want a herd of grandchildren?"

Words came to me in little gusts of sometimes maybe often never. But Mom carried on. "I'll send you out some things. There're some baby clothes around here still. And I can get a few more from Adrian. They say they're not having any more. Mostly girl things, of course, so if it's a boy, he'll be dressed in pink."

"Maybe it will be a girl. That would be nice, but I haven't thought about it that much, boy or girl."

"Do you have names picked out?" Mom asked.

"Roger for a boy, with Daniel for a middle name, after Dad, of course. Maybe Frances for a girl. Maybe Frances Danielle."

"Those are both nice, very nice. Your dad would be happy. Maybe Roger is a male form of Rose, is it?"

"I don't think so, Mom, but maybe. I hadn't thought of that. Anyway, I should go. I need to get some groceries. I do most of the cooking around here."

"Can't that Lucy girl do some of it?"

"She does, that Lucy girl does cook. I'll call in a week or two. Okay?"

"Bye, then."

"Bye."

I turned on the TV and turned it off. Snow was falling now. Something like shame pulled on the space below my diaphragm, not precisely shame, but it would know where to find it. I would love to have been able to see what went on in there, how the muscles heaved and hoed when a person felt like this. I wondered if those organs and tissues wished they would get some light or air just once, for clarification.

six

ON MAY 4, 1981, the day Roger was born, Lucy drove me to the hospital and stayed with me. She was my coach, and we had a midwife. The birth was relatively easy, I was told, probably because Roger was small, just over five pounds, and his head wasn't entirely round. I did not have to scream or beg for a painkiller. The midwife, Mary, showed me how to exhale in an animalish deep groan, reaching into my qi, she said, which minimized the pain; it was a miraculous intervention,

I could hardly believe it worked. Roger breathed and was able to breastfeed, so nobody made a fuss. Later, looking back, I think the hospital staff may have thought he was unusual but what would be the point of saying that then, to the two moms? Enough was enough. Besides, there were some other babies in the nursery who looked a little funnier to my wondering eyes, although probably not *dysmorphic*, I had to admit. I looked at one, then another, then another, then another, then at Roger, and like all the other humans, I could see there was a problem, and on the second day, I said so. Lucy said, "Your hormones are all over the map, you have postpartum ovaries; they don't know what to do. Don't pay attention to anything you're thinking. Pay attention to what I'm thinking." Lucy said we should have him circumcised, and I agreed. She is so persuasive with her slightly southern vowels, that after day three, when, because of the extra-large pads, I remembered coatex protection, and after day four when the doctor said Roger was a beautiful boy, I felt all would be well.

Once we were home, away from the comparison group, I apologized to Roger for thinking such wild diagnostic thoughts about him, explaining to him it was the psychologist's way. In fact, I apologized more than once, and always when Lucy was out of the house. I started to love him, every day a little more, until the love was almost an amphetamine in that its intensity kept me awake, even when he was sleeping. In his crib, near our bed, I could hear Roger breathing and was unbelieving and also proud to be responsible for this moving container of life. Lucy seemed to love him as much as I did, although I could not know, and still to this day do not know if that can be true. I don't think I could have loved a child she had borne, not in the same way. But. As the days passed, I couldn't help it, I wanted to know if she saw anything funny in the way Roger looked, and after six weeks, when his face had grown into itself a little, I ventured to ask Lucy, directly, "Does he look a little unusual to you?"

And in the voice of a baby enthusiast, she replied: "I guess if you call a little button or a bug unusual, because he is as cute as both." The corners of Lucy's mouth angled down at about thirty degrees, and I knew this to be the mien of indisputability. In the days following, when she caught me watching anxiously, my mouth pursed in skeptical concentration, she said, "Rose, Rose, Rose," in that tone of voice, as if calling me out of a dream or coma, which sometimes was the case. She was so lovely, I loved her.

Every time I went grocery shopping, I took Roger with me. Other babies, I noticed in the Co-op grocery store, even the less pretty, had rounder faces and looked more alert, the baby adjective most likely to be used for sorting purposes, although the ones I studied closely, I reminded myself, were in magazines or on TV; much as I might have wanted to, I couldn't approach Roger's cohort of live infants with a test kit. The first few times, when I took him out in the Snugli, he wanted to push his face against my chest, almost as if he did not want to see or be seen. I wondered if some radio waves from my sternum had advised him his mother was anxious about his face, and to compensate, I tried to position his cheek against my chest, looking out at the new world sideways, but he stubbornly preferred to face forward, so I said, okay, then. Still, this face-hiding behaviour seemed kitten-like to me, aberrant for a human baby with open eyes, and I wondered if I had done that as a child, so I called my mother. She said she didn't remember anything like that, but that I would have been in a buggy not a Snugli, because I was born in March, and no one carried their babies around on their chests back then, so they didn't need to look sideways.

"Well, this is June, and people like me are carrying their babies around on their chests," I said, in our defence. Then I added, "Maybe I should get a *buggy*."

Mom ignored this and said she'd had compliments on both of us, me and Adrian, and that we had been better-looking babies than most. In the easement, while Lucy smoked, I told her I was not sure we had had any unequivocal or gasping compliments yet on Roger's appearance.

"Gasping?" Lucy asked.

"You know, like a sudden intake of breath because he's so cute."

"Have you ever delivered a gasping compliment to the parent of a baby?"

I had to admit I had not.

Carmen had said that he was sweet, but of course he was sweet. Unless you believed in original sin, what else could be said of a blank slate of human tissue?

Lana, the neighbour on the other side, who spoke with an unspecifiable accent (and whom we called Lana the language barrier) had said he was *pracious* and a *dohll*, and I clung to her choice of words, carted them around with me as if they had their own Snugli slings on my chest. Lucy's mom only glanced at him and asked if he had all ten fingers and toes. I asked Lucy why she had said that, in particular, and Lucy insisted her mother meant it as a compliment, as in, if he's got all ten fingers and toes, he's fine. She's not interested in babies, Lucy said, or anyone other than herself, really, she expects the *Calgary Herald* to have stories about her.

"Why?"

"I'm kidding, Rose. Because she's self-centred."

"Oh, I see."

Maybe I was hypervigilant, to use Peggy's phrase from her seminar presentation on anxiety. I sent pictures to Mom and Adrian and awaited a verdict via the telephone. Adrian already had two precious and doll-like daughters. With his visual and spatial awareness, he would notice anything out of whack, but then would not likely say anything, because he didn't like to criticize and was more on the hypo-vigilant end of most scales.

Roger was two months old when we went for his first shots, and the doctor, Dr. Suleiman, displayed no concerns, but asked, "Is he suckling well?" I said, pardon, and she asked again, "Does he suckle well?"

Seeing this as an opportunity to get a positive report on Roger's fledgling permanent record, I answered, "Yes, very well, better than average, I like to think," and the doctor looked pleased and wrote a word or two in the file. I told Lucy, jokingly, that I wished there were a suckling competition we could enter, as I was sure Roger would win. She wrinkled her forehead and took Roger from my arms. We were in a mall, at the Bay, after the appointment, buying more cloth diapers; we both hated the disposables. I said, "I wasn't being serious, just now, about the suckling contest."

"I know that," she said, "I know you don't want to put him into a *suckling* competition." A woman holding the hand of a toddler turned to look, actually nodded as she passed by as if she understood what we were discussing.

"I think it's just, sometimes I think you might be judging me, the wrong way," I said, my face reddening from the confession Lucy didn't hear, being ahead of me by then, holding Roger, boarding the escalator to the children's section. Undaunted, I carried on a brisk, mental exchange. 'You think I think about this all too much, don't you?' 'This?' 'You know, me, Roger, Roger, me, looks, compliments, dys...' 'Don't say it!' 'Someone has to.'

At the top of the escalator, Lucy said, "Let's get him a couple of outfits. I'm in the mood for Roger shopping."

"Yes, let's," I said, and I kissed her cheek and Roger's head which smelled of baby and utter helplessness, and my heart was ransacked by tenderness.

WHEN ROGER WAS ten weeks old, Mom came to visit; she had had to put off the trip because of a choir obligation. I went to the airport on my own, in the Oldsmobile, because Lucy was at work. By then Roger was smiling, he could, of course, but he didn't that often, only once in a while, and I hoped he would for Mom, at arrivals. But during the walk from the parkade to the terminal, he had fallen asleep with his forehead on my chest and his chin drooping like a little plum, and so I missed the one time Mom might have made an unguarded comment or flinched. I knew her face, obviously, and it gave away information like a notice board. As we waited at the carousel, reminded no doubt by all the bags circulating, Mom said, "You haven't told this friend of yours about my bladder bag, have you?"

"No," I answered. For once this question did not irritate me. I wanted her to hold Roger, wanted to press him into her arms, but being in the Snugli, still asleep, this was an impractical plan. Instead, I said, "He's a good little breastfeeder."

Mom said, "That's good. You and Adrian didn't have any problems with the bottle."

"Oh," I said. We watched the circling bags and Roger woke with a startle.

"You knew your grandma was here, so you decided to wake up," I said, and I couldn't stop myself, I undid the Snugli and worked Roger out of it, handing him over to Mom. I had an idea I resembled a wild animal, my hair, my eyes, my still spottily menstruating vagina, and yet I smiled an uncontrolled and broad smile at the woman next to me, who was not my mother. She smiled back.

Mom pronounced Roger solid and a bit like the Drurys around the eyes. She said she hoped he didn't have the March heart and wanted to know if they had checked it at the hospital.

I said, "I don't think they have a specific test for the March heart."

She said, "You don't have to be persnickety. I just meant did they check his heart?"

"Yes, I think they did. Which Drury does he look like? Grandma?"

"She was the March."

"Oh, right." Roger was studying Mom, his head wobbling a bit but with a half smile. I was thrilled. "What about your side? The Lowes? Does he look like them? Or the Kernighans?"

"I can't really see it." He was stretching out his arms and yawning, trembling a little with the intensity. Mom smiled and gave him a little kiss.

"Do you think he's cute?"

"Very nice looking," she said, without going into specifics.

Her bag came, and as we walked to the parkade, I told her Roger and I would sleep in Lucy's room; to be accurate, I said, Roger and I sleep in Lucy's room, but she didn't care, she wasn't listening, and, I said, she could have the spare room, there was a cot from IKEA.

No response from Mother. As we waited for the elevator to the sixth level, I said to Mom, "I think he likes the parkade. He's really looking around. He doesn't always like to do that."

She said, "Babies like to look around, that's what they do best."

"I just said he doesn't always like to do that."

"I guess I didn't hear you right. My ears are still funny from the plane."

MOM LIKED TO SAY the things she shouldn't say over the phone. After she'd been home for three days, she called in the evening and asked if I remembered a girl from Flax named Donna McBeel.

"I don't think so."

"She was a little older than you. The family moved to England when Donna was maybe seven or eight."

"No," I said, "I don't remember her. Why?"

"Well, I probably shouldn't say anything, but she had a water head."

I knew what she was talking about. "You mean hydrocephalus?"

"I just started to think after I left that Roger's forehead seems a little pronounced."

"Well, they didn't say anything at the hospital, and the doctor measured his head when he got his shots. It was a bit big but in the normal range." She could tell by my voice I was on the defensive. Roger's own grandmother!

"I should keep my mouth shut," Mom said.

"That's okay," I said, softening up, grabbing a tea towel to wipe my nose. "I wondered a bit about his head myself, until the doctor measured it." Roger was in his bouncy reclining chair. The front door was open to let the breeze through the screen, and he was watching the top page of a section of the newspaper on the floor flutter and fall on the air. I loved watching him observe these mundane mysteries. That same breeze reached my face and neck where I sat beneath the kitchen window, on the floor. From across the street I could hear a sprinkler going through its semi-circular program, which by the end of July was almost pointless.

"I'm sure he's fine," Mom said. "A lot of the Drurys have big foreheads, like your uncle Angus."

"That's mainly because he's bald, but never mind. Have you been talking to George? Did you tell him you were here, and you met Roger?"

"Yes," she said, brightly, and I thought, I wonder if she's in love with George. "He wanted to know how you were doing, if you had remarried and I told him no."

"Remarried? I'm not like him," then I thought of Lucy and considered maybe I was. "He didn't ask about Roger? I told him I was pretty sure I was pregnant before I left Guelph."

"He seemed not to want to delve into much, just wanted to make some plans for fix-it jobs."

"George is not one for delving," I said. "He didn't happen to mention if Petrie is really his last name or if it's the name of the foster parents he had down near Longview?"

"Well, I'm pretty sure it must be Petrie. Why would he go by somebody else's name?"

"Well, that's what I'd like to know, Mom. I'll have to call him one of these days. I'd like Roger to be able to fill out a family tree when he's in Grade 4 like everyone else, with accurate information and names that go back two or three generations. Or if you think of it the next time you talk to him, could you get him to write it down, make a little tree?"

"He's coming up this way next weekend to prune the actual trees, so I can ask him then."

"Thanks, Mom."

That very same day, I had Roger with me at the Co-op, buying groceries. He was awake, for once, and looking around rather world-wearily at the rows of cans and boxes of cereal when a woman, probably in her forties with very pink lipstick, stopped her cart next to mine where I was standing, inspecting the canned fish. She looked at Roger and emitted a one-syllable type of bark. It sounded like "Rowf." Holding a can of tuna, I stood, cataleptic or wondering if I might be.

Then she said, "That's an unusual-looking little sausage," regarding me with chagrin, as if I were the hapless caretaker of a baby-shaped link of meat.

"Don't listen to her," I advised the top of Roger's head. Fight adrenalin rushed to my hands and feet.

"Oh, I didn't mean to be rude," said the woman, whom I had by then noticed was wearing perfectly matching green socks and running shoes that looked to have been dyed.

"Well, you are," I said, looking directly into her green eye shadow. "You were."

She made a face of mock injury. I dropped the can of tuna loudly into my cart and pressed ahead, saying nothing. Later, in the detergents aisle, I saw her again. Still furious, I thought of running my cart into the back of her green ankles but did not at that precise moment have the emotional vigour. Instead, I held back until she rounded the corner, then studied the cleansers for a good five minutes. "Some foam while others do not," I said to Roger. Having had enough of shelves, he pressed his face into my sternum. "I know," I said, "the Co-op can be a bit much." By the time we approached the coffees and teas, I could see my enemy was in the express line and would soon be gone.

Outside, I mentioned to Roger that I hated everyone. While we were in the Co-op, the hot, dry weather had come to a dramatic end, and dark threatening clouds were skittering in from the northwest, along with a bracing, cool wind. I tied Roger's hat on and, once across 16th Avenue, race-walked home, planning my call to Lucy. I hate everyone, I was going to say, not scream, I did not scream, just a comment, I hate everyone, all of them. But now the heavy raindrops, large as bumblebees, were falling, and Lucy, after all, was at work; I couldn't bother her with this sort of thing. The optometrists couldn't possibly want their receptionist spending her time soothing callers. She'd be looking at the rain, too, which was pleasing.

At home, I closed the windows and changed Roger's clothes and lay next to him on the bed. With my face close to his, I said nothing, I kissed his cheek. With his grey-blue eyes he regarded me, then moved his hand from his mouth to mine. His little fingers against my teeth were about the circumference of a drinking straw, so breakable. "I wish I could fold you up somehow, and put you inside my skin," I said, pulling up my T-shirt and undoing the nursing bra. I loved the feral ferocity with which he latched on, and I looked forward to it and was never disappointed. Roger's mouth and my nipple were members of a very old organization which had welcomed us, no questions asked. Then I pictured the woman in green shoes and imagined punching her with leather boxing gloves. "Roger," I said and stroked his fluffy head. If someone gawked at Roger again or made a *rowf* sound, I would simply stare back. Roger was fine. Mom had left her old Dr. Spock with me, and the other book on infant development, *Up the Years From One to Six*, the ones I had used to hide my coin collection. After Mom left, I didn't want to look at them, but eventually, one day, allowed myself to leaf, once, quickly, through their old-fashioned pages. I was a furtive mother, I guess. Then I put them away. Dr. Suleiman had said not much was expected in the first six months, except for eye contact and reaching and grasping, both of which Roger already did in his own wavery way. He liked my hair and Lucy's. He grasped and held on, he was hitting his milestones, hewing to his own round-eyed wavery routes.

I WENT BACK to school. Mrs. Marini, across the street, babysat on Mondays, Wednesdays, and Fridays. On Tuesdays and Thursdays, I had no classes and could start work on my thesis, I thought, with Roger, somehow. By then, he was drinking formula some of the time. I'd given up on expressing milk, which could take half an hour to produce an ounce or even less. I couldn't bear to sit still that long with a pump, with a bottle, with all those contraptions. My final attempt, I threw the bottle at the wall, it was plastic, I knew it wouldn't break, but Lucy came running from the living room to the bedroom. Never before had I thrown anything in frustration, at a wall, I mean, but pumping my own breasts forced up titanic and opposing wave actions of thought: Yes, I am a thing that may be pumped; no, I am not. Lucy volunteered to call the La Leche League. I said, "No, I called them once before, and they wanted the address, the address of the breasts.

I told them no, you can't have that address, and I hung up, well, I just pushed down the receiver buttons."

My female classmates insisted on having a baby shower for me. In our Ed. Psych. program there were twenty students, twelve of whom (including me) were women, and they were all invited. Attendance at the shower was good, with all but one guest showing up, and she, Elizabeth, had a good reason, her dog had been hit by a car and killed, and at first this cast a pall on the celebration, as everyone knew the dog, Amber. Elizabeth had brought her to class twice and was subsequently told by one of the secretaries not to bring her again. We all rallied around Elizabeth in her overwrought anger and pain and disappointment. She had thought Amber would get a degree with her, and now she was dead. The good thing was, Roger seemed to listen to the chatter about Amber with genuine interest, which impressed my classmates, especially Peggy, who said, "Look at him. He's got a great fucking attention span already!" I beamed with pride, naturally.

Debbie, the hostess, had been to an ashram, and this was the explanation for almost everything Debbie-related, such as saris and a bare midriff as well as a slight, sing-songy accent. She was also a vegetarian, so the food at the shower was vegetarian. There were gifts, and everyone seemed to be impressed by Roger's *alertness*, and this cheered me immensely, all of these women being half-trained observers of children. Certainly no one seemed to be taken aback by Roger's appearance, and I know this because I vigilantly, I hypervigilantly, watched for signs of taken abackness, that is, peering with greater than average intensity, eyebrow movement, uncertainty of the mouth musculature, and so on. The gifts were all clothes and books, and I was grateful and moved by their interest and care. I said so. Then Debbie asked about my husband. She said, "Your husband must be very happy with this little guy." It wasn't an explicit question, but everyone stopped talking and eating and the room was like a united audience, awaiting my reply. I had told Peggy my husband and I had reconciled, unsure if I had said his name was George or Jeff. To others, Debbie and Elizabeth, I had mentioned Jeff, SAIT and culinary arts. To many, I was vague, and they were too polite to press for details.

"Yes," I said. "Jeff is very happy. He had the summer off from SAIT, so he helped out a lot. Now he's back, of course, for more cookery." I repeated the word cookery, and my forehead warmed slightly, glowed, I imagine, and a drop of sweat rolled down my back, between my shoulder blades.

Hooray. Teresa wanted to hold him. She was a stocky woman in whose arms Roger seemed vulnerable, and I wondered what the doctor would have in store for percentile ranks when we showed up for the four-month visit I was already putting off. Was it possible for the head circumference to surpass the one hundredth percentile rank, I wondered, and apropos of this, said out loud, "I guess there's nothing beyond the one hundredth percentile rank, is there?"

"You're not already thinking gifted, are you?" Teresa asked. Everyone laughed.

Margo, who bought almost everything second-hand and was famous for the pilling on her overly washed sweaters and for the faded armpits of her rayon blouses, took Roger from Teresa and said, "Hi, little Boo Boo. Are you a little Boo Boo?"

Maybe because Margo was addressing him with a synonym for mistake, or maybe because she was holding him with genuine warmth, I said, "Oh no," began to cry, and flopped my head onto the shoulder of the woman next to me, who happened to be Peggy. One can imagine ten graduate students of psychology ministering to a weeping member of their cohort. The verdict was I just needed a good night's sleep. And then we had cake.

Back home, I greeted Lucy with, "Hi, Jeff!"

"Uh oh," she said, "you didn't tell them the Dr. Chan story?"

"Yes, I did, and I hope you don't hate me for it."

"You gave them details about Jeff Drury?"

"Only briefly. When asked about him, I said he was helpful. I don't even know why. It's not as if I'm afraid to tell them about you, or that they would care about my personal life. I think it has to do with Dr. Chan, I need to keep my story straight, I can't tell her one thing and everybody else the truth."

"It doesn't matter," Lucy said, I think she meant it, but then, at that very moment, Roger leaned toward Lucy's arms. This was the first time he had leaned toward either of us, and it may not have been intentional, I am certain it wasn't, he was only four-and-a-half months old, he sloped toward Lucy in my arms, and I handed him over. Moments later, I decided I needed to go for a walk, I love the fall, I love nature, I need a moment to myself, I said to Lucy, after that shower event. I walked to Tom Campbell's hill, which is a kind of undeveloped park nearby covered with fescue grass, a type of grass that grows in the West, Carmen had told me. It likes to grow in clumps, which must be an adaptation to dryer climates. Whatever its evolutionary story, watching the fescue grass on Tom Campbell hill could be a recreational balm.

I sat down on the one bench and wondered, is it possible that I am more immature than Roger? Is it? He sloped toward Lucy, and I felt infinitesimally excluded. He didn't even *with volition* slope, I had tilted him in the direction of Lucy, he had no choice, he is matter, gravity drags on him. Admit: I felt a pang, a drop of lemon juice on a fresh and open cut, and as a convoluted response to what should have been a non-stimulus, I thought of Joe and a sleeping bag and a tent. Yes, a miniature departure would be the thing, or a break. That's what they had all said at the shower, I needed a good night's sleep. Roger loved formula, truth be told, it would be a good thing for me to get away. Of course, I couldn't tell Lucy I was going to spend a warm fall night at the copse. I would think of something. I could go and come right back and feel better for it, bathed at the open-air homeless spa. Roger slopes toward Lucy, I slope toward Joe's old place. I didn't even think I would do it, given my fears of cougars and rabid bats, but I did. Monday, when Lucy was at work, I made preparations, I bought a little tent, blue like Joe's, and a toque. I already had the sleeping bag Joe had used, so I bought a foamie for support. I kept all of this, my kit as I called it, stored, secreted to use Anastasia's word, in the basement behind the furnace, and when I looked at it, I felt a whoosh of delight.

Yes, I needed a little getaway. I was doing too much. I was reading for my literature review and taking three courses, one of which was an independent study with Dr. Berrigar on what we were calling Lives Lived Differently, where I hoped to be able to use my Joe interviews but, often, instead, found myself veering into genetics, looking through books and monographs with sad and clinical black and white pictures of babies and their many potential reasons for living life differently. That's where I really got familiar with dysmorphia, that's when I first learned of fragile X syndrome. One of the babies in one of the pictures looked a little bit like Roger, and I looked and looked, held the picture close to my face, swallowing and wincing. This was the week I had assembled my kit, and as I sat in my seventh-floor office, I wanted desperately to hold Roger close and away from photographers, away from scientists. It doesn't matter, I said to myself and to Roger, it doesn't matter, it doesn't matter, it's only a picture, and I love your little face, your round eyes, the way you flap your arms with glee, and there in the educational psychology building, milk spurted from my nipples. It spurted. I was an animal in school, a brainy wolverine in a desk with a notepad in its paw, thankful her officemate, Karen, was nowhere in sight as she dabbed at her eyes and nipples and bra.

The Saturday after the walk to Tom Campbell's hill, I was able to sneak the tent, the sleeping bag and the foamie into the trunk of Lucy's car. I had told her I was going out with Elizabeth because I hadn't seen her at the baby shower and her dog was dead. And I liked Elizabeth, she was the only other fellow student who objected to the SES talk. We both hated it. Elizabeth's grandmother was Blackfoot from out by Gleichen, and she said the SES talk was code for Indian. I was beginning to think she was right, but I wasn't meeting her for a drink to discuss this. She was going to Edmonton for the weekend with her boyfriend, so there was no chance of her calling while I was out. I told Lucy if I drank too much I would stay over at Elizabeth's. I think she could see I was lying. From her optometric work, she's very comfortable looking into eyes, almost as if she can read a very small font in there, the size of the smallest letters in the smallest eye chart and mine were saying: I'm going to the copse.

The formula was made, Lucy was excited about being alone with Roger, so I took off, but I had to go to Juliet's Castle to kill time, eighty-thirty was too early and half-bright to pitch a tent in the druggy copse. Juliet's Castle is a bar in a strip-mall on 16th Avenue. I had the impression only men went there, but I walked in anyway and sat at the bar, trembling like I had upon my arrival at the gay and lesbian dance. I ordered a gin and tonic, Lucy's favourite drink, and abruptly gained control of my sympathetic nervous system. As my eyes adjusted to the gloom, I noticed there were two other women in the bar, both around my age, one playing pool with a guy and the other dancing by herself in front of the jukebox. I judged them both to be of low socio-economic status, but they were both blonde, so Elizabeth wouldn't care. I felt homesick for my office at the university and thought of going there instead of the copse, to read and highlight and find pictures of babies and children looking like Roger, babies identified as examples of genetic flawlessness, or babies who had a temporary problem that resolved itself by age twelve months, but I did not. Three times, I said to myself, just forget about it.

Having declined a second drink, I drove to the parking lot at the head of the copse trail, exited the car, and looked at the sky. The moon was up, just, not full, almost, and piercingly solitary without a cloud in sight. The sun had been down for a couple of hours, but in the west, when I turned to look, the sky held onto a lighter quality behind the blackness of the mountains, a blue a person might want to enter if it were a room with a door. I sighed and pulled my kit from the trunk. Conditions were fair with a bit of a breeze. Most of the leaves still clung to their trees. The path, the flight path, was a lighter grey against dark vegetation and shrubbery, and the smell of the night had risen, whatever its ingredients, open-eyed insects, plants exhaling, nests perhaps crumbling, leaves shuttering themselves for the season. The steeper spur path to Joe's old home was visible enough, and I walked slowly, grabbing lilac and willow branches for stability. No one in sight! Upon arriving at my camping spot, I was disproportionately relieved, as if I had been rescued from a collapsing building and carried to this private haven. Apparently, you had all the right insurance, ma'am.

I rolled out the foamie and spread the sleeping bag on top. The sleeping bag smelled a bit like Joe, like old soup and hair and clothes that needed washing. I hoped to god he was still alive, put on my toque, and wormed into the bag, unsure if I would bother with the tent. The leaves were fluttering, and I wanted to see them, and I felt safer this way but a little scared my potentially March heart wouldn't make it through the night, and then what? By wondering what was it exactly about the March hearts, I distracted myself. Were they more loosely attached than others' in their owners' dark breasts? Did they tend to let go before fifty and flop like a dense fish onto a cage of ribs? I shivered, wondering, then stopped and watched the moon, but not for long.

Mentally, I moved on to fragile X syndrome, thinking maybe Adrian had it, he had a large head and other symptoms, his reading problem, for example, his general impulsivity. Maybe he had *some* of the extra repeats of the amino acids, that's what caused it, too many As and Gs and Cs, so stretched you got a weak spot. Carried by the mother, in this instance, and there was a phrase that would make you want to take some scissors to your own helixes. To consider there is a deficiency with your own DNA is to invite the ocean in to wash you away and start over with a new stab at evolution. Yes, Mom, you had a fragile X and now you are a clam. Just as well. A gust of wind came through, and the topmost branches above my head went slap happy, clattering like midway rides the lower branches had improvised for them: have fun, you kids, don't break your necks. Don't get fragile, fragile X.

My spot was free of stones and root protuberances and was likely the very place where Joe had slept within his tent, but outside like this I could see beyond the crest of the hill to the north, where the lights of the Elks golf-course clubhouse emitted a reassuring glow, a guiding illumination should there be a crisis in the copse, a cougar, a rabid bat, a heart incident. I lay on my back, staring skyward, and put on my mitts. In my core, I was at peace with the trees, with Dad's idea of heaven, with the proximity of the clubhouse, but in my extremities, I was nervous. They shook again, then stopped when I heard voices coming from the direction of the clubhouse. It must be one a.m., they were closing their bar and restaurant. Shortly after, their lights went out, and the copse became darker, which is when I stood up, rolled the foamie and the sleeping bag, carried my kit to the car, put it in the trunk, and sat behind the wheel. Now the moon was high and down in the coulee, cars drove by on Deerfoot Trail, fast and furious, their occupants smoking and listening to music, some, no doubt, with a diagnosis.

Roger was in his own room now. Back home, I looked at him, then I woke Lucy and told her I'd been to the copse, that I had gone to see it on my way home from Elizabeth's place.

"You went right into it? In the night?" Lucy asked.

"Yes," I said, glistening I think I was, like someone covered in a Vaseline of instability.

Lucy was up on one elbow. "That's out of bounds," she yelled, like an official at an athletic event. She was fully awake and smelled like a cigarette in clean sheets. "Don't go there alone at night. Don't do that. That's dangerous."

"It's not really dangerous, is it? I mean, it's a copse in Calgary."

"You know what I mean, incautious to a bad degree."

"I wanted to hear the leaves, I mean, at this time of year."

Lucy examined my eyes for signs in the same semi-haunted way I had, once or twice, with Anastasia, observed the Ouija board's reports.

"Don't do that again, okay. Go there in the daytime, with me. Don't do it again."

"Okay," I said. "Okay."

seven

ROGER'S FIRST CHRISTMAS was memorialized in his baby book with a photo of the turkey, Lucy, Lucy's mom, Carmen, and Janet and Andrew, a couple Lucy had met at the community association meetings, where she was an executive member-at-large. In the photo, taken by me, Roger, held by Lucy, is facing the camera and smiling. He looked average enough, to me, by then, although a little reedy. That was the word I had come up with, maybe because he reminded me a little of the reeds along the side of the road to East Flax, with their narrow, elongated tops and generally pleasing movements. His hair was becoming browner, the colour of bulrushes.

There was a second photo, of Lucy with Roger on her lap. Roger was wearing black plastic glasses frames from Halloween. The nose and mustache had been removed, and Roger tolerated the glasses well, likely because people laughed at his serious little face. (Not too far into the future, by the time he was two and a half, he would begin to love to make people laugh.) Lucy was trying to get Roger to hold onto a single, blank piece of white paper, which created a blur in the lower foreground. She wanted Roger to hold the paper while she pretended to be a TV news reporter with a southern U.S. accent. She was wearing black, plastic glasses, too, and rattling off a news report, things like, early morning found Roger Drury trying on a new snowsuit, most likely appropriate for next winter. He displayed a *lot* of interest in his new stacking cups, watching his mother create a tower and whack it over with enthusiasm. "Roger likes to watch things," Lucy said. "He seemed to enjoy the aroma of a roasted bird, a turkey. His nostrils worked appreciatively throughout the afternoon. When asked to comment on his day, Roger Drury was, as usual, aloof but not dismissive. His eyes spoke volumes. They always do."

I carried that photo with me and often took it out of the zippered pocket in my purse. There they were. The sights and sounds of Lucy still made me melt, elicited a jangling in my mind similar to the letdown reflex when I was breastfeeding, but from a spot closer to where joy overlaps with crying. If I were a pigeon, when I looked at this photo, I would have cooed. Sometimes, I showed people. I showed Peggy and told her I wanted to be honest, I was divorced and with Lucy. I told Elizabeth, and she said Dr. Chan didn't need to know Jeff was a made-up character. After these disclosures, I assumed my classmates all knew. We went to one more of the dances, Iris and Barb came for dinner; Roger took a shine to them. Lucy brightened every day for me. She was on an even keel, she had no endocrine shakeups. She stayed with the optometrists and developed her ideas for "One Thing," her community newsletter column. I sometimes worried she would fall in love with someone more like her, someone she interviewed and photographed, whose photo she kept in a zippered pocket. Occasionally, I sneaked a look in her briefcase, and in her wallet, then sat down, swooning with situational guilt.

Lucy didn't pressure me to take Roger to the doctor. He was fine, he will be fine, and he is currently fine, she said. He's healthy. I took him for the prescribed shots, albeit a bit tardily, and at nine months we went to see Dr. Suleiman, because Roger had croup. Dr. Suleiman commented that she thought he looked a little floppy. Was he sitting up well? she wanted to know. I was noncommittal. As babies with croup will do, Roger was breathing noisily, and the doctor apparently did not have the heart to administer a sitting test under those conditions.

"At nine months, he should be sitting on his own with ease, at least some of the time," she said, jotting notes at her little shelf.

"Well, he does," I said, "most days." With pillows on either side of him.

"Aaah," said Dr. Suleiman, as if to say, aaah, it is easy to see you are a lying mother. And I was. I knew not sitting at all at nine months was a sign, I had looked in the books, but Lucy said he's fine, he will be fine. I can't blame her, though, for my decision to stop taking Roger to see Dr. Suleiman from ages nine months to twenty-seven. He wasn't sick, he has not been sick, I told Dr. Suleiman in August of 1983, when we finally went to see her, but she put a black mark on my file, a notation, I'm positive.

I had continued to see her occasionally, because I had heard if a patient made no appointments for a year, she or he would be struck from the roster. When Roger was twelve months, and sitting semi-confidently, I went to Dr. Suleiman with an anomaly on my foot. It's plantar wart, she said. Have you been in a public pool? Yes, I had. For moms and tots, I said, expecting praise, not adding we had dropped out. Dr. Suleiman sent me to a dermatologist. I returned again, alone, when Roger was seventeen months because I was going deaf in one ear. She blasted out some wax with a syringe full of water and reminded me to make an appointment for Roger's eighteen-month immunizations.

"Yes, of course."

"Is he walking?"

"Yes." I can't explain myself. Almost, I said, I whispered.

"What was that?" Dr. Suleiman asked.

"Nothing."

He wasn't walking, but that was still considered normal. Dr. Suleiman followed me into the reception area to listen to me make the appointment, which I later cancelled. Instead, I took him to a clinic, the Market Mall clinic (where Helen the doctor had told me I was pregnant) in December, a week or so before Christmas, when people would be generous and maybe lax about asking a lot of developmental questions. They might even be drunk. At the clinic, I made up a story about my general practitioner being on a six-week holiday. The nurse asked, of course, if he was walking or talking, and as we were right there, Roger half out of his yellow snowsuit, I had to say no to both. "We're late walkers and talkers in my family," I said, "but then we become quite good pedestrians. And we never shut up."

"Can you let him stand?" the nurse asked.

"He gets quite nervous in doctors' offices," I said, "so he may not want to stand."

"Hey, Roger," the nurse said. She was wearing a set of matched scrubs with panda bears, her hair was curly all over, short and almost black. Siobhan, her name tag said, was taking Roger from me. "Can

I see you standing up? Can you do that for me?" His little boots were glossy and incriminatingly clean. Roger stood. He could do that, but he took no steps. He did smile, radiantly, and Siobhan made a note. As Roger turned to climb back onto my lap, he fell sideways onto his bottom and made a new noise he liked, a little squeak, like a twenty-pound mouse. Siobhan made another note, and we finally got the damn shot. By then I suspected alarm bells were ringing in Siobhan's mind, I even thought I saw her pressing a concealed buzzer below her desktop. In the hallway, I expected to be waylaid by a psychometrician. We hoofed it out of there and into the mall. Roger and I were going back to Ontario for Christmas. We had to buy a few things. We were euphoric to have that ordeal over with.

I WAS NOT in any way an anti-science lunatic, a home remedies or home-schooler devotee, but this came to me as a message from the television. I was watching TV, waiting for Lucy to come home. Roger was sleeping on the couch with his feet in my lap. It was late afternoon, the day of the immunization, and he was wearing yellow corduroy pants and paler yellow socks, the ones I called cracker socks. I had got into a habit of inventing colour names by association. I don't know why, a mistake I guess, because he still calls pale yellow *cracker* and light blue *bird egg*, after broken pieces of robin's egg. His feet, I wanted to touch his feet, but I also did not want to wake him up. I wanted to coddle him, mainly because we would be leaving the next day, to see Mom, of course, and Anastasia, and others. Mom had been to visit in July and had not made mention of hydrocephalus or of feeling sorry for Roger. She beheld him in a new way, though, I think, with caution and gravity and a checked sadness; it came off her like a perfume only I could smell. She had smiled more than usual and read to Roger and brought him a Care Bear, which he had thrown to the floor, more interested in the travel alarm clock she had brought along, with its illuminated dial, the very one I had taken with me on my overnight stay at Mesmer High. Back in Flax, George was renovating the dentist's office, at last. No one had wanted to rent it for anything, and the equipment had been sold.

Lucy was out interviewing people for her community newsletter column, "One Thing" (stories only, no opinions). The next column would be her fifth, and she was becoming famous in Renforth, the community-association equivalent of an Olympic medalist or national tennis star. The neighbourhood was falling in love with her, and I was a little jealous and proud. Roger, Lucy, and I: we were a happy little trio.

That day, on the CBC, for no reason, filler I suppose, an old NFB documentary came on, only a few minutes long, on the topic of threshing on the family farm. It had nothing to do with Christmas or winter other than it was black and white, from the fifties and nostalgic, and I was reminded of the Van Epps' farm in all seasons but mostly summer. Anastasia and I used to walk through the fields thick with moths and grasshoppers and monarch butterflies, to the chokecherries and back. We liked to lie down in the fields when the grass or the grain was tall, just to disappear like animals and leave a trampled spot behind when we left. We imagined someone might be tracking us.

I remembered us lying once head-to-head in the grass that would become hay bales, and Anastasia telling me about cats and neighbours' dogs who had lost legs when the mower came through. If we just stayed there, watching the sky until the mower came, her dad wouldn't see us until it was too late, and unlike a dog or a cat who lost a limb, we would be sliced, a top layer would be sliced off like baloney. We would be sandwich filling. And later, when the barley was tall but not yet entirely ripe, in August, we'd do the same, and now the combine would be the threat. We'd be eaten up by the combine. Again, Mr. Van Epp wouldn't see us until it was too late, and we'd be chopped up and left to dry with the straw then scooped up by the baler and knotted into a tightly bound parcel. Maybe in the winter they'd be throwing some straw under a cow, and one of our heads would roll out. I liked these scenarios. Then, close to threshing time, the sky was bluer, the bugs were bigger and noisier, and nothing could be stopped. Machines and fall were on their way. But head-to-head in the grain, within its bakery fragrance, on certain days we were both out of the wind and in it, and this arrangement even Anastasia admitted to enjoying. "It makes you want to be cold blooded, the same temperature as the air. We could be snakes," she said once. "Likely the combine would sail right over us, although I have seen a snake in a bale. Dead, natch."

By the time we were in high school, Anastasia no longer wanted to lie in the grass or the grain, I did, but she didn't, and she told me I was a peasant, I was cut out to be a peasant even though she was the one who lived on a farm, and I was the town girl. I had forgotten that until the threshing documentary. I think she may have been right. I would have preferred a smaller world for Roger and me, the two of us clomping around in our rubber boots, once he learned how to walk, growing beets, with no real expectation of school for Roger, all of the neighbour ladies in their kerchiefs saying, oh no, he's better at home with you, never mind this therapeutic hullaballoo, all these Carmens and Lanas who want him already in swimming or daycare. They would have accents, maybe Russian, and they would advise me to stay home and make soup with Roger, boil turnips, even if he wears a bright yellow kerchief on his head, so what, he's only little. They'd laugh and say, oh, that Roger, he should just take care of the lambs, maybe, no? Even *they* would judge, according to their values, I supposed, but that day I decided to remain firm in my cloistering of Roger; no, no to daycare, Mrs. Marini was just fine.

I had tried, Roger and I had tried, we had enrolled in moms and tots swimming lessons, in August, when he was fifteen months.

At that age, he was the senior member of the class, *our old man*, the instructor, Shawn, called him. The others were all five months, six months, eight months. Within this group, for our first lesson, I could clearly see that Roger was a different-looking person with his long-ish head and roundish eyes and fine brown hair that stood on end. Moms held their babies and stood in the water, bobbing up and down. Roger was in plastic pants, and his cloth diaper immediately became sodden, as did the disposables others were wearing. I asked Shawn, "Do they have to wear diapers?"

He answered, "It's a pool policy," and I looked to the mother next to me for eye contact, for a moment of solidarity, and she looked at me as if I were an avid supporter of turds in public pools. Maybe I was premenstrual. I looked away, and the pool blurred, the large windows along the west wall became edgeless coronas of light, reminders of the other world beyond the Renforth Recreation Centre. I splashed water on my face and recovered, and by the end of the thirty-minute class, Roger was smiling at another baby, who smiled back. My heart melted and crackled like butter in a frying pan. The next lesson was not so bad, we went through the same routine, splashing and bob-bing, and Roger seemed to remember the boy he had smiled at last time, Noah, the eight-month-old, and smiled at him again, as if to say, hello, friend. But this time Noah's mother said, "There's Andrew, look, Noah, there's Andrew," as they drifted in the water, right past and away from us.

I'm a baby myself, I guess. It's nothing, after all. Noah's mother didn't notice Roger was smiling. It's nothing, but he looked different, there was no denying that, and something rose up from the water between Roger and me and the others, a recognition in the bulbs behind the nose of inarticulate organized flight. And I knew I could not take him to a place where he might be rejected, where he *would* be rejected, and his little heart might suffer its first beating. At the end of the class, I said goodbye to the other moms in a jolly voice, knowing they would wonder at our absence next week, and someone would say something, and Shawn would call, concerned but also perhaps relieved. I didn't tell Lucy we dropped out, and wouldn't you know she made a surprise visit to the spectator gallery for lesson three, and we weren't there. I had to explain, and I did, I told her about Noah and his mother. She said, "Maybe you're being too sensitive." Then as she was untying a knot in her running shoelace, she looked up at me and said, "I understand," and I cried like Dad at Grandma Drury's coffin, but I did not fall to my knees.

When Lucy came home, smelling of cold Calgary air and eggnog, I said, for likely the fifteenth time, I wish you were coming with us to Ontario.

LUCY STAYED IN CALGARY that Christmas because her mother, Caroline, had died suddenly in late October. Lucy found her in the bathroom, on the floor. It was a Saturday afternoon, and I was at home with Roger. She called and said, "I think Mom's dead. I've called an ambulance. It's okay. I've put her on the couch with a blanket. She doesn't weigh very much; I'm surprised at how little she weighs."

"Do you want us to come over? Are you okay on your own?" My forehead was sweating. I had never had to manage a corpse or a girlfriend with a dead mother. "Are you very sad?" I asked.

She replied that yes, she was, but she was fine on her own. She was calm.

She had had to organize the funeral and have the house put up for sale, and this had meant taking days off work. The optometrists, although liberal about the concept of us as possibly lesbian parents, were not overly generous with employee benefits, and now Lucy had to make up days absent. "All they have ever really wanted is to sell me and you, and likely Roger, glasses," she said one evening in December.

"I guess that's the business they're in," I offered, feebly. "I wish you could come with me to Ontario, though. I don't know how Roger will be on the plane or how Mom will be, in her house, with Roger. And I'm going to see Anastasia and probably George. You could charm them all while I faded into the wallpaper." Lucy's face responded to the mention of George with what I would call grit, as if he were an unfamiliar track and field event.

"Do you care that I'll be seeing George?" I asked.

"I would like to hate him, but he did contribute something of himself to the construction of Roger, so there's that, and despite that, Roger will be the one to charm them."

"I hope so." Outside, the wind was blasting, and the west-facing window rattled in its frame. Roger was asleep, and we were in the kitchen, protected and prepared, because the furnace had been cleaned and the filter changed, my kind of comfort: with Lucy, I derived deep satisfaction from the booking of maintenance, the changing of oil and filters and the vacuuming of ducts and refrigerator coils, maybe more than I used to, as Roger moved through time, indifferent to scheduled progress.

"The furnace sounds better," I said, "don't you think?" Lucy nodded. She was at the stove, stirring, making a rock candy syrup. We had a new tradition, the drink of the month, and for December it was the Rum Daisy from her tattered booklet, *Fancy Drinks, How to Make Them*. The Rum Daisy was made of rock candy syrup, lemon juice, orange cordial, and rum. For a winter's night, perfect. We were cozy and alive.

"Speaking of tell," I went on, "I'm going to tell Anastasia about us, you and me, when I see her."

"You don't have to, you know," Lucy said. "I'm not bothered, I'm not exercised."

"I know. Anastasia and Adrian. I'm going alphabetically." Then I asked, "Do you miss your mom a lot, I mean with the thought of Christmas and you being here alone?"

"It's more wondering where she is than missing. I know she's somewhere, the essence of her, I mean, here and out there." She gestured toward the window with the rum bottle. "I admit I look for her, like my cat in the tree, only with Mom it's when I drive around in her old neighbourhood. Then I think, maybe she's back in Lexington, closer to Howard. She always felt guilty about him and the boarding school. I think I might go back to Kentucky one of these months or years, see my relations. You and Roger would have to come." She was doling out the rum. I thought, if it weren't for Lucy, I, too, would be someplace else, likely back in Flax, living in Mom's house, watching her watching Roger, occasionally discovering her measuring his head with the tattered fabric tape from her sewing box.

"I'm still a little hurt none of the cousins came to the funeral," Lucy said. It had been a small affair with a few neighbours, and from Kentucky, Aunt Belle, Caroline's sister and Uncle Fritz and Lucy's brother Howard, of course. He was, as Lucy had told me, deaf, completely deaf! He taught at a school for deaf students, the same one he had attended.

"But it was so nice to meet Howard. He smiles just like you. I love him," I said to Lucy, after my first sip of Rum Daisy. "I love how he kind of connected with Roger. You told him that, didn't you? That I noticed a connection?" I had said this before, and I was saying it again. Although I didn't think Roger was deaf, he could hear me opening a bag of chips from two hundred paces, and Lucy's car door closing from the other side of the street, I wondered if there might be some kind of auditory issue getting in the way of words making sense. Howard had tried to teach Roger some signs, but his hands flopped (they *were* floppy) downward, fingers uninterested. I could see from his eyes though, that he wanted some further conversation, and I told Lucy to tell Howard, and I assume she did, in sign language, she knew some ASL, although who knows. "Yes, I told him," Lucy said, "I told him Roger liked him. He called Roger his little nephew."

"I like hearing that."

On the plane, Roger was good as gold, as people around me said. He had two watches for the trip, his usual little Timex and a Mickey Mouse Lucy had bought for him (and altered with an extra hole on the leather strap) as a bon voyage Christmas gift. Lucy and I did not know what he loved about watches, but he spent most of the flight staring at them, both on his left wrist. Of course, I wondered if he might be a nascent genius, inferring new ideas about time and space. At the same time, I had my doubts. Once, when Roger looked up at me from my lap, I noticed the whites of his eyes were visible above and below the irises, and before I could stop myself, I thought, he looks like a fledgling of some sort, the spawn of a heron and an owl with his round eyes and thin limbs and his diaper bulge, his sparse and feathery hair. I no longer spoke to Lucy of Roger's appearance; she had told me to stop, but incurably I thought about it. FLK: funny-looking kid, Margo had told me one day after a class, not about Roger, of course, just in passing. "That's what doctors, pediatricians, write on the file when they think something's wrong, but they're not sure what. I guess more often than not it's an indicator," she had said.

"Of what?" I had asked.

"Soft neurological signs," she'd said.

"Soft?"

"Nothing major or conclusive." I felt as if she were unintentionally kicking sand at the back of my eyes.

We landed. As the plane braked and shuddered, Roger made squeaking sounds, and people smiled. I rented a car, and off we went into the southern Ontario evening, past Guelph and George, past farmhouses lit up, alone and charitable with their light displays, and I pictured the Van Epps' place, always bedecked, and shivered with nostalgia and pain. Anastasia and her husband had a daughter, Maisie, twenty-one months and talking *a blue streak*, Mrs. Van Epp had said over the phone; I had pictured a tiny blonde savant clutching a slide rule.

Mom was obviously happy to see Roger, and she said nothing about child development, directly or indirectly, when we arrived or at any time *during* the visit. Roger sat in our old wooden high chair and smiled at his grandmother. "I think he remembers me," she said. I thought so, too, from when she'd been out for the Stampede. He loved her rice pudding and held his dish out for more, which pleased Mother, I could clearly see, and my head pulsed with circulating and conflicting messages of pride and trepidation. After dinner, Mom carried Roger around and, looking out the living room window, said, "George will be up tomorrow."

"To stay here? Overnight, you mean?"

"No, he said he's going to get a room at the Mesmer Arms. I asked him if he wanted to stay here."

"Well, I'm glad he's not," I said.

Mom continued talking as she sometimes did, with her back to me, still holding Roger, looking out at the yard. She said, "You shouldn't be so hard on George, you know, there are things you don't know. Things he's had to put up with."

"Like what?" I sat on Dad's old chair and waited for her answer, but she handed me Roger and said, oh, never mind.

NEXT AFTERNOON, we had to make a *quick trip* to the Van Epps, Mom's idea, just to say Merry Christmas, but when the time came to leave, she decided to stay home. At the Van Epp home, nothing had changed except Anastasia was now married to Mel, whom she'd met at U of T. They were both studying at Cornell, working on PhDs, Anastasia in history, Mel in chemistry: he had stayed in Ithaca because of the time-sensitive nature of his atomic meddling, Anastasia said.

We hugged, she was in khaki pants and turtleneck and looked like an L.L.Bean model, and Mrs. Van Epp, very much unlike other farm or town women in Flax, even during the holiday season, was wearing a black velvet dress and silver jewelry. Her hair was cut short, and she looked like Mia Farrow, greeting Roger as if he were an adult, saying pleased to meet you and shaking his narrow hand. "I like your watches," she said, and as Roger extended his wrist for her to get a closer look, I swooned with love for him and for myself, because I had dressed him in a white shirt and clip-on bow tie.

Maisie came down the stairs quickly the way young children do, having to land both feet on each step. She was in a T-shirt and underpants and spoke with the poise of a twelve-year-old. "Are you Roger?" she asked, taking his hand while he was still in my arms. "I was waiting for you. Come to my fort." I put him on the floor, and he followed Maisie, crawling at top speed to the Van Epps' den, where white sheets had been draped over easy chairs and sofa pillows to create hiding spaces. Anastasia said, "I guess I'll force her into this outfit later," placing a red frilly dress and white leotards on the newel post.

"No Abby?" I asked.

"She decided to stay in B.C.," said Mrs. Van Epp. "She's doing a forestry practicum."

"Yes, how to grow magic mushrooms in an old-growth forest," Anastasia said with a straight face. Mrs. Van Epp made no comment, she maybe did not know about that type of mushroom, she most certainly did not know. For just a moment, my heart was gulping at the air: I had missed the smell of that house. "Where's Mr. Van Epp?" I could never call them by their first names. "Shopping," said his wife. "Eggnog? Homemade with rum."

"Of course."

Later, I said to Anastasia, "I have something to tell you." We were outside in the snow with their old dog, King. He was eighteen now, so they said. "Isn't that one hundred and twenty-six in people years? I'm getting used to doing mental math, because Roger's doctor always speaks in terms of months. Anyway, never mind. No," I said, "forget never mind. He's not walking or talking yet. I'm kind of worried. So, it's really me more than the doctor who's thinking in months. I've been avoiding her, truthfully. He's had his shots, and really, he's very healthy. How often do you take Maisie?"

The sun on the snow was blinding, and I looked at the barn for relief, then the whistling pines in the laneway and beyond them to the field where Anastasia and I had lain imagining death by combine. "Never," said Anastasia. I wasn't sure she was listening. "He'll be fine," she added, "he's got lots of time." She was wearing black earmuffs and a black wool coat and black mitts that looked as if they had been made of King's fur. He flopped onto his side in the snow, and Anastasia said, "Let's put him in the barn. It's too cold for him out here."

But when she tried to lift him, he wouldn't stand, he would not budge. She disappeared into the garage and returned with a toboggan and a ragged orange blanket with frayed satin trim. King agreed to sit on this while Anastasia and I hauled him to the cool dark barn and laid him in a passageway, then Anastasia got him some water. Had she not said to me, "What was it you wanted to tell me?" I may not have mentioned Lucy after all.

I didn't say, oh right, as if I had forgotten. I leapt in. "I'm in a relationship with a woman. Her name is Lucy. I like her a lot. I think I love her." King lay on his side again, fell onto his side really, as if muscle use were too much bother.

Anastasia said, "Oh my god, I think King is dying." She placed an ear to his ribcage while my eyes shifted here and there. A lone cow stood in a stall, and I remembered Lucy's cowhide. Bossy and I regarded one another sympathetically.

Anastasia raised her head from King's pelt. "No, still ticking. Well, that's big news."

"Yes, we're living together. She's crazy about Roger."

"I have a friend Nora who's a lesbian. She's always calling herself a dyke."

I nodded. We were both on our knees beside the living King. "Some people do that," I said, a hint of science in my voice.

"Did you tell your mom?" she wanted to know.

"No, not yet. I'm going to tell Adrian next time I see him."

"Well, I won't tell my mom then, or anyone in Flax, or anyone anywhere."

"Thanks," I said. "Your mom is watching Roger and Maisie, right?"

"Oh, yes, of course, don't worry. She'll be in the fort with them. They'll be wishing she would go away."

THAT EVENING, George arrived. The plan was for he and I, Anastasia, and Adrian to go for a drink in Mesmer; Mom would babysit Roger. George had his timing organized like I suspected he would. He'd said he would arrive at six-thirty so he could see Roger, but he had been held up getting out of Guelph, and was sorry to be so late, "Almost nine, I can't believe it." I stared, obviously dubious I'm sure, at his face while he made this allegation. Roger was in bed. "Do you want to sneak up and see him?" I asked.

"Oh, no. I wouldn't want to wake him up. I'll see him tomorrow. I've got a room at the Mesmer Arms."

"You could have stayed here," said Mom.

"Oh, no, it's better this way. I like hotel rooms. A George in a hotel room is a happy George." I knew right then he would leave Mesmer the following day without meeting Roger. Seeing Roger would asphyxiate George with responsibility and connection and commitment. Inside that flat-backed hard skull was a compartment made of wood.

I couldn't be bothered with a seasonal hug. Adrian had been at Mom's for hours, waiting with me, so we got into George's car and left, picked up Anastasia, who had already had a couple drinks, and drove to the Mesmer Bar. I had questions for George, otherwise I would have stayed with Mom, listening to her Bing Crosby records. From the backseat, Anastasia said to George, "Isn't Roger cute? You must be so proud!" I wondered about my face at that moment, how it looked, and I imagined — like an old friend listening to another old friend exaggerating.

"He's a great little kid," Adrian added. Great little kid was the phrase Adrian had settled on.

George said, "I didn't get a chance to see him tonight. Tomorrow, though."

"Oh, you have to. You'll love him." Anastasia was still herself, slip-sliding around on her figure skates. She was making fun of Roger, I thought, or maybe not. I wanted to stop at a side road and walk toward a farmhouse or a barn but we arrived at the bar, and I smoked one of Adrian's cigarettes. Things improved. When it would have been close to eight-thirty in Calgary, I went to the pay phone on the wall and called Lucy. She might be in the easement, or at Carmen's or a community association party with Janet and Andrew, but she answered on the third ring.

"I love when you accept the charges," I shouted. "And also, I miss you. I've only had two drinks. I'm at the Mesmer bar. I just called to say I love you, ha ha," I half-sang.

"I love you, too. Are you sure you're not in the notorious Mesmer lesbian bar? How come I can only hear women talking in the background?"

"Yes, I'm sure. Some guy just played Gloria on the jukebox and asked Anastasia to dance with him; that's how lesbian it is here at the Mesmer Arms."

"And is she dancing with him?"

"No, she's not." I was going to say George is here, she's talking to George, but instead I said, "Roger misses you."

"Does he? How do you know?"

"He looks at his Disney watch and then we look at your picture. I brought your picture with me. I didn't tell you that. We talked about you at bedtime last night."

"Oh, you're making me verklempt. Which picture?"

"The one from last Christmas, with the glasses. Remember?"

"Yes, of course. I can't wait for you guys to be back here."

When I returned to the table, George had his arm around Anastasia, comradely, I supposed. To Adrian, I said, "I wanted to let you know my roommate Lucy and I are in a romantic relationship. She calls herself Roger's dad. She wants to adopt him someday. I really like her. That's who I was just talking to on the phone. Mom's met her. She calls her *that Lucy girl*."

Adrian did not entirely roll with this punch. Taking a long swig of beer, he looked away, then back at me, at my forehead rather than my eyes and asked, "What about George?"

"I don't know. I guess nothing, nothing about George." George wasn't paying attention. He was telling Anastasia a story about fighting fires in Guelph.

"That's okay, that's good, actually. Now I can be the normal one. Cheers!" he said, tapping his bottle against mine.

"Yes, cheers," I said. "And I'm more than happy to take on the mantle of abnormality."

"So when is this Lucy girl coming to visit?" Adrian pretended to want to know.

I had no idea. "Maybe next summer or next Christmas. She's paying the bills right now. She's the worker, at least until I finish my thesis and get chartered as a school psychologist. You don't need a PhD," I felt the need to tell Adrian, "in Alberta."

We drank too much, we each likely had six beers and were at the point of building a pyramid of bottles and pleading with the waitress not to take it away or knock it over. No one could drive, I had warned Mom this might happen, so we stayed in George's room with the two double beds and a cot that Adrian set up between the credenza and the foot of George's bed, the *door bed* George called it, where he could protect us if the cops or organized crime showed up. Organized crime sometimes made an appearance in places like the Mesmer Arms, he said. "Either or both of you can climb in with me, if you want, if you're scared." No response. Anastasia and I took the bed closer to the bathroom, the *bathroom bed.*

All quiet. As soon as the light was out, we all fell asleep, I believe, although I woke up around three, expecting to find Anastasia in bed with George, but no: I felt the approach of a hangover. The blue deodorizers in the toilet gave off a strong scent of coverups, and the bedspread smelled as if it had been washed with pineapple Jell-O. I fell asleep and woke up again, got up and found the bathroom door shut, light leaking around its hollow edges. In the boozy dark of a hotel room I imagined illuminated with the flakes of other people's skin, I could easily see George's bed was empty; knocking very gently on the bathroom door, I pushed it open. The light in there was bright enough for surgery or intricate embroidery work and George was on the toilet in his boxers, doing a crossword, with a pen.

"Do you want the toilet?"

"No, I just need a drink of water."

"There are Dixie cups, in a dispenser," said George, in his firefighter first aid voice.

"Yes, and a lot of air fresheners in this place," I said.

"The air has maybe been breathed a few times."

"Let's not think about it."

Four little paper cups of water later, I said, "I'm going to get a ginger ale first thing in the morning."

"There's a machine in the lobby, I could get you one now," said George.

"That would be so great." He didn't stand up to go, however, furrowing his brow at the crossword. His chest was bare, white, and hairless, his right shoulder shiny as if he had been rubbing it with ointment. I took the opportunity to say, "George, tell me honestly. What's your family history, I mean medically? Do you have any relatives who are learning disabled or neurologically different in some way?"

Without any hesitation, George answered no. "I have an Uncle John who is a lawyer, and Uncle Archie sells boats, in Alberta, maybe that's a sign of a learning disability. My Aunt Helen is a secretary in a school in Lethbridge. She knows how to type with speed and accuracy, I imagine. My cousins seem okay, Randolph is a cop, Linda is a nurse. And I think I've told you my sister is a chiropractor in Picture Butte. Christine Petrie-Pomeroy. The Petries and the Langfords are neuro-logically similar to others of their kind, I would say."

"Well, you told me your sister had a brain injury; now you're telling me she's actually a chiropractor in Picture Butte?'

"I know. It's all true. She had a brain injury such as a concussion, and now she's fully recovered. That's how the brain is. I can't explain it. Can you?"

"So it was just a concussion?"

Silence from George.

"And Langford is your mother's name?"

"It was before she became a Petrie." For answering questions, George adopted a semi-serious vocal pattern, as if all inquiries were taken from a prying government pollster.

"What about your dad?"

"Short fuse syndrome? Or no fuse at all?" He continued to work on the crossword.

"How are you related to those Petries who had the cabin?"

"Second cousins somehow. I don't even really know. They were paid for keeping me, until I turned eighteen. They wouldn't have, otherwise, although they did allow me to stay in the cabin, until I left. There is no family loyalty amongst the Petries! Maybe that's a learning disability. It's something in the blood or missing from the blood, you could say. For the Petries, blood is not thicker than water. Petrie blood would not float one of Uncle Archie's boats."

"Why do you say that?"

"What's a five-letter word for pig-like animal?"

"I don't know. Could it be tapir?"

"Yes! That's it." As he penned in his answer, George's dimples almost crackled with delight.

"Would you get me a ginger ale right now," I asked, "if I gave you the change? I don't think I could be in the lobby without vomiting."

George sighed and stood up. "I guess so. Never mind the money. My treat. Rose needs a ginger ale. All of life must come to a halt."

"Thanks. I'll stay in the bathroom, in case, you know, of barf." We shimmied past one another, and he opened the door into the stale bedroom and closed it gently behind him.

As predicted, George went home to Guelph the next day without seeing Roger. Christmas Eve, Adrian and Susan and their daughters, Laura and Lisa, came for dinner. They were going to her family for Christmas Day. With his cousins, Roger seemed to have discovered his social appetite. Maybe it had been whetted by his afternoon with Maisie. He crawled madly from living room to kitchen, up and down the stairs after his cousins and at some point, upstairs, he squealed his first fully formed ear-piercing squeals, the first of probably thousands of what we came to call his *detectors*, named for the shriek of a smoke alarm test. Roger produced detectors when he was excited, very happy, or anxious. On that Christmas Eve of 1982, I didn't mind, I was momentarily crammed full of joy. A year and a half later when he was in preschool, I was not.

He hit another type of milestone the night before we left for Calgary. Mom and Roger and I had dinner, and that evening I told Roger we were going home tomorrow, on the zoom plane as I called it, to see Lucy. From the way he looked at me, knowing and inward, like an older child with a serious set of plans, I think he understood. "Let's call Lucy," I said. "She needs to hear our voices. Plus, we need to remind her what time to be at the airport." Holding Roger, I dialed, and she picked up right away. "It's us," I said, "we can't wait to see you. Roger wants to talk to you." I held the receiver to his ear and said, "It's Lucy." Roger listened, and I could hear Lucy saying that she missed him, and his bed missed him and the couch and Carmen, and Mimi was meowing more than usual, looking for him. Roger listened! His eyes moved from the receiver to mine, and he smiled. He had picked up on the scent of connection that can't be seen, the togetherness that passeth all understanding. When I took the phone from him, he latched his arm around my neck to confirm that Lucy and I were his and he was ours. That was my most joyful moment as Roger's mother, and as Lucy's girlfriend, but I didn't tell Lucy until much later, a few days after I kissed Asa on the Stampede grounds.

On the thirtieth, two days after our return, Mom called. My heart lurched when I heard her voice, and it was right to lurch, it knew, here it comes. "You made it home safely?"

"Yes, the flight was fine, Roger was really good. How are things in Flax?"

"Oh, the same, pretty much the same as always." Then came the pause. "I was going to say, about Roger, maybe I shouldn't say anything, but he seemed a little forlorn, being here, maybe he felt a little lost."

"Oh? I thought he had a really good time with his cousins. Why would you think that?"

"The look on his face, I mean."

"What was it?" I asked. "What was the look on his face?"

"I don't know really. Sometimes he looked a little sad faced. I couldn't help but feel a little sorry for him."

"You don't need to feel sorry for him. He's happy." I wanted to scream.

"Did George get a chance to talk to you about his family?"

"Sort of. He told me about his aunts and uncles. Why? What do you know about his family?"

"Oh, that, not much, same as you, I guess. He has lots of relatives out there. In Alberta, I mean."

"I know. I know. He told me."

"How's the weather there?" Mom asked.

eight

IN JANUARY OF 1983, I took the bus to Banff, having ruminated too much on my mother's call, Maisie's advanced skills, Laura and Lisa's angelic three- and four-year-old faces, the swim class, Noah's mother, and people at the Co-op who looked twice. The bus left from the North Hill mall and was primarily for skiers going to Sunshine, but it stopped in the Banff townsite. Roger was with Mrs. Marini. Lucy thought I was working on my thesis and had to get a very early start.

All the skiers smelled good. Most were likely high school students, because the holidays weren't over yet. My seat was next to the window, so I could watch the city, then the country, the Morley Reserve, roll by while the girl next to me talked to her friend across the aisle about the biology teacher and Math 31 and the University of Alberta. In Banff, I disembarked at the bus station with a middle-aged man, who strode away. This was my third time in Banff, and I wanted to go to the bookstore, I wanted a coffee from somewhere, and I wanted to walk to the Banff Springs for a glass of wine at the Rundle Lounge. It was ten a.m., but the main street was already busy with tourists, healthy people in fur coats and impressive boots, even fur hats. I had a coffee at McDonald's, because it was open, and sat for a long time and went to the bookstore and browsed, and I suppose I didn't notice, but the little wet towels of dread were most likely slapping against my heart by then. I didn't notice. So that when I began my walk to the end of Banff Avenue and left up the hill to the hotel, my field of vision was narrowing as if I had a case of sudden-onset retinitis pigmentosa, the outer edges of my experience were darkening, but still I didn't notice, I was looking ahead, directly forward, at the bridge, at the people with their pink cheeks, but I was afraid, I guess, in my capillaries, presumably because they were closing down, turning off their cell-sized light bulbs. I continued walking, and I could hear my feet on the sidewalk and the snow, and that sound was good, was robust even, but also might have been from other feet, behind me. The mind knows what it's doing, I suppose, although it is slippery, and it's wet, and it's in the dark, except for the peepholes; it must have seen I was very close to the Banff Mineral Springs Hospital, because that is when I had the jolt of vertigo spin at me, and I found I could not breathe in enough to satisfy my desire for oxygen. I seemed to be dying, so I walked in the front door of the hushed and brilliant hospital and saw reception and told the woman there who had white hair beneath a white cap that I was having trouble breathing, and my fingers felt strange. She called a nurse from somewhere, and that nurse led me to the emergency window, where, for better or for worse, I was the only patient. I say for worse because in my final moments I wished for one other casualty, someone with an open bleeding wound I could watch. A different nurse took my blood pressure and told me to breathe in to a count of three and out to a count of four. I struggled with this exercise, but was able to comply and began to recover. Then I was flooded with warmth from my hands to my feet. "Do you know what a panic attack is, Rose?" I heard the nurse ask me.

"Yes," I answered, "theoretically."

"Ever had one before?"

"No."

"I'll get the doctor to take a look at you, but I'm pretty sure that's what's going on. You were hyperventilating."

Immediately, I wanted to stay and seek employment as a nurse. I sat in a cozy cubicle, breathing in to three and out to four, and the doctor came, Mike, although the name tag said Dr. Bartok. He said, "Had a bit of a scare, did you?"

"Yes, my breathing went wonky, and I felt as if I couldn't see, although I could. I could see, but everything looked strange."

"Feeling worried about anything in particular?"

"No, not at all. Maybe my thesis, getting it done so I can get a job."

"What field are you in?" Dr. Bartok had the look of a man whose photograph might appear in a genetics text with the caption *I am right, and you are wrong.*

"Educational psychology. But I came here today to get away from it. Not here in the hospital but to Banff."

"On your own, or with a friend?" Clearly, he was getting at *are you always alone like this, on the fringes?* I removed my black toque and felt numerous alarmed hairs fan outward with electricity.

"Yes, yes, I'm with a friend, but she's at the bookstore. I just decided to go for a walk, and the next thing I knew I was, ha ha, feeling like I was dying."

"Do you want to give the store a call and have her paged? We can get the number for you."

"No, no, I'm fine. I'll head back into downtown." Finding an old used tissue in my coat pocket, I took off my glasses and gave them a wipe, leaving a mucous-based smudge.

"Well, you're good to go, but I suggest you mention this to your GP in Calgary. And you'll have to give your healthcare number to that lady right there," he said, indicating a woman in a plexiglass booth.

"All roads lead to doctors," I said. No, I did not. I said, "Will do," and I did, and carried on up the hill to the hotel lounge. I was ebullient! The danger had passed, and I tucked it away like a credit card, like a kleptomaniac because I would not be telling Dr. Suleiman. Having navigated my way to the Rundle Lounge and ordered a glass of red wine from the handsome waiter, I reassured myself Dr. Suleiman did not need to know about panic or Banff. The reassuring sun was still above the mountaintops, and for one second, I thought my eyes were closing in on themselves again, but the thought moved on, and I made a plan to call Lucy from a phone at the hotel, to let her know I wouldn't be home until maybe sometime after seven (when the bus got in) and that I was getting lots done on my thesis. I didn't like lying, and I had always thought I couldn't do it, but it was starting to seem like nothing more than a skill requiring patient practise.

ON MARCH 3, two months shy of his second birthday, Roger started walking, and this seemed good enough to me, and to Lucy. I don't think he had seen any point, any advantage, until spring, when he decided he might like to go outside to chase a rabbit; there were several bounding here and there in the neighbourhood of Renforth.

I understood everything about Roger, I truly did. To celebrate this milestone, Lucy created a surprise weekend away for the two of us. Roger would stay with Carmen; she would have access to our place in case Roger got homesick for the house, but he would sleep over in the cot and seemed excited about staying with Mimi the cat. Also, Carmen had a new tenant in my old place, Robert, a law student, who had seven younger brothers and sisters he said he'd run away from, and in whom I saw potential as a relief babysitter if Carmen had a stroke or fell asleep and did not wake up, not that Carmen was either negligent or sickly. The night before we left, I ran up Robert's outdoor stairs and asked if he could just keep an eye out; my travel anxiety had arms and legs wanting to be useful.

We were heading to Missoula, the weekend after Easter, and we left Friday at noon. Carmen had the afternoon off from her mapmaking job, and Roger went with her cheerfully, jubilantly (jub-u-lantly), I would say, entering her house to chase after Mimi and have ice cream. With the car loaded, we were about to take off when the letter carrier came by with the mail. I got out to get it — why? I do not know — and there was a letter from George I tossed into the glove box to read later, expecting nothing really, the usual rationales, maybe mention again of why he had left without meeting Roger, why he wanted to do more work on the dentistry, as he called Dad's old office, why he was half-living with Mom. I wanted to appear uninterested, and I was, because Lucy had let it be known that she wasn't happy I had spent the night in the Arms with George. On Valentine's Day she said outright, "Don't do that again, spend a night with George."

I said, "Adrian and Anastasia were there, and we were all drunk."

"You could have got your own room, you and Anastasia." I had to admit that had not occurred to me, and I did admit it to Lucy.

"He's just kind of a given," I said, "and by that, I mean he's just going to be around in some fashion. I know this, so I plan a kind of

no-stimulus-response way of dealing with him. It's a way of not react-
ing when you're implementing a behaviour-change program, very
similar to ignoring, only the person doesn't know he or she is being
ignored. Besides, I was with my brother. It was just silliness."

Lucy said, "Don't do it again. Promise me."

And I did. I had bought her a bag of licorice allsorts that day, and
we were eating them in the kitchen. I think I had black licorice on my
teeth, and I felt a weakness that she might leave, she might take off
with Roger.

Before we had gone very far on Highway 2, tumbleweeds appeared,
blowing fast and easterly, grey ones left over from the fall, I supposed,
freed by the April wind from fences and ditches and wherever they
passed the winter months. I had never seen so many before. "Will
they get stuck on the undercarriage of the Oldsmobile?" I asked.
"It's a low-slung kind of car."

Lucy was distracted. A vicious gust of wind slammed at us from
the west, and she yanked at the steering wheel and said, "Can you
read me that letter?"

"Sure," I said, a little frantic in my breathing suddenly, and I
thought of Banff, forcing a long exhalation. I had nothing to hide, my
sweaty palms wanted to say, as I retrieved the envelope. "See, it looks
like he's drawn a bear or a cat over the seal because, you know why,
because he steamed that letter of mine open, the one from Nancy and
he's still thinking about that."

"He has the obsessive capacity of a serial killer," Lucy said. I was
impressed with her observation and at the same time experienced a
sensation, a dart with feathers, passing by my mind's eyes.

"I really don't think he's a killer," I said, "that's a bit extreme.
Anyway." I ripped the envelope open and began to read. "Hello Rose,
and in brackets Lucy."

"Oh, for Christ's sake," said Lucy. "For crying in the shithouse."

I laughed.

"*Your mom is well and sends her best.* Really? I can't picture her sending her best. He just makes that kind of stuff up. He *is* compulsive about putting on a good social face. Anyway, *I've been cleaning the eaves and pruning the lilacs in my spare time. Adrian and Susan and the girls were here last Sunday, and I made a roast.*"

"Adrian and Susan and *the girls?* He made a roast? Has he moved in with your mother?" Lucy asked.

"No, he's just there a lot. I don't understand it myself. Really, I don't."

Lucy said, "My head is already spinning from the tone of this letter. Who does he think he is? Your elderly aunt? Aunt George?"

"Well, he goes on," I said, with firm resolve. "*I had some time to think after the dinner, about family and so on, and I had a kind of brainwave which is a phrase I think Nancy used to use back in Fort Smith.*" I rolled my eyes. "No, she didn't. Because it's a letter he has to bring up Nancy. This is his MO."

"What an asshole," Lucy said, pushing in the cigarette lighter.

"Anyway, to go on. *When you were here, Rose, you asked about my family, my uncles and aunts, and I forgot to mention one person I should have. It's who I was referring to, or to whom I was referring, when I said what I said about not much loyalty among the Petries.*"

"Whaaat?" Lucy asked. "What's he getting at?" Smoke swirled around her head as she lit the cigarette. Uh oh. I had already scanned the next paragraph.

"Well, it's like this," I read aloud. "*I have a brother. His name is Dennis, and he lives in Medicine Hat, in the big centre there, the Wild Rose Centre. My parents put him there when he was five, because he's handicapped, mentally, I mean, not physically. Well, physically, too, but that's not why they put him there. I guess the schools didn't know what to do with him, and the doctor said it was the best thing, so that's what they did. I was just little myself, Christine my sister was eight. We didn't want Dennis to go, but that was the last we saw of him. I know you wanted a sort of family tree, your mom told me, so that's another branch. The branch of Dennis Petrie. My parents' names are Stan and Martha. Yours truly, George. P.S. Your mother already knows about Dennis."*

At this news, my eyes looked westward to the bright mountains, and I pictured the nurses of Banff and breathed out to four. "That's why he said not enough loyalty in the Petrie blood to float a boat. That the Petrie blood wasn't thicker than water."

Lucy inhaled her smoke and said nothing.

"Do you see now how my worries aren't totally unfounded? Problems on both sides of the family. Adrian with his learning disability and George with his brother."

"Okay, I just want to say this one thing. George is not a *side* of the family."

I exhaled, deeply and wearily. "He's a *side* of the DNA."

"Fine, let's use that term."

I did not reply. I wanted to remain silent. Part of me actually may have felt some relief at the news of George's brother.

"And it's neither here nor there, as my Aunt Belle says," Lucy went on, "because Roger is not handicapped or heading to a centre in Medicine Hat. Roger is Roger, he's walking, next step will be talking. He's not even two. He looks fine, he does not look funny, and he never will, case closed, give me that letter. Give it to me." She grabbed at the air in my direction with her cigarette-free hand and I offered up the letter. I had read it twice, that was enough, I could remember the particulars. Steering with her elbows, Lucy crushed the single piece of paper, then rolled down the window and threw it onto the highway, where it took off like a headless white bird in a generally eastward and ragged direction.

"There's a fine for littering," I said. Lucy shook her head in what was apparently exasperation. We weren't even past Okotoks yet on our surprise weekend. The wind continued to buffet us, intermittently and aggressively. I couldn't say anything, I couldn't make the points I wanted to, I couldn't operationalize dysmorphia, so I abandoned the topic: I don't think Lucy particularly liked me at that moment.

"Okay, let's calm down," I said. "It's windy. We need to concentrate."

"I like wind," Lucy said, "and no, I won't calm down. Wind helps me concentrate."

Don't you need to calm down to concentrate, I wanted to ask, but instead I took her right hand from the steering wheel and kissed the first knuckle, but she pulled it away, and I was hurt. We were having a constrained fight, I realized, our first.

"Let's sing along with somebody," Lucy said. "Play Mellencamp."

"Okay, okay," I said, rummaging already through the tape case. But we didn't sing, we listened quietly until Claresholm, then south of there the wind died down and Lucy said, different now, recovered, "I heard there's some kind of gay bar in Missoula. Esmé told me."

"When did you see her?" Esmé was a famous lesbian in Calgary.

"Out on my beat, doing the column. She was at somebody's house in Renforth, in the yard."

"You didn't tell me."

"Because Missoula was a surprise. What would I say? Esmé says there's a gay-friendly bar in Missoula. What would you have said?"

"I likely would have said we should go there for a surprise weekend."

Lucy placed her right hand on the back of my neck and squeezed, which gave me goosebumps. "I'm sorry I yanked my hand away from you like that," she said.

"That's okay," I said. Then the drive became *fantastic*, a word I never used, it was Lucy's kind of word. When we returned, she would say that she and I had had a fantastic time together.

Montana was more rolling and flashily ranchy than southern Alberta. Not long after crossing the border, we agreed we could tell we were in a foreign land, which happened to be Lucy's homeland. At least three times, Lucy said, it's like in the book, meaning the book she was reading, *A River Runs Through It*. We stopped in Helena for something to eat, and I looked at the map, listing off the National Forests in the area, Lolo, Bitterroot, Flathead. "The U.S. always feels so different, even without maps you can tell you're south of the border," I said. Even if someone drove you blindfolded or transported you in a trunk and dumped you in a national forest, I thought, but did not say. The American-ness is an electro-magnetic strip of confidence and allegiance to the flag resting at a height of about five feet seven inches, the height of Lucy, so it gets easily into your eyes and ears. It's arousing. I was glad our fight was over. We drove on.

The hotel was a retro type of place, without trying to be, on the Clark Fork River. The property included a rocky little beach where one could stand and listen to the river or watch it from the window of room number 109. Lucy said we should learn fly fishing. Maybe it's too cold, I said. We agreed neither of us cared what hotel employees thought. We didn't care if they wondered about us checking in together, and we agreed that we loved hotel rooms no matter what the condition; they were full of promise and mystery, crimes, loneliness, and so on, dirt.

Outside, from our stony beach, we could see Missoula. It was like Shangri-La, or how I had pictured Shangri-La in the ninth grade when we read *Lost Horizon*. The city was flat and surrounded by large foothills and a couple of bigger mountains that were hazy and protective. Nothing could go wrong in Missoula, I said to Lucy, hopefully. We wanted more to eat and to drink, and Lucy asked at the desk where we could find the AM:PM, the supposedly gay-friendly bar.

We could walk there! We wondered, should we change, dress up in some fashion and decided don't be ridiculous.

As it turned out, there were ten people at the bar, all men, plus us and the bartender, Greg, who called himself Gretchen, to us, sotto voce. Gretchen had been to Calgary, had been to the Stampede, even, and to a gay rodeo somewhere nearby. He had friends all over North America, friends in San Francisco and New York City, and two of them had died, already, from the disease called AIDS. Lucy said, yes, she knew what he was talking about. One of her friends in Kentucky was sick. She had never mentioned this to me. She proposed a toast to him, and Gretchen's friends and I joined in, but I felt like Bonnie Edwards or someone else from Flax, someone listening in.

We walked back to the hotel in silence, me holding Lucy's arm.

In bed, there was an uneasiness with us, Lucy was distant, I told myself she was lachrymose from booze. In bed she said, "People are dying, you know, of AIDS."

I said I know that.

"I don't think you care like I do, necessarily."

"I'm not personally affected by it like you. Maybe that's the difference," I said. She turned her back to me and prepared to fall asleep. I thought we would be having sexual fun in the hotel room, but now it seemed not likely. I wondered about that deer George had seen in the Missouri River, if that story were true, and if so, why would a deer venture out into such a wide river. Maybe to hide its tracks, I thought. I wondered about Dennis and at the same time did not know how to wonder about him, who to picture and in what circumstances. I thought of Roger in his cot at Carmen's and experienced the distance between us as a map to Calgary with street lamps. On our special weekend in Montana, Lucy and I fell asleep rather slowly.

I HAD SAID to the doctor, Dr. Suleiman, when she asked how Roger was doing, that for a two year old, he was pretty childish. Then I had laughed. This was the summer of 1983, when people had curling iron hairdos, but not Dr. Suleiman. Her hair was long, black, and straight, it matched her black, laced shoes. Of course, she did not laugh at my joke. She said she was a little concerned that Roger had not started walking until twenty-two months. All time was in months for Dr. Suleiman. I told her I was three hundred and thirty-nine months, and I still had trouble walking in snow, having calculated my age in months prior to the appointment because I knew we would be speaking that kind of math. She said to me, "It's not funny," but only as an aside, not really with eye contact. "You should have brought him in at eighteen months," she said, "why haven't you been in with him?"

I said, "I wound up having to take him to a walk-in clinic for his shots, just because of time constraints. He's healthy. You know we're not supposed to make unnecessary visits to the doctor's office. Waste of healthcare resources and so on." I felt we were yelling at one another in a civilized manner, and if there were a graph of the decibels of communicative assault, the trajectory would be rising sharply.

"We need to think about an assessment," she said. So, *she* thought about it right there and got out a memo pad and wrote an official referral, to what she called the developmental clinic at the Children's Hospital. There's always at least a six-month waiting list so he'll be thirty-two, thirty-three months by the time he gets in, which is what we want, according to Dr. Suleiman.

I said, "I don't know if that's what I want." I felt very selfish, like a cad must feel, then wondered quickly why a cad is always a man or a dad and never a mother. Was I perhaps the first fully fledged mother cad?

Dr. Suleiman said, "It doesn't matter what you want." (That was how she spoke; to a degree, I was used to it.) "I'm his physician, and I need to know if there is a developmental issue or something motoric if I'm going to provide the right treatment. And you need to know as his mother so you can pursue the proper interventions."

At the sound of the word *interventions* I felt weak, as if I were being compelled to enter the sweaty tent of a faith healer and hand Roger to a shifty-looking carnie who would assure me this'll be fine, don't worry, Dr. Glockamorra is a great guy, fabulous. I said, "Okay, fine, you know best, Dr. Suleiman," but feeling a need to assert my diagnostic expertise, carried on to ask, "What do you know about fragile X syndrome? I was wondering if Roger might have it, a bit of it."

"Does he have a lot of problematic uncles, or great uncles?" A cloudy vision of Dennis appeared before my eyes. "No, well, one uncle who had a problem learning to read, and my grandmother may have had what they call the March heart, it's a weak heart, or some such thing she got from her dad, and I guess my dad clearly had it because he died four years ago, suddenly, of a heart attack. He was forty-six. My uncle Angus had a slight heart attack last year, I think. I mean, their mother with the March heart lived to be eighty, so she didn't suffer any effects, just maybe carried the predisposition of the March heart, kind of like fragile X." I smiled.

"Hmmm. Well, let's leave it to the clinic to decide what, if anything, is going on."

If anything: With clammy hands, I clung to those words. At home, I thought of not telling Lucy but rejected that autosuggestion and, immediately upon her arrival, I said, "Roger's going to the Children's for an assessment, in six months or so, because of the walking, and the talking." He was in the living room watching cartoons.

Lucy didn't, as she liked to say, get exercised. She said, "That's okay, isn't it?" That's what she said. She didn't grab me and hug me to her chest as if I or Roger had been diagnosed with a wasting disease.

I said, "I guess so," although it was nothing like okay, there was no other mother of a twenty-seven-month-old who would think it was okay. All other mothers of twenty-seven-month-olds receiving such news would be at home and, one way or another, having a drink, a drug, or a moment with her god or superego. She would not be saying, that's okay, isn't it? Leave that to the aunt or good friend, the cousin or someone removed by one or two degrees of intimacy.

Two days later, Roger grabbed my wrist to look at my watch. He did this often, examined watches, his and others', maybe twenty times a day, and Lucy and I always told him the time, precisely. It's four-ten o'clock, we might say, or it's eleven-thirty-five o'clock. On this occasion, before I could utter eight-thirty o'clock, Roger said, "O," clear as a bell. This was his first word! I was incredulous and euphoric. "That's right, "I said. "O'clock." Roger held my wrist, clearly wanting more information. "It's eight-thirty o'clock," I said, then "Lucy!" I yelled, "Roger said O." She was on the couch, in the living room, and I was getting Roger ready for bed. He ran to Lucy (and her wristwatch) in his pyjamas, took her arm and said "O" once more. I was right behind, following his teetering gait, acting as security guard: since learning to walk he crashed and bashed his way through the indoor and outdoor world like a firefighter with poor balance.

At the couch, with Lucy as his adoring audience, Roger asked, "O?", clearly gleeful with his accomplishment and hoping for an answer to his first articulated question.

"He wants you to say what time it is. He's saying O, as in o'clock. He's talking!"

Lucy sat up and said, "Eight-thirty o'clock. Listen to you. You're a little talking time machine. Listen to you." Squeaking and laughing, Roger ran back to his room, Lucy said, "Let's have a drink," and we hugged and jumped up and down and, when Roger was in bed, drank our gin and tonic. That was early August and the beginning of Roger's own signature brand of "One Thing," viz., words containing long o sounds and an array of ineffectual words somehow associated with long o sounds. Soon he was saying poncho, o'clock, poncho-clock, and snowy o; also crick crack cracker jack, presumably because he liked the sound.

IN LATE AUGUST, I returned to Dr. Suleiman, having booked an appointment furtively for a time when Lucy was at work. I can't explain why, other than I was protective of my problem, my problem child. There was a phase during labour when I wanted everyone to leave me alone, even Lucy, and in mammalian isolation, I groaned the deep abdominal qi groan the midwife had taught me. As long as there was a hint of a problem, I was still in labour, I supposed. Lucy didn't need to know everything, she had never been in labour. Before Dr. Suleiman was seated on her rolling stool, I told her Roger was talking, I had counted twenty or so words, including poncho, snowy, cocoa, loco, crick, crack, and cracker jack.

"Poncho?" Dr. Suleiman said. "Loco? Does he say any words that might have more utility?"

"He has a way of asking what time it is," I said. "He holds my wrist and says O, for o'clock in a kind of questioning way or cadence."

Dr. Suleiman rolled closer to the notepad on its shelf. "Have you considered putting him into a daycare?" she asked. "There are several therapeutic daycares out there. I could find out what might be close to your part of town."

"No, I haven't thought of that," compressing the sentence into what sounded like one word.

She reconsidered and said, "Well, any kind of daycare would do. He could benefit from exposure to peers. Does he have any play buddies?"

"He has me, my friend Lucy, his babysitter Mrs. Marini, our neighbour Carmen and her kitten, Robert her tenant . . . no kids his age, I confess, although he enjoyed seeing his cousins last Christmas."

She nodded sagely. "I would think about it if I were you."

"I *was* thinking about his great-uncles, like you mentioned, and their heart problems, and I happened to come across some information about Marfan syndrome. Do you know anything about Marfan syndrome, or anybody who has it?"

Dr. Suleiman, in still-life position, observed me for ten or maybe more seconds. She had the empathy of a clock; I could almost hear her ticking. No wonder Roger liked her more than I did. "You should hear from the developmental clinic in a few months," she said.

ABOUT TWO WEEKS before Halloween, I bought a sewing machine and made a costume for Roger. It was a ladybug outfit made of two sections, a body of red furry material with black circles of a felt kind of fabric on the back, and a red toque with black circles for eyes. The day before Halloween, Barb and Iris came for dinner and exclaimed over my creation, then insisted I dress Roger in it, which I did. Accepting the attention with grace, he sat on Iris's knee, gazing with tired concentration at her wristwatch. Togetherness with Barb and Iris seemed to call for this type of observation, so I said, "I think the woman who sold me the sewing machine was flirting with me."

"You never mentioned that," Lucy said.

"Keeping secrets," said Iris.

"No, it's not that. I'm just never sure what's going on. She touched my arm twice, it didn't really register until I left the store with my Brother brand machine."

"Didn't register," Barb said. "Ha ha. Well, you know what they say, it doesn't matter where you get your appetite, as long as you eat at home." Ugh, I thought, that was vulgar, but maybe Barb would think it's okay I'm getting my appetite from a man at the gym named Asa.

I had been running, doing some working out at the Renforth Athletic and Recreation Centre more regularly since August and had been nurturing a passing acquaintanceship with Asa, last name unknown. We had said hello, how are you today, windy out there isn't it, and nothing more. Still, I thought about him as if he were an unexpected windfall heading my way, a sizable cash prize or a voucher for a trip to Italy. And, I didn't think this was a repressed false memory, it had returned to me as I picked up Roger from Iris's lap: I had run into Asa before, before I started going to the Renforth gym regularly, in Chinatown, probably more than a year ago on a Saturday morning when I had gone out to the Rainbow Bakery to get three coconut buns. Asa was ahead of me in the lineup; I'm positive it was him. We had a conversation about coconut buns, he said he was going to get three, and I was there for the exact same reason, and he said, "Kismet." The entire interaction was a little sexual, with him saying, "Enjoy your buns" and winking when he left, giving me a quick up and down once-over. Next time I see him I'll ask if he likes coconut buns, I almost said out loud to Barb, or just bring him one and say kismet, prompting him to respond with what I have occasionally thought to be his withering expression, as if to imply everything between us is imaginary, which it is; he is my imaginary appetite stimulant, and I am perhaps his object of recreation, maybe tomfoolery. I really can't say. I've rehearsed asking Asa to come with me to Medicine Hat, to see the place where Dennis lives, perhaps to meet him. It's important to allow yourself a number of impossible thoughts and motives, maybe that's what keeps Halloween alive.

nine

ROGER'S APPOINTMENT FOR the Developmental Clinic was to be April 11, 1984, at nine sharp. He would be thirty-five months by then, which I was sure would please Dr. Suleiman. The clinic had called on Monday morning, January 9, with an appointment in late February, but I said no, that date didn't work, which was a lie, any date would have worked, as all I was doing was writing up my thesis. I found reasons for no workable dates until April, allowing three months for the developmental burst I anticipated. I didn't write the appointment on the Co-op water birds calendar because I was planning not to tell Lucy until one or two days prior, or if she asked, but when she got home from work that day, in the snow and the dark of January at six, before she had her boots off, I had told her. "Roger's appointment at the Children's Hospital is for April 11." Although Roger was standing with me, sucking his thumb, he was not listening, waiting as he was, with confidence, for Lucy to pick him up and ask, *I wonder where Roger is?*

From the boot bench, Lucy looked up at me, nodded and asked, "Why are my socks wet again?"

We wouldn't discuss the appointment that day, or the next, because there was tension: I had changed my thinking about Roger's clocks interest since our neighbour Robert, on January 1, had given Roger, as a New Year's gift, a miniature Big Ben with authentic sound. At the sight and sound of this clock, Roger had tensed up his little body with inexpressible pleasure and squealed, producing a sound worse than his squeaks, a new type of shriek, reminiscent of an exotic jungle creature in ecstasy, one step away from a howl. The next day, I suggested to Lucy that maybe people needed to stop giving Roger clocks. In response, Lucy had said, "People? Only Robert and I have given him clocks."

"And my mother. But anyway. He needs other interests," I said. "Obviously my Christmas campaign failed." Using Lucy's money, for Christmas I had bought him a soccer ball, Lego, Perfection, a Playmobil train track and three interlocking puzzles suitable for three year olds. Boxing Day, I had caught Roger trying to write what I inferred were numbers on the face of the soccer ball, and, wrongly, I admitted later (after the shriek-howl) I drew a misshapen clock face on the ball. The Lego and train track, he had since ignored. Occasionally, he sucked his thumb and watched while Lucy assembled the puzzles.

"He has other interests," Lucy pointed out. "He's interested in you and me and hockey. He likes the Flames even though he doesn't say much about them. He likes the Stampeders. He likes Mimi."

"Those are all things you like," I said. "He just gets pulled along in your undertow."

"Well, he likes them, too. Isn't that kind of typical for a dad/son relationship?"

Stop with the dad/son, I wanted to say, just once, but I held back. Where would I be without Lucy? At a shelter, on a pallet, next to Joe Travolta?

"But the thing with the clocks and watches, it's starting to be too much. He has four watches and an alarm clock and a clock radio and now the Big Ben."

"Who gave him the clock radio?" Lucy asked.

"Okay. I did, fine."

"So, stop with the too much," Lucy said. "You go on too much about too much." Roger was in bed. Lucy had gone to the bathroom and closed the door. It was another, what one might call, fight. Through the bathroom door, I said, "I don't go on too much about too much. Too much is measurable. What can you do with a clock or a watch if you can't tell time, other than stare at it? At least the clock radio has a radio function." I could hear her peeing in there.

"Well, I guess to him it's art," Lucy said, with emotionless reason. I wasn't even sure why I was arguing, my case was shaky, as Lucy had already pointed out. The issue to me was, if *Robert* were giving him clocks, next it would be the entire neighbourhood. I knew how these things could mushroom. "I'm going for a walk," I said and went outside. On that day in early January, already the Christmas lights looked like too much. Too much *is* a quantifiable construct, I barked to Lucy in my mind. But when I returned home, I was calm and apologized for the clock comments. We made up, but there was after this fight a little crack of separation or perhaps more like a few lines of crazing in an older dish. I wanted Lucy to feel worried, and maybe that's why I was actually eager to tell her about the assessment date.

But once she knew, days passed, and Lucy said nothing about it, and neither did I, and the silence was compounding the dread that was growing in my stomach like a cobwebbing, presumably embalming some of the food I was eating, as bits of it seemed to stick in there for longer than usual. On many days and in diverse situations, I breathed in to a count of three and out to a count of four and kept the full-blown panic at bay. One warm chinook evening in the middle of February, after Valentine's Day and an exchange of identical boxes of Pot of Gold chocolates, outside in the easement, I started talking, thinking Lucy can listen or not. I said, "I know how we'll look and how the parent interview will sound. I'll have to say I was married to a swinger, for one thing." (I had confessed to Lucy about Larry and Irene on the drive back from Missoula.)

Lucy looked up from the melting snow; knowing I was referring to the assessment, she said, "No, you won't have to say that."

"If they ask, I'll have to tell them."

"Why would they ask if you were married to a quote swinger unquote?"

"They'll ask if I drank or took drugs while I was pregnant. They have to ask that. They'll ask if there are any relatives with psychiatric or developmental problems. I'm not telling them about Dennis; I'm not. I'll tell them about Adrian, but not Dennis. Then I'll have to mention Joe was staying with me. I know the things they have to ask."

"So, you had a few sips of one beer. And what's Joe got to do with anything?"

"I don't know, other than Roger still looks like him a bit. And they don't really know the effects of one or two drinks, or a half. But it's not that, it's just that if I look at me through their eyes, I see a woman who had an unbecoming sexual experience with Larry and Irene, then with an estranged husband, lived with a homeless Joe, moved in with a Lucy."

"A lesbian, you mean, you might as well say," said Lucy.

"No, that's not what I am wanting to say or even thinking."

"Yes, you are, of course you are."

"No, I'm not." Where I sat on the steps with my head in my hands, slumping forward, Lucy, as I had hoped, came and sat next to me and wrapped both arms around me. At times when she could have hated me, she was often kind. "No," I repeated, "I'm not thinking about them thinking about me or us being lesbians, maybe a little bit, but *moreso*, what I'm thinking is I don't really know anything about George. How will I explain that? I don't know if what he said about the brother Dennis is even true. I don't even know if his last name is Petrie. He could be a Jute or a Kallikak."

"A what?"

"Never mind. I shouldn't say that. It's just a reference to genetics, eugenics, never mind. And then there's the fact you're supporting me, financially."

"It's not really me, it's my resting-in-peace stepfather who is truly supporting us, if you want to tell them that, but I can't see how that's relevant."

"It's a package; they'll be judging me, for sure, like my colleagues would: one of them might even be there, on the panel or whatever it's going to be, as part of a practicum placement."

"The appointment is for Roger, not us."

"Oh, no, it's for us, too," I screamed in a whisper. The veins in my neck no doubt protruded, and I would have been happy to tense my body all over, like Roger at the first sight of his Big Ben, only out of fear rather than ecstasy. "You don't know how these things work. They will be judging, they will be well-intentioned people, like us, or like me, I mean, as in, trained observers such as psychologists and so on. They have to judge, that's what they're paid to do. They'll meet with us, they'll do some tests with Roger, and then they will gather behind closed doors to discuss *us,* the three of us." And, I didn't say this to Lucy, but the prospect of them discussing us behind closed doors or a two-way mirror filled me with a dense anger, the type that might assume mass, in space, and be discovered with its own startling gravitational field. I don't think Lucy had any notion of this anger because she was too good, she was not a mother, and she had the capacity to rise above the judgments of others. Lucy let go of me, sighed, and distracted both of us with her ambition. She wanted to pitch her "One Thing" column to the city's daily paper, the *Calgary Herald.* She knew someone who knew someone who had given her a contact. I said I thought it was a great idea, and I could see Lucy doing it, and I could see the paper being interested, but my skull was heavy with the effort this enthusiasm required.

A week later I went to Medicine Hat for a night, feeling guilty, of course, as if I were meeting a lover, as if I were a traitor. I told Lucy that Margo, one of my student colleagues now living in Medicine Hat, was having a party and wanted to get the *gang,* I said, in italics — lying details seemed to be a specialty for me — together for a party on Saturday. I took off in Lucy's car on a Saturday morning and found a room at the Satellite Motel, right on the Trans-Canada but well within the heart of Medicine Hat. Part of my story was true, in that Margo did live in Medicine Hat now. I had called her and asked about the centre for people with disabilities, and she knew about it, she had even worked there, and at that news a sensation passed through me, as if a buzzer had been pushed and released. Should I ask if she knew a Dennis? "Where is it?" I asked. "What's it like?"

"An institution," she said. "The grounds are nice, I guess you could say. I guess that's the best thing you could say."

No, I couldn't ask about Dennis.

Mentally unprepared for the nice grounds and because, for February, the day was almost warm, I drove around Medicine Hat until I found a park on the river, Police Point, an otherworldly kind of place filled with cottonwoods, quite possibly Dad's idea of heaven on earth. The visitor centre was closed until spring, but there were postcards of the park in a stand beneath a shelter. I took one for Lucy, thinking she could place it on her desk, in a frame, as a little joke on Cottonwood Optometry. According to the park brochure, the cottonwoods had hitched a ride on the river, and that's why they were in Medicine Hat when they should have been farther south, in Kentucky for example. Police Point was full of them; despite their rickety build, they had muscled out others, and to me, in the slanted sunlight, they seemed like evening trees, reaching, with their frail arms, for a hat or a menu. Sitting on a bench and watching the frozen river at Police Point Park, I lost my will to see the Wild Rose Centre. Instead, I drove to the Dairy Queen, got a cheeseburger and a chocolate milkshake, proceeded to the Satellite Motel, ate, watched TV, slept.

In the morning, as is so often the inexplicable case, life was different; I drove by the entrance and the sign, Wild Rose Centre, did a U-turn, plunged right into the grounds, and sat in the visitors' parking lot for a while. I wondered if someone would come and tap on my window. Ma'am? Ma'am? But no one did. I saw two people on the walkway, employees I assumed, as they seemed to be wearing uniforms and did not appear to be dysmorphic or to have an unusual gait; nor were they holding clocks or screeching. I supposed the residents, or orphans as I was thinking of them, stayed in the buildings, maybe moving between rooms and activities in secret hallways; why I thought they would be secret, I cannot say. I felt a terrible sadness for Dennis, and I realized then I had, somewhere, a copy of my marriage certificate and, as a member of the Petrie family, I could make a claim to see him, if he existed, and if a claim were required. I could bring the marriage certificate and demand, as a Petrie, visiting rights. I rolled down the window and could smell fresh snow mixed with the dispiriting exhaust fumes of Lucy's oil-burning car. Did the windows of the Wild Rose Centre ever open, and if so, what scents might be familiar to Dennis, what might he like to smell, through an open window? Did any specific pleasures, I wondered, cause him to squeal loudly? I listened, I thought I heard trays clattering, then rolled up the window and left, driving home in the Alberta cold, which had returned in the form of a weather system called an Arctic dome.

East of Bassano, I stopped at a rest centre to stand outside in the unkind frigid air, breathing in to three and out to four, when a thin and shivering dog appeared from behind the washroom building. He was black and short-haired, big-eared, the size of a beagle, and when I opened the car door, he jumped in on what looked like frozen paws. I turned on the heat full blast, and he jammed himself between the steering wheel and my lap, shivering, and I said you poor thing, you poor thing, Lucy would love you. Then I took off my coat and wrapped him in it, calling him King Two although Anastasia's King was bigger and fluffier, and there was little resemblance.

In Calgary, Lucy greeted King Two as if he were one of her old family dogs, born again; "He has poodle hair," she said. "Maybe he's part poodle, part beagle, a beadle." Roger stood back, in the living room, watching, sucking his left thumb while protecting the watch on his wrist with his right hand, creating a kind of shield as if King Two might decide he wanted nothing more from us than a timepiece. With urging from Lucy and me, Roger finally approached our new dog and, with an outstretched index finger, touched him on the head. "Like this," said Lucy, taking Roger's hand and running the palm along King Two's skull. She insisted we needed to go to the emergency veterinary clinic, where our new friend checked out fine; he had no identification, no one they knew of was looking for him, he was ours. We all, as Lucy would say, she and I, loved King Two; he smoothed over some of the cracks and crazing between us.

ten

BY APRIL 11, the developmental burst had not occurred, despite my many self-mumblings that *we* would show *them* what development was, or is. Roger could still walk, of course, what I called steadily or in a steady forward direction, he was halfway toilet trained, and he could clearly articulate his collection of long-O and crick-crack words. He might agree to run after a soccer ball if Robert kicked it. He preferred bright, girlish colours in clothing, and already at the age of two years eleven months, would not allow Lucy or me to select his clothes. If we tried, he would screech. He had a way of knowing colours by association. He had held, for example, a sleeve of his orange turtleneck next to Mimi and squeaked knowingly. A similar connection had been made between his white jeans and the snow. For the hospital, he wore those very garments, his Mimi-coloured turtleneck, as we now called it, and snow jeans, along with the turquoise jacket I think he wanted to call bath after the usual dyes of his tub water. Not wanting my son to look so eccentric, earlier, with Lucy in the shower and King Two by my side, I had suggested blue jeans, but at the sight of them, Roger had stared defiantly into my eyes and said no, a long O word he pronounced clearly, like a chirp, with no prelude or postlude. I put the jeans away, knowing there was nothing to be gained from a wardrobe conflict.

Away we went in Lucy's Oldsmobile. Most of the snow was gone, the sky was blue and the temperature mild for April in Calgary. Roger had on his *always* watch and his *car* watch and had been told, by Lucy, he could, just for today, wear his car watch into a big place called a hospital, to meet some interesting people. He seemed content with this prospect. I had flattened his hair down with water, but enroute it was already popping up in dark, brown clumps, like a determined kind of spring foliage. As we entered the parking lot, all of my pores at once began to shed a fine layer of sweat. I said, "Whatever the first appointment is, can I just go by myself with Roger? I think if I can get through the first one on my own, I'll be better equipped for the rest, but if you come with me, I'll start blubbering."

Lucy steered into a parking spot and said, "No, I'm not sitting in a waiting room with an old copy of *Ladies' Home Journal* while you're talking to the professionals. What kind of parent does that, especially for the first appointment, which will likely be with the psychiatrist?"

"The psychiatrist? Who said anything about a psychiatrist? They said psychologist, speech and language pathologist, occupational therapist, physical therapist, and pediatrician. You think they're planning to shuttle us into the psych ward the minute we arrive?" I was smiling a little bit, but I was filled with dread, and I told Lucy that for me, dread management was a solo affair.

She said, "Okay, I just got the psychs mixed up, I didn't ever hear there was a psychiatrist, and I don't see why it's got to be a quote unquote solo affair right off the bat." But she knew certain Roger-related arguments with me were as fruitless as wardrobe conflicts with Roger, so she agreed, as long as I explained to the first examiner who Lucy was, why she was waiting outside, and stressed that she was neither negligent nor in denial. I nodded and wiped my forehead with a handkerchief.

Appointment number one was with the *developmental* pediatrician, neither a psychiatrist nor a psychologist, Dr. Von Daniken. Lucy stayed in the waiting room, waving farewell, and naturally Von Daniken assumed she was a friend offering support, but in the office, with the door closed, holding Roger in my arms, I told him she was my girlfriend and partner and co-parent of Roger, but that I had decided to soldier through the first appointment on my own, because I needed to rally up my own strength. I don't know why I used the words soldier and rally: was I under the influence of extraterrestrials, I wondered, and suppressed an urge to ask the doctor if he was related to the notorious Von Daniken, surmising he had fielded that question a trying number of times since *The Chariots of the Gods*, and I did not want to try him. I really thought I might faint, and had there been a warm mound of grave mud to hand, I might have. Grave-mud fainting, I thought, is a kleptomemory, one I would rather keep to myself and very briefly, I thought of Constance Tandy.

Taking a chair, with Roger on my knee, I lurched onward, telling Von Daniken I didn't know much about Roger's father's genealogy, because he had been in foster care for many years and was estranged from his family of origin. I told him we were divorced. On his clipboard, Von Daniken wrote something, then looked up, directly into my alienated eyes and asked, "Can you undress him, please?" The office was warm. My sweat, I imagined, made my skin shine like a stone from one of those rock tumblers. When we got to the plastic pants and diaper, I said, "He's seventy-five percent toilet trained." For his part, Roger seemed unworried about being naked in the doctor's office. He sat on the paper, on the table, and I hoped his little ass was still clean and I wished for Lucy to be with me so I could tell her I was on the cusp of a rigour, I breathed out to eight and composed my surface. Roger was allowed to keep on the two watches. He sat quietly with his round eyes watching me as I talked. Seeming to infer the formality of the occasion, he neither grabbed at Von Daniken's watch nor said *o'clock* or any other word.

Von Daniken asked Roger, "Is it okay if Mom sits over there?" indicating the chair opposite the table. He nodded, and I abandoned him to the examining table.

Von Daniken measured Roger's head, his length, tapped on his torso, checked some reflexes, listened to his heart, observed that his testes were descended, then swivelled his upper body to speak in profile. "His features are a little unusual. Does he look like his father? One should never jump to conclusions about these things. The circumference of his head is in the normal range, although at the ninety-fifth percentile. The shape is a little atypical. I'm sure I'm not telling you anything you haven't already worried about." Still the profile speaking.

My eyes filled with tears. "I wouldn't say he looks like his father. No." I considered asking about the contagion of facial features, mentioning my time with Joe, but I knew this was ridiculous and did not want the pediatrician to think *Mom* was a crackpot.

Von Daniken then picked Roger up and turned to face me. "He's healthy?"

"Yes," I said, "nothing serious except for the croup once. He started walking at twenty-two months and talking at twenty-five-and-a-half months. That's not that bad, is it?" I asked, pathetically and desperately. "He looks kind of pale," I went on, "maybe he needs more sunlight." In Von Daniken's arms, Roger's legs dangled like two parsnip-coloured roots pulled easily from sandy soil.

"Well, it *is* April," the pediatrician said. "And it's been a long winter. Can you touch your nose?" Roger complied.

"I don't think you should ask a lot of questions like that. He gets pretty nervous when he thinks a person's testing him." Knowing how defensive and absurd this comment sounded, I removed my glasses and rubbed my eyes, as if my judgment may have been momentarily clouded by a migraine or a mote. Von Daniken carried on. "Who's that right there?" pointing to me.

Roger looked and smiled, entirely cherubic in his nakedness and willingness. Smiling even more, he flung his hand toward me. In the chair, I pulled myself closer and held his fingers, feeling as if I were in my own chair-sized basement, filling with water.

Von Daniken handed Roger to me, asked more questions, wrote more notes, and said, "You can dress him now. We'll talk in conference at three, but I won't say anything there I haven't told you here. I'll make an appointment for you with genetics. It won't be for a couple of months at the earliest. Usually nothing shows up, but there may be some idiopathic condition, and as you've said we don't know much about Dad. He's still young, of course," and for one moment I thought the doctor was referring to George, but naturally he meant Roger, "and his height and weight are reasonable, but there's a good possibility there's a delay, well, clearly there *is* a delay when we consider mile-stones, but we don't know what this implies, could just be motoric. The others will do some standardized testing, so they will have more empirical news for you. Later. The receptionist will advise you where to go next."

Clearly there is a delay. This utterance tripled my weight, I was a heavy thing being buried. Dr. Von Daniken left the room.

The remainder of the visit was a Jacob's ladder of failure. Immedi-ately following the pediatrician, I had to concede a need for Lucy's companionship and intervention. We travelled from one small room to another, some with two-way mirrors, the better to see you with, and some without. For the speech and language part, I was invited to stay with Roger, and Lucy elected to watch from outside, through the mirror. With her long brown hair and high forehead, the speech and language pathologist reminded me of Alice in Wonderland. She called Roger a little fellow and asked him to point to pictures and name things. I warned her, Sophie, that Roger did not respond well to testing, I could not stop myself from repeating this despite knowing my maternal craziness was filling most of the space in the small room. I pictured myself as a bulging, leaking propane tank, about to light a cigarette. After the third picture, Roger stopped talking and for the next test, after the sixth picture, stopped pointing. I said, *"Roger,"* in a voice of frustration and demi-churl, to which Sophie said, "It's okay, Mom. Lots of kids clam up. It's an unfamiliar setting."

I had imagined any potential intelligence testing would be the worst, but in fact watching Roger with the physical therapist was the most disastrous agony. She, Martha, threw a beach ball to Roger. It bounced off his forehead as he clapped his hands together, again and again. He could not walk along a yellow piece of tape. He wanted to look at her watch. He wanted to climb up her body as if it were a pole. He could not jump over the yellow line. He bent his knees and smiled.

He failed every task. I said to Lucy, "My son will be entering kinder-garten in the can't-catch-a-beach-ball stream."

Lucy said, "Don't say that about Roger."

"Does it make it different if I don't say it? "

"Yes, it does. It diminishes Roger if you say that. It makes him less than Roger."

"Well, no matter what I say, he can never be less than Roger unless he has a degenerative condition."

Lucy walked away from me, stomped really, down the hall and returned and entered the physical and occupational therapy room. She chased a delighted Roger, saying, "C'mon Roger, show them how fast you can run."

After the fine and gross motor assessments, I let Lucy know she would have to escort Roger to the intelligence testing. I needed to sit on the other side of the mirror and wring my hands.

Lucy gave the history again and sat quietly in a chair in a cor-ner while Roger pointed, made a tower of blocks, pretended to feed a picture of a doll, and gazed adoringly at the clock on the wall. After this, they came to find me and we had mini pizzas and sat until three, when we set sail for the conference room. Roger would stay in a play area with a nursing assistant while we met. As the pediatrician had promised, there would be empirical news, and it was parsimonious, as we liked to say in psychology, yielding one repeating figure: the third percentile rank! For intelligence, receptive and expressive language, fine and gross motor ability, everything except head size, length, and weight. To my surprise, Lucy began to cry. I had never seen her cry and had not been sure she was capable of it; I had even wondered about the possibility of blocked tear ducts and asked Dr. Suleiman about symptoms on one of my infrequent visits. Even when she had once whacked her thumb with a hammer, not a tear, only the welling up that one time when I bought the ring.

"It'll be okay," I said, loudly, to the room, taking Lucy's hand. "He's still Roger. Nothing changes, quoting Lucy."

The psychologist, Kathy, nodded and said, "That's right." I appreciated her approval, but of course everything *had* changed, and I stopped listening as they advised us who to call, and what to expect, and when we would hear back from genetics for an appointment. My ears and eyes felt as if they were opening into hollow, uninhabited space, then I heard Lucy blowing her nose and someone saying they would send us the assessment reports. Fine, go ahead, I thought, wanting to find Roger wherever he was with the nursing assistant, to sieve through paint and drywall and all matter, and leave and be gone.

As we strapped and buckled ourselves into Lucy's big car, I said what I had to say about dank submission and my resistance to being clubbed, with Roger, into same. I imagined running furiously away, with Roger, without Roger, either way, the Trans-Canada Highway was right there, a stone's throw from the parking lot. "I know what my mother's going to say when she hears about this percentile business. She's going to say, well, Donna McBeel . . ."

"Never mind," Lucy said. "I know. Never mind. Let's not talk about it right now. We all love you, Roger. We're talking about you right now," she went on, looking at him in the rearview mirror, "about how much we love you." He didn't care who we were talking about, he was still happy to be wearing both watches, and apparently, studying them carefully, at that moment decided to say, "Four o'clock," which it was!

"Did you hear that? Roger just said, *four o'clock*. It's four. He can tell time," Lucy said. I was too clubbed and depleted to rejoice, and truth be told, at that moment, as I have said, I thought his accuracy no more than a lucky coincidence. But not Lucy. She unbuckled herself, got out of the car, removed Roger from his car seat, and holding him in front of her, shaking him a little, like a newspaper, she said, "You can tell time, Roger! You're incredible. You are at the top percentile rank." I opened the car door, but I didn't get out, because I wanted to run, even if it was just to the end of the lot and back, so I closed it again and waited.

"Can we please, please go?" I asked.

ON THE PHONE, Mom asked, "Do you want me to come out there for a bit?" This had not occurred to me, but now it seemed not a bad idea. This was a significant family event, not a death or a birth or a marriage, but a metamorphosis, Roger A to Roger B.

"I guess that would be nice."

"Well, for Pete's sake," she said.

"What do you mean?"

"Well, you don't want him to be at the third percentile, do you?"

"No, I'd rather he was at the eighty-third percentile, obviously."

"I'd better at least come for a visit then."

She made arrangements but cancelled them, which was fine with me and Lucy.

eleven

IT SEEMED ONLY days after the assessment, Roger began to talk in
sentences that usually made sense. We began some enriching activities. I took Roger to swimming lessons again and endured two entire
sessions, and he progressed from pollywog to tadpole, along with
everyone else. But while other children were leaping from the pool's
edge into their mother's arms, kicking and swimming underwater
with their eyes open, Roger was holding onto my neck with such

desperation his little biceps, I think, took on more definition, and that was progress, I supposed. Also, the day after he turned three, I signed him up for the Saturday library group for three- and four-year-olds. Most mothers and the one dad left their children and looked around the library or went next door to the coffee shop. I stayed, because Roger gripped my hand and said, "StayMom," one quick word, as if I were a mother doll sold by Mattel. Every time, the exact same request, and I was so touched and immobilized by his need of me, I stayed with him right there on the floor, listening to stories about Arthur or Clifford, the big red dog. Roger never let go of my hand. I don't know why the library scared him. The other children sat listening, autonomous as university students and always, at least once, I had to move a finger beneath my glasses to press at a tear.

By three separate community associations, I was told Roger was too young to join pre-T-ball.

He could reliably tell time to the hour, but three (years) had no meaning for him. He detested calendars, months, and weeks, assaulting them when he could, slapping away pictures of lambs or mountains. "No, I don't want Friday! I hate it." Calendars were rectangular and static, unlike the repeating twelve-hour unit, the hour hand, the minute hand and the smoothly sailing second hand. Roger understood that time circled on, it was not a rectangle. *Just say I'm two*, he had been trained to answer; becoming three made no sense. "I'm two," he insisted, "o'clock, o'jock, o'poncho," concluding with an emphatic shriek. Some nights I had to pretend he had a windup stem on the top of his head to persuade him to walk to his bedroom.

Despite Roger's various needs, his special needs I found myself trying not to think, I felt I should find a job. Lucy was still supporting me financially, although nothing, except for Roger (which was a big something, Lucy said), was stopping me from finding a job. I had finished my coursework and my thesis was mostly complete, I had only to do my chartering, after which I could work as an educational psychologist. Why was I not elated or even chipper? The thought of completing these steps and seeking employment was like putting on a wet bathing suit on a cold winter day, worse, in the walk-in freezer of a high school cafeteria on a cold winter day. Maybe I was lazy. Lucy said, don't bother getting a job. Not yet. She was now an optometric assistant, and she'd met with an editor at the *Herald* who had asked to see samples of her column from the community paper. She was almost famous; soon she might be. She had fans in the community, and I wondered if she might be seeing someone else. Our neighbourhood in particular seemed to have a greater density of lesbians than others, or even straight single women, and everywhere (it seemed) we went, they greeted her, because they wanted to be in her column, I told myself. I developed a mesh of poorly articulated suspicions.

One day, I looked in her purse. There was no appointment book with coded entries (meet DC at 4?), and the smell of her battered privacy stayed with me for days. I vowed never to do that again until I did it again. Another time, I left Roger with Mrs. Marini and took the bus to the optometric clinic and walked the alleyway to the parking lot, just walked by quickly, thinking Lucy might be outside with someone; I had an image of her back there, in her long-sleeved white shirt and black hair, with some other woman. I guess she was at her desk, because she wasn't outside hugging anyone. I took the bus home feeling ridiculous, got off at the video store and rented a movie, *Tender Mercies*, knowing nothing much about it. That night we watched it, and Lucy said to me, seriously, "Roger has an immortal soul just as durable as yours and mine, only probably shorter, in stature, I mean."

"What do you think it looks like? Does it have a shape?" Like your cat in the tree, or Constance's great aunt by the pump, I wanted to say, but stopped myself.

"It's beyond our ken."

"I know, the ken of science."

"It's rugged," she said, "a rugged little soul."

"Like an old rugged cross?" I smirked. I couldn't tell if we were half-laughing or half-serious, but I resolved not to walk by the clinic parking lot again; Lucy was incongruous and lovable, whereas I was perhaps not.

"You need to sign Roger up for preschool," she said.

"I know, I know, I know."

Many of those long spring and early summer days, I thought of Joe and his thin jacket, his worn-out shoes, his blue cap, and his potato-eating, *Sure, I'll finish off the potatoes if nobody wants them,* the salve he left in the bathroom, which was for his eyes. They were often crusty in the morning, and I used to worry bits of his eye crust would fall onto his toast. I was nauseous then, and nausea insists on a nauseating storyline. The tube of salve was rolled up tightly to squeeze out the final bits. It was a prescription, and I tried to read the name on the label, but it was worn and folded away to specks of blue. Where was Joe now? Surely, he had a job and a place to live and some new clothes.

We never did go to the genetics clinic. I cancelled the appointment and did not reschedule like I said I would. Postponing forever ate away at me, but that was the price I paid. And what would they have found in my DNA or Roger's? A broken spring?

Lucy started to make short movies for me; they weren't for Roger or anyone else, and for this, I loved her. She spoke in accents from the southern U.S.A., not necessarily Kentucky, because she said they more or less talked like me except to say law-yer and you all. She imitated specific people, once even her grandmother Fairfax, and I felt warmth envelop me. I watched and rewatched this video, then listened sometimes without looking while she spoke in her grandmother's accent about how she had always wanted to learn to skate. It was a regret.

So, in the warmth of mid-June, we went shopping for skates and made plans to go to Bowness Park in the winter, the three of us.

One good thing, maybe as a side effect of practising pre-T-ball with me and Lucy, Roger developed a new interest: balls. One day at the Co-op, he zeroed in on a pile of soccer balls, and Lucy bought him two, with the stipulation we could not draw a clock face on either. He and Robert began playing soccer in the alley. Then he asked for a basketball: Roger had a new interest! As summer came on and arrived, I felt more limber, I felt my cartilage relax. He would have friends, there was no doubt, I said to Lucy out on the steps while she smoked. I was emotional in my sternum. "Thanks so much for getting him started with the soccer balls!"

"It was him. He got himself started," Lucy said. "He's good at that. But he can't get himself started to school, that's one thing he can't do." A couple days later, she left me the pre-kindergarten video, which I watched while Roger was in his room looking at his basketball, and Lucy was at work.

In the video, Lucy was sitting in the car, that's where she sometimes made her movies, with King Two after they'd been to Nose Hill park. She had on her hat with the earlugs, to be funny. She said, "I had a sort of friend in high school named Linda Louise, so we called her Linda-Lou, who stands out in my memory for her use of the phrase *in two shakes of a lamb's tail*, because it was her way of saying she wasn't going to do something. This was in a physics class, and I had asked her if I could borrow her slide rule because I guess I had left mine at home. She was in the desk in front of me. Surely, she said to me, in just two shakes of a lamb's tail. So, I sat there waiting while everyone else got to work on the problem. She was good at physics, and she was finished soon, but then she just sat there, clutching her rule, and looking a little out of the corner of her right eye at me, to see my reaction. I wanted to smack her, but instead I asked Hugh Herbert who sat across from me and was also good at physics, and he handed his slide rule over just like that. And after, I wondered what kind of point Linda-Lou was trying to make but I never mentioned it to her. It wasn't worth the effort. Anyway, I had entirely forgotten about that incident until someone at the clinic used that phrase in two shakes of a lamb's tail, but in her case, it was in reference to a credit card, and she did find it promptly.

"What I'm saying is, you need to register Roger for pre-kindergarten. You need to call the school in two shakes of a lamb's tail and not be a Linda-Lou. It's almost the end of June, you need to go before they all shut down for the summer."

I didn't want her to think of me as a Linda-Lou, so I looked up the number of the school and called. The pre-kindergarten was part of the elementary school, but it wasn't called pre-kindergarten, I had an idea it was perhaps therapeutic, to use Dr. Suleiman's term, because in the phone book, under Peter Lougheed Elementary, it had a separate listing: Early Start Program and Preschool. The receptionist answered, and I asked for an appointment with the principal. I said I wanted to enroll my son in preschool, I added that he might be a little different, but that I lived in the area, as if that explained it, and I had a report from the Children's Hospital. The secretary said, "Yes, certainly, tomorrow afternoon, Dr. Cove can see you at 3:45. Bring your son. What's his name?"

She has a PhD, I thought; or can she be a medical doctor? Had Dr. Suleiman been in touch with them?

"Roger," I said. "Roger Drury. I'm his mother, Rose."

"Great, Rose. We'll see you tomorrow afternoon!"

That was June 20. I called the next day and rescheduled for June 25, cancelled that, and said I would come by on the twenty-eighth, but I didn't. When I called on the twenty-ninth, the last Friday of June, no one answered.

I HAD TRIED, but failed, to forget about Asa. After Roger turned three, as a wrong-minded reward to myself, I began attending the gym at the Calgary Athletic Centre at the time I thought Asa might be there, which was around eleven. I would deliver Roger to Mrs. Marini at ten, have a shower, fuss with my hair, and go. Usually, I ran on a treadmill while Asa was on the indoor track, and when he stopped to cool down and walk around the track, minutes later, there I was. I could tell he liked me, he wanted to be noticed.

Asa was bombastic, and he was ribald, and I didn't always know what to say, so one day, mentally sifting through topics, I asked him what he thought about the DNA being cloned from an extinct animal called a quagga. I had planned to comment on the Oilers winning the Stanley Cup, but I think the extinct-animal angle was wiser; he was flattered that I might want his views on popular science. He admitted he knew nothing about this animal, but he said, well, if they can do that, can they take some DNA from me and grow a younger version? That I can slide into? He was forty-five, he had already told me, and divorced, and seeing a woman he called the Dolly, who was thirty. "I can't keep up with her," he said. This set the tone for our conversations. I was agreeable, he shared untoward intimacies; I listened, he went too far then became aloof; after five days or a week, he would apologize and embrace me in a sweaty hug. At the age of twenty-eight, I developed a lurid crush on him, which was fine, because he was seeing the Dolly, and I had Lucy.

I liked the way he talked, particularly his use of old-time words such as skedaddle and dilly dally, enunciated always with a slyness as if he were borrowing them from the minds of their most probable users. We had a flirtatious friendship, that's all, I said to myself, although he likely didn't think so. Once, after we had finished our runs, we walked the track and our arms brushed together, four times. Another time, he held my hand for about three seconds, he just grabbed it when we met up in the foyer. My body became thirteen years old. Had there been an autopsy in the gym change room, the coroner's report would have said, what a loss, look at that adolescent heart, not what you would expect in a late-twenties mother who worries all day every day.

One July afternoon, we went to the Stampede. I was entering the gym, and he was exiting, and our paths crossed in the parking lot. The gym was up the hill but not that far from the grounds, and if the wind was right, you could hear the screams from the midway as you walked to and from your car. Every year it was the same midway and the same screams, but it was nevertheless alluring, as screams tend to be when mixed with the smell of frying oil, and I had said to him, "We should go to the Stampede, just for an hour or so, and go on a ride. We could line up and go on the roller coaster and get thrown around a bit."

He said, "Rosie, you're talking to the right person. A client just gave me two passes to the grounds. Let's go. Carpe diem." Moments later, we were in his vehicle, a leather-scented interior with many extras. I had not yet been in a vehicle with him and was very happy, in fact, joyous, to be travelling in the same conveyance. Outside of living together, this was as close to shared domesticity as one could get, with the little garbage bag, the box of Kleenex, distant food smells, and evidence of musical preferences, manly sunglasses. I felt instantly very guilty, and my bowels churned, then settled. I thought the words *explosive diarrhea.*

"Where are your cowboy boots, Rosie?"

"I don't have any. Do you?" He didn't answer, distracted as he was, driving and looking for a parking spot. I wondered what if Lucy were doing the same thing, and we ran into each other, she with one of the optometric clients. Would we just split up on the spot? Who would Roger choose?

"Look, this guy's leaving. Are we lucky or what?"

"We are lucky, Asa, we are. I can pay for the parking."

He didn't argue. It was ten bucks. "I guess that's a lot for people looking for one midway ride only, but we're an unusual breed, Rose, that's what we are. An unusual breed."

"Maybe like some kind of water dog," I offered, "like a poodle. Or my dog, which we call a beadle."

"I was thinking something better looking than poodles, Rosie. Look at us. Pretty good looking for our age, I mean my age, not yours. I'm bragging. Sorry."

"Go ahead and brag!" I almost yelped. Asa had his own very specific look, with a face that rested into grouchiness, but somehow smiled lovingly.

He kissed my cheek and one bar on a graph in my mind darted upward, and we stepped out and onto the hot pavement and hot sidewalk, crowded with the carnival bound, people going to the fair, loaded with a very specific type of anticipation, other bars and graphs.

The complimentary tickets were accepted without question by the boy at the turnstile, and we were in. "We'll need midway tickets," I said, "there's a booth. I'll go get the minimum amount needed for a ride."

"No, no. I'll get the tickets. You got the parking. Don't be a spending martyr."

"Okay. I'll wait here and admire the crowds."

When he returned, he was with a man and woman, foothills-aged, to use Leonard Cohen's classification, tanned and wearing the full plaid shirts, jeans, boots outfits. Asa introduced me as his friend. They assessed me, I assessed them, and they left.

"Who are they?" I asked.

"My ex-neighbours; Sandra my ex-wife knew them better than I did. He's a dermatologist, and she's a real estate agent. They don't approve of me. And by extension, you, I'm sorry to have to say."

"They were a bit overly tanned. You would think a dermatologist would eschew that kind of thing."

Asa said, "I think he thinks of himself as a skin advertisement. I mean, you don't want to go into the dermatologist's office and see a guy who looks like he lives in a crypt. Do you? Would that put your mind at ease, Rose, if you had a suspicious mole?"

"Maybe not."

"Let's go to the roller coaster."

"This reminds me of my very first date," I said, "to the fall fair. A daytime date, because I was too young for a nighttime date. It was exhilarating, actually." I could feel myself revving up on talk.

"Actually?"

"Yes, actually."

"So, who was this first-date guy?"

"His name was Robert. He was in Grade 10, and I was in Grade 9. He had rosy cheeks and a thin nose, features which maybe don't sound like they go together, but he was cute. Then suddenly it was okay for me to go on a nighttime date, my parents did not have rules, or if they did, they changed them between one offer of a date and the next. So we went to a high school dance. I can still remember the smell of his sweater, or the effect of the smell of his sweater during the slow dances. It was kind of swoon-inducing. For fabric softener or whatever it was."

"Oh yeah? Swoon-inducing? He was probably hoping for some other effect."

"Ha! No way. I was pretty puritanical at that age. There was no effect that would have had any effect," I replied, idiotically.

We said nothing more as we charged toward the lineup and took our place at the end, the oldest people, as far as I could see, if you averaged our ages.

"And?" I said. "Your first date?"

"Mary Lou Park. We went to the drive-in with my buddy and some girl he knew, and they were in the front seat necking up a storm, and Mary Lou wouldn't allow so much as a chaste kiss. Mainly what I remember her saying is *off limits*. She was like a damn referee. That relationship didn't last very long."

He was quieter now, not the booming voice but the confidential ear-level one. "We're moving fast here, Rosie. We're gonna be on that track in a matter of minutes. Good timing. They'll be able to hear you screaming over at the top of the Husky Tower."

The usual carnies were in charge, thin and smoking and dressed in black; their indifferent attention to safety was thrilling, snapping the bar into place and moving on, a form of animal husbandry. Ever so faintly, you could smell the barns.

The ride was intense, of course, and brief. By a higher power, I was pressed into Asa's shoulder and shirt. I wondered if he would scream in a masculine sort of shouting way, or swear, but he did neither. I laughed, not being a screamer either, and soon the cars were braking, and we were climbing out, and not wanting him to feel disappointed with life after rolling and coasting, I said, "Let's go look at the animals for a while, in the barns, the cows and pigs."

He said, "Okay, for a quick visit," and kissed my cheek and asked, "You still going for a workout after this?"

"Yes, I am," I said, thinking *workout* was his word, not mine, and my eyes became prickly with tears contained within the sockets.

"This way to the barns," he said.

"That's a sentence I like," I said, but he didn't hear, he was ahead by a couple of strides, and sometimes I had noticed he did not hear that well.

Why was he kissing my cheek? Why was I betraying my beautiful and loyal Lucy? Don't think I didn't wonder what the attraction might be. Everyone analyzes, psychoanalyzes, that is. Now I had my own DSM, third edition, required for the part-time job I would be starting in August. I needed the diagnostic manual to be up on all the criteria, not that I was diagnosing much, I would be working for the province, auditing files in schools to make sure the necessary paperwork was in place to qualify students with problems or conditions or disabilities for grants, so there would be extra money for extra help. The file needed to have a doctor's diagnosis and other supporting documentation, audiograms for the hard of hearing, ophthalmology reports for the visually impaired, psychology reports for the learning disabled, the mild, the moderate, the severe, and the profound. Genetic details. I looked forward to carrying the DSM in my briefcase. It would be like a concealed weapon.

Asa strode ahead. I caught up to him and said again, "I like that sentence, this way to the barns." He held my hand, and we followed the scent of animals.

AFTER THE STAMPEDE outing with Asa, I was bulbous with guilt, convinced my face showed, like they say of pregnancy. In mirrors I had rarely noticed before, on the visor of the passenger seat of the Oldsmobile, in the bits of glass on the hat rack Lucy had hung in the hallway, I checked my reflection for signs of betrayal and pimples. Then I told myself surely this kind of thing happened with lesbian couples and was not a big deal. Then I recalled Lucy skeptically accepting the ring I had bought her, *you straight girls*. No matter how one looked at the situation, even an anti-lesbian evangelical Protestant minister would say, well, that Rose girl is in the wrong here.

I shuddered and shook myself like Kings One and Two. As our July drink of the month, Lucy had selected the Palmetto Cocktail, and the evening I decided to confess, I stirred up two for us. My hands steadied as I poured, perhaps because my limbic system knew in a knot of ganglia tucked beneath my hippocampus, I was not going to say a word about Asa. We were in the kitchen at the table near the open window. Roger was in bed, tired out from swimming lessons and T-ball 'practice' with Robert. It had been a good day. Lucy was brown from being outside, tending her easement flower beds and killing dandelions. She was enjoying a week of holidays, a good reason for me to stop going to the gym for a while.

I said to Lucy, "I never told you about my most joyous moment of being Roger's mother." Then I did begin to shake a little, in my ribcage and diaphragm, because I am the kind of animal that knows it will get caught, before it gets caught, or even if it doesn't get caught, explicitly.

Lucy said no, what was it, R?

For the first time in our relationship, Lucy called me R, and I very sternly told myself: get rid of Asa. I had Lucy, he had the Dolly. If the genetic scientists working on the quagga scraped some DNA off an old piece of my muscle, would they grow a Rose, an R, without a heart or a moral compass, as they say? I needed to make amends, I needed to confess to Lucy while the sky was still a little pale, everything the colour of a light bulb at rest and unilluminated. The days are long in Calgary in the summer. I had lots of time. I stopped shaking.

"It happened a long time ago, when I went to Ontario at Christmas, when Roger was a year and a half. I had that picture of you with me, the one I always have, it's in my purse, the one from Roger's first Christmas, you know, the one with the glasses."

She knew. I don't think Lucy fakes interest or attention as much as I do. Sitting there listening, she looked like I was going to say she had been chosen to represent all of Canada and the United States at an emerging journalists' event, with prizes. That's how heartening she can be, or at least look. "It was the day before we were going to come home, I think, and I showed Roger that picture and said we're going to call Lucy, on the phone. And you talked to him, and he got it. He got that it was you. And while he was listening to you, he put his arm around my neck and it was as if he knew you were there with us, on the phone, that the three of us were an us. He knew that without any empirical evidence, he could fit us together out of thin air, and I wasn't sure he would be able to do that, maybe ever, and I felt so happy right then, to have him and you."

Lucy placed her hand on mine. "That's so sweet," she said, and I continued talking.

"My heart melted like a candle that day," I said, "I think it melted into a new shape." Lucy kissed my forehead, then my hand, the hand that had held Asa's. And that was my confession. Why rock the boat? It was nothing, and it is over. Still, I worried intensely for at least another week, imagining the friends of Asa I had met at the Stampede, both of whom wore glasses, might be patients at Cottonwood Optometry. I pictured them noticing my and Roger's pictures on Lucy's desk, I envisioned one of them saying to her, I think we met that lesbian friend of yours at the Stampede grounds. She was with Asa. He left his wife not long ago, or, more accurately, she gave him the boot. He's already got a girlfriend, and now this. I guess you could call him a swinger.

For the remainder of July, I stayed away from the indoor track. The weather was great for running, not too hot, and August 6 I started my half-time job with Alberta Education. I wanted to be able to tell Dr. Cove, the PhD at Peter Lougheed School, I was working, in education, when I met with her to register Roger. In two shakes of a lamb's tail.

twelve

EARLY AUGUST, I returned to the gym, and there we were, walking together and brushing arms again. I told Asa I had a job and one of my first missions was to go to Pincher Creek for a meeting. "Do you want to come with me?" I asked, realizing I was laying the groundwork for inviting him to come to Medicine Hat with me, one day, thinking for sure he would say no to Pincher Creek, but he said "Sure, there have to be some advantages to being your own boss. I have an old client in Pincher, maybe I'll track him down."

A week later, we met early in the morning at the gym parking lot. I didn't feel guilty, because now I thought my friendship with Asa was dedicated to the mission of meeting Dennis Petrie and solving the mysteries of Roger Drury. "What is it exactly you do?" I asked him.

"Wholesale," he said.

"Of what?"

"You name it, I sell it."

"Okay. Well, here's my new car," I said, "it still smells new inside." I had bought a Toyota on a five-year payment plan.

"Why don't we take my car?"

"Because I get paid mileage."

"You can pretend you drove, submit the mileage, buy me a hamburger on Tuesday."

"Then I'll pay for your gas."

"If it'll make you feel better," he said, so we took his vehicle. The eastern sky was pink, and, despite being nervous about my new job, despite being a questionable person, I felt happy. We got coffee to go from a place on Macleod Trail and motored on, a southbound secret. The heater was on, the morning was cool. Against the backdrop of numerous small strip malls and Super-8-calibre hotels, Asa's semi-bald profile was an irresistible sight.

I asked, "In your opinion, or experience, what does the phrase 'to have one under your belt' mean? As in 'at least he got one under his belt.'" Seemed like a reasonable question at the time.

"You're trying to turn the conversation to sex already, Rose? We just got on the road. It's not even eight o'clock."

Like a flirtatious fool, I smiled.

"It's a comment I overheard when I was probably fourteen, and I just want you to confirm what I suspect it meant."

"Well, what was the context? On a golf course, it might mean at least he got one hole in one before he collapsed from a massive stroke."

"The context was a funeral. Four guys I went to school with died of carbon monoxide poisoning after getting stuck in a snow bank, with the exhaust pipe in the snow bank, and I went to the visitation, four coffins in one room arranged in a square. It was a bit much, especially since one of them was the first guy I ever had a serious crush on, if you can call a crush serious. And I was standing there, staring at one of the bodies, not the guy I had had the crush on, and a man behind me said, 'Well at least he got one in under his belt.'"

"Okay, Rose, now what do you suppose that meant?"

"I took it to mean he had had sex with someone, once. But I think I remember it so clearly because I wondered how that guy knew."

"How do you think he knew?"

"You're just like a psychiatrist, Asa." He smiled, and I said, "I think he knew from guy talk, or guy lying," I said.

"See, you knew the answer to your question. You just wanted to bring up the topic of sex."

"Like I said, you're very much the psychiatrist here." Then I added, "You could just as easily say our topic is death, high school death." I thought of Lucy and "One Thing."

Asa adjusted his rearview mirror.

"Did you know any kids who died when you were in high school?" I asked.

"As a matter of fact," he said, looking into my eyes with a slightly irritated intimacy, "yes, I did. Paula Bee, I called her. I believe I have already mentioned her to you, the girl I beat in all spelling bees in the second and third and fourth grades. She lost her academic crown, and in the tenth grade got hit by a car while she was riding her bike."

"And killed?"

"That's our topic, apparently."

"Did you go to the visitation?"

"No, I did not. We weren't what you would call friends. She was a teacher's pet, but I didn't entirely dislike her. She always respected me on some level because of those bees. Anyway, I'm pretty sure she had not had the opportunity to get one under her belt."

"No, not likely, or at least I hope not."

This was one of Asa's loutish comments for which he did not apologize. I felt we had had some sort of tussle, but *what* sort I could not readily say, so I sipped my coffee, and we were quiet then to the city limits. He may have thought he had offended me, or he may have been thinking about sales, the Dolly, I don't know. In profile, his lower lip protruded above the upper, and this was worth studying, at carefully spaced intervals. He looked like he could have a criminal mind, like he could have posed for one of Carl Jung's archetypal mug shots. This, I decided on the spot, was my male type, a compact type with shoulders, able to get younger and vibrant or possibly trashy girlfriends, most probably because of an aggressive demeanour. Nothing mysterious there. No doubt he viewed my non-Dolly characteristics, my disinterest in high heels and ankle bracelets, open-toed shoes, nail polish, and nearly all makeup as perhaps a challenge or as perhaps a friendly distraction. When compared to what I knew of the Dolly, I was practically a man. What would he say if I told him about Lucy?

"Since you like topics, Rosie, how about staying with the first under your belt?"

"The first time I did it? *It?*"

"Yes, the tale of your lost cherry. Entertain me with that story." What an inglorious turn our conversation had taken.

"Is this going to be a reciprocal arrangement?"

"I can't guarantee anything, my friend. We may be tired of the topic by the time you finish."

In a bisexual display of hand strength, I crushed my paper cup and asked, "You expect it to be that boring?"

"No, that's not what I meant. You know that's not what I meant."

You know that's not what I meant. I liked his speculating that I knew what he knew.

"Well, in the annals of cherry loss, I believe my story may be unusual."

"Good, good. Go on."

I wasn't sure I should go on. To the west, the mountains were illuminated as if from within, by lamps, up early, and thinking: Rose Drury is a poor example of a mother and girlfriend and employee of the Alberta government. We've seen all kinds on the Highway 2 South, and she is at a very low percentile rank on many scales. We're not laughing, we're not even chuckling.

"Okay," I said, and I began my story. "I had a boyfriend in high school named JJ, whom, were I to meet now, which is not impossible, I heard he moved out West, were I to meet him now, I don't think I would like him at all. He was a cheapskate, never bought me so much as an order of fries, and very conservative in his views, socially, I mean. Like for example, he always used to say, *would it be such a big deal if you got pregnant?* And, *I want to have ten kids.* When he made these comments, I felt angry, but I never expressed my anger, I was not an anger-expresser, I just said nothing, but obviously, they made an impact, as I remember many comments he made of that ilk. And he never seemed to have a condom but wanted to have sex in a desperate way. I didn't want to have sex, because his penis was too big. I didn't know it then, but his *member* was quite a bit larger than average, and it seemed impossible that anything that big could fit into a space I had a hard time shoving tampons into. I didn't want to have anything to do with it. I equally did not want it in my mouth, I can't believe I'm saying all this to you, but anyway, I felt in love with him at the time. I knitted a scarf for him one Christmas, but never mind, that's another story. I did like him a lot. My heart used to leap when I saw him at school. It leapt around."

Asa looked at me. "The old leaping heart gets us into trouble."

"So, anyway, one day, it was winter or late fall, it was kind of cold, and I guess I was in Grade 12 and seventeen years old, and we went for a walk in a wood lot, down a concession road, a place nobody went, it was a road that didn't even get plowed in the winter, and we did something approximating 'it' against a tree. Except it wasn't really what you would call getting one under your belt, I think it was just a partial event. Anyway, he came, and as far as I knew he told his best friend we had done it, because the best friend said to me on Monday, I hear you two had a good weekend. Congratulations!"

"See? This JJ told his friend he had finally got one under his belt."

"But he hadn't really. We hadn't done it in the full sense of . . . it. And then about a week later, I cheated on him with this guy I had gone to elementary school with years ago who had moved away and come back and had a much more reasonable-sized penis. We did it in his car several times and in several back roads over the course of a few nights or weeks. He had a gross of condoms. That is not an exaggeration. He ordered them from somewhere. So that's really how I lost my virginity.

"Then JJ and I broke up after the following Christmas, because he gave me the worst gift ever given by a boyfriend to his quote high school sweetheart, but I can't describe it at this time. It still makes me feel frankly clammy, and as a result I'm too at-risk to describe it, the effects simulate the symptoms of a heart attack, from what I know about heart attacks, from my dad, dying of one."

"Oh, I didn't know your dad was gone, Rose," said Asa, solemn and kind. Then he crammed his empty cup into a plastic shopping bag he had hung from a knob.

"Yes," I said. "He is. Gone."

There had been several dry, hot days in August, and already the topsoil was blowing away, dramatically now, across the highway in a clique of dark ghosts trying to get somewhere east of there.

Asa said, "To reciprocate, I lost my cherry in the parking lot of the Mount Pleasant outdoor pool, after a high school, Crescent Heights, dance. I was sixteen. My dad had a tradition where he'd let you book the car for a night as a reward for getting your license. Then after that you were pretty much SOL in the wheels department, because there were five of us kids, all boys, and I was in the middle, although the older ones got out as soon as they could."

"Why?"

"Because there were five of us! Plus, my parents in a three-bedroom house. You had to get up in the middle of the night to jerk off, and even then, you had to go to your special *haunt*. Actually, where we lived was at the end of a street in Varsity, and there was some undeveloped land on the ridge next to us, which I guess was useless because of the grade, but now I'm pretty sure it's being developed for some *terraced* condos. People would walk around there with their dogs, but mostly not at all, it wasn't like now where people walk their dogs everywhere, there was a lot of off-track terrain in the summer, and the wild grass would grow as high as your waist, and I would go out there and look around briefly like a prairie dog, then flop down on my back and go to it. Then I'd clean up with a Kleenex or a leaf. Sometimes I'd fall asleep. I got to like grasshoppers.

"But anyway, the night of the dance, since I had the car, I had to think strategically. I'm pretty sure you won't approve of this, Rose, but I zeroed in on Elizabeth Morris. I don't know why, that is, I don't know what makes a high school bad girl, maybe you can explain that, you're better at understanding why people do what they do, but she was pretty much like everyone else until the tenth grade, maybe because Paula Halinski died, they were kind of friends, I never put those two together before, but in the eleventh grade, it was like Elizabeth Morris decided she was going to fuck every guy in the school. More power to her, I guess, but I'd have to say she occupied an unusual social position, because she was also a big deal on the track and field team, could run like crazy even though her legs weren't that long. Never mind. You get the picture. You went to high school just like everybody else.

"So, having the car, I zeroed in on Elizabeth at this dance and asked her if she wanted to go for a ride. For all I know, she maybe expected my overtures, likely knew all about the Byrne-family tradition."

"That's your last name? Byrne?"

"Yes, it is. So, we drove around, I bought her a chocolate milkshake and some fries."

"See?" I interrupted to say. "You bought her a chocolate milkshake and some fries. You weren't a cheapskate."

"No, I was not. Thanks for the accolade. Anyway, it was still warm, September, the first school dance of the year. Then I drove to the pool parking lot. Turns out we both had rubbers, so we did it twice. The first time I lasted maybe ten seconds, the second time maybe five minutes. I had this idea she had this chart at home with us all rated on a five-star system, and I got one and a half stars. The second time we did it outside with her kind of on the hood. I was pretty proud of myself for that. There was still water in the pool, and we looked at it for a while. We put the rubbers in the garbage and Elizabeth said, 'I've always liked you more than most guys.' That's how I figure I got the one point five. She may have said that to everyone, but I don't think so, because on Monday morning she gave me a bag of red licorice."

"I would have given you allsorts. But anyway, what's she doing now?"

"No idea. She went to school somewhere in the States on a track scholarship."

"Because of the track and field," I said, in the manner of Lucy, as if I could conjure her up there with us.

"Mainly because of the meat," said Asa. "Remember mainly because of the meat? Remember that?"

"The meat the meat the meat," I sang and then we sang the old jingle together. What was it even for? A supermarket chain? Then I said, "There are the mountains. It's funny how our minds get pulled toward them, and yet there's not much to think about them; they're large rocks standing still. That's all."

"So, tell me about this cabin you were locked in down this way. It was down around here, wasn't it?"

Oh, yes, I had told him about that.

"That's when my dad died," I said, "when I was in that cabin. It was west of Highway 22 a little bit, but about this far south. It's surprising, but I found it once when I was at U of C doing my masters. I had actually driven around once looking for it but couldn't find it, and had concluded I never would, or it had been torn down or struck by lightning. Anyway, I had to do a practicum course for Alberta Mental Health, going to what they called halfway houses for people transitioning from the hospital in Ponoka to the community. I had to rent a car, even. I was interviewing a whole lot of patients and what they called proprietors. The proprietors were the people whose houses or basements or Quonset huts or cabins the patients were in, preparing for real life, outside of an institution. And as it turns out, the infamous cabin was housing a depressed woman who happened to be on my list. I had directions: go south go west go south go west, and there I was, at the Petries' house. They were still there. They had got religion, or maybe had had it all along, maybe that's why they took in my ex-husband, George. I had to interview them, they didn't remember me, it had been six years, and even so they had seen me as a hippie, and now I was in a skirt and nylons, probably my eyes weren't swirling in my head like when I met them the first time from the jubilation of escaping combined with the worst news of my life."

"So your dad dies when you're in a locked cabin?" Asa turned his head to look at me, and it was almost as if for one or two seconds he could see all of my ingredients.

"Yes, and I missed his funeral. It was all very, very strange. But to get back to Mrs. Petrie, when I asked her why she had taken in a patient, she said that one day she had opened up the Bible and it fell open to a page *exhorting* her to call Alberta Mental Health, apparently, and take someone in. I got to hear a lot of stories like this. So anyway, she did; she took in Annette. I remember her name because she was the worst of all the patients I interviewed. Most of them seemed to be doing not too badly. The proprietors often seemed more, well, eccentric than the patients, talking about their amateur therapies and so on, one woman pronounced it theerapies with a long e, or experimental cures they were working on. Diets." And I repeated *theerapies* to myself and laughed, wanting to tell Lucy, wanting her to reply with a word of her own, overheard somewhere, like *obeast*. She had told me, a woman at the optometry clinic had said about her sister and her diabetes and her glaucoma: *And to add to it she's terribly obeast.* I opened the window for a blast of fresh air, closed it, and carried on with my story.

"Well, Mrs. Petrie walked me over the little bridge and along the footpath to the cabin. There were still horses. It was exactly the same. Exactly. Mrs. Petrie opened the door, and she yelled, 'Annette, there's somebody here to see you.' Then she left. That was the protocol."

"This was summer, and Annette had the blinds all closed and the wood stove going. There was no padlock on the door. She was sitting on the couch doing nothing. There was a radio and a TV, but they were both off. She was sitting looking at the floor. She would not answer any of my questions. She embodied death in life. I have no idea who judged her to be at the halfway stage."

"The powers that be," Asa said. "Clearly."

"Yes, those powers," I said. "But, I was not above taking advantage of her. I asked if I could look around. She said nothing so I got up and took a look. The bedroom was the same, and on the bed was the same heavy warm quilt I had loved so much when I was there. I wanted to steal it, but of course I couldn't take it from Annette. But at least I knew where the cabin was, and knew I could invent a reason to return."

"Wait a minute, to take this quilt?"

"Yes, I wanted to steal the quilt."

"So did you?"

"No, the fact I wanted to was enough. This is the thing about the human mind, Asa. You never know what desires are lurking in there, in those wet lobes, which is sometimes worrying, for me, anyway. Maybe not everyone. Annette probably."

"Annette probably did or didn't worry about her wet lobes?" Asa asked, smirking.

I didn't rise to the double entendre, I rarely did. Instead, I sighed. The foothills were closer and gentle; if you wanted to sleep outside, they were there for you. I said, "I wasn't supposed to do this, but I told the Petries that Annette wouldn't talk to me, and maybe her meds needed looking at. They said, 'Oh, she gets like that sometimes. She can be very stubborn. Tomorrow she'll be out riding with us.' They even offered to answer the questions for her. They were wearying, so I'm not sure what prompted this, but I said, you probably don't remember me, but I met you once. I was here with George, after we'd been up north working together in Fort Smith. You came back from vacation, and I was here with George, and your husband drove me to the airport.

"Mrs. Petrie took off her glasses and looked at my face. She actually squinted as if I were hazy. Then she said" — and I performed a somewhat realistic impression of Mrs. Petrie's cigarette-ravaged voice — "'Oh, yes, well, George left not long after. He just up and left.

We never heard from him again. Did you? Did he get in touch with you?'

"And I said no, Asa, I said no, even though when George left, he went directly to my parents' place in Flax. You might as well know the worst about me. And actually, that's not all. I did go back to get the quilt. Their place was at the corner of a range road and a township road, so really the best way to get to the cabin was from the range road, from the west side of the buildings. You couldn't be seen from the house, because the cabin was in a little dip in the field. I went there three times, in the fall, sneaking around when I should have been working on the practicum, driving my rented car, and putting on unnecessary kilometres. I figured Annette wouldn't last long there, and the Petries would go away to Europe."

The radio produced a burst of static, and Asa turned down the volume; he was listening.

"So, the first two times I went, I parked and walked from the road down into the little dip and hoped the horses wouldn't come running, which they didn't. It was always late afternoon by the time I got there. The first two times, Annette was there. The blinds were all down, and there were billows of smoke from the chimney, so I knew. But the third time, the blinds were up, and there was no smoke, so I just walked right up to the place. From the front porch, you could see the Petries' house, but there were trees kind of obstructing the view. No vehicles in sight though. And more importantly, perhaps symbolically, there was a padlock on the door, not a combination lock but a padlock. I moved quickly and got a biggish stone from the creek, dried it on my jacket and smashed the lock five or six times and it broke. I went inside, Asa. My heart was pounding like I have never heard it pound. It was very confused about fight or flight. I just sat for a moment and waited for the Petries to enter the cabin with two guns, but nothing happened."

Asa laughed with a roar, like Carmen, so I smiled. "I went to the bedroom, and there was the quilt. I folded and folded it until it was a rectangle I could sling over my shoulder, then I left. I threw the rock in the creek and set the broken lock back in the latch and walked casually back to the car and left. I was really kind of off-kilter for about two hours, but I had the damn quilt. At first, I thought they owed me this quilt, they owed me something, but a voice said no, they didn't, you just took it. Okay, I thought, I did. So what?"

Asa was quiet. Then he asked, "Why did you want that quilt so badly?"

I rolled the window down a few inches and up, down again, up, and said, "Well, you know how you can call a quilt a comforter? Well, it was like a comforter to me, I guess. That's the only reason I can come up with. I keep it in the basement in a suitcase. I don't even use it." To change the subject, I asked him about the Dolly, did he have a picture? How did they meet? He didn't have a picture, and they met in a bar.

"Do you think about her a lot?"

"I think about her some. Let's go back on 22," he said. "I want to eat lunch in Black Diamond, and I want to get some beef jerky in Longview. How does that sound? A late lunch if your meeting goes late."

I said that sounded good to me.

I arrived early for the meeting, and waiting in the staff room, I thought about Lucy and her cowhide, how we once in a while lay on top of its cool, deceased surface and sometimes under it, Roger and Lucy and I, and at those times I wanted to get the quilt from its basement hiding place in my luggage and tell Lucy I had it, tell her that George had been a sort of hostage-taker, but that I hadn't entirely objected. I didn't want her to hate him, though, at least no more than she already did, because he was Roger's biological father, after all. The effort involved in speaking and clarifying, going back and explaining, saying yes, I know, yes, I understand, yes, my motives seem murky at best, weighed on me like snow in an avalanche: I had heard it was like concrete, even up your nose.

The resource teacher entered the room and shook my hand. She was wearing an expensive-looking pantsuit, glossy shoes, and red lipstick. "I'm Wanda Youngman," she said. "We're really glad to see you. We've got quite a few questions about the files." Following Wanda to the main office, I thought, her hair reminds me of Lucy, her walk, too. And as I spent the morning sifting through binders and reading reports and taking notes, I thought, Lucy, let's just forget this day happened. I'll have lunch with Asa, we'll call it a day, we'll call it a night, we'll call it a mirage. And when I arrive home, I'll say to you, tomorrow afternoon I register Roger at the nursery school. I meet Dr. Cove. I get it done. You'll see.

thirteen

"YOU PROBABLY SHOULD have registered him last December," Lucy said, "not to mention last week." She was leaving for work, I had stepped outside to say goodbye. Roger was inside watching Power Rangers, wearing his soft velveteen rabbit pants and turtleneck with rabbit motif, ready to go across the street to Mrs. Marini's. Outside, the world was blindingly bright, although most lawns were now brown, people had given up watering, fall was on its way.

"I know," I said, "I know I know I know. I had to work up to it, as you know. They're *required* to have a spot for him, I've told you that, we're in the area, and I have the reports from Children's. I'll look bad, I know, compared to all the other mothers who registered their little people months ago, but I'm not like them, I guess, *we're* not like them."

"They're not all the same," said Lucy, opening the Oldsmobile door, releasing the scent of warm leather. Manly, I thought, Lucy was manly compared to me: well, who wasn't, if manliness were next to decisiveness? "They're not a homogeneous entity," Lucy went on. "Were your parents like all other parents just because you were in school? Mine certainly were not. School isn't for parents. You don't have to sit in a desk and give people Valentines." We weren't arguing, we were speaking conversationally, and although the morning sun was beating with an end of August fury, we were in the shade of Lana's mountain ash, which helped me to remain calm. The clusters of seeds hung like party favours, and I warmed at the thought of Roger's new friends, his new start in life, and my new start at goodness: I had not seen Asa for nine days and planned not to see him for nine more, maybe ninety.

"Yes, yes, yes. But you know as well as I do, it will mean evaluation of him, and me, maybe you and me. It's like a coming out in society, I mean, not like in the gay or debutante sense, but there will be scrutiny as we trot around in our cold-comfort neighbourhood."

"Trot?" Lucy said, and laughed, causing me to laugh a little, too. "And it's not a cold-comfort neighbourhood," she went on. "Carmen is virtually a third parent, and Robert is a fourth, and Mrs. Marini is a surrogate grandmother. They love him at the Co-op. Don't say it's cold comfort, it's like every other place, maybe even warmer and more comforting."

Lucy was wearing a white shirt, she always wore white shirts to work, and in her white shirts she was pretty and competent in appearance, one who knew her own mind, and I knew she wanted me to be brave and outspoken, and I was not the opposite of those, but I was something more at a right angle: here is brave, there is cowardly and in between is Rose, hedging. Here is outspoken, here is silent, and here is Rose, holding back, then blurting.

"Do you want me to come with you?" Lucy asked. "I could likely get off early."

"No, I'll get him on the list. It will be done this afternoon; he *will* be a registrant. Go to work." She got in the car, slammed the door shut, rolled down the window. "I love you."

"I love you, too."

Inside the house, I called Mrs. Marini and asked if Roger could spend the afternoon with her as well. The plan had been for him to be there for the morning while I was at work, then I'd pick him up, we'd have lunch, hang out, and go to the school together, by which time I knew, I would be soggy, I would be like his water wings in the bathtub, half-deflated. I wanted to meet this Dr. Cove fresh from work and seeming to be too rushed to have collected Roger from wherever he was undergoing enrichment, with peers. And I wanted to take things in the manner of successive approximations.

Two-forty in the afternoon, as I climbed the concrete steps of Peter Lougheed Elementary, I wondered if I would tell Dr. Cove I had just arrived from B.C., and this was why I had not yet registered my son with special needs. Maybe.

Dr. Judith Cove was short and shaped like a rain barrel, she had a British accent, her lipstick and jacket were fuchsia. Instead of lying, I told her the truth, that he had been assessed at the Children's Hospital, and I brandished the reports in close proximity to her desk phone, not letting them go. Roger was at the third percentile rank in most domains, I told her, and I had not wanted to send him to preschool because I was convinced people, other kids, even adults, would make fun of him; I told her that he was very naïve and honestly had no friends except for his two cousins in Ontario, and many days I didn't know what to make of him.

Dr. Cove said, "Why, you mustn't be ashamed of your son," the way people from the UK will often speak, comforting and at the same time certain of their position and correctness.

"I'm not *ashamed*," I said. "It's not that I'm ashamed, at least I don't think I'm ashamed, I'm worried he'll be judged, unfairly," I said, nodding my head, surprising myself with my serenity. Then I added, "I'm a school psychologist, in the system, I mean, I will be soon."

"Then you must know he may be judged, as you put it. That can't be helped. But we will be here to support him and you. That's what we're here for, and to provide an education, obviously. We've had several children with special needs in our program. We can accommodate any student in our catchment area, and we take pride in our integrated classrooms. I trust you support integration for all students?"

"Yes!" I said. "Of course I do, in theory, but in practice I'm a little bit wanting to keep him at home on the farm, if you know what I mean," and I laughed in a way I had never exactly, precisely, laughed before. Dr. Cove smiled and said, "It's a difficult transition."

"Yes," I said, with the serenity of a psychologist trained in the science of difficult transition. "But!" I went on, I didn't think Roger would need anything extreme like an educational assistant, just a kind and firm teacher who would not allow him to talk incessantly about clocks, and who would laugh only once at his one joke, which wasn't really a joke but a gag, I said, explaining that he liked to pretend that he'd tripped and say whoops I almost fell, even though he hadn't. She'll have to nip that in the bud, I said. I told her that he knew the numbers one to twelve. I hastened to add that I had a babysitter who spoke Italian. And that Roger had been to the tots' library group. Then I stopped abruptly, feeling like I was with a representative of the Canadian Border Services and had declared more than enough.

Dr. Cove told me to bring Roger in the next day, she would like to meet him.

"Okay. That's just fine," I said.

"He'll have to be assigned to the afternoon class, because the morning one is full," she warned. Then Dr. Cove shook my hand and said, "Don't worry, Rose," and I said, "Thanks for not saying don't worry, Mom." I don't think she knew what I meant, regarding me as she did, with a frankly puzzled, or bemused as the British might say, facial expression. Walking quickly, as if heading to a gathering of psychologists who knew more about education, integration, and inclusion than any principals, I left the building. Outside, on the sidewalk, to myself, quietly but aloud, I said, "I'm not ashamed." This was a practice I had started, defending myself to an imaginary group. It felt a bit like a tic. The day was sunny and not yet three in the afternoon, and as I walked to Mrs. Marini's to pick up Roger, I decided we should go to Big Hill Springs Provincial Park with King Two. "Maybe we'll stay there," I said to Roger, in the car, "even if there is no camping."

"Where?" he asked. We were about to leave, he was in his car seat holding a stuffed animal, a black cat with yellow eyes, and with his and the cat's eyes he was looking at me in the mirror.

"The Big Hill Springs," I said. "Remember we went there with Lucy in the spring to see the waterfalls? Remember? We're not going to stay there, I'm kidding, I just feel like staying there. Sometimes I just say things. Like you. You just say things sometimes, and you don't mean them." Roger pressed the cat's face to the window. King Two barked for at least thirty seconds every time we took off in the car, his only really irritating habit, a long series of rowfs delivered up with a metronomic rhythm.

Big Hill Springs was close to Calgary, not far from Cochrane. There was something a little spooky about the place. Lucy and I had both noticed it, back in the spring, even though the day had been warm and breezy, the type of day you want to shelter behind a rock or large tree and listen to the branches moving and watch the shadows. The place is sequestered in a coulee. And Lucy had said, "We could say it's Transylvania. Transylvania means beyond the woods, that's all it means, I learned that when I was with you-know-who, Meredith. It's pretty simple, Latin, *trans* — beyond or across, *sylvan* — woods."

"You impress me," I said, and kissed the back of her hand.

We followed a trail that day, holding Roger's hands, and she said, "You can feel some kind of mystery here, as if something good or bad happened, something halfways momentous to more than one person." I listened. And then she said, "And they were transfigured," and I said hmmm. And she said, "You're against that sort of thing, aren't you, metamorphosis?"

"No, I just wonder where and when does it happen."

And she said, "Roger, that's called tufa," pointing at the slippery limestone in the stream.

Now Roger and I were back at Big Hill Springs, and I, my super-ego, must have hoped for transfiguration. Only two other cars in the lot. We didn't go up the hillside, but when Roger ambled into the grass, he found a little violet and picked it. I said, I practically shrieked, "Roger, you're not allowed to pick the flowers here!" and, as if it were poisonous, he threw it to the ground and examined his hand for residue. Poison was a new concept for him, an all-purpose threat he had latched onto, his gateway to anxiety. I knew what he was thinking, and I said, "It's okay, you didn't know. And it's not poison. We can take little sticks though," I said. "For Lucy. It's her birthday in two days, so we'll get her thirty-seven sticks or stones, or both. King Two can help us."

Then I picked up the flower and threaded the stem through a buttonhole on his shirt and said, "Never mind." He had recently begun to request button shirts, like Robert's and Lucy's, and I was happy about this development, what I called the Robert effect, even if most boys his age preferred T-shirts. I ran ahead of him a bit and pretended to trip over King Two's leash — "Whoops, I almost fell," I said, looking back at him, and he screamed with laughter, then ran ahead, pretending to trip over his own feet, looking back at me, waiting for my laughter. For some reason, I think I will always remember the way he looked that afternoon, that specific expression that said *I want you to laugh now, Mom*. It gave me an ache in my diaphragm, so I said to Roger and King Two, "Let's calm down, we need to calm down," and we did and went to the trail. As I had expected, the stream was quiet, but the trees were whispering, whispering aspens.

At the first waterfall, we stopped, and I said we'd better not whoops, I almost fell here, thinking Roger would laugh, but instead he looked alarmed. Even though it wasn't at all deep, the water was gurgling and rattling like something with an appetite, he likely surmised. Who can know all the moments your child will want safety? I would never have guessed, and I knelt down and said, "We won't fall in." I put my arms around him and kissed his warm cheek. "I was kidding. I would never let you fall in or eat poison." Then he looked stricken. Dear god. He put both arms around my neck, and I said, "The water makes the rocks look funny. It's called tufa, remember?"

Pulling away from me, Roger said, "Tufa clock?" A joke.

"It could be tufa clock, I don't see why not, somewhere at least, as they say."

Later, back in the warmth of the car, before we left for Cochrane, and ice cream, I said, "Tomorrow we're going to go to the school to meet someone. She's called the principal, and she's the boss of the school. She wants to meet you, and do you know why? Do you know why, Roger?" I was turned sideways talking to him, in his car seat once again. Holding the black cat, he pointed its face at me, as if it might be on the verge of growing teeth. I repeated, "Do you know why?"

"No," he said, in a kind of abrupt meow, like an angry cat, was his intention, I think.

"Because you're going to start school there in September, in just a few days. You'll be in early, early kindergarten, and you'll have friends and a teacher. That'll be fun, won't it?"

He moved the cat's head up and down, nodding.

"Lucy's going to love her sticks, I think," I said. "We have an impressive collection."

No response. "Should we go and get some ice cream now?"

"Meow, meow," Roger said. King Two started up with his rowfs.

OF COURSE, I had to confess to Lucy that I'd gone alone to the school and would be taking Roger the following day to meet the *inimitable* (as I began to call her) Dr. Cove. Upon hearing this, Lucy gazed into my eyes for ten seconds of Episcopalian judgment, then, after dinner, said, "Roger and I are going to the Co-op to get chocolate sauce and bananas and pineapple. You want to come?"

"No, I'll stay here. I want to sit outside, in the yard, in the warmth. It's supposed to cool off tomorrow." Which for five minutes I did, until I called George. I had his Guelph number, and if he wasn't there, I would try Mom's place, but he was there. I had probably not called him since, I couldn't say, since the seventies, or maybe once or twice from a university pay phone in 1980 to say I had picked up dessert or bread at the farmers' market.

"Hello," he said, in that somewhat fake, tentative voice he affected on the telephone.

"Hi, George. It's Rose."

"Rose! I was just talking to your mother. She'd like a rec room in the basement, a rumpus room! She wants room for a rumpus."

"Really?" Instead of replying, I am pretty sure he took a silent bite of soft ice cream or a cupcake.

"Yes, really," he said, eventually. "Why do you call?"

"Dennis," I answered, without so much as a blink in time. "I was hoping you could tell me something about him, what he was like, what he looked like at the very least."

George breathed out through his nose, swallowed, and said nothing. I believe he had taken a sip of tea.

"Are you there?" I asked.

"Yes, of course, I don't hang up on people as a rule. I'm just... I haven't seen Dennis for twenty years or more."

"Well, what can you tell me?"

"I can tell you... what... he was afraid of everything. He cried and wailed and could only say momma, even when he was five. He was afraid of mascots and fireworks, the wind, snow, rain, bugs. It was hard on my mom to have him and then probably to lose him, and it was hard on me and my sister. Mom and Dad took him one day in the summer before he would have started Grade 1. End of story." George delivered this information in the style of a news reader.

"Did you ever go and see him?"

No reply. I could hear Carmen outside, laughing. George's cup may have been placed into a saucer; he liked cups with saucers. I heard a distant tink.

"No."

"Did your parents?"

"Not that I know. I think they advised against it, at the centre. I heard Dad say that once, that they advised against it, visiting."

My throat began to hurt for Dennis, and for his mother. I said, "I'm thinking of going to see him. Do you know if you have to be a relative? A blood relative? I still have our marriage certificate. I'm thinking that might be enough."

"Tisk," said George, rather than using his tongue and the roof of his mouth. "I don't have any idea what the rules are. I assume Mom is their contact, the next of kin. Dennis might be dead, for all I know, but I imagine Mom would have contacted me or Christine if that were the case. Or maybe not, we don't talk, as you know, Mom and me. Have you thought, Rose, about what if he wants to go with you? If you meet him and he wants to go with you? Have you considered that? Maybe it's better to leave well enough alone. He's in a wheelchair, he can't even likely get into the car with you."

"It's just a thought I had, George. Just a thought. I'm not sure I'll act on it. I drove to Medicine Hat one day and looked at the place, but I didn't go in."

"My sister did that once. She took the bus from Lethbridge to Medicine Hat to see the place when she was maybe fourteen or fifteen. She told me she didn't go in, but I've always wondered, because she looked so pale when she got home. She had walked from the bus depot, and no one else knew where she'd been, only me, she had told some lie to explain her whereabouts, and she walked home from the depot, and she was a little darker than a sheet of paper, so at the time I was sure she had seen him, but she would never say. A Petrie never says. That's our slogan, and we're not changing it. How's Roger?"

"He's fine," I said, thinking I guess he'll never meet his so-called Petrie grandparents. Because, would they advise sending him to the big house in the Hat?

"So you still haven't talked to your parents? Not since you left Lethbridge?"

"No."

"How come?"

"You know what I'm going to say, Rose. A Petrie never says."

"Okay."

"How's Roger?"

"You already asked that, and I said he's fine, starting preschool soon next week, right after Labour Day."

Again, there was silence, and I pictured the sky between us changing from pale yellow to orange to red then red with indigo stripes, to indigo with moonlight. George said he had better make his lunch for tomorrow, he'd better get his nightgown on.

LUCY ARRANGED TO go into work at two so we could take Roger to school together on the first day. I wonder if she thought I would require an ambulance. I did not think it impossible, despite maintaining composure through the morning and during lunch, egg salad sandwiches that I choked down dryly, like a snake swallowing a cork plug it had mistaken for a toad. Roger wore a turtleneck with small airplanes motif and his soft, black velveteen pants; he had three pairs. Roger liked his clothes. Robert had dropped by on his way to work wearing a white shirt and tie with dress pants, and Roger, pulling on the tie, had asked, "What it is?"

"That's a necktie, Rog. I'll get you one the next time I'm in the men's store. What colour do you prefer?"

"Bird," Roger said, meaning bright blue, and I began to worry he would balk, at the final moment, insisting upon a necktie for school, but he did not. We walked the three and a half blocks to Peter Lougheed Elementary and entered by the side doors up the stairs and into the kindergarten end of the hallway, and the atmosphere, thick as a greenhouse, of the fear and elation of three- and four-year-olds ready for pre-pre-kindergarten as I liked to call it.

Roger seemed not at all anxious, and we were proud of him, considering he had only ever been in the care of us, Mrs. Marini, Carmen, and Robert and never on his own in a group. He had a hook for his egg (pale blue) jacket and hung his empty pack there, too. Miss Emily, whom Lucy and I had met, said, "He'll be fine," and we saw him into the room, staying close to the door, observing him stand uncertainly for a moment, then step toward a table of books. "Take a book,"

Miss Emily said to him, "and sit down anywhere, and we'll get started in a minute. Moms and Dads, you can stay for a while if you want." But most were leaving, this seemed the most practical, Protestant sort of route. No one was crying, so Lucy called out, "See you later, Roger," and she waved. I followed suit and waved and blew him a kiss, and at that moment I saw a parent, a mother with straight bangs to the middle of her forehead, round-framed glasses, a scientist or a judge, perhaps, look at Roger in the way look changes to watch, then seek me out, the mother, *Mom*, then look away. Gazing emptily into my private tank of motherhood, I swallowed and looked at Lucy for first aid. I wanted very badly to rest my face on her neck or that of an omnipotent observer, and beg for assurance, but I did not flinch. I guessed I was like Dad, flinchless as a dentist.

To pick Roger up, I arrived at 3:15 on the dot, because I did not want to wait in the hallway with my cohort of parents, especially the one with the precision bangs. Besides, a few were familiar from the community association, and they would want to ask about Lucy and her column, and I wasn't in the mood for pretending I enjoyed small talk when I was worrying my son might be trampled or thirsty or considering the poisonous qualities of chalk. Inside the doorway, the children were lining up, giving Miss Emily a hug if they wanted, or a handshake, on the way out. I could hear her asking each one, by name, her voice sweet and loving, and suddenly there was Roger in the hallway, with a black marker streak on his right cheek, his hair a little sweaty and up at the front, his turtleneck untucked, but there he was, independent, looking first for his hook, his jacket and pack, then for me. I was so proud. He understood conformity! He inferred the routine! And he was proud of himself, I could see in his shy smile. Approaching me, he said, "Hi, Mom," and jumped up and down, stiff-kneed, and took my hand. "Did you have a hug or a handshake?" I asked.

"Hug," he said, as if it were nothing out of the ordinary.

HOWEVER, LUCY WORKED almost every afternoon, so either I, depending on my work schedule, or Mrs. Marini was the one to drop Roger off, but usually I picked him up, and each day a few more quiet cells were added to my ruthless body of comparisons. It was either an inward growing body or it was forming elsewhere, independent of the white house, as we called our place, roosting in the copse, or fermenting beneath a floor board at the community centre. No matter where it might be stationed, this body was a good communicator, always in my ear, commenting. If I drank three glasses of wine or two gin and tonics, or three Campari with soda, or Lucy's drink of the month, it might shut up for a bit, but it awoke, later, alert and chatty.

In the company of his twenty peers, Roger was very clearly different. Oh, they're all different, everyone is unique, we all have our strengths and weaknesses, I say, with no conviction, to the audience in the stands. Emma knows all of her letters, Jacob can snap together Lego with foresight and finesse, Martin is on a real little hockey team, not pre-pre-hockey, and Hayley's a little fish, she got the swimming award in her tadpole league. Some of the four-year-olds can sound out words, or they're starting to get the idea. As soon as possible, I had signed up for parent volunteer duty, printing my name in all caps, as they say in schools, on the calendar square for September 19. My supervisor would allow me to work the morning instead, she didn't care when I worked, as long as I did my job. And now there, I stood with my hips resting against the sink, arms crossed, watching the carpet time. Once in a while, someone misbehaved a little, usually Jamie, who had been given two reminders and with a third would have to sit on the thinking chair.

Roger sat a little too close to Miss Emily and touched the hem of her skirt, twice. He wanted to touch her wrist, then her watch, but had been warned somewhere along the way, had maybe even been to the thinking chair, and was exercising restraint. Now a third time, his hand moved toward Miss Emily's wrist and hovered until the boy next to him, Ryan, half-barked with authority, "Roger, don't!" and Miss Emily said, "Ryan O., never mind." There were two Ryans, and this was Ryan O'Hanrahan, in Roger's mind an adorable form of missing link or digit from the O'Clock family. After his second day of school, Roger had mentioned Ryan O., with a tensing of his body, at the sound of this enchanted name.

Carpet time was over, and they were allowed to pick centres, according to a process they already understood. First Reindeer, then Foxes, then Ducks, then Goldfish surrounded Miss Emily while the others waited, and made a selection from some pictures, then placed the picture in a pocket. Roger was a Goldfish, and he wanted dress-up but had already been to dress-up on Monday and Tuesday, thus had to make a different choice: crafts, store, blocks, or play dough. What did he want? Roger was saying something to Miss Emily, and, as she was asking for clarification, Ryan O. interpreted: "He wants the necktie." Roger smiled confirmation at Miss Emily. "He wants the necktie in dress-up," Ryan reiterated.

"Thank you, Ryan," Miss Emily said. "Roger, you can have the necktie again next week, on Monday." She showed him Monday on the large calendar. "Now you need to pick a different centre — play dough? Store?"

Roger chose store.

I was preparing to move from my spot by the sink, when Ryan approached me, slaloming his way among tables and chairs, holding high the necktie he had managed to liberate from dress-up. "This is the tie Roger likes," he said, holding it close to my eyes. "You just hang it on your collar like this. It's not a real tie like my dad has." He clipped it onto his T-shirt and gazed upward into my eyes.

"I see," I said, "Very nice."

"You should get Roger a tie like this," Ryan advised, earnestly.

"He really likes it." Ryan was charming and lovely, with black curly hair and goldy-brown eyes.

"Maybe I should," I said. I was supposed to help out at crafts and was wanting to move in that direction, to the table bearing water, paints, glue, and pasta shells. Roger, spying the tie, left store centre in a smiling and panicky rush to get to Ryan so as to attempt to grab the tie from him, but I told him, "No, it's part of dress-up, and you're at store," realizing, with a fatigue in my shoulders, the absence of any transcendent value to this regulation. "What if everyone wanted the tie while they were at store?" I asked, aiming for the larger and improbable good. Even Roger saw my example as valueless, he being the only child who wanted the tie. Nevertheless, I placed it out of reach on the jigsaw puzzle shelf, and Roger protested, squeaking the smoke alarm sound he resorted to at times of frustration. Many of the children stopped what they were doing and looked, already familiar with the source of this dolphin voice. "Roger!" I said, warningly, and he did it again.

"It's just Roger squeaking," someone said. No one laughed, but several pairs of eyes watched closely for what might come next. I anticipated a shriek. Miss Emily called him to her to remind him to use words and not squeaks, while Ryan offered to "just sneak the tie back to dress-up." I liked this little boy.

After the clattering and mayhem of everyone rotating through two centres, the class went outside. Roger moved slowly and was distracted, putting lids on paint cans and rinsing his brush forever. He didn't want me to help him with his jacket. "Go, Mom. Go outside with the kids." Was he ashamed of me? No. No. Independent. I was outside before he was, and by the time he had made his way down the stairs to the playground, Ryan and his group had run to the climbing apparatus. Out on the field, another group of boys was kicking a soccer ball around. Roger took my hand and beheld my face with joy. Maybe he had wanted me to be outside so he could join me, or so I could see him manage on his own. I didn't know, but I felt I should. Behind me, a voice asked, "Are you Roger's mom?"

I turned around and saw Betty, who was five and in full-blown kindergarten. She had poor vision and very thick glasses, and, I surmised, a larger-than-average-faced watch to help her read the time, even though she admitted, as soon as Roger reached to look, "I can't tell time. I just have this big watch."

"It's very nice," I said.

"Thank you. It's big so I can see it."

"I understand," I said.

"Roger comes with me at recess," Betty said in the voice of an administrative assistant. I wasn't keen, but I nodded kindly, then felt I had to speak.

"He might want to go on the climbing apparatus."

"No, he doesn't. He told me."

Roger had his head bent at an awkward angle, following Betty's wrist like a bird of prey. "Well, you two go and play, then. I'm supposed to be supervising."

"Come on, Roger. Let's walk around." And off they went, the two little oddballs, I had to think. From about twenty paces, I could see Betty was getting fed up with Roger's interest in her watch. I think she wanted him to chase her. I looked the other way and observed the soccer players. That's how the day went, not so terribly.

SEPTEMBER IN CALGARY was a good month for running outside in the evenings and avoiding Asa, the rec centre, and the indoor track. But after the first parent-volunteer preschool visit, which I had told Lucy went swimmingly well, listing the positives, Ryan O.'s protective friendship, Betty's overall niceness, Miss Emily's understanding ways, I wanted a sighting of Asa. I said to myself that apparently, for me, one good emotion must lead to another, like a scavenger hunt, with Asa, not necessarily as the prize, but the lush crush associated with him. Yes, that was it, the lush crush in my limbic system required fertilizer. He was probably still showing up at around eleven, and I could easily take Roger to Mrs. Marini's without much notice, and if she said no, so be it, but she said yes, and Asa was there, eventually, arriving at the track as I was preparing to leave.

"Where have you been?" he asked, in his loud voice, layered with simulated and genuine concern. "It would seem you're not as dedicated to your regimen as I am, although you're looking trim. You're not cheating on me at some other facility, are you?" I smiled like a woman fool, my face and underpants sharing sister moments of involuntary bliss. I wanted to tell him about Roger and Lucy right then, I should have, of course, the shoulds were stacking themselves gymnastically, somewhere beyond my field of vision, but I said, "No, I only have eyes for the Renforth Athletic Centre, that's it, but I have been running outside a bit because it's been just right in the evenings. Have you eaten all your beef jerky? Did you share it with the Dolly?"

We were both at the railing, watching the runners and walkers, holding our little towels; mine I liked to swing around, while he had his over his shoulder. "No, I didn't share one damn bite of it. I took it to work and put it in my desk drawer, and now it's gone. That means we need to go on another road trip, someplace with butter tarts. This likes to be fed," he said, reaching for my hand and placing it on his firm but ever-so-slightly rounded belly, causing for me a moment of horror, because I thought we were heading for his penis. Bad enough, the belly was next door and sloping precipitously. I guess I blushed.

"You're blushing, Rosie," he said. No one took any notice of our carrying-on by the mats, by the railing and the stairs to the gym below; it's always hard to believe no one can see concussion stars floating above one's head from the impact of forceful flirting. Nevertheless, my vision stalled and turned inward, and I saw the Van Epps' barn and a bloated cow Anastasia had once shown me waiting for the vet, and I momentarily saw myself as a Holstein with four stomachs filled with compliments and the smell of Asa and the track and the grass clippings of a lush crush. I reached for the banal. "I might have another part-time job soon," I told him, "with the school board, doing assessments." Watching the runners and walkers, I added, "But we could still maybe go to Medicine Hat someday. I have a meeting coming up there, for my other job. No date for it yet, but sometime in October or November at the latest. That would be a good road trip for us. I've heard they have butter tarts in Bow Island."

He winked at me and said, "Gotta run, literally," and off he went around the track. What a prick.

"See you soon," I said, to no one, to my gas bags of emotion. I needed a veterinarian, *stat*, with a sharpened device, sterile and logical, to impale me. Having told Mrs. Marini I would be working in the morning until noon and would pick up Roger for lunch before taking him to school, I needed to drive around for half an hour, putting in time. First, I stopped in at a 7-Eleven and bought some beef jerky to put in my desk drawer later, and the ridiculousness of this adolescent behaviour calmed me. Heading west on Memorial Drive, the sun shone on the river, the sky was solid blue, and the news on the CBC was good, some might think upbeat, even, as it was all about Reagan and Mulroney and their restored special relationship, which made me want to gag. And right after the news, Stevie Wonder, "I Just Called to Say I Love You." Maybe meant as a joke about the president and the prime minister; I would tell Lucy later. I sang along, headed north and back east along 20th Avenue. My little Roger was waiting for me, my lovely Lucy who believed all things were possible would be home by five.

fourteen

DROPPING ROGER OFF at 12:45 with the other parents, I began to wonder if they were perhaps eyeing me with a consensus of tepid hostility.
They may not even have been aware of their solidarity, but I viewed
it as botanical, like trees sharing the same root system. Nothing was
said. The woman with the precise black bangs, thin and rooted to
her one habitual spot in the hallway, observed Roger and me as if we
were wildlife. Discomfiture was a word I wanted to try out with Lucy
but held back.

In mid-September, the birthday party invitations had begun to appear in the students' letter boxes or cubbies. First, from little Dorothy with her retro name and hippie parents. Nothing for Roger, but that was fine; she was a girl and in the other pre-kindergarten class. Then Jamie; no invite from him, either, but he spent so much time in the thinking chair, he might be a bad influence. But when Arthur appeared to have excluded Roger, buzzing around at arrival time with his envelopes, shoving them into cubbies as we waited for Miss Emily to open the classroom door, after all the parents had left and the children were in the classroom and settled on the carpet, I actually lingered in the hallway to examine the back of Roger's cubby. I was positive the invitation had been pleated into easy-to-missness, or, had slipped through the interstices at the rear of the cubbies into Scott's below, and searched even there with a fresh type of guilt, but found nothing and left the school with my forehead sweating as if I had just finished hiking the Larch Trail. Roger did not notice or seem to care. Since Robert had given him two clip-on neckties, he had been wearing them to school, alternating the green plaid, or boxes as Roger called the design, with the solid red, aka fire 'stinguisher. I wondered if that was why he had not been included on Arthur's guest list.

Lucy believed everything Roger would turn out fine, he's just himself, she said, an original. Once in a while she called him sui generis. Optimism was easy for those who had nothing to do with schools, I told myself, and therefore did not realize that schools are not benign. Can you point out to me, I wanted to ask Lucy, any other building so filled with so many people in training? Certainly not your mild-mannered optometrists' offices. In a crowded junior high hallway, on a Wednesday afternoon, the density of people per square metre could evoke associations with disaster preparedness, I had once told Lucy.

In late September, I was indeed hired by the Board of Education as a type of intern to do some work under the supervision of a chartered psychologist, My first assignment was an assessment of a junior high school girl named Daphne. Daphne had Down syndrome but was high functioning, as they say. She would be going to high school next year, so the system wanted an up-to-date assessment (IQ score, how much support does she need) as well as what they called a social/emotional (why is she acting like that?). She was in Grade 9, in a special class with an acronym name standing for life skills and communication and community living. I arrived at noon to meet the assistant principal, Hugh, who wanted to talk to me. He had a gym class at 1:05 so was dressed in grey track pants and a white T-shirt with the school's crest — a lynx seeming to be jumping through a hoop. Around Hugh's neck was a metal whistle. He shook my hand and before I had managed to sit down said, "I hope you can do something about her talking to herself. Even if you can determine if she's hallucinating or just imagining characters or could benefit from some meds. She'll stand in the hallway with her back to the lockers talking away to beat the band. It scares the kids. If you could do an observation, will you be here for the break at 1:50?"

"Most definitely."

"You'll see what I mean."

Hugh went on. "She's no trouble. Not defiant or aggressive at all. It's just the talking to herself. Not to put too fine a point on it, but it makes her look batshit crazy," he said, picking up a badminton racket from behind his desk. "I mean you want to spare her the indignity, right?"

"Yes, of course. Does she have any friends?"

"Well, that's the thing. No, not really. In three years here, she hasn't really connected with any of the kids in her class. Most of them have one good buddy. And we tried to set her up with a buddy in the school, but she wouldn't buy into it. It's almost like she knows it's not the real thing; well, she does know. It's not Coke. You're giving me Pepsi." He withdrew a birdie from a desk drawer.

"I talked to her parents on the phone, her mom. She seemed really concerned about high school, life after high school. She was in tears, actually. They're great people. Great. Very supportive. Her older brother Luke was in track, won the city four-hundred metre two years ago, no, three. Her parents want what's best. So do we. But she's going to be ostracized in high school if she's out in the hallway talking to the spirit world. Do you know what I mean? I like the kid, but there's something about her that can be a little eerie. Do you know what I mean?" Bouncing the birdie, Hugh searched my eyes as if the half-baked school psychologist must surely be an arbiter of all things eerie.

I said, "Yes, I know how the other students might see her," and waited for Hugh to say something cruel, but he didn't. His eyes were very brown and seemed kind. He had a hundred details to attend to, Daphne was one of them. A janitor who happened to be going in the right direction led me to the classroom, and I met the teacher, Miss Bell, who introduced me to her class, eight students eating lunch at a round table.

"Everyone, this is Miss Drury. Can you welcome her to our school and our classroom?" Miss Bell said one, two, three, and the group, setting aside juice boxes and sandwiches, sang out to the tune of Queen's *We Are the Champions:*

Welcome Miss Drury to our class

Welcome Miss Druuuu-ry to our class

Welcome Miss Drury, we hope you have a good time

Welcome Miss Drury — pause, pause, pause — to our class!

I listened and smiled and thought Lucy is never, *ever* in situations such as this. Everyone in the class had an intellectual disability, maybe a genetic condition or a condition of unknown etiology as they said, or were in some way *syndrome-y*, as one of my former classmates put it. Some people approved of this type of class, while others were violently opposed. I supported a *continuum of options* I liked to say, but if asked by Miss Bell, Ruth, did I want Roger in her room, my answer would have been no, never, not on your life. The teaching assistant stayed with the class, and Miss Bell and I went next door to the kitchen to talk. On the counter were plastic bowls, oats, raisins, and measuring cups. "We're making cookies this afternoon, we sell them," Miss Bell informed me.

"Does Daphne like cooking?"

"No, as with most things, she would rather watch." Ruth Bell had short, black hair, she was tall and thin and blinked frequently as if trying to position her eyeballs more deeply inside her skull. I must have been gawking because she explained, "I'm blinking like this because my eyes are for some reason dry. I don't know why." I thought of mentioning Lucy's optometrists, but Miss Bell pulled some Visine from a pocket, thrust her head back and squeezed drops into each eye, then looked at me and laughed. "Sorry you had to witness that," she said.

"Maybe it's from chalk dust," I offered.

"I don't use that much chalk, but you never know. Could be ambient." She was holding a tissue to her nose. "Many things are, most things, really. Anyway, I'd like you to figure out who Daphne is talking to. And why she won't interact with the others. She's very remote, and I want to know what to do about it. Her family has the same problem at home. They take her to activities, and she goes into her own world. The world of Daphne."

"And what is there?" I asked.

"Mildred," said Miss Bell, laughing a little and imitating what I presumed was Daphne's pronunciation. "That's her best imaginary friend. I have no idea where the name comes from. The lesser lights are Bonnie and Roy. But Mildred is the big cheese."

I told Ruth Bell I would spend some time in the classroom observing and some time with Daphne doing some testing. And in the hallway. Lurking.

"I'll stand in the hall with you. I'm always talking to people in the hallway — actual people — so you won't look out of place."

When break time came, I was able to see Daphne with her back to the lockers, talking to Mildred and the lesser lights with enthusiasm. The other students gave her a wide berth. At one point, she threw back her head and shouted *Mildred!* as if she had made an off-colour comment, then laughed. Daphne in the corridor was unlike Daphne in the classroom. I could only interpret it as a defence mechanism, a rudimentary protection against social expectations. I could say this sort of thing, I was the psychologist-in-training. Daphne seemed sensitive to social expectations. To Miss Bell, I said, "She needs social skills."

"We work on those every day," answered Miss Bell.

One on one, in the little meeting room down the hall, I asked Daphne to tell me about Mildred. Her cheeks reddened, and she volunteered no information. From my briefcase, I withdrew a sixteen-piece jigsaw puzzle of an elephant, and we worked on that together. I asked what she was looking forward to in high school, and she dipped her head and giggled and said David Bowie.

"Do you think he'll be there?"

"Maybe." She shrugged her shoulders. "Yes." Then she looked at me gravely and said, "I want to be a baby forever." Immediately I suspected this might be an echo of her parents' warnings, but it might also have been Daphne speaking from the heart.

I said, "A lot of people feel that way."

FOR STUDENTS BETWEEN the ages of seven and sixteen, such as Daphne who was fourteen, there was the WISC-III, the third version of the Wechsler Intelligence Scale for Children. For younger children, we had the WPPSI, the Wechsler Preschool and Primary Scale of Intelligence. One cloudy afternoon, I signed a WPPSI out of the test cupboard, telling myself I should practise administering it, knowing I had a subject at home. The person administering the test, the tester, needs to be well-versed in the subtests, the process, the starting points, the cutoffs and so on, but the subject, the individual being tested, should not practise an intelligence test, of course. This results in an invalid and probably inflated score.

I left the kit in my trunk for a couple of days, where it glowed (in my mind) like a plutonium bundle of potential. If Roger and I *reviewed* the test material once a week for one hundred and fifty-six weeks, without actually *rehearsing*, in three years' time, when he would almost certainly be assessed again, he would score in the gifted range. And although IQ scores aren't everything in an assessment (they're not, despite what the IQ-test-naïve public might think), Roger was singular enough that school administrators, principals, placement people might find his anomalous change in scores plausible. He's just a quirky kid, they would say. We can try him out in the regular stream until division two, someone would suggest, then look at the gifted programs, pending another assessment (and more practise). In my imagination, I saw Roger in a Grade 12 physics class, wearing a tie, squeaking when he made mistakes, being compared to Glenn Gould without the musical talent.

On the third day, I brought the kit inside, where King Two sniffed its vinyl case as if it were a fellow canine, and to prevent distraction and the likelihood of him gnawing on test materials, I locked him in the bedroom. Lucy was at work, and Roger was watching TV, oblivious to all forms of psychometricity. After much literal to-ing and fro-ing with the case itself, picking it up, setting it down, carrying it to the table, returning it to the hallway, I got out some of the blocks and placed them on the living room floor where Roger was lying, mesmerized by Mr. Dressup. I asked, "Do you want to play with these for a while?" Propped on one elbow, he stacked them into a tower and returned his attention to the screen. I put them away and asked, "What's a coat, Roger?"

He did not reply. I repeated the question, and, with a little shrug, he answered, "Time to go outside." Not bad, I thought. With a query, a kind of verbal prod to say more, he might get a point or even two, but I didn't continue. I sat on the floor with Roger and looked out the living room window at what looked like rain clouds. So much of everything was beyond the third percentile rank. Evidence of this fact accumulated in my soul, to use Lucy's construct, like a one-million-piece jigsaw puzzle taking shape. I put the blocks away and felt a wave of regret, as if I had shown Roger my own id wrestling with its superego. And besides, were he to practise, were *we* to practise, the future psychologist, and there would be a future psychologist, would know. Seeing the blocks, Roger would say, "My mom has these toys!"

"So, your mom works in schools, does she?" Beth or Harriet would ask. "She's not Rose Drury, by any chance, is she?" riffling through referral and consent papers for parent signatures.

"She has a car," Roger might say.

"Okay. So, your mother *is* Rose Drury. And you've *played* with these blocks before?"

"The clock is wrong," Roger would say, grabbing onto the psychologist's stopwatch.

"It's not actually a clock," she would say, "it's called a stopwatch."

"I want it," Roger might whisper, maybe even standing up, shrieking, possibly even heading for the door, making a run for it, the tester's nightmare scenario, chasing a child, hunting a child down, pleading, please little person, let's just co-operate, because I don't have a lot of time, nor do I have a timepiece with which you may play.

I didn't do it again, the borderline rehearsal testing, and for the wrong reason. I pictured myself written up as a case study on ethics, a textbook case, literally, eventually known as the Rose Effect, or the School Psychologist Mom, perhaps even illustrated by a blurry photograph of me, Rose Drury. *She skyrocketed her child from the third to the ninety-ninth percentile rank after weeks and weeks of so-called play with a commonly used IQ test.* They say fear was her motive. They say that, unlike her girlfriend, Lucy, she was unable to relax in the present psycho-educational moment. She whirred her thinking ahead to a special-education class in an undesirable corner of the school, she anticipated a lazy, C-type of teacher in track pants, and, rather than accept this eventuality, she was prepared to push her son with a motherly brutality back into the regular classroom. Whatever it took, she would be quoted as having said, in the textbook, or textbooks.

There *had* been progress. Roger had stopped saying whoops, I almost fell, partly because Lucy, intuitively understanding the process of satiation, played a falling game with him at home; almost every day after dinner she would rise from a chair or the couch or move away from the sink and fall to the floor. She was a trained faller, or so it seemed. "I've been to the school of hard knocks," she said to Roger and me. Every single time she fell, Roger became breathless with laughter, he became so charming, and I laughed, too, relieved and adoring. As long as he could laugh like that, he would be surrounded by goodwill.

At pre-kindergarten, as with everything, there were ups and downs, possibly a few more downs. I considered Roger's choice of clothing to be increasingly foppish. Added to the ties, he wanted matching socks and pants, fridge-colour socks, fridge-colour pants, bird-egg socks, bird-egg pants, yolk-colour this, Principal-Cove-colour that. Rather than getting closer to a conventional understanding of colour words, he seemed to be getting farther away. Dead leaf was his latest, meaning yellow brown. I said to myself and Lucy, it's learning by association, it's another way of categorizing. She said, "It's a prototype."

He *had* to be in Ryan O'Hanrahan's group for all activities, and of course he was not. Oblivious to his own peskiness, Roger secreted, to use Anastasia's old word, his centre marker in the same envelope as Ryan's daily, more than once. Directing Roger to the appropriate centre had become not exactly a class joke but a pre-kindergarten amusement. At the same time, he became interested in insects, particularly bees. I wondered if possibly he saw them as belonging to the same underdog class as he. This was not entirely farfetched. The other kids knew he liked bugs and sometimes pointed out dead samples to him in dusty corners or behind small appliances, sometimes advising him, in the voice of a teaching assistant, not to touch. *"Roger!"* one would warn. "Just look, don't touch!"

Then Miss Emily called about the Squeaking Program, an intervention she wanted to implement to discourage squeaking and encourage other ways to communicate strong emotion, joy, frustration, anger. The speech and language pathologist, Laura, had recommended it, and Emily suggested I *touch base* with her for more details, giving me the number for the health unit. I didn't call, didn't call, then I called. In her frank way, Laura said it would be all about modelling, redirecting, reinforcing. "If you could follow up at home, it would help immeasurably. Just saying things like, I feel happy because, oh, I don't know, because I saw a horse today." Laura laughed and said, "That's a bad example, but you know what I mean. We don't really talk like that, much, but we're supposed to." And she laughed again. "I mean as opposed to squeaking or shrieking. Not that Roger shrieks, well, sometimes it's close to a shriek. I think Emily's going to tie a reward system to it. For every half hour he manages without noises and with real words, he'll get a sticker. If you want to try something similar at home, I can help you set it up."

"Okay, sure," I said. I was energized, actually. I thought it *would* help and thought Lucy would, too, and she did. We made a chart.

I think I imagined, this is it, the fix. After one week, Emily sent home Roger's completed sticker chart, afternoons neatly divided into segments, the majority of which were stickerless but covered in pencil messages such as Try Harder or You're Doing Your Best (contradictory) or Use Your Words, Roger. From twenty possible spaces, there were four stickers on the chart squished into Roger's backpack, which I always grabbed from his hook before proceeding down the hall to the after care he had started attending. Usually, by the time I arrived, only a few wan children were running around in the unflattering and prison-yard light of the gym. The pick-up moment was always a little fraught, as I blurrily took in Roger's fringe-dweller status. But he was invariably thrilled to see me, often to the point of trembling, and in return I wanted to tremble. What a pair, I thought. Shakers and not movers. I always hugged him and smelled his sweaty child head and was reminded of recess in Flax, indoor or outdoor, the heads would sweat. Always, he pulled the sticker chart from his pack and, with honest and smiling pride, showed me his results.

IN OCTOBER, I volunteered at Roger's class again and met Greta, another *mom*, of course. She introduced me to her daughter, Lisa, who was four and thought Roger was "a riot." Roger was busy wearing two neckties in the dress-up centre, so I pointed him out to Greta, and for a Satanic reason I will never comprehend, I said, I whispered, "He's a little developmentally delayed," confidentially, as if I were the mom with the severe bangs. As my mother would say, I was shamefaced, I know I was, for talking about my son as if he belonged to someone else, as if he belonged to a mother who had a bad seed in her groin. Greta must not have noticed. "Oh," she said, "I have a sister who's developmentally delayed, so I know all about it. She has Down syndrome."

Miss Emily asked if we could get the painting smocks out of the supply room down the hallway, they were supposed to be in a cardboard box marked ECS PM Smocks, but they might not be. Greta said sure, for both of us, and we left the room and entered the hallway where jackets hung, and children's voices could be heard singing "Four Strong Winds." Greta had the key for the supply closet and couldn't get it to work, and in turning to me for help, smiling and saying she was a key klutz, she saw that I was crying. She touched my arm and asked if I were okay, and was it about Roger? She saw through me. "Lisa talks about him all the time. She really likes him," said Greta.

She got the key to work, and inside the supply room I began to sob in a way I had not sobbed since the day in the car with my mother. It was a response to Greta's kindness, I think. "Oh, dear," she said and found a black, rubbery, rolling stool for me to sit on. I sat and put my face in my hands and let go, cried like someone wearing away the brake pads of restraint, someone who was getting down to the wheel wells, right to the metal. Given any more encouragement, I could very easily have made screeching sounds or begun keening. Thankfully no one else entered the supply closet. Crouching next to me, Greta asked if she could get me anything, or if I wanted to talk to Dr. Cove.

"Dr. Cove's not a psychiatrist," I said, in a palsied voice, "but maybe you should get her." On the one hand, I didn't want to scare away Greta and her sister with Down syndrome and all that she might know, while on the other, I wanted to be escorted out of the art supply closet and the school and perhaps the city of Calgary, like an invalid.

"I'll see if I can find her," Greta said, leaving me alone in the narrow room full of shelves. Despite my condition, I was able to find the box of PM smocks, tore part of a ragged sleeve from one of the painting shirts, blew my nose on it and stuffed the remnant into a pocket. Then I snapped out of it. Greta returned with Dr. Cove, her face warm and understanding, and I regretted my wild display of hopeless ideation. I bucked up and apologized and said, "I think I must be premenstrual or something. I don't normally behave like this. I think maybe I should go home. Maybe it wasn't the best day for me to volunteer. Look at my badge, it's all scrunched up and even a bit wet."

Dr. Cove offered to make me some tea, she invited me to come to her office, she offered to drive me home.

"No no, no no. I can walk."

Greta delivered the smock box and returned with my jacket and purse, for which I was so grateful. I said, "Thanks so much, Greta," and saying her name triggered a new set of sobs, more pleasurable than the previous, escaping from my back and shoulders into my throat, like large birds getting loose after sitting on a roost for days or even months. *Thank God we're out of that madhouse.* Then I stopped as abruptly as I had begun, and I told Dr. Cove I would walk home and be fine in an hour and a bit, when it would be time for Roger to come home, time for me to return to the bleak reality of percentile ranks.

I walked home. I unlocked the door and went to the phone. Lucy answered. "Cottonwood Optometry. How can I help you?"

"I'm having a nervous breakdown," I said, "or maybe just a breakdown. I don't feel nervous. I was sobbing at the school, Lucy. People saw me, the principal and this woman named Greta who has a sister with Down syndrome. I'm sure I alienated her."

Lucy said, "Just hold on. I'll turn on the machine. I'll put you on hold, and I'll find an empty room. Hold on."

There was no music or advertising for those holding for Cottonwood Optometry. My head ached from whatever was going on in there. Kittens were scratching at the backs of my eyes. Lamely, I thought, I'll tell Lucy I need a CAT scan.

The voice of Lucy. "What's happening? Why are you suddenly having a breakdown? Just because you're crying doesn't mean you're going off the deep end."

"I know, I know."

"What is it? Tell me."

"It's Roger, at the school. He's so different. He'll never fit in."

"Sure he will. He'll fit in as much as I do," Lucy said. "I don't fit in, but look at me. I'm a receptionist at a reputable business! I've never fit in. That's why I'm so happy to be Roger's dad. And I know you think I'm being kind of ridiculous when I say that, but I do want to be his dad. I can't be his mom, but I envy you."

"Don't say anything nicer or I'll slip more deeply into my breakdown."

"Roger's an interesting person. Don't feel bad that he's not exactly like the others. There's an infinite number of others."

"All going to birthday parties with other others. He never gets invited, Lucy. I haven't mentioned that to you, but the others get invited, and he doesn't." I was talking now in an uncontrolled voice, as if I were a large-throated bird with a wobbly cry.

"Okay, but things have just started up; the kids are getting to know each other. And we'll have a big party when it's Roger's birthday, and we'll invite the whole class and the teacher and this Greta and her sister and Dr. Cove. It'll be a big event. Mention might be made in the *Renforth Bugle*."

"Mention," I said, witheringly, "honourable mention."

"What's wrong with honourable mention? I had honourable mention at the science fair, several times. I never won a prize, but I kept entering my projects, Rose, because I had an indomitable spirit. I kept going back and climbing the ladder of my science dreams, and look where I am now. I am at reception."

I tried to laugh and said, "You're funny. I love being around you."

"I have to get back to my desk. The optometrists will wonder where I am."

"Okay," I said in a quavery voice. Roger and Lucy could never know what I'd said to Greta, the sneaking reference to a little developmentally delayed: not what but *how* I'd said it.

ONE FRIDAY AFTERNOON, even though the clocks had not yet been changed, by the time I picked up Roger at the school's after care, the early gloom of evening was imminent. I was in an anxious state I had not *used my words* to dispel, having had a hateful meeting with a mother whose child I had suggested might have ADD. The child, Joel, was already being treated for hyperactivity, but his mother objected to the *label*. She said her pediatrician had assured her Joel did not and would never have ADD, despite having prescribed medication to treat its symptoms. She insisted that, from the results of a *brain scan*, the pediatrician had deduced that Joel could not possibly have ADD. I hated this kind of talk, there was no brain scan for ADD, and when confronted with pseudoscience, I wanted to respond like Lucy in the Peanuts cartoon, *just shut up and listen to me*, but I did my best to remain pleasant. The principal was sitting in on the meeting.

However, after three iterations of ADD would not really show up on a brain scan, there is no blood test for ADD, it's a group of symptoms, all countered by the irrational arguments of a mother to whom I should have listened more *actively*, I said, "Okay, I give up." I could feel my face warming, and I wondered if the principal might call my supervisor to report me, for something. By way of concluding the meeting, I suggested to Arva, Joel's mom, we just agree to disagree, arranging my mouth into a smirk, and in response, Arva tossed my report onto the table, causing it to flutter like an unhealthy white bird before it landed upside down. And off she went. To my relief, the principal said, "That went better than I had anticipated."

But driving away, I was saddened and rueful. Why had I become so het up, to use one of Lucy's phrases? I could simply have said, okay, let's not call it anything. Or let's call it what you want. What does it matter? But, *but*, why should *I* acquiesce, after seven years of schooling, as I liked to ask myself, at least two of which had been dedicated to the irrelevant study of American and Chinese history? The truth was I had not liked Joel's mother, because she had wanted to argue, and because she was obviously uneducated, had frizzy, permed and thinning hair, and was wearing a ski jacket that stank of baked-in cigarette smoke. SES, the old grad-school code for you are not as good as me. Couldn't she see I was nothing more than the Lucy character? I wanted to call the real Lucy, but she was at work until nine.

Roger and I went home. He was excited about a drawing he had completed, a drawing of a bee. His bee was small, well, life-sized, black and yellow, and in the very centre of a large piece of paper. I told him it was convincing. By then, I was forgetting my meeting and my red-faced need to be authoritative.

Inside the house, while I let King Two out in the yard and threw a couple of sticks for him, Roger went upstairs to the bathroom, flushed, and yelled for me, "Mom! The water!" he said. Upstairs, I found the toilet filled to the brim. A healthy, medium-sized turd and some paper floated, gently tapping the side of the bowl. Roger stood nearby, transfixed. "Look!" he shrieked. Pooping in the toilet was still an accomplishment for him, as was independent, usually inadequate, wiping. As well, he had never seen such a curious toilet malfunction and was obviously taken with his excrement's bid for freedom, because he flushed again.

As the water rose and crested the banks of the bowl, I shouted: "Roger, are you an *idiot?*" *Whee*, he must have been thinking, briefly, watching the paper and shit slide merrily to the floor, before he registered *idiot* and my harsh tone of voice and began watching me closely for my next move. His eyes filled with tears, which, heartbreakingly, did not spill. Then he smiled at me, like someone about to pet a dangerous dog.

"Oh, Roger," I said, stepping into the toilet bowl runoff in my leotard feet. Picking him up, I said, "I'm sorry, I'm sorry. I just lost my temper because of the poop spilling out. It's nothing. I can clean it up."

"That's okay, Mommy, that's okay," he said, patting my face.

I carried him to his room and threw my leotards into the hamper, and we rolled around on the bed. I stood up and fell over, bouncing on the mattress. I kissed him repeatedly, I said Mom's a dork, I said, poop likes to get out of the toilet once in a while. We lay on the bed for a while saying nothing, and then, while Roger watched, I cleaned up the bathroom. The turd had held together, and the water level in the toilet had magically receded. I sopped and bleached and wore yellow gloves, which I threw out. There, I said, but Roger's face still had a look. "Where's at Lucy?" he wanted to know.

"Still at work. She won't be home until after bedtime." I went to the closet and got a mask Lucy had bought for Halloween. It was Goofy, and she was saving it up, as she put it, for October 31. I put it on. When I entered the living room, Roger shrieked with pleasure and ran at me with his arms wide open, *wide* open like I had never seen them before. We hugged and laughed, and he put on the mask, and we looked in the bathroom mirror, and Roger shrieked once more from behind the mask. We had canned baked beans with cheese and mashed potatoes, Roger's favourite meal. Then we returned to the bathroom, where I gave Roger a bath and washed his thin hair. When he was in his blue and white striped pyjamas, in front of the mirror, he said, "I'm a geek. I look geek."

My heart: a small jackknife snapped open inside it, scraping the valves. "No, you're not, don't say that. You're my smart and handsome boy! You're getting smarter and handsomer all the time. Let's brush your teeth."

Once Roger was asleep, I sat on the couch with the mask, waiting for Lucy. I would have to tell her I hadn't been able to save it up for Halloween.

fifteen

GRETA CALLED on Sunday morning, the weekend after Thanksgiving. She was meeting Betty's mom, Marilyn, for a coffee at the Beanie on 17th Avenue. I whispered to Lucy, "Should I go?"

"Yes," she said, "Roger and I need some alone time." Were they all colluding to point me in the direction of therapeutic social activity? I didn't know. I couldn't confess to anyone I had called Roger an idiot on Friday, and he had not yet squealed on me. I actually don't think he possessed the cognitive lineaments to *tell*. For better or for worse, his mind moved forward in first gear, looking straight ahead for clocks, Ryan O'Hanrahan, candies, and velveteen clothing.

"Sure," I said to Greta. "I guess we're kind of a group," a comment I don't think she heard or chose to acknowledge.

"Two o'clock okay?" she asked.

"Yes, see you."

"I guess we're an unaffiliated group, it seems, Greta, Marilyn, and me," I said in the hallway to myself, before I stepped outside, as they say, where the weather was sunny and warm enough for a sweater, nothing more. Too early in the day for raking and there were church bells coming from somewhere. Carmen's window was open, and I could hear her on the phone; Robert looked out of his upstairs window and waved with an oven mitt hand. Maybe because of the church bells and Lucy's influence, I thought, *I prepare a way before you*. We, Lucy, Carmen, Robert, me, we had had a way before us, prepared by the mathematics of what we can achieve and what there is available, an equation that works for most. All of life's treats splay out before the average and the above average, those who walk forward together with the phone, the garden tools, the baking pans, the coffee plans, into the vessel, the funnel of everyday, while the ones at the edge, the outer left edge, are sliced off; the way is not prepared; they fall away, like Joe, like Roger will if he does not use his words.

I inhaled the dusty air, exhaled with panic, looked to the south where the path was clear, and ran-walked to the Greek Orthodox parking lot, to the wooden stairs, down to the other part of 6th Street and back up, not even panting. Cars were entering the lot, but they saw me as a walker or a runner on my prepared path. What if, I was wondering, Roger were sliced from my protection, fell from an edge, rolled from the borderline? Borderline: so that's what it really meant, rather than what we psychologists laboured to explain, oh, borderline means just below the average range, on the border between this and that, between the fifth and sixteenth percentile ranks, above the damn third by several rungs of Van Daniken's ladder.

Behind the Greek Orthodox Church I shook my head, turned away from the cars, and slapped myself in the face. Snap out of it. Greta was kind, but Roger did not have Down syndrome like her sister, and I wished little Betty would stop hounding my son and find some girlfriends with thick glasses, because Roger was just now beginning to want to play soccer with the boys, he was starting to show more interest in the Flames and hockey, he was inching closer to the prepared way. My breathing became normal, and I returned home.

During lunch, Lucy and I used our words to convey emotion. "I feel happy when Lucy makes the tea biscuits with cheese," I said.

"I feel silly when my sock has a hole and my big toe is out, looking around," said Lucy, placing her right foot on the table. With a pen, she drew a face on her toe and said, "Hi, Roger, I'm a toe, and I'm using my words even though I don't have a mouth."

"It's Lucy," said Roger, "it's Lucy saying for the toe."

"Ha," said Lucy, dropping her foot to the floor. "Well, Roger, it's your turn. How do you feel? About anything? Today?"

With the attention, the formality of our speech, the toe's ability, the performance anxiety, Roger's face very briefly conveyed a tight little lust for squeaking, but he swallowed it. He repressed! Wobbling his head back and forth, Roger said, "I feel crick crack. I feel buzzing."

"That's good," I encouraged, "like a bee."

He went on. "I feel grabba, boo-moo, pee-pee, no-no." Then a tiny eek, like a bat being stuck with a pin.

"That's pretty good conversation, Rog," said Lucy. "You kept the ball rolling, you did. We're all happy about that, and now your mom has a turn."

"I feel okay, right now, maybe a little bit excited or riled up, about seeing Betty's mom and Lisa's this afternoon. At the coffee place. I'll bring you both something, a muffin maybe."

Greta and Marilyn were at the Beanie before I arrived, Greta with her braid and Marilyn, as usual, dressed in black with her startling and prematurely white bouff of hair. I wondered if she had a syndrome, and I wanted to say this to her, with her, and laugh, but needless to say, I did not.

Standing up, Greta said, "We were just talking about my sister, Molly. Here, have this chair," and she dragged a third chair to the table. "I talked to her on the phone this morning. I'm being chirpy, I'm being a good sister, and I ask, 'What are you doing today, Molly?' and she says, I don't *know*, just like that, *know* like that's a ridiculous question, as if I had asked what's the weather going to be like six weeks from now, like I was a fool for asking. She does that once in a while, and it always makes me laugh, so I said you don't have to be a grouch. I'm not a grouch, she says, like a grouch. She's a funny girl."

I smiled and smiled. Greta and Marilyn already had coffee, so I went to the counter to order, my hands in a sweat. I was in the disabled moms group, and I didn't want to stay, but I couldn't disappear out the back door: that would cause a ruction, to use one of Lucy's words. When I returned to the table, Greta was still on the subject of Molly. "It's funny how one day she can have great conversational skills, and the next she's like the troll under the bridge. I mean, some days she can really surprise us all, she can talk about movies forever, nothing in depth, of course, she's not going to be sharing her thoughts on cinematography, but she knows her actors and her favourite movies, and they're not little-kid movies. She loved *Ordinary People, Kramer vs. Kramer*, that's the kind of things she likes. She follows the plot. She gets it. I guess what I'm saying is, she has Down syndrome, but she also has some complexity to her, and people don't see that. It bothers me. It makes me mad."

Feeling as if I were practising conversation, I said, "I'm supposed to be working on Roger's speech, or, I guess it's more like helping him to express himself more appropriately when he's excited or angry or frustrated. The speech pathologist set up a kind of program, and we were just working on that this morning at home, Lucy and me, my partner, maybe you've met her or seen her, she hasn't been able to volunteer yet. Anyway, we were taking turns at lunch, I feel happy about, I feel excited about. It felt really fake to me. I mean, when was the last time you said I feel happy about something? Well, maybe people talk like that, maybe kids do. I'm trying to do the right thing."

"You have to do what the professionals tell you to do," Marilyn said, with sarcasm. "When Betty was little, they told me to make up this little room out of a big cardboard box full of lights and random objects for her to look at. I tried it . . . I busied myself" (Marilyn mimed busyness with frantic hand motions) "and I put the fourteen-month Betty on her back in the box room and thought, this is nuts. This isn't real life. You don't lie in a box and look at a fork and spoon. I don't listen as well as I used to, since that. And Betty's only five. I've got a long road of oppositionalism ahead of me." Beneath the white hair was an angry mind. "Betty's in love with your son, by the way. I guess you know that," Marilyn said to me. "It's Roger this and Roger that."

"Oh, yes. Roger loves Betty's watch. And her," I hastened to add. "I didn't mean he just likes the watch."

But Marilyn laughed. "Oh, I know all about the watch. It's okay if he loves her for her adapted timepiece. And I'm pretty sure he's getting tired of her commandeering him around the playground. Just tell Roger to tell her, I want to play with the boys. Pretend I'm the speech pathologist. She needs to be in the real world," then she laughed again, "like I am. Sort of.

"I mean, I worry about her," Marilyn went on. "That's the real world. My husband's away a lot, in Texas, sometimes Newfoundland, even Nigeria, where the oil is, so most of the school and CNIB stuff falls on my shoulders. And I'm not going to say I shouldn't complain, because actually I love to complain. He, Nick, he's pretty good, he likes to do research on Betty's condition, he'll be in Houston and call up some eye centre or just drop in to an ophthalmology department. I don't know why I'm going on about what Nick does. Oh, yes, because sometimes I feel like he doesn't really know Betty. She's not really Daddy's little girl, she's Mommy's little girl, so I hope she doesn't go boy crazy if she isn't already. I actually think she has a crush on Roger, and I already worry about her with boys for a funny reason, because she can't see very well except for close up, so one of my big worries is that boys will be making fun of her, and she won't know, because she won't be able to see it on their faces. That's my big worry I confessed to at the hospital when they asked me about my nightmare for Betty. Kind of a shallow worry, but that's it." Marilyn's eyes were dry and brown.

"I understand," said Greta. "Maybe this doesn't seem like a big deal either, but to me it was. I was with Molly once, this was after high school for both of us, and I was at university, and she was still living with Mom and Dad. It was over Christmas, and I had taken her skating. She's not bad at ice skating, and we were leaving the arena, and I realized I had forgotten my skate guards, so I told Molly to wait for me and went back in, and when I came outside, just outside the door, some kids were talking to Molly, some teenagers, and I thought great, they seemed to be being nice to her, so I held back a bit until I picked up on what they were saying. They were telling her she was beautiful. One of the boys said, Yeah, you're really pretty, and the girl with them said, Have you ever thought of modelling? And I heard Molly say, No. She knew they were making fun of her, but, of course, where would she go? She was waiting for me. I was so mad, but I didn't want Molly to . . . I didn't want to legitimize their making fun, so I just took her arm and said, Let's go, Moll. And in the car, she said, I'm not pretty, in her flat, gravelly voice. And I said, They don't know you, Molly. Just forget about them. You always look nice. You look pretty. No, I don't, she said. She didn't say much for the rest of the day, she always gets quiet after that sort of thing. So, if Betty can miss out on any of that, you know what I mean, Marilyn, I'm not trying to be glib."

"I know. I know."

Betty, Roger, and Molly: that's what we talked about for nearly two hours.

NOT MANY DAYS LATER, I made an ill-advised plan to see Asa, for a turkey sandwich, at his place. Wednesday morning at the gym, he had handed me a scrap of brown paper, maybe from Tuesday's lunch bag, with his address (not his phone number) and said, "Come over Sunday afternoon if you've got the time. I'll fix you a sandwich made of frozen turkey meat. We can sit outside on my fenced patio. The fence is so high, we can sit outside, but no one will be able to see us. They'll just hear us chomping. You'll see."

"Why should no one see us?" I asked.

"No one should not see us," he said. "Anyone could see us if they were determined to. I'm just a proud patio owner."

"Are you someone who gets drunk in the morning and talks crazy talk?"

"Not in the least."

"Okay, I'll come over." I had nothing planned and anyway, I wasn't likely going to go, but I did.

Sunday morning, I sprang a false engagement on Lucy and Roger, claiming I was going to meet Peggy at Nose Hill for a walk, then possibly a coffee or drink, whatever happened to be on my breath when I returned from Asa's walled patio. Early afternoon, in jeans and hiking boots, I left the house. Recklessly, I had *secreted* a skirt and my

Frye cowboy boots in the car. Beneath the jeans, I was wearing black tights. My id told me to drive to the Nose Hill parking lot and change there, not that difficult as the parking lot, although small and often full of cars, was usually empty of people, not to mention that some changing of clothing was not entirely foreign to the location. I simply stood between the car's driver side open doors, took off the jeans, put on the skirt and boots, closed the backseat door, and sat myself in the driver's seat, a little shamefaced and shaky. Where does crazy desire come from? It comes from a root cellar of the soul, a cold room, from behind a wooden door, not a place of warmth, but one of storage and preserves, and even though it is half-full or half-empty, and there's no urgent need for any more supplies, you think, maybe I'll just drive over for the sandwich anyway. I'll put on a skirt in a parking lot, a long-sleeved T-shirt, black, and tights also black, and my old pair of boots and resemble a person I am not sure I ever was or could be.

Asa lived in a neighbourhood called Bankview, fifteen minutes away by car. Bankview, I had read in the *Calgary Herald*, had the highest density of single people in the city. I worked with a woman, a psychologist, named Vera, who told me a lot about her sex life. I couldn't tell if I appeared entirely conventional to her, and so she wanted to shock me, or she had inferred I was unshockable. Vera met men through newspaper personals, and she had visited one in Bankview. She said he worked for Occupational Health and Safety, and this is why she felt comfortable going to his apartment. His apartment was a sty, ironically, hardly safe for occupation, she said, a studio with a king-sized bed taking up all the space in the living room, a rusty tub and sink in the bathroom, and clutter everywhere. He had offered her oral sex, no need to reciprocate, he said. Vera told me this in her office space on the other side of the mustard-coloured divider between us, late one afternoon when I wanted to go home. "He wasn't bad looking," Vera said, "and I had to admire his forthrightness, so I said okay.

Then after I couldn't wait to get out of there. He phoned again, and I told him he must have the wrong number even though he said, that's you, Vera, isn't it? I could hear him saying my name as I hung up." Surely Vera knew that her story would elicit visualization; she was the one who had told me about the reading comprehension program called Visualizing and Verbalizing. I told her I needed to get going and pick up Roger from the after-school care program.

Would a patio-proud man live in squalor? No, he did not. Asa lived in a condo behind a palisade-like wooden fence. He had said reach over to undo the latch, which was easy enough, then three steps down into a little courtyard or more accurately patio with a few spindly trees growing along the perimeter. It was exactly as he had said. Asa had set up a narrow table with a pale blue tablecloth and dark blue dishes. He gestured through the window for me to come in, and I opened the door and entered, very nervous, and as per usual, trembly. I was not faint, but my legs became weak, and I thought of slipping onto my knees to prevent a head injury. But my feet held firm; I was aware of them as flat, reliable surfaces, maybe the way a wild mammal must take note of its paws while standing before a mesmer-izing sight such as a wide and wild river.

"Rose," said Asa, walking toward me in his plain white apron, a trifle stretched over that pleasing belly. He put his arms around me, then kissed me on the lips, once, chastely, then a second time with some passion and tongue — a moment of rejoicing followed by a brief worry that he might make an offer of unreciprocated oral sex. Could this be the Bankview protocol? I hoped not, I was there, frankly, I told myself, for a genuine penis. But he did not. We had a glass of wine and ate the sandwiches at his outdoor table. Most likely, the turkey had been roasted by the Other Woman, but I did not have the stamina to inquire. I pictured her, I wanted to tell Asa, to be a little like a turkey herself, large breasted and with a beak.

Asa and I often spoke of firsts and mosts. Outside at the patio table, with a mouthful of half-chewed turkey and bread, I asked, "Did I ever tell you about my most spectacular turning down of an offer?"

"Go for it," Asa said, pouring me some water. The turkey was a bit dry. "But I have to say, I'm not encouraged."

"Oh no, don't be discouraged," I said, blushing at my unintended implication. "Okay, well, this was when I was in high school, when I had my first real boyfriend, the one I told you about in the cherry incident."

"The one with the too-big thing."

"Yes, his name was JJ, and his father was an accountant. Not sure if that has a whole lot to do with the story, but money consciousness did, and likely if you have an accountant for a dad, you get specific money ideas drilled into you as a pipsqueak. So JJ was, I think I already told you this, JJ was a cheapskate. I mean, in the days when the social etiquette was your boyfriend, especially when he had a paying job at the rink, might buy you the occasional order of fries and a Coke, he, more often than not, had forgotten his wallet or hadn't had a chance to get to the bank or only had enough money for one ticket at the movie theatre, the Lyceum."

"A not unfamiliar type," Asa said. "I have a couple of buddies with that syndrome or ex-buddies, or at least guys I try to avoid."

"Yeah, dating him was not what I had been trained to expect from Ann Landers and *Tiger Beat* magazine."

Now Asa poured himself more wine, but I said no, thanks.

"Regardless," I went on, "he was considered cool, so maybe that's why I liked him or loved him. We were together for almost two years, so this was the Christmas of my last year in high school. By then we had gone all the way, as we used to say. JJ would stow a tarp and a blanket in the trunk of his dad's car, which miraculously he allowed him to use. As a result, JJ did have to buy condoms, which I think was his rationale for having insufficient funds for Coke and movies, etc. Although his best friend worked at a pharmacy owned by the best friend's dad, so I suspect he got them for free or at a reduced rate. Most of our dates concluded with a drive down a specific and rarely used country road that ended in a woodlot, where we unloaded the tarp and the blanket. That was the routine. I liked it, to be honest."

"Money isn't everything, Rose." Asa flashed me his mock-wise face.

"Yes, true, ha ha. Anyway, Christmas drew nigh, and I decided to knit JJ a scarf. My mother helped me or at least got me started and fixed my dropped stitches. She was just starting to feel completely better from her cancer, she had been declared totally cancer free, and she seemed excited about this dumb scarf I was making. And I had told JJ I was making a scarf so he would know and could reciprocate with some kind of handcrafted thing.

"Anyway, the scarf was hideous and too wide and too bulky to even fold in half lengthwise, but I gave it to him, and in exchange he gave me a joke gift."

Then I said, "Oh, oh, I think I'm going to cry. I wasn't expecting that. Why do I care so much about that stupid joke gift?"

Asa looked stricken, he could be very dear. "Don't make yourself sad over it," he said. "I don't need to know about your most spectacular turning down of an offer or a joke gift from ten years ago. To me, it's great you accepted my sandwich offer. Look at you. Here you are."

"Okay, no, I'm all right. No crying she made. Ha ha. You know what? Never mind. I think I'm telling the wrong story."

"No. I want to know what happened. I just don't want you to be crying."

"No, I'm not crying, I'm fine. Okay. To get back to the cheapness angle, I didn't say anything to JJ about the gift, but the next time I was out with him and stopped at the woodlot, before he had a chance to get out of the car and open the trunk, I said, if you want to have sex, you're going to have to pay for it. He said, What? In his most faux manly and horrified voice, using an inflection I'm sure he thought thousands of men lounging in their La-Z-Boys across Canada would have tried out in similar circumstances. So, I repeated, if you want to have sex you have to pay me." And at that very moment, from a nearby tree, rather convincingly a raven asked, whaaa whaaa whaaat?

"You mean faux like fake?" Asa wanted to know, as the raven, perhaps attracted by the scent of bird sandwiches, perched on the fortress-like fence.

"Yes, I mean faux like fake," and I exhaled deeply, a zephyr of turkey breath most likely. "I have no idea where this proposition came from. I had not planned it. Mostly likely my association with my best friend Anastasia was the root source, it was the type of thing she would have done. Then I said, I want to go home. And he drove me home with his fuming face visible in the car's dashboard light. At school on Monday, he brought me the scarf in a brown paper shopping bag with handles. I hung it in my locker and left it there until the big locker cleanup in June, when I threw it into a metal trash can in the middle of the corridor. So that was that."

"That was that for the cheapskate JJ," said Asa, and the bird took off.

"That was it." Then I added, "And the next boyfriend was George of the cabin, whom I married and divorced." (I had not yet told him about Roger.) "And then Lucy. I love Lucy," I said to Asa, I ventured forth. I think he imagined I was referring to the television show. I don't know what he thought, and the moment slid by. "Did the Dolly cook this turkey meat?" I asked.

He sighed. "Yes, she did. But never mind. Let's go in and see if we can find some football on TV. I've got some good Scotch. It's kind of cool out here."

"Sure," I said. I had to go into the bathroom to sit for a moment and blow my nose.

Then, we sat on the couch. We found a game, football, the Stampeders against the Roughriders. I was tense and wished I hadn't told the story, felt in fact that I should make up for it, felt that I should leave and buy some mints. After a *spectacular* touchdown, in the seconds after we had both cheered and yayed, Asa leaned over and kissed me, and I kissed back in a moment of delirium and swooning. I wondered if I could detach this moment from all the others, tear it away like a perforated sticker and put it in a book, the situation was ideal, Asa had the Dolly, I had Lucy, just do it once, have a good old-fashioned shag as perhaps Dr. Cove would say, and go home, but I knew I would not be able to endure the guilt and deception, I knew I would confess and ruin things for Roger, and me, and as Asa was squishing my left breast, I said, "This is a bad idea. I can't do this, I'm in a relationship. I can't."

"For fuck's sake, Rose." Silence. We were still lying on the couch. "Why didn't you tell me?"

"I thought you had guessed, deduced. Truthfully, because I'm with a woman. Lucy. That's what I meant when I said I love Lucy. I guess I'm bisexual, because I definitely want this . . . with you." The moment had certainly lost its charge. There was a small water stain on Asa's living room ceiling, likely from a leak in the upstairs bathroom, and it reminded me of me, so I sat up. We both sat. The Stamps made an interception and got another spectacular touchdown. We didn't cheer. Asa downed his Scotch, and I said I guess I'll go.

"Stay if you want," Asa said, dismissive, "I'm going to watch the game."

"No, I should go," and I stood up and arranged my clothes.

"Well, I can't likely compete with a woman in bed anyway," Asa said, seeming to be relieved he had dodged this challenge. "But do you want to take something with you at least?" he asked, standing and moving in the direction of his tray of sandwiches.

The absurdity of arriving home with Asa's leftovers made me laugh. "No, better not. I'm supposed to be on a little hike at Nose Hill with my friend Peggy."

"Okay, go then. Get out," he said, a little like play-acting a dramatic scene.

Leaving, talking through the screen door, wanting to make it up to Asa, I asked, "What about the road trip with me to Medicine Hat? There's a place there I'd like to see more of."

At this, Asa half-scowled, half-smiled. He threw a plastic spatula at the door and said, "No, Rose. Get out. Go home."

"Okay," I said, and exited the patio. I retraced my route to Nose Hill parking lot, where I changed back to my jeans and went for a short walk.

sixteen

LUCY HAD A COLUMN in the *Herald!* "One Thing" had run in the *Renforth Bugle* in September and been *picked up,* as they say, presumably by some pipe-smoking Daddy Warbucks type who had snapped a few ink-tipped fingers and made it so.

I was proud and worried she might become a smart journalist with an insider group of friends, and at the same time inexplicably aroused by the prospect she might leave me alone with Roger, and we might climb into the car and head out, to somewhere. Great Slave Lake? The column, Lucy's poise and kindness, were all evidence that she was a bigger person than I, emotionally and intellectually, and someday soon she would cough up a bit of phlegm and notice.

The subject of the column was Flora, a deaf woman Lucy had met at the clinic. Flora had come in for the usual reason, glasses, and because Lucy knows some ASL, they were able to communicate, and Lucy did a semi-competent job, as she said, of interpreting between Dr. Moroz, the optometrist, and Flora. Then they had a smoke together outside, and Lucy described "One Thing" and asked Flora if she would be willing to appear in the column. Lucy took her lunch early, and they went to a coffee shop, where Flora had to write some things down, Lucy said, "for me to get what she meant." She was so animated as she described her conversation with Flora, so vivid, I knew I would always remember her face from that day. Lucy always had her camera with her, and she took Flora's picture in the parking lot behind Cottonwood Optometry. Her face seemed maybe twenty-eight years old and large, her glasses were frameless, and her hair, although seeming to be tied back, sprung up in a curly border around her face. She looked as if she were used to measuring people with her eyes, but I may have been making that up because I knew she was deaf.

For "One Thing," Flora told Lucy, I wish my parents could communicate with me better in ASL, especially my mother. I realized when I was eighteen, maybe sixteen, or even younger, that I was missing her all along, that I couldn't make her understand anything I wanted to say with two or three meanings, like I could my deaf friends. Do you know what I mean, Flora had asked, and Lucy had written *ambiguous*, and Flora had nodded, vigorously. I love my mom, Flora had said, and my dad, but they took two sign-language courses, and because I can speak some, I can use my voice, which I would prefer not to, I think they think, that's it, that's me, that's their daughter. I mean, they think what I say is me, and they'll talk away to me, but it's just a bit of sound, sound conversations. I don't know how else to put it. They live in Kelowna, by the way, so they won't see your column, and if they do, that's okay. I don't mean to be mean. It's just, you have to be able to communicate on a level of depth about everything. Like this: I had a dream a while ago, you know how every so often you have a very strong, long-lasting dream, that Mom and I could communicate without effort, without speech or sign, through a kind of pulses, like heartbeats maybe, but each one was a meaning, a subtle meaning, and she could understand that I have this intimacy with her but also isolation. And when I woke up, I felt glowing, and Lucy had added *radiance*. So I called Mom on the TTY and told her my dream, and she said she understood. She said that three times. Maybe she did understand. I came from her, but we come from two different countries. But can I say two things? If you see this, Mom and Dad, I love you. I'm happy to be deaf. Don't feel bad.

The column was in the Saturday *Herald* "Life" section. On Sunday, I thought Lucy might leave me. She can connect with people this way, and look at me, I'm a pinched affair, my glasses are scratched and grimy. I look out and see the potential for horror where I imagine she sees beneficence. I've been wondering if that's really why I want to see Dennis. Maybe he's a horror, maybe he's nothing but a big water head on a bed, a lake surrounded by bone, or a big, blubbery body with a tomato-sized head and a squeaky helium voice. There is no end of ways the human body can assemble itself and survive and then furiously want to carry on.

Then I tell myself Roger is not and never will be Dennis, and Dennis's life will not be Roger's, but it might have been, I think, thirty or forty years ago, when a funny-looking kid not talking properly and shrieking about clocks might have been problem enough to go to a centre forever. He's getting better all the time, I tell my mother and

Adrian. Last night he wanted to stay up and watch hockey with Lucy and me; he likes to know the goalies' names. While Lucy and Roger were getting cookies, I looked at the column for the ninth or tenth time. I told Lucy I was proud of her, and all day Sunday I ruminated. So absurd. Monday morning after Lucy left for work, I called the Wild Rose Centre. My heart was beating like Flora's pulses; I thought Roger might be bothered by it in the living room. After five rings, a receptionist answered, and I told her I was Dennis Petrie's sister-in-law and asked if I would be able to visit someday.

"Certainly," she said. "He doesn't get a lot of company."

"Is there any day that would be better than others?"

"Every day here is more or less the same as the previous one, so the day isn't an issue. The hours are, though — visiting hours are two to four-thirty, every day, unless you make special arrangements."

"Okay, thank you," I said.

THE FIRST REAL progress report and parent-teacher interview happened in mid-November on a Friday morning. We didn't bring Roger with us, I was not modern enough for that, and neither was Lucy, and on this we were in agreement. Our appointment was at 8:45; we walked to the school, past grass coated in frost and beneath empty branches and a morning sun low in the east. Peter Lougheed Elementary was an old school, recently renamed but with few renovations. The stairs were worn and slate, the handrails brass, and on the second storey was a stairway to an attic apartment, originally intended for a live-in janitor. Without children in the hallways, the school gave a strong impression of the secret lives of mice and bats, in ascendance no doubt during weekends and holidays.

The two pre-kindergarten rooms were on opposite sides of the south end of the upstairs hallway. Miss Karen's door was closed, but Miss Emily's was open, and we walked right in, my stomach empty and dropping like an elevator full of chalky air. Dr. Cove was present: surely, she did not, *could* not, attend all the interviews, so Roger was undoubtedly already on the special list. Also present: Laura Flynn, speech and language pathologist, with her file, and Miss Emily, with a stash of notes. Kindness conjoined with preparedness blasted toward us from the school team at their low round table. Lucy and I took our places on the small chairs, and Laura Flynn began, with apologies for her time constraints. She had to get to the next meeting in ten minutes, and I thought, good, there are other children, worse, forty-two-month-olds who may not be able to form a single word. Too bad for them. I was as hostile as a cornered wolverine, sweaty beneath its pelt, whereas Lucy's forehead, I could see, was dry and unfurrowed as a plate.

In her periwinkle silk blouse, Laura began. "First of all, let me say Roger has a made a lot of progress already. His *r* sound has really come along, but that's developmental, so I can't necessarily take any cwedit for that. I mean credit," she added, laughing, and we all laughed. I liked her, but the levity made me want to cwy, I mean cry. I was tedious in this regard, Lucy had told me, and I knew she was correct. I needed to buck up, and, in that moment, I bucked my shoulders, upward. "Aaaaannnd," Laura went on, "we're making good headway with the affective program, the expression of emotions. Emily has the data on that, that tells us he's talking about his feelings more, squeaking less. Are you noticing any changes at home?" she asked. Her hair was in a type of bun on the very top of her head, with strands of stray hair on every side, as if she had forgotten to let it down after a steamy bath.

Lucy answered. "Some," she said. "Right, Rose? We were just saying last night, he told me he was feeling hungry, which was new, I know that's not one of the words we're working on, but didn't he say he was angry, when he was with you, Rose?"

"Yes, when he was in the bathtub," I said. "He said he was angry at the water for going down the drain. He was slapping at it with his hands. Well, I modelled it for him first, then he imitated me, and we slapped at the water as it was draining away. That was probably the wrong thing to do. We don't want him slapping, obviously, when he's angry."

Dr. Cove smiled. Her silence made me uneasy. I wondered if she was thinking this mother is unstable, a water slapper.

"Getting excited seems to be the biggest issue for Roger," Miss Emily said. "When he sees a bug, sometimes, especially if it's dead, or, of course, Ryan O., I mean not if he sees Ryan O., but if he's in his group for centres. And since we introduced mystery numbers — it's a guessing game — he likes to guess eleven, or if he's revved up, he'll say mystery number instead of making his little screaming sound, which is okay. It's ..."

I interrupted to ask Laura, "Do you think you'll be doing any assessments this year, before Christmas? I only ask because at the hospital he just clammed up, he wouldn't say anything, well, he wasn't talking nearly as much then, but he's changed so much. I just wonder if you think he would still be at the third percentile rank. Does he really seem to be there to you, Laura?"

Lucy crossed and then uncrossed her legs, causing some upheaval for the low table.

"He's making gains," Laura said, "so I would like to just leave it until June, then I can do some testing. It's the language component I'd be looking at, not the speech side of it. Is he acquiring concepts? Does he make inferences and predictions? For now, apart from the intervention we have in place, just talk to him lots, which I'm sure you do already, read to him, of course, model inferring. Miss Emily is reading *The BFG* to the class, so if you wanted to do the same at home, that would help." She smiled and put her file into a plastic bag.

"My briefcase is at the cobbler," she added, grinning, "being cobbled. Anyway, sorry I have to run. I'll let Emily take over now. I want to stress Roger is doing great, and he's a delight to work with. If you have any concerns, just call, you have my number. Fridays I'm in the office."

Dr. Cove said, "Thanks, Laura," and they exchanged a look that seemed to imply impending thorniness, a problem, a snag? My inferences failed me, and Dr. Cove carried on. "Rose, Lucy," she said, "before Emily begins with her summary of Roger's progress, I need to introduce to you the possibility of an individualized program plan, or IPP, for Roger. Rose," she said again, ominously, "I'm sure you know what I'm talking about. We're thinking Roger would benefit from the more structured approach of an individualized plan that would address his unique needs." And quack quack bleat bleat she continued, about funding and signatures and nothing *really* changes. Emily can review this colossal document with you and so on and so on. At the conclusion of this exposition, Dr. Cove removed her glasses and placed them on the table, as if she had been reading her own inimitable thoughts.

I knew what I was hearing, I had already sat in on similar meetings and read IPPs in the files of five- and six-year-olds, fat like a tax accountant's dossier. And, I had forecast this moment in a dream about Dr. Cove ice-fishing, from which I had awoken when she commented to me, serene above a frozen lake, "We try to find the right fit for all of our students."

I had asked, "Do you mean the right fish?" and at this question, she had flicked her hook in my direction.

"So, is it acceptable to the two of you if Emily proceeds with her goals and her progress report, after which we can discuss next steps?"

"Can we wait just one minute?" I asked, rubbing a spot above my right eyebrow. "Are we maybe not focusing too much on Roger's deficits? I can tell you right now, predicting and inferring will make many people agitated, many older people, and he's only three and a half, so I'm not sure I'm ready to commit to IPP status just yet, on the basis of . . ."

Here, Lucy leaned into the tabletop and said, "But Rose, we need to get on top of this. He can't be screaming in Grade 1 and chasing Ryan O'Hanrahan around the room because his name starts with O. You have to be reasonable." In her black turtleneck, with her slight Kentucky way of talking, she looked and sounded like an authority flown in from the USA, someone with a book titled *Giving In To Your Special Child:* a look at twentieth-century incarceration rates. As well, I had never heard her use the phrase *to get on top of,* as in, to curb. I was sinking, I felt, below the surface of the yellow-topped table, with no one; soon I would be among the ankles and knees of the women in charge.

"We're not really expecting him to infer and predict," Miss Emily offered, her cheeks and throat pinkening. "If you could just trust me with this, Rose, and take a listen to this proposed, I repeat," she said, smiling, "proposed, IPP, I could get your input on the goals and strategies. We're a team here, you know."

"I know, I know," I said. "I just get the feeling, I am *inferring*, that we're being railroaded here."

"But it's for Roger, to help Roger, it's not about us," Lucy had to say. "It's not about us."

"You don't know the system like I do," I practically hissed, so that Dr. Cove felt she needed to interject, with her glasses on again, peaceably.

"You don't have to make any decisions right now, Rose. If you would like to listen to what Emily has to say, look at the document, take it home and read it over, then decide. The decision is always the parents' to make, but we enter into the conversation knowing we all want what is best for Roger." Dr. Cove nodded to Emily and pulled on the left cuff of the white blouse beneath her cerise jacket.

Emily began. "Roger is coming along nicely," she said. I cast my eyes upon her inevitable documentation, and I composed myself and swallowed and cascaded downward in my soul, like a vertebrate who has made the move to a lesser phylum after millennia of struggle with an unyielding backbone. Miss Emily carried on with her goals, and they made sense, and I agreed right then and there and signed to it, as did Lucy, of course.

We left the school and walked home, and Lucy spoke first, on the sidewalk. Now the morning was fully under way and the sun was in our eyes. She said, "Don't worry. It'll all work out. Don't feel bad."

"I'm not feeling bad," I said.

"I know, but you will, and you have to keep in mind that Roger is not worrying. Roger is not sad. If he were hurting or writhing in pain, I could see it, yes, worry, fret, but he's not, he's fine, he's learning, he's just a little behind the curve, that's where he is, he's behind the curve but he's going to catch up. You'll see."

"I'm not feeling bad. I am just a deep worrier. Someone has to be."

"Consider the lilies of the field," she said, smiling at her church history.

"Isn't that in reference to clothing?"

"No, it's in reference to anxiety."

"Well, consider the dead frozen grass of autumn in Calgary."

"Same thing," Lucy said, "it toils not, neither does it . . . spin."

"I'm not spinning."

In front of our house, I said again, I'm not spinning, and she kissed my cheek, got into her car, and drove off to work. I crossed the street to the Marinis and got Roger; it was only 9:45, and I had an office afternoon and considered calling my supervisor and claiming to be sick, but on a Friday afternoon with the system shut down for parent-teacher meetings, I would be a laughably obvious malingerer.

Roger and I spent the rest of the morning on the couch, watching TV. I think he sensed, I guess he inferred, I was peculiarly hollowed out by how the big world viewed my small son's mind. I was defeated and ashamed of wanting him to be more like me, and I said to Roger three times, "You're so good!" reinforcing him not for his behaviour, but for his self. "Can I get earmuffs?" he asked.

"Sure," I said.

"Betty has them. That's what Betty has. Pumpkin colour."

ON TWO SEPARATE November afternoons, I walked to the golf-course pathway. I wanted to listen to the grass in the wind, and the leaves, many of which had fallen, their yellow corpses dense on the ground and the scent of everything dustier and sleepier than spring or summer. I still thought I might see Joe if he happened to be in the nearby trailer park or even camped in a more distant stand of shrubbery. I'd read about a virus, CMV, and wondered if he had had some symptoms, maybe there had been an outbreak of something at the shelter; a virus can live forever and commit acts of sabotage. That's what rubella did.

seventeen

A MONTH AFTER the parent-teacher interview, the Peter Lougheed Elementary Christmas concert came to pass. Roger wanted to wear two neckties, but I said no, and Lucy concurred. She said, "Robert's coming with us, and he'll be wearing his necktie, so that makes two." We waited outside for him to creak down the outdoor stairs, and as we began our walk, half a block from home, the power went out. And the night was clear and starry, even in the city, for a minute, and we didn't care if the concert had to be cancelled. But the lights came on, and the city returned, and the stars vanished. At the school, dropping Roger off at his room, we were pleased to see most of his male classmates and one of the girls, Hayley, in neckties, pleased to believe Roger had the cachet to create a trend.

Since my own high school days of glee club, I realized, the Peter Lougheed Elementary School Christmas concert was my first experience of being in a gymnasium filled with parents, grandparents, and siblings, all emitting a particular yearning for a particular child. The yearning is a melancholy thing, I thought, almost like looking at the night sky because in those numbers of young bodies, the parent must confront the unexceptionalism of her own Lisa or Betty or Ryan. Roger might have been absent, but the group of three- and four-year-olds would easily close in to fill his space. And so you yearn for your child to live forever, even at the lower percentile ranks. You think, maybe this generation won't die after all. That was the feeling in the gymnasium crowd, I'm pretty sure.

We found three seats together halfway back, with me on the aisle next to Lucy and Robert beside a grandfatherly type. I wanted to be on the aisle in case Roger needed rescuing, or, if at the final moment, Miss Emily called on me to explain him in a few quick phrases: George, the open marriage, the train, Joe, Lucy, Dennis in Medicine Hat, Robert and his fashion choices, Lucy again. We're different, we have a tenderness you might not see, but if you would care to listen to my preamble . . . In my ribs, I felt some hyperventilation and did the counting, in to three, out to four. The lights dimmed, and I settled down. Dr. Cove took the stage in a gold and purple dress and told us to be proud of our beautiful and caring children (our eyes met, I think) and to be appreciative of the ability and dedication of our teachers. We applauded and at the tumult of sound, I wondered if, when his class's turn came, Roger would squeak or screech on the stage.

We hadn't talked about the stage out of an anxious awareness of perhaps planting the impulse in Roger's mind. Impulse control was a phrase with which I had become very familiar, incredulous at how much the average three-and-a-half or four-year-old had in storage in their limbs and mouths.

Roger's class was second up, after Miss Karen's. They rambled and marched onto stage wearing Bristol-board antlers, and there was Roger for everyone to see. I had a desire to fly from my chair and twirl around the rafters like a deflating balloon of motherhood pride and fear. Lucy took my hand, and I said, "Roger is so cute." After some signals from Miss Emily, the class sang "Up on the Rooftop" to generous applause and some whistling. Roger knew the words to the song and sang with such gusto, his cheeks were red. I didn't see anyone else on the stage. Lucy observed that Jamie, the bad boy, seemed to have been ousted from his position by another boy, Harvey, who stood in the front row with his arms crossed, scowling. The children returned to their classroom and played, maniacally I assumed, for the remainder of the program, there being insufficient seating for three hundred and some children. I could have played maniacally with them but stayed and slowly returned to some point on the high-average end of the bar graph of human excitability. After the show, we returned to the kindergarten class to enjoy tarts on paper plates and Tang in Dixie cups. But it was none of the bad boys who came to find Lucy and me, with our mouths filled with pastry, nor was it Ryan with whom I had already spoken in an attempt to measure his possible tedium with Roger. It was Scott, to whom I had paid little attention, and about whom I had no opinion other than to know his father worked for a television station and usually dropped Scott off at school, dad and son both occasionally wearing bow ties, which I was surprised Roger had not noticed.

Scott must have been watching me and Lucy. He must have walked toward us with determination, but neither of us noticed.

There he was, in a little blue sports jacket and jeans, a white shirt and bow tie. As he was regarding me with intensity, I said, "You guys did a great job with your song."

Then, I know this for sure, he checked around for the whereabouts of his teacher, Miss Emily, and asked with a mature sense of authority, "Did you have AIDS and that's why Roger looks the way he does?" The room was very full, because parents from the morning class were there as well, but I don't think anyone other than Lucy heard, and Roger was far away, preoccupied with the newly opened train centre.

Gazing downward at Scott with a sociological detachment, I did not reply, and Lucy, in her cool weather reporter's voice, without a trace of anger, said, "No, Roger's mom did not have AIDS, but more to the point, that's an inappropriate question. Roger looks just fine the way he is, in fact, he's very handsome. I suggest you move over to where the tarts are, and get yourself one. They're very good. I think Miss Emily went to a lot of trouble to bake them."

Scott, entirely unintimidated, studied me, then Lucy, and me again, before threading his way toward the tarts. I searched the crowd for his parents, but could not locate them. Was he perhaps there alone, having dressed himself and headed along the sidewalk during a power outage with an unstoppable need to ask his AIDS question? I didn't find out. Of course, I had wondered what was being said in the neighbourhood about Lucy and me, but I had no interest in caring, I told myself.

Of Scott, Lucy said, "He's just a kid."

"I know."

"Are you okay?"

"Yes, of course." At that moment, Betty's mom, Marilyn, shouted hello in my left ear. "Didn't they all do a fabulous job?" she asked me. People were beginning to smell crowded. I placed my arm around her but for a moment could not speak. This room was the world, and the world was this room.

Lucy said, "They were terrific. Betty looks gorgeous in that dress."

"Yes," I added. "Betty looks so pretty, and her dress is beautiful!"

"Oh, thank you," said Marilyn.

"You and Greta and I should go for coffee again soon." I was shouting above the din.

"I'll call you." Marilyn mouthed the words as she drifted off in the direction of the tarts.

eighteen

MOM CALLED TO tell me George was visiting. "He's here right now," she said. "He's upstairs. I don't know if I should say anything, but he said he'd like to get back together with you, even with Roger. I shouldn't say *even*, but you know what I mean, even though you have a child. There aren't that many men who would step up to the plate like that. Anyway, he's upstairs having a bath, so I thought I'd call. He could give you a call if you like."

"Roger is his child, did you forget?"

"No, of course not. I didn't forget. Do you want him to call?"

I could so clearly picture George in the bathtub. He had likely brought along his inflatable bath pillow, upon which his shampooed head would be resting. George believed in leaving shampoo in for two to three minutes, as if it were a treatment. He would likely be thinking about cake: he liked to have his bath after dinner and be clean and sweet smelling for cake at nine. I knew Mom would have got him a cake or more likely made one.

"No, Mom. I'm not interested. I'm happy here. Lucy helps me out." I said goodbye, ending the conversation abruptly, not having yet explicitly told Mom that Lucy and I were *paramours*. I told Lucy Mom didn't need to know. I told her I was queer enough with Roger, and I was. She didn't understand the mathematics of acceptance in Flax and area. Evincing one oddity was okay, but with two or more you were simply making a display or had something seriously wrong with you. Lucy had grown up in a city, albeit Lexington, which undoubtedly had a different social abacus with which to snap beads of judgment back and forth, but regardless, anonymity would factor in, lovely warm and comforting anonymity.

Lucy did not hector me. If Mom had lived in Calgary, she would have, hectored, but if Mom had lived in Calgary, I would have been more open with her. I told Lucy what Mom's friend, Eve, had said about a lesbian couple (heroically) living in an apartment on the main street of Flax. She'd said, "Why do we have to look at that?"

Even Mom had gone to the defence of the women: "Well, they have to live somewhere."

"Yes, but right on the main street?" Eve's objection seemed to spring from a fear the lesbians would be seen on the main street, and all of Flax judged, consequently.

"Seen," I said to Lucy, "making a to-do, which could be just as easily done on a back street, far from the holiday traffic." I was pleased with my corroborating case study. "You see what people from Flax are up against."

"But your mom was supportive, relatively speaking."

"She felt sorry for them. That's her emotion. I've told you that."

"Well, we can make her feel sorry for *us*. We'll tell her the community association wants us to move."

"That would be a lie."

"She doesn't need to know that. You phone her up and say, 'We're having some trouble here. The community association is kicking up a fuss about us living here.' She'll say, 'Because of Roger?' And you will say, 'No, because we're in a lesbian relationship.' She'll say, 'What's that got to do with anything?' and you will say, 'I guess they're a lot like Eve.' Then you ask her, 'Do you want to talk to Roger?'"

"Ha, sure, next time I call her," I said.

Two or three days later, George called.

"Hi, Rose."

"Hi, George."

Silence.

"Christmas is coming!" George announced. "Will you have a turkey? Did you have a turkey for Thanksgiving?" This was his way of prying.

"We had a small turkey."

"Who is *we*, if you don't mind me asking?"

"Roger, Lucy, and me, Carmen from next door, and Robert who lives in my old apartment." Silence. "What did you do?"

"I spent the day with Brian and Jean." Friends of George who were on and off, on and off.

"They're back together?"

"For the time being."

"How's Mom? She told me you were visiting. Are you still there? Did she bake you a cake?"

"I'm back home. She's fine, and yes, she did, a banana cake with frosting. Very good. Of course, a frosted cake is a ... what?"

"A happy cake?"

"You remembered."

"Not easy to forget."

"You and Lucy stick to yourselves, except for the neighbours, do you?"

"No," I answered, a trace of annoyance in my voice, "we have friends. We even have *lesbian* friends. We're going out with a couple tonight."

"What are their names?"

"What difference does it make?"

"I like to know your friends' names."

"Barb and Iris."

"Do you like them?"

A brief exasperated silence prefaced my reply. "Yes, George, they're my friends. And, I have to go now. Lucy needs some help with Roger. Good to talk to you."

"What are you going to do with Barb and Iris?"

"We're going to a club. It's called the Green Room. I'm telling you because I know you will want to know. Anyway, I have to go. Lucy needs me."

Quickly, like someone speaking around a closing door, George asked, "So, you're not moving back to Flax?"

"No. I have to go, George."

"I see I'm getting the bum's rush."

"Good to talk to you. Bye."

Lucy did not need help. Roger was excited about seeing Tracy, his babysitter, later. She always showed up with a jigsaw puzzle and was able to engage Roger in watching her jig it together, for hours sometimes, a pursuit he rejected with Lucy and me. He and Lucy were in the bedroom, looking through her clothes, planning an outfit for the evening.

"Lucy doesn't know what to weaw." He still had trouble with r's, despite the good news of Laura of the plastic bag briefcase.

Lucy's colours were black, white, and grey, but she had a red silk shirt Roger liked, and he was standing on the bed, holding it in front of him as if checking for the fit. "Weaw the Principal Cove one, Lucy," he said.

"That's not exactly her colour, Roger. This is just plain red. Hers is fuchsia. Do you see how this is red?" I asked. I wanted him to start using just one routine colour word.

Roger said *cracker jack*, tossed the shirt at me and flopped on his knees to the mattress. Then he shrieked. King Two ambled into the room and waited for something to happen.

"Okay," I said, "don't go silly now. This is red, this blouse is red so just say red, Roger. Say it."

His miniature Big Ben gonged, eight times, and Roger began rolling from side to side, laughing and squealing, "It's eight O'Hanrahan! It's crick, it's crack."

Deciding to interrupt before he got to smoke detector status, I placed my hands on his shoulders and said, "Stop rolling around and listen to me, Roger. It's a red shirt. Just say that, please. Then you can go back to rolling around."

"No," he said, in a harsh high-pitched bark like a Chihuahua. "Your face is red."

"Okay, fine, good use of the word red. You can go back to flailing."

I wasn't angry, but I was stern. Then Lucy decided to wear the red shirt, saying, "I guess I'll put on the Principal Cove shirt."

"Can you just call it red? Help me out a bit here?"

"You're being rigid," she said, "colour is subjective."

"I *know!*" I said. "I know about colour!"

That was when we both felt the bed shaking and saw the eeriness of Roger, rigid and bent at the arms, pale and leaving us for his own subjectivity. That was the day he had his first seizure.

NOT LONG AFTER, I got the urge for going, again, to quote Joni Mitchell. Even though Christmas was in the air, even though the lights and alcohol could be seen through the windows on the street, I lied to Lucy and wondered: why the lying? It resulted in guilt and misery. Were these *my* two emotions? I had told Lucy I was going to a meeting in Red Deer, I was staying overnight, but was not yet sure where. I might bunk in with a colleague named Sandy. The decision to go was spur of the moment because one of the other psychologists had backed out but really, I should have offered to attend earlier, because the meeting concerned inclusion for students with disabilities in all Alberta schools. I needed to be more of an advocate for Roger. Righteous lying was easy; any flushing of the face could be attributed to the passions of selflessness. As for my job, what I would actually do, how I would cover my tracks, I supposed I'd call in sick from a pay phone somewhere.

I had selected a day when Lucy had to be at work by nine, delivered Roger to Mrs. Marini, and returned home to pack up the tent, the sleeping bag, the stolen heavy quilt, a pillow, toiletries, and one new set of work attire for tomorrow. I also gathered up several sections of old newspaper and matches, then made cheese and raspberry jam sandwiches with the bread I had baked. I was feeling rather jaunty. My hands and legs seemed to believe I was going for good: they always fell for that same story.

Destination: Red Lodge, a provincial park near Bowden, home of a Vietnamese restaurant where I was planning an early lunch. By then my extremities wouldn't know exactly what was going on. I was right about that, and the pho was delicious. And I wondered if pho had the phonological qualities to become one of Roger's favourite words, if he would like to hear that, in Vietnam right now, it's pho o'clock. Yes, he would like to hear that, he would love to hear that, and he would maybe almost trip and almost fall, or really fall and start to shake. Weather-wise, conditions were better than expected for mid-December, sunny and clear as if the light were actually manufactured within the fields and structures and trees by a whitish-yellow chemical. I looked forward to lying outside, inside my stolen quilt.

The park was empty, no cars, no trailers, no oddballs in tents conducting social psychology experiments or studying the flora for a master's degree thesis in botany. I thought I would pay the park fee, but I didn't. I had visualized someone watching me pay from behind a verdant screen, but once the tent was up, I visualized no one watching me not paying. Did I not pay in taxes? And this was not the camping season, and there were no services, although the taps worked, the outhouse had paper and the Little Red Deer River ran as if it were late fall, which it was, technically. Not enough cold days or nights yet to freeze it.

The Little Red Deer River may be the world's most soothing river. It's likely the one Joni Mitchell would have wanted to skate away on. It is never rushed but winds and has, farther west than Bowden, by dint of shallow and modest flowing in soft terrain, created deep coulees where you can imagine the Indigenous people standing and watching the Europeans travelling toward them with their world of things. At the Red Lodge Park, the river has a pebble beach, and, with my quilt, I walked to it, a five-and-a-half-foot baby. The river made faint sounds like water falling asleep. No breeze moved the branches of the trees. Their roots probably extended into the riverbed, and I pictured them, at least the spruce, beneath me, drinking water. The others were senescing, no doubt.

The earth beneath the pebbles was dry, and I opened the quilt and folded myself inside, placed my head on the pillow and stared at the sky. I was aiming for peri-senescence, which I thought to be free of obligations and yet more conscious than the peace that passeth all understanding. Inert, I lay on the stones for a minute, maybe two, until I simulated a seizure; I shook my arms and legs for maybe fifteen seconds, then stopped, then started again, tensing my neck and torso as well and holding my breath for as long as possible, likely no more than forty seconds. I gasped and lay with my eyes closed and said, "Roger. Roger."

We had gone to the hospital, of course, and they had said seizures weren't that uncommon among young children. They had taken his temperature, and it was 102 Fahrenheit. Had he had the fever for long, they wanted to know? I said I didn't think so, because I had no idea. Well, he has one now, the nurse said. Lucy said, as far as we knew he hadn't had one for any length of time. She reminded me of a calm goose, hissing in slow motion.

"It's called a febrile convulsion," said the nurse.

"I was under the impression you needed a very high fever to trigger a convulsion."

"I wouldn't say trigger is the right word."

"Cause?" I asked, tentatively.

To the nurse, Lucy asked, "What word would *you* use from your thesaurus of hospital verbs?"

"You know, if you're going to be abusive or hostile . . ."

"No, she's not," I said. "We just want to know what to do."

Lucy mushed her face into Roger's hair and emitted a high-pitched squeal. Roger smiled and said, "Lucy makes the sound!" He was fine. He had regained consciousness on the way to the hospital and now seemed refreshed. We were behind one of many curtains in a long, narrow, and enervated room. "The doctor will be here shortly," said our nurse, and left us. I said, "Lucy, don't antagonize the medical people."

"She was implying Roger had had a fever for days and we hadn't noticed."

"Maybe he did."

"No, he didn't. Of course, he didn't. I check his forehead a lot."

"Oh, I didn't realize. Why do you check his forehead a lot?"

She didn't answer, and I felt incompetent and of below average intelligence. "Did someone tell you and not me he might have seizures?"

"No, of course not."

"You just thought of it and checked his forehead accordingly and a lot?"

"Do I have the caesar?" Roger asked.

"We'd all like a Caesar," I said.

"Caesar is the name of a drink," Lucy said. "It's also a person's name and sometimes it's a dog's name," and this information seemed to satisfy Roger. "It can also be the name of a Roman dictator," Lucy added. She was sitting on a metal folding chair, speaking authoritatively about all subjects, while Roger and I sat on the examining table. Roger rested his head on my shoulder and looked upward at me with glassy eyes and raspberry-coloured cheeks. I sighed. The hospital is a structure that will diminish you. Just give in to it.

For a moment, we sat in silence, and then Lucy came to life. Looking at Roger, she said, "I'm a dictator dog, and my name is Caesar; I do what I want. I stomp all over the Rubicon."

"Lucy can stomp," Roger said, smiling broadly.

From behind the curtain next door came a shhh. Lucy stood and repeated, "I stomp all over the Rubicon." She licked Roger's cheek, dog fashion, and he laughed. I said, "Maybe it's best not to get him all worked up."

In response, Lucy made stifled barking sounds. "They gave me a surgical mask, and now I sound like this," she said, barking raspily into Roger's neck until he shrieked, of course, which is when the doctor entered our cloth emergency bay. Abruptly ending her routine, in a whoops, I almost fell motion, Lucy returned to her chair.

Dr. Park with his grey crewcut was older than I had anticipated. He looked as if he had had a career as an astronaut, gone back to school and found the classes unnecessary: Tell me something I don't already know, was his demeanor. "What's the problem?" he asked.

"He had a seizure," I said, "and apparently he has a temperature of 102."

"What do you mean by seizure?"

"I mean stiff, twitching, and jerking for about forty-five seconds, turning kind of blue."

"What's your name?" he asked Roger and listened to his heart, asking, with a sideways head, "Otherwise he's healthy?"

Roger said, "Roger."

Looking directly into the doctor's eyes, I decided I was not going to mention the developmental clinic, and the decision felt good, as if briefly all of my speaking apparatus were made of polished silver. "Yes."

Dr. Park wasted no time delivering his advice. "A seizure is alarming, but not uncommon. Watch him. If he has another, we'll do an EEG. For the time being, give him two baby aspirin to bring the fever down. Lots of water. And I'll give you a prescription for some antibiotics, just in case. Okay?" That was that.

Watch him. Bustling my silver-lined throat out of the way, these words shone in a neon white and did not demonstrate a capacity to turn off or burn out. I sensed they might occasionally tip backwards, singeing some tissue in my visual cortex before righting themselves. Of course, we had to tell Principal Cove, Mrs. Marini, Miss Emily, Laura Flynn, the after-school ladies, Carmen, and Robert. This would complicate all the playdates I imagined to be imminent. You have to watch him, you have to watch for the electrical malfunction. A little spark on the surface of his brain, and away he will go. You have to watch his head as if it were a barn with delinquent kids inside, smoking. The lenses in my eyes were wearing out or down.

By the Little Red Deer River, I fell asleep and woke with the sun in the branches of a bare balsam poplar. Maybe I was in Dad's idea of heaven, those black limbs filled me with pleasure and relief. Had a tree root ever had reason to rise to the surface of the earth, a riverbank let us say, and gently absorb a human body, digest it for the liquid and the nitrogen? You would think trees might have thought of that, although they weren't big on adaptation other than growth. Theirs was a simple formula: stand your ground. Without the vulnerable spinal column, remain unbreakably upright. Were there other life forms so effectively equipped to stand and wait? They might not be watching, but why would they? I think I knew then, although I did not make a resolution or sign a proclamation, that I would not, no, should not, skate or swim or run away or leave for another lying overnight junket.

I walked and ate the sandwich I had brought with me. I sat beneath the quilt on a bench and watched the sky change. I loved to be alone, but, later in the darkness, in the tent, and wasn't there a prison near Bowden, I may have had a rigour, and I unzipped and checked and unzipped and checked and finally slept until awakened by the sound of a group of ducks, roughhousing at dawn in the placid Little Red Deer. I tore down the tent and threw it in the trunk and drove to a coffee shop in Olds. From there, I timed my arrival home so that I could smell the remains of Lucy and Roger's breakfast when I opened the door. They were gone, Roger to Mrs. Marini, Lucy to the optometrists'. King Two greeted me with passion and devotion. I could be at work by one, I told him, let's just have a nap.

LUCY WAS DOING more columns. Every other week, "One Thing" ran in the *Herald*, and, of course, she had her regular monthly piece in the *Bugle*. For the *Herald* column, she travelled farther afield, to other neighbourhoods, videotaping. Any topic was allowed. People might talk about their dog, someone else's dog, streetlights, cousins in B.C., fly-fishing, Rice-A-Roni, anything. Five times she had been recognized in places outside Renforth, a coffee shop, a movie theatre, two restaurants, and the zoo.

On Christmas Eve, as we waited for Robert and Carmen to come by for drinks, Lucy got out her camera and interviewed Roger. She said she would put him in the paper, and he shrieked and said he didn't want to be in the paper, taking her meaning literally. "I can't fit in the paper."

"I mean your picture and your comments."

He was in the living room in his Pluto pyjamas. Ryan O. had told Roger he wanted Pluto pyjamas for Christmas, and ergo so did Roger. They were new for Christmas Eve. Roger's forehead was shining, and his hands were warm, and he was warming up in other ways, running up and down the hallway with King Two, semi-shrieking his favourite words, *cracker jack* and *screech owl*, weaving them into his answers to Lucy's questions. Lucy had thought the video camera might slow him down, I admit, she did say that, but it wound him up. She should have turned it off, but she, and Roger, and King Two, and I, could not stop what I called afterwards, to myself, the buffoonery, and to Lucy, *your acts*, as if she were the subject of a book in the Bible.

"What are you hoping Santa will bring you?" Lucy asked. On the recording, there followed a longish pause, Roger's breathing as he glanced at me, Lucy, me, Lucy and said, "Lego castle, alarm o'clock, a snowly owl, no a screech owl . . . cracker jack." With cracker jack, he shrieked like someone being stabbed. Truthfully, we all laughed through five or six variations on this story. King Two came and went in the frame, looking a bit like a sock puppet, licking Roger's cheeks. "What are you going to leave for Santa and his reindeer?"

"An apple, a carrot, a cookie, a cracker jack, a jick jock..." and so on.

Lucy's appetite for this kind of perseveration equalled Roger's. They shared the same plumbing for repetition, as if they both had a sink or flushable appliance they could fill, empty, fill, empty, forty-five times and still enjoy the whoosh. Whereas I eventually began to imagine Roger's shrieking on a playground repelling peers like a whistle with a bad seal.

"Maybe we should stop the interviewing," I said, after jick jock entered the conversation for the third time, commanding King Two to sit on his big pillow, but they carried on to another tier of giddi-ness while I went to the kitchen to get eggnog. From there, I could hear Roger calling to me:

"Mom! Mom!"

"What?"

"Mom!!"

"What, Roger??"

"Cracker jack o'clock!"

Which was when, on the videotape, the five times I have watched it, I was able to see Roger suddenly tire, place his head on the arm of the sofa and seize up, stop breathing and turn white, then inhale with a superhuman need for oxygen. Of course, right away, Lucy called for me, "Rose, Rose, come here." I heard her from the kitchen and again on the video, the camera on the floor, my voice saying, *Oh, no, not again. Is he hot? Does he have a fever?* Was I irritated? Why did I sound irritable? The seizure was over, and Roger lay there, me kneeling with my hand on his head, Lucy sitting, holding his feet.

"I can't go to the hospital today," I said. It's on the videotape, we forgot to turn it off, five minutes of the living room floor and wall, a corner of the Christmas tree.

"We don't have to. They can't do anything but order up the EEG," Lucy said. Roger moved and sighed and said *Mom* in a whisper, and I wished I had a pouch for him somewhere on my skin.

"I'll get a blanket," I said. Then, "Maybe I'll get two."

"That might make him too hot," Lucy said. "It's already warm in here with the oven on. We need to take his temperature."

"It won't make him too hot," I said to Lucy, using a tone of voice I might have used with Adrian when he was ten, or George when I was sick of him.

"Okay," she said. "Okay, okay."

Returning with the blankets, King Two's toenails clacking behind me, I asked, "Why do you have to get him so worked up?"

"Worked up?" Lucy said, in her manner, as if being on the defending side were unheard of, for a Strike, from Lexington. Her mouth hung open. "He was sitting on the couch, talking. He was being interviewed for 'One Thing.'"

"Can you be serious for once?"

"I am."

"I mean with your choice of words."

"My choice of words is how I talk. It's my *choice*. So I caused the seizure because I made him laugh? What about you harassing him about colours and feelings?" There we were, attributing causes, arguing about fault, all on the videotape.

"Harassing? I'm just following Laura Flynn's orders. Which don't include rewarding Roger for saying *jick* and *jock* and performing crazy acts."

"Acts?"

"I mean actions. I just said a minute ago maybe we should stop the interview. I knew it was too much, too much carrying on."

"Carrying on? What does that even mean? If *carrying on* and causing Roger to laugh and get a little wired brings on a seizure, then I guess he has a seizure disorder. He can't not laugh."

"No, I realize that, but he doesn't need to get so worked up he's saying the same stupid words over and over and screaming like a wild man."

"How are they stupid words? They're just words he likes the sound of."

"You don't think *jick* and *jock* are stupid words, especially when strung together in the context of nothing?"

"Jick," Roger whispered.

"No, I don't, actually," Lucy said. "Plus, jock is a word."

Wrapping a blanket around Roger, I said, "Go and check on the pigs in a blanket. I'm going to be here with Roger and make sure he's warm."

"*I'm going to be here with Roger and make sure he's warm.*" She was mimicking me. Roger was too dazed to notice. Lucy went on, "No, I say no to pigs in a blanket. You can check on them. I'm going for a goddamned smoke. I wouldn't want to *carry on* with the stupid pigs in a blanket."

"What's that supposed to mean?"

"Nothing."

"Fine," I said and muttered into Roger's hair, "Go for a smoke. Walk around and be famous in Renforth." All quiet for a moment as Lucy pulled her coat from the front hall peg.

"What was that you said?" she asked. At her feet, King Two wagged his hind end, expecting a walk, and she looked so lovable, tromping back into the living room in the winter coat she'd found at the Goodwill with its big collar and covered buttons in one of Roger's preferred colours: chocolate icing.

"I'm sorry," I said. "Let's not argue. There's no point."

Lucy didn't answer, but she also didn't slam the door, not that she ever had; she closed it gently. Outside in the easement, she smoked a cigarette and talked to King Two. I looked out the living room window and saw her; as evidence, my feet appear on the video, and later we laughed about that. When Lucy came inside, she turned off the camera. Roger, all of us, were back to normal by the time Robert and Carmen arrived.

ON A COLD SATURDAY in January, with the smoke rising straight from the chimneys and twirling in tight curls from exhaust pipes, Marilyn called to say we needed to talk, then she said hold on for a minute; there was a crashing sound, and she set down the phone. I didn't want to go anywhere. Lucy had been to the Co-op in the morning to get eggs and a chicken and onions and carrots. The food was planned, and we had a movie, *Splash*. Roger had not had another seizure, and Dr. Suleiman was on to the referral for the EEG. We were becalmed, we were like people with felt linings zippered to the furniture; even the cars were plugged in for coziness. Roger had a six-pack of suckers, a treat for going the entire week at school without once screaming.

Marilyn returned to the phone. "Sorry, that was Joel trying to get the roasting pan out of the drawer. He's trying to be helpful." Because Marilyn had had two older sons, then Betty, she was a veteran of motherhood, a zoologist who had studied children and maybe even defended theses. I always took her advice. She said, "Can you meet me and Greta at the Beanie? Around two? It's kind of important."

"Really? What's going on?"

"I can't explain it over the phone. It's too . . . vague."

"Is it about R-o-g-e-r?"

"Yes, indirectly. Greta can come. Can you be there?"

"Sure, okay." Roger and Lucy promised to wait to watch the movie. "It's Marilyn. She needs help with something."

Lucy put the Flames toque on my head, and I entered the white and blue day and my car's stiff interior, manipulated the reluctant gear shift, and drove on frozen tires. That degree of cold is silencing and alienating, and you marvel that the radio stations are functioning.

Greta and Marilyn were there at the coffee shop, and so were others drinking coffee as if the cold were just a flavour, and I congratulated myself and warmed to my own hardiness. They had a chair waiting for me, and I got a coffee, and no one even mentioned the weather, the big blue Arctic sky and the rime on the Beanie's big window. Greta was wearing a beret pulled down over her ears, and I wondered momentarily if we were going militant, if we would be putting a board of education superintendent into the trunk of a cold car. We exchanged weather pleasantries, and without a transitional change in facial expression, Marilyn asked me if I was at all aware of what was going on with Roger.

I was alarmed, of course. "What do you mean? He had a good week. No screaming!"

"Greta and I are able to be there more than you," Marilyn said, and Greta nodded. "And we've been noticing some things we thought you should know about."

"Well, what?"

"There's a little group," Greta said, "that not exactly picks on Roger, but they try to exclude him in sneaky ways, when Emily's not watching."

"But it's their so-called gym class where it's not so subtle," Marilyn said. "Mr. Morrison is the gym teacher, which is weird in itself that they have a separate gym teacher, but that's when Emily has her prep time. He's used to older kids, and he doesn't notice stuff like I do. Scott's the ringleader, but there are others; Arthur, Joel, and Harvey are the principals, and it's like they have a kind of radar for each other. When Mr. Morrison is busy with his whistle and his instructions, they get themselves positioned so that when it's time to choose partners, Roger can't find one. I've seen it happen half a dozen times on three different occasions. So Roger winds up being Mr. Morrison's partner, because there are twenty-one of them, and nobody ever seems to be absent on gym days. Plus, I really hate to tell you this, but I overheard Arthur saying, 'We have a special name for you, Roger.'"

"To Roger, you mean?"

"Yes, right while they were all sitting on the circle, and Mr. M. was getting the soccer balls from the storage room."

"Oh." My stomach felt like a close relative of roadkill, a trampled animal still breathing in its final spot. "Arthur said that?"

Greta tried to console. "Don't inflate it in your mind, Rose. Kids say stupid stuff like that all the time, every day. Marilyn and I have just happened to notice a pattern, and we think you should be aware of it."

I picked up my cup, trying to sip, but my lips were stiff, so I set it down again, and Greta placed a hand on my arm.

"What's happening with the birthday invitations?"

"So far, there's just been Betty's, but Ryan has promised to invite him to his, in March."

"And Lisa, too," Greta added.

I was fluttering around in my ribcage, inside the coat I had not yet removed when I realized I *had* to move up a notch to where Marilyn and Greta were, beyond crying, and a cold day was a good day for it. I could be stoic, anyone could, that was what psychology would tell you.

"Maybe take an afternoon off when they have gym and just sit and observe. You have every right to do that. Tuesday and Thursday they have gym. Just keep on top of it," Marilyn advised.

"I will, I will," I said, and my lips unstiffened. "I'll ask Principal Cove on Monday."

"No, just call Emily," Marilyn said. "Cove will get on their case and make it worse. Call Emily, and say you're following up on a physio appointment, gross motor blah blah blah."

"Should we have a physio appointment?"

"No, no, just *say* that."

"Okay." I was so grateful for their friendship, I couldn't remember ever having felt such gratitude. For a Christmas gift? For roadside assistance? I was in their group now. I said, "I'm so grateful for you two and your help." And we talked about other things.

In the car, I waited a full fifteen minutes for the engine to warm up, even though Lucy had told me the optometrists had told her two minutes was plenty. I did not shiver, neither did I shudder, but contemplate the children in Roger's class, I did. Were they in reality little pack animals? If this were a nature film, and they were bobcats, bobkittens, would they just kill Roger? No, I didn't think so.

The windows weren't frosted over, I had only been an hour and a bit, but the temperature was sinking with the sun. Three-thirty, and already the downtown was looking dusky, but I was revving at the higher notch, or the first notch, of imperviousness; still, I would have hated to have to drive to Medicine Hat at that hour and in that temperature. And I wondered if Asa was warm with the Dolly in Bankview, and what Dennis might be doing, and what he might possibly look like. As soon as I got home, Lucy would pull me into the bathroom and ask, so what was the big deal? And that is what happened. I answered, "Marilyn just wanted some advice on something that's going on with Betty. She's insensitive to others' feelings sometimes, just once in a while."

"Who isn't?" Lucy asked. "Plus, she's four, isn't she?"

"She's five, actually."

"So Marilyn just wanted some free psychological services?"

"More or less. We're an informal support group. Anyway, let's watch the movie. I need a drink, maybe some rum." In the living room, King Two lay on the floor, at my feet, sometimes on my feet. I held Roger while he sucked on lemon- then grape-flavoured balls of sugar on a stick.

nineteen

I BEGAN AN ASSESSMENT of a girl named Jody. She was thirteen and had cerebral palsy, walked with a walker, and talked slowly. She had what Laura Flynn, SLP, would call a dysfluency. "I think, I think, I think, I think, I think, I think about cheese a lot," Jody said to me. There may have been one or two more *I thinks* before we began our cheese conversation. Jody liked curds and Swiss cheese best. She was pretty. Her movements were slow, especially on the right side, but she was able to complete the testing, even the timed subtests, although the results would necessarily be viewed with *caution* because of the motor limitations. Still, her IQ was measured at the 0.5 percentile rank. Ninety-nine-point-five percent of people would score higher. When Jody was six, her IQ was at the fourth percentile rank. Now it was lower. Why? Because the norms are looser when you're five or six, even more when you are three or four. "This is likely where her IQ will stay," I told her mother, Carolyn, explaining the elasticity of childhood norms, wondering what team I was on.

Carolyn didn't seem to care about the percentile rank. She shrugged it off, she said, "Pffft." I was impressed with her presentation of self. First of all, in her pea jacket and rust-coloured wide-wale corduroy pants, she appealed to my middle-class SES. Secondly, as I have indicated, she was, or appeared to be, uncowed by norms. "Jody's Jody," she said. "You know what I think?" she asked. "She's a pretty girl, and that has probably, more than anything else, helped her get along."

We were completing an adaptive behaviour scale, a questionnaire pertaining to practical and social skills. "She's been to the junior high sock hops, although she doesn't do much hopping with that clunky walker, but there are always other kids around her. They say kids are cruel, but I haven't found that to be the case. If they are, they're no more cruel than adults." I nodded, I made notes and asked Carolyn to rate her daughter on her domestic and social skills, could she do her own laundry, could she tell if someone was making fun of her? "Of course, I don't want her to have a serious boyfriend ever," Carolyn said, laughing. "But that's not just because she has a disability; I feel the same way about her older sister who's fifteen."

I asked, "Do you know anything about the Wild Rose Centre?"

"Ha," Carolyn said in reply. "I know the doctor advised me to place Jody there when she was six months old. He said, she's going to be retarded, it won't make a whole lot of difference to her where she is.

You need to think of your other daughter and your husband, your family life, as if Jody were a creature from the lost lagoon."

"Oh," I said. "That's more than a little bit heartless."

"I didn't follow his advice, needless to say."

I wanted to know if she had visited the place, but why would I ask that, implying she had considered institutionalizing her daughter. Carolyn went on, "Although I've heard things have improved in the past few years, that they have group homes now, and I'm not saying Jody won't have to live in a group home someday."

"I have a son," I said, "with a delay. He's only three, almost four, but he's definitely different from most of the kids. Plus, this doesn't help, he's a little funny looking, he's an FLK, I guess the doctors would say, a funny-looking kid."

"Oh," Carolyn said, "I didn't mean to boast about Jody being pretty."

"That's okay. I'm glad she's pretty. No offense taken. Anyway, some friends, parents of two of the other kids in the class, told me a few of the kids were ganging up on my son in gym, kind of collaborating so he couldn't find a partner when the gym teacher tells them to pair up."

"Oh, dear," Carolyn said.

"So I went and observed them in gym, and nothing happened, of course. They were all being nice to Roger, and he didn't have any trouble finding a partner for the activities, so I don't know what to think."

"Don't think anything," Carolyn said. "I mean, just think some of the kids are little assholes some of the time."

A bell rang, and the hallway sounds began, junior high school voices and bodies wanting to get to the next thing, then the next after that.

"Three months ago, I would have been crying, telling you about my son. Now look at me, I'm not. But anyway, I'm supposed to be listening to you."

"I'm happy to listen," Carolyn said, "and if you want some advice, when you have a kid with a disability or a lasting problem, you have to grow a, not a hide exactly, you don't need to be insensitive, what you need is to develop a second brain, one that's all reason, no emotion, and let it sleep most of the time, just wake it up for meetings and those times when you have to make major decisions." Using the notepad she had brought with her, Carolyn sketched a pencil-coloured brain, tore off the page and handed it to me, and we shared a bit of a laugh.

"I'll keep this," I said, then tallied up the score from the adaptive scales and, incredulous and uneasy that I had become a calm purveyor of rankings, told Carolyn, "Jody's still at the fourth percentile rank for practical skills and social skills."

"Well, she's holding her own," Carolyn said. "I suppose that's a good thing." She didn't say pffft.

SINCE THE THROWING of the spatula incident, I had seen Asa three times: once in November, again in December before Christmas, then not again until March, and always at the gym. He would never do anything like change his habits or routine to avoid someone, he was a pylon around which others altered their course, which I did, half-consciously. Were the three run-ins random or unexpected? Yes, maybe. I gave myself the sort of advice a lying despot gives a minion, and in response, I told the despot I was a special case with idiosyncratic and idiopathic drives and desires, or, desire; I had only one, and it was well-contained, no one knew about it, and no one ever would. It was a hobby, really, more assuredly pleasurable than most and damaging to no one. Just seeing Asa in November at the track, seeing his glaring face, and hearing his unfriendly hello had sustained me until December 22, when he had relented and said, "Oh, for God's sake, Merry Christmas, Rose," and given me a sweaty hug, after which I had felt golden, as if a flashlight were training a golden beam onto my stunted heart.

Then not again until March, the day after my birthday. I had been too busy, I had a sore ankle, I really did not want to see him frequently, because if I did, I might have to drive to the hospital, to emergency with no evident symptoms, nothing seemingly real, just a psychological swelling or two, I had babbled (words to that effect) in the direction of Asa's smiling and uncertain face, concluding with, "So now I'm almost thirty, as of yesterday."

Asa nodded, took my hand. "I'll buy you a coffee. Come on, Rose. No hard feelings, no hard anything."

In the little café at the gym, I said to Asa, "It's not that I don't want you to have any hard anything for me, it's just that I haven't been totally honest yet, still. You told me about the Dolly, and I told you about Lucy, a little, but there's more. How is the Dolly?"

"She's well."

"And she's still the Dolly?"

"That's how I think of her. It's probably wrong, but that's how I think. Her name is Stella, and she knows I call her the Dolly."

"Does she mind?"

"She hasn't said so, and she's no shrinking violet. She told me to lose ten pounds."

"Your belly?"

"I took that to be her meaning."

"I like your belly."

This conversation took place, whisperingly, in the coffee lineup. We found a half-clean table, swept off the sugar granules and sat down. I said, "Well, the actual story is I'm in a relationship with a woman named Lucy, like I told you, *aaaannd* I have a son, whose name is Roger. Roger's dad is George, the man I was married to for a couple of years in Ontario. He's still there. He gets along with my mother better than I do. He's actually from Alberta, but he seems to have emigrated to Ontario. Anyway, Roger's got a problem of some sort. He had an assessment, he's only three by the way, almost four, he'll be four in May, but he had this assessment at the Children's Hospital, and he didn't do very well, he was at the third percentile rank for everything, right across the board, a true developmental delay."

"Ah, he'll catch up," Asa said. "My cousin Carl was slow, he didn't talk until he was four, and then he turned into a kind of weird genius, reading everything in sight."

"Mmmm, yes, maybe, I don't know if he'll catch up. I'm trying to get used to the idea of him not."

A gust of chlorine smell passed into the café; through the window to my right, I could see the moms with their little ones, bobbing in the pool. "Do you like the smell of chlorine?" I asked Asa.

"I do," he said. "It reminds me of summer and cannonballing in the water, back in the days before I had to lose ten pounds."

I smiled at him. I said, "Roger's a little bit funny looking. People sometimes do a double take when they see him in a store or at the library."

"That's when you tell the bastards to take a picture because it will last longer." Right. This was what I thought of as Asa-bluster.

"I know, I should, but I can't. I can't get into fights over my son's face or the shape of his head. Much as I'd like to deck someone at the Co-op one day, it likely would not advance the cause of Roger in the neighbourhood."

I paused and with my lips made the convincingly equine noise Roger had recently begun to find hilarious, then carried on. "Anyway, to tell you everything, I've spent a lot of time wondering about causes, and it turns out George, the father, has a brother, Dennis, who's also disabled in some way, and the family put him in the Wild Rose Centre when he was five, the Wild Rose Centre in Medicine Hat. And I called, and yes, he's there, Dennis Petrie is there, and I'd like to go and see him. I'm curious to know if he looks like Roger, if there is some here-tofore undiagnosed Petrie condition, but I don't want to necessarily go with Lucy, because she's not that excited about the connection, about somehow soldering our little situation with the Petries via a relationship with Dennis, which I can fully understand. I mean, the last time I talked to Mom, who doesn't yet know I'm in a girl-on-girl relationship with Lucy, she told me oh, by the way, George would like to get back together with you, with Roger, of course, not all men would do that, she said, take on a child, and I had to remind her that Roger was George's child. Of course, she said, I know that. So, I had to stress that that was not going to happen. I told her I had Lucy to help me out. 'That Lucy girl,' she always calls her. She says, 'Does that Lucy girl do anything to help out?' Yes, I always say, and I want to say, well, she paid all the bills for about twenty months, but I haven't made the situation explicitly clear, as I have said. I will though, soon, it's on my list."

Asa sat with his lower lip thrust ahead of his upper. I was feeling pretty flirtatious, I admit, gelatinous in my organs and vigilant, watching and noticing hands, fingers and shoulders, buttons straining on shirts, the chin.

He said, "Hmmm. I don't want to complicate your situation, or more importantly mine, ha ha, but I'll go to the Hat with you some-day, I can work it out, if all you want is to lay your eyes on this Dennis guy. I might stay outside and wait in the car, though."

"Well, I was hoping you would come inside with me. You could impersonate a Petrie. I've thought about looking at a lot of disabled people in one place, and it kind of scares me. Kind of. I'm afraid I'll be appalled. Because what if he looks like Roger? Or Roger looks like him? What if? I might pass out."

I had really only fainted the one time on the grave mud, but I was playing that card.

"Okay, okay," he said. "I'll go with you, I don't know about inside, that's up for negotiation, but I need advance warning. We can talk about it next time we see each other and in the meantime, we'll carry on with whatever this is, our meatless affair," he said, laughing. "That's what Stella called a vegetarian party she attended not long ago. We'll go to this place in the Hat together someday."

"Thank you so much," I said. "Thank you, thank you."

He stayed to read his paper, and I left for work, entering my car in a dither. Lucy would come with me, obviously, if I asked again, and if I told her it was important to me. But apparently I loved a tentative plan with Asa. It was in the anticipation, like looking forward to a vacation in an undiscovered city. Nobody knew this place was here? Incredible.

Roger would still be at Mrs. Marini's; in ten minutes, she would walk with him to school. Lucy was with the optometrists, and I was on my way to work, where I would begin my *psycho-educational* report on Jody. This was good, report-writing calms a person down, and I required calming. I was like someone with six or seven full jars lined up on a shelf in her chest, awaiting a squad, someone to begin shooting so as to splash the contents together, to free them, to pool them, to watch the glass fly to other shelves. I breathed in to three and out to four again and again; parking became the new conundrum.

My desk wasn't exactly where it should have been, it felt closed in because the divider between Vera's and my space had been shunted from its usual spot. Repositioning the orange wall, I wondered if Vera had moved it to accommodate a newspaper-mediated tryst, at night, in the mothballed school. Or the janitor? Drake had been fired from Mesmer High, Mom had told me, for having booze in his cleaning supplies cupboard. All things are possible. I had a new bag of beef jerky in my drawer and ripped it open, withdrew a chunk and began to gnaw before I found Jody's file and sorted through my papers.

twenty

RYAN O'HANRAHAN'S FIFTH birthday was on the last Saturday of March, the invitations having appeared in the cubby mailboxes a week and a half in advance. Not everyone was invited; just some of the boys, including Roger, and the bad-ish girl, Hayley, and Betty. Had Betty become inexplicably popular as the year went on, or was she being invited as a default companion for Roger? No one could or would say. Moms and dads were also invited to stay; there would be a pitcher of sangria, and Ryan's dad, Tim, to drive anyone home needing a lift. Party hours were from two to four-thirty. The razzle dazzle of preparing, buying a gift, which had to be a soccer ball, buying a new tie, taking escalators, red-cheeked running from room to room the morning of the party, squeaks progressing to shrieks, exhortations to use words, all had Lucy and I worrying about a third seizure, which did not occur. *We* had been seizure-free for three months now, the EEG was booked for May, and we were happy. We had also found a Sylvester necktie and what Roger called a Sylvester-colour shirt. "It's blaaaaack," I said to him, and white, I added, as he got dressed, bleating the word, thinking this might make it stick, and that was his outfit: black velveteen pants, black shirt, Sylvester tie, and Mickey Mouse wristwatch.

Lucy never wanted to be early or on time. King Two watched forlornly from the living room window as we left the house at 2:10. We walked the four blocks to the house of Ryan O., knocked and entered via the backdoor mud room full of shoes and boot smell, added ours to the jumble, and entered the kitchen. Four moms and Betty sat around the table. Betty, as fashion-eccentric as Roger, was wearing a very orange dress with exuberant crinoline, lifting the skirt of her dress from her lap like a sunrise. Presumably the dress got in the way of playing with the other children at the party. Introductions were made, Lucy positioned herself against the counter, near the sangria, and I led Roger to the living room, where Mr. O., seven or eight boys, and Hayley were assembling an expensive-looking train set. "Wow, Roger," Ryan said, "you look fancy."

Tim O'Hanrahan introduced himself, said "Nice tie," to Roger, and I happened to notice Scott, from the Christmas concert, looking up at me with a four- or five-year-old's manifestation of fear and loathing. Roger squeezed into a space among the kneeling group, and I returned to the kitchen to stand next to Betty, who needed to explain that she could not sit on the floor in her crinoline. For the first time, I realized that Betty, in her dress and glasses, looked like Dennis the Menace's girlfriend, Margaret.

Now where was Scott's mother?

Ryan's mother, Maureen, whom I knew worked as a nurse at the General, was of course present, thin and muscular, with her long orangey-red hair; and the others were Arthur's mom, Hazel, wearing a cowboy hat and plaid shirt, I knew not why, Hayley's mom, Ellie, whom Lucy and I would later call the over-laugher, and Jamie's mom, Tracy, who kept her ski jacket on. A folding chair was offered, and I placed it next to Betty and as close to the living room as I could, filled with a precarious energy and a need to check and check again. "Can I have a turn?" I heard Roger ask twice. Then Ryan's voice, "It's not ready yet." Then what I presumed was Scott's voice, "Don't *wreck* it," followed by a low mumble from Tim.

Hazel said, "Well, it's the famous Lucy Strike in our midst. One thing about me is that I read the *Renforth Bugle*, religiously, but that wouldn't make for much of a column, would it? Unpaid advertising for the *Bugle*, I suppose it would be."

"How do you choose your . . . subjects?" Ellie asked, with a laugh some might call a shout. Clearly, they all wanted to be chosen by Lucy, just like me. After a period of rapt listening to Lucy, still leaning against the counter, now holding a glass of sangria, I asked in a neutral sort of whisper, "Has anyone met Scott's mom?"

"She's a surgeon," answered Betty. "She operates on sick people."

"Oh. I guess that's why I've never met her. Where's *your* mom?" I wanted to know.

"She went to the store to get a card," said Betty, taking a long swig of grape pop.

"No one has met Scott's mom," said Tracy, skeptically, as if Scott's mom were a rumour.

"Much like Principal Cove's husband," added Ellie, with an un-restrained ha!

That's how the talk went. From the living room, relative quiet, as I craned my head around the door frame at regular intervals. Lucy smiled at me from her spot, and I experienced a whammy of love. And Marilyn showed up with her card and stood by Lucy at the sangria bowl, and while the others were talking about skiing, I leaned close to Betty and asked, "Have you ever heard anyone call Roger names?"

She belched and asked, "Like Roger?"

"No, like making-fun-of-him names."

Betty turned her grape-mustached face to me and considered. "Nope. Well. Bughead. Sometimes they call him Buggy Bughead, be-cause he likes those dead bugs." And at that instant, Marilyn came to shoo Betty from her chair and into the living room, from which soon after came cheers and the faint sound of an engine moving on tracks.

Moments later, pouring herself a coffee mug of sangria, Maureen called out, "Are you guys ready for cake and gifts?" They weren't, really, but Tim herded them away from the train and into the kitchen where the moms stood up and the kids sat down, sharing chairs, pair-ing off, Hayley squeezing in next to Betty's crinoline, Ryan as the birthday boy on his own chair near the cake, Roger in an agonizing few seconds with no place to sit until Ryan and Maureen, together, said, "Roger, right here," indicating the half-chair Ryan had available.

We sang, and the gifts were torn open. I was proud of Roger for thinking to get Ryan a soccer ball, which emerged as the obvious favourite of the gifts. The snow had been gone for at least two weeks and would no doubt return, but for now the backyard was bare, and after the candles and cake, they all went outside. Maureen made coffee. Tim returned to the living room to play with the train set, Betty followed him, and Lucy finally sat down and made everyone laugh with her story of a "One Thing" woman who said she had been hoping Lucy would come by, because she had Five Things and wasn't going to compromise. I needed to go to the mud room and look out the window to the yard. The kids seemed to be in teams, running after the ball, and Roger was following along, veering in towards the ball and the action, then away as if he either wasn't sure what to do or didn't want to get kicked or to dirty his velveteen pants. I watched only briefly as my son, my creation, maneuvered the dumb surface of the grassy earth, appearing to be routinely buffeted from the human edge, the verge, I thought, Lucy's word. "Well, the third thing," Lucy was saying, "was the person who had parked in front of her house the day of the street cleaning."

"I can see that," said Tracy in her solemn voice.

twenty-one

WHEN I ARRIVED at the school to pick up Roger, he was missing. The staff in the playroom thought he was in the gym, and the gym staff thought he was in the bathroom. That's where he told them he was going, but he wasn't in the bathroom, and his coat and backpack were on his hook. Miss Emily was still at school, and was worried, of course, when she heard the news. He was surely outside in the yard, we thought, it was a warm day for April, and he could be waiting for me and ready to go, walking the perimeter, checking the time and waiting for a bus to pass by, but he wasn't. Some boys from the neighbourhood were playing on the apparatus, as it was called, and Emily asked them if they had seen a boy in a long-sleeved red T-shirt, with the Flames insignia. No, they said. Their politeness caused my eyes to prickle. They even checked inside the tube slide, as if he could be clinging in there. They hadn't seen him standing by the eastern steps, either, where he sometimes liked to watch the little grocery store across the street.

We went back inside and looked in the washrooms and all the classrooms upstairs and down. Every space where he was not increased my panic. I have read somewhere that a person never forgets being lost; searching for someone missing, someone who is your child, must be the other side of that primal fear. The eyes are alarming the rest of you, and the rest of you is detaching from the eyes and asking: can this be all the light has to say? It can't be.

Dr. Cove had had to leave at three for a meeting downtown at the board office; we called, and the secretary tracked her down, and she said she would be there in five, everything would be fine. In the meantime, I should drive home, follow the usual route, and check the house; she'd been through this before; it's what the cops would advise. Then if he wasn't at home, come back to the school, and we would call the police. While I did that, they would continue to look in the school.

I drove toward our house on 6th, along 12th Ave. and then north on 5th St., along 13th, then up to the Trans-Canada. My eyes were feeling like fingers in a bad dream, grabbing at streets and sidewalks and shrubs and slipping away with no strength. Roger, Roger, Roger, I said, pulling up in front of the house. He didn't have a key, but he knew where the hidden one was, under a flat stone in the poppy bed on the west side of the house, not that he had ever used it or would likely know how to. The key was there. I replaced the stone and went inside anyway, and there was King Two, shaking his ears because he'd been asleep, wondering where Roger might be. "I know," I said, "I know, we'll find him." The interior of the house, so still and familiar, seemed full of a cozy and yet sickening nostalgia for five hours prior. Roger, I said, and looked in every room and under every bed. I was calming down, or dying a little like people in the cold, I really could not tell. The order of events in time was accordioning out and snapping inward to a stop. Was this how Einstein came up with his ideas? Altered by the search for a missing child? I had to call Lucy, and we had to call the cops. Why hadn't I called Lucy?

"Cottonwood Optometry, this is Lucy, how may I help you?"

"Lucy, Roger's missing."

"What? What's going on?"

"We can't find him. He's not at the school, and he's not here; I'm at home looking for him. His things aren't gone from the school, his coat and his backpack are on his hook. Dr. Cove told me to come here and look. So I'm going back to the school, and we're calling the cops. I want to call right now, but I also don't want to until I'm with the people at the school."

"I'll be there in fifteen minutes. They'll understand here."

"Come to the school."

"Yes, yes, of course. But we need someone at the house in case he shows up at home."

"Right, right, you're right. I'll ask Carmen."

Carmen was at her place and of course willing to wait at home for Roger. She would call the school immediately if he showed up; in her white T-shirt, she looked like a nurse or someone prepared for an emergency.

We called the police, or, I called, with Dr. Cove and Miss Emily and Esther from after-care all sitting with me in Dr. Cove's office.

Death was hovering in the atmosphere, the way it can materialize with minds in a group; it was there, I was not imagining.

The constable on the phone asked questions, how old was Roger, had he possibly gone with a friend somewhere? No, his best friend had left earlier with his sister and his second-best friend had gone home with her mother right after school. He didn't have any other friends. Did Roger have any problems at home? At school? Yes, he's a bit below average, I said. He's a bit eager to please, I suppose. What was he wearing? What colour is his hair? Now it all seemed excessively real and floodlit. Does he have any particular interests, any places he might have wanted to go to? The Saddledome, maybe, I said, we haven't been in it yet. Or any number of places, really, places he might not have mentioned, with outdoor clocks that make a noise.

He said he would let the cars out on patrol know, they would be on the lookout. It was too soon to consider him missing. We needed to look some more and make some calls to classmates' homes and to his friends, then get back to him. His name was Sergeant Bloomfield.

Now the outside was becoming dusky — it was a lovely evening — and everything appeared situated and contained except for my own body, which required a reinforced supply of atmospheric pressure to tamp down the billowing agony. I looked at my hands, and they did not know what to do. Lucy arrived at last and became managerial. She said, "I'll call Betty's house, and Ryan's; they might know something. Roger might have said something to one of them, or both. Knowing Roger." I said I had to go to the bathroom, and Lucy said, go, go, it's okay, it's going to be okay. The hallway was brightly lit for the janitor and the large quiet broom he'd left leaning against the wall, so he could look in all the locked and little-known places. But instead of the bathroom, I went outside, holding the door so it would not lock behind me, and looked at the spaces and lives carrying on and longed like a swimmer to plunge into the undisturbed sidewalks and traffic and life behind windows. Take me with you, indifferent citizens and illuminated porches. Could Roger be walking to the Saddledome? Would he be there by now? He'd have had to take Edmonton Trail, where Carmen's dog once was hit by a van, then cross the Langevin Bridge and pass by the Cecil Hotel. Could he possibly know the route? He half-knew his traffic and safety rules, didn't he? No, not really. His clothing was bright. But he would be excited, with all the cars, the sky changing colours, and what if he had a seizure? There he'd be lying on the sidewalk. What then? Someone would help him. Surely, they would. I could see his little body moving along with people on the sidewalk, people looking sideways at his face, wondering if he was a homeless kid or a kid preparing for homelessness and walking in the direction of the homeless shelter. They wouldn't think *that*. Someone would help, a helpful man or woman, there were lots, maybe an aimless person would help him out, maybe even Joe. Don't be imagining everything. It'll be okay, like Lucy said. He might even have gone in the opposite direction, to the Co-op. There was the kids' ball pit there. Could Roger possibly know to cross 16th Ave. at the light? That's what we always did. He might know, and there he would be, in the ball pit. And there was that book there he liked, *Thirteen*, with all the pictures within pictures. He might just be there by now, with Maria the clerk with the salt and pepper hair, filling out the necessary paperwork for a lost child at the Co-op.

Lucy had talked to Marilyn, who quizzed Betty, but she knew nothing. Marilyn said she would go out and drive around, then come to the school. She said she'd make a few phone calls first, if that was okay, and Lucy said yes, without reservation. Would I have said no? I'd rather the whole community did not yet know my son was missing? Lucy reiterated, yes, that would be so helpful, thank you so much. I heard this as I returned to the classroom and imagined burying myself in the foothills. The soil had been soft near the Petries' cabin.

"What about Ryan?" I asked.

"No answer," said Dr. Cove. She had called the hospitals and now was calling the police again, asking for Sergeant Bloomfield and handing the phone to me.

"Okay," he said, "we'll start looking now. I need to know, does Roger have a best buddy?"

"Well, he wants to. His name is Ryan."

"Have you called Ryan's place?"

"We just did, but there was no answer."

"Kids don't always answer."

"I'll walk there," I said, "right now. It's just down the street."

Sergeant Bloomfield said to call him back and let him know what we found out.

Lucy and I were at Ryan's house in less than two minutes. We knocked, and Ryan's junior high sister, Julie, answered. No, Roger wasn't there, she said. She yelled up the stairs to Ryan, "Did you see Roger at after-care?"

Silence. "Yes."

Ryan came down the stairs, leaned over the railing looking a little unusual, we both thought later, maybe a little like a five-year-old with an imaginary concealed weapon. Julie asked, "Did he say he was going to go somewhere?"

"No." Ryan was wide-eyed with sincerity. He ran back upstairs. I had an urge to ransack his room for clues, but we needed to get back to the school, where we looked some more, up in the old janitor's apartment, even though it had been locked. There we found a bat coming to life on a window sill. The janitor, Mike, said, he's bound to be here in the school somewhere, he's playing a game on us, and Lucy said, I think so too. We'll find him. He's okay. You have to think of the best outcome. Think it, she said to me, in a commanding voice. The bat moved its head as if in response, and we creaked our way down the narrow stairwell to the second floor, and back to the office.

Norma the secretary had returned to the school to phone parents, and I sat next to her. She dug in her purse and gave me a pill. Lorazepam, she said, it calms the nerves. Put it under your tongue. I did as instructed and sat in a chair near her, where students sat if they needed medication at noon. Norma was the dispenser, she was the sensible solid crux of the school, and yet she had a nerve pill. I wanted to clutch onto her, I wanted to be pinned to her like a brooch. Lucy, Emily, and Dr. Cove were in the office, strategizing.

After each call, Norma said, "No sign," with efficiency, without emotion. I was wishing she would choose a different phrase, but she had volunteered to come back to work at six-thirty in the evening. I guess I thought the pill had given me permission to free associate. I said to Norma, "They say it doesn't signify, sometimes, in British novels, to mean it doesn't matter. Just, you saying no sign made me think of that." My voice was going vibrato, like someone in a Halloween production.

"Well, it does matter, obviously," said Norma, dialling.

"Of course. I'm really grateful you came back to work. I just meant it does signify when there's no sign. Never mind." I was thinking of the boy in high school, dead near the selvage, his still face in the woods. For several hours, I was the only one who had known he was there. His poor bereft parents. His poor, poor parents. I looked around the office, so usually busy but now only bright, and in the fluorescence of the room, every single thing was decidedly not Roger.

Lucy said, "Come in here, both of you."

"Not right now," said Norma, striking names from her phone list. But Lucy pleaded, and Norma relented and in Principal Cove's office, Lucy said, "Let's pray."

"Good idea," said Principal Cove, and with the four of us standing in an unlikely circular formation, Lucy led us in an abnormal prayer, saying for God's sake, God, help us out, help us find Roger, lead us to him, and thanking him, God, for the help we had not yet received. My heart swelled for Lucy and her worried face; she loved Roger as much as I did, I could see, at last. And I felt the pill start to help, although I could not be convinced the prayer would make a difference.

Norma returned to the phone. Sergeant Bloomfield dropped by and said nine times out of ten in these situations, the child shows up at somebody's house, there's a miscommunication. They'll call. He drew a pie chart on a movable blackboard Principal Cove had in her office, divided it into ten parts and coloured nine of them with yellow chalk. That's to help you remember, I think he wanted to say, your odds, but he held back.

The pill was definitely helping, more than God, although some would argue God had created benzodiazepines. I said, "I wish we had switched to daylight savings this past weekend. A week from now, and it would still be bright outside." Although, now that darkness had fully arrived, was no longer creeping toward us, I felt a little more confident. The streetlights were on, the evening was warm, Roger had long sleeves. Long sleeves against the world.

Norma completed the phone list, and we sat waiting. I called Carmen, and she picked up on the first half-ring. No news. At 8:15 the phone rang, and it was Tim O'Hanrahan. Principal Cove put him on speaker phone. He had called our house and spoken to Carmen, who had said to call the school. He said Roger was there at their house, and he was fine. It had been a gong show of an evening. Julie had just told him we'd been there looking. She was in the basement getting ready for band camp and had gone out with Maureen as soon as she got home to get the things she needed. Ryan was upstairs playing, as it turns out, a game called giants that the kids seem to have made up, which involves no adults, adults not knowing the rules.

"So apparently, what happened is Roger saw Ryan leaving with Julie and ran after them and got here and just went upstairs to Ryan's room. Julie was downstairs in her room and didn't hear any of this, then, like I said, she went out with Maureen. I made some dinner, and Ryan insisted he would eat upstairs, I didn't really care, I wanted to watch the hockey game. He came down for about three helpings, so that should have told me something, I guess. But it's not that I didn't go up to his room, I did, but I guess Roger was hiding in the eaves, we have eaves we use as storage space along the south wall of the two upstairs bedrooms, and in Ryan's room there's a little elf door into them, we call it, so that's where Roger was most of the time, being a giant, apparently. He just wandered downstairs three minutes ago and said he was ready to go home. They were done playing giants."

"Rose and Lucy will be right over," Principal Cove said.

"I've spoken to Ryan," Tim said. "I'm really sorry about this. I feel awful."

"That's okay, we'll be there in a minute," Lucy said.

I TRIED TO SEE it as developmental progress, that Roger now had the capacity to make his own plans. He had managed to follow Ryan and Julie O. home via a combination of lying and subterfuge. "I'm going to the baffroom!" "I was quiet in my shoes!" "I walked in!" (To the O'Hanrahan house.)

And giants is a game where kids stand around the model train in Ryan's room, straddle it like giants, and everything becomes small so you could wreck it if you want, but grownups can't know about it because they're the other giants, and if the grownup giants find them, the train track giants will be put in the zoo. Hence, Roger had a Nerf gun in his hiding spot, and Ryan brought him food. "Then I went small again," Roger explained to us, "and went downstairs." Apparently, it was a good day for him; "I had a fun," Roger said.

twenty-two

IN LATE JUNE, after the pre-kindergarten school year had ended, we, Lucy and Roger and I, went to Medicine Hat to meet Dennis. We passed the yellow fields of canola, formerly known as rapeseed, and in and out of their pockets of smell, a little like feet. In the backseat, Roger was quiet, the drive lulling with the sun and warmth and the nearness of summer dust and insects. Although the landscape was wide open, you could imagine yourself in a mile-wide nest.

Dennis had been told to expect us, but we had no other knowledge of what he knew about his visitors. We had been told he was in a wheelchair and *could get around* in it. The day I called to make the appointment, I had been told it was Dennis's birthday, June 15, the same day as George's. Dennis is turning thirty, the woman on the phone had said, whispered in fact, as if it were a secret. Were they planning a party? I asked, and she had said, oh, no, as if that were implausible. George and Dennis were twins, but George had been too sad-faced or shamefaced to admit it, I guessed. I told Lucy I was not surprised. "So, Dennis might look like George and have George's DNA and be doubly related to Roger, but I can't say I care, because Roger looks nothing like George." Lucy lit a cigarette. I was more worried they were fraternal twins, and we would be meeting a living and institutionalized vision of Roger's future. At that possibility, my mouth went dry.

The Wild Rose Centre was large and quiet, with no sign of life at all, unlike the last time I had taken a look at the place. It had the atmosphere of an abandoned college with a few remaining quarantined students, or Three Mile Island. We parked and told Roger, this is where your uncle Dennis lives. It might be a kind of funny place. The staff on the phone had said Dennis would be ready for us at the front reception desk — no doubt they did not want people snooping around — and we did not want Roger frightened by a *parade*, as Lucy had said, of people with *infirmities*. I had not quibbled with her choice of words, because I agreed.

We approached the front door in silence, I think because the place gave off a kind of roar of pasts, presents, and futures under blankets and in chairs, but inside we went. The light at reception was bright and artificial and reluctantly mixed with sunlight, and the smell was tiring — food, bleach, and Mimi's litter box, masked but present. To the left and right of the front desk: doors, closed. But there was Dennis, a wizened version of George in an electric wheelchair. I could see immediately the same long eyelashes. Behind the desk, Ruby, in a white dress with name tag, said, "You're here for Dennis?" and did introductions. We took turns, Roger, too, shaking the cool, thin fingers of Dennis's left hand, his right being drawn up to his chest. Instead of hello or happy to meet you, Dennis said, "I hope we're going to Dairy Queen."

"We could," I said. "Can we walk there from here?"

"Yes, of course, I wouldn't have suggested it if we can't walk there. I go with Joan." Dennis took a deep breath after every fourth or fifth word. When he finished his sentence, he frowned.

"Okay, who's Joan?" Lucy asked. Roger watched Dennis with interest, as if he were an exhibit. He wore a watch on his left arm, and, with movement, it rode up and down his broomstick-thin wrist.

"Joan's a staff," said Dennis. "Are you coming here to be staff?" he asked Lucy.

"No, we just came to visit. This is your sister-in-law, Rose, and your nephew Roger."

In response to this information, Dennis said nothing; he fiddled with a control on his chair.

I asked, "Do you know your brother, George?" Unsure if this was an advisable sort of question, I looked to Ruby for guidance, but she didn't seem interested; she was on the phone to someone on the other side of one of the closed doors, I surmised, from which came banging sounds. Dennis did not answer. "Are you coming to be staff?" he asked me.

"No, we're visiting to see you."

"I guess *he's* not coming to be staff," Dennis said, pointing toward Roger and laughing like a cough, his skeleton moving in his chair from the efforts of his muscles.

Ruby hung up and said, "The Dairy Queen's just up the street. Dennis knows where it is. You should take this bib. He can be a little messy with the chocolate dip," handing me a dome-fastened, adult bib that I draped awkwardly over my forearm, then shoved into my purse. Dennis buzzed out the door, and we followed, along the Wild Rose's concrete pathway to the sidewalk. Lucy maintained pace with Dennis, while Roger and I speed-walked behind.

The DQ was not busy, and the staff there knew Dennis and his ordering habits, which was a help. We all got small chocolate-dipped cones, found a table and a space for Dennis's chair. "I'll need the bib," Dennis said in an impatient tone of voice. I affixed the bib, while he commanded Lucy to get more napkins. "I'll need more than this! Didn't you get any training?" Lucy got napkins, and Roger ate, watching.

As Dennis bit into his ice cream, bits of chocolate landed on his bib, four times, and each time he blamed me. "You dropped that piece of chocolate, you stooge." "Pick it up, you're fired!" "I'll have you fired in no time," and so on. I plucked each fallen shard from the bib and placed it in Dennis's mouth, feeling the softness of his inner cheek. Against the boniness and hostility of the rest of him, this vulnerable bit of flesh warmed my heart to Dennis.

"Who did you say you are?"

"Rose. Your sister-in-law. I was married to George, your brother. I guess you don't remember him."

Again, the empty look. "Are you in trouble with the law?"

"No, I'm not."

"Well, you should be."

"Why?"

No answer. By then, he had ice cream on his chin and in his beard stubble. "Do you want me to wipe off your face?" Lucy asked.

"Okay, go ahead."

With the eating, Dennis's watch had inched up to the bend in his left elbow, and Roger, still chewing, had moved as close to the chair as possible in an attempt to read the time as it might be conveyed by this unusual man and his unfamiliar watch.

Dennis shouted, "You can't have my ice cream!" His lips constricted, he looked furious. Roger can be unresponsive in the right way at times, and on this occasion, he was. "I don't want it," he answered calmly, "I'm liking your watch."

"It's a piece of junk," Dennis said, ice cream dripping from his chin to the bib. "If you want to get me a present, buy me a watch and a jigsaw puzzle, and don't say I can't do them, because I can. I'll have you fired." This time he smiled, so Lucy and I laughed with relief and extra gusto.

twenty-three

AUGUST 22, 1986, we took Mom to the airport, came home, and sat in the easement. She'd been with us for ten days, during which she decided she wanted to meet Dennis. We had been back one other time after the first visit, before last Christmas, when we took him a watch and two puzzles. That day, the sidewalk was too snow-covered for a trip to Dairy Queen, and, after accepting our gifts, Dennis had left in a huff to a place of mystery behind one of the big metal doors.

With Mom, he was pleasanter. Her one emotion beamed out of her, I guess, in a genuine worry and sorrow for Dennis's well-being. She promised more puzzles, in the mail. George was living in Mom's basement now and working at the creamery. Mrs. Drury was running a type of foundation for lost Petries.

Also, while Mom was here, Joe showed up. He knocked on Robert's door, got no answer, then came to the house next door. He could only stay for a few minutes, because he had a ride to Olds he had to meet in the Co-op parking lot. He was going to find a place to live there, because he was starting school at Olds College in September, studying landscaping. He looked the same, as unusual as I had remembered him, and Mom studied him with curiosity and said nothing, and I wondered to myself if she would call in a few days to offer an observation she shouldn't make (I just thought it was kind of odd how much Roger looks like that Joe who dropped by). I so hope she does not. Roger had a good sophomore year at pre-kindergarten, but Mom can't really understand what that means. He was invited to six birthday parties, for Arthur, Harvey, Hayley, Ryan, Betty, and Lisa. He shrieked less this year, he told a variety of *jokes*. He'll not likely be ready for Grade 1 when the time comes a year from now, but there will be accommodations, Dr. Cove has said. This fact is a dust storm in my lungs, but Mom doesn't need to know. No one does, although Marilyn and Greta surmise.

I ran away again, having abandoned the resolution from Red Lodge Park. In the spring, after a year of staying put, I went to Lethbridge, for a legitimate reason, a Psychological Association meeting, and stayed an extra night: the usual. I brought the tent, the quilt, the foamie, and so on. After the meeting adjourned on a Friday at noon, I motored south to get closer to the Sweet Grass Hills. They are a vision: they appear like a monument, like a Stonehenge or ruins from a complicated time enveloped in the unknown. They are in Montana, but I decided crossing the border would be too much, so went east toward the point of entry, as it is called, Aden. The road is gravel, but there hadn't been a lot of rain, so nothing impassable. I had my usual feeling of being illegal, doing wrong. I drove and stopped by the side of the road. The hills are in fact called buttes, I had learned. I had brought binoculars and sat in the passenger side with the door open to look.

In May, the sun was already hot. Looking through binoculars can be transcendent. Everything was covered in grass, but drawn up close you can take your place among the stalks, imagine your roots in the cool old earth and your body waving sideways in the wind. I went further east, then north and over the Milk River and back west to the Writing-on-Stone Park. Too early by one week for camping, but I did pay for a day pass on the honour system and walked and stood on the Hoodoo Trail and watched the hills from there. I went into Milk River and ate at the Chinese restaurant and returned to the park and sat in my car feeling unsure.

No one ever tells you if you belong. That's what Lucy said, belong in a good way, that is. They'll tell you you belong behind bars or in a psych ward or in rehab or in a zoo, but not in the big herd, not in the larger tent.

And I didn't put up the tent. Other people appeared, because it was a warm Friday night, they looked at petroglyphs and stayed until sunset, past nine-thirty, but they were all gone by ten. They likely saw a woman alone in a car. I pulled the quilt from the backseat and returned to the Hoodoo Trail and sat and could still see the Sweet Grass Hills from my spot, a darkness against a brighter darkness. The moon came up, the half-moon, and at midnight I left. Lucy asked, "What are you doing home at this time?" It was about three. I said I had decided not to stay for the breakfast meeting. This seemed plausible, a crowd of psychologists eating toast and discussing the categories and rankings. I wondered if I smelled like limestone. Lucy went back to sleep and got up early with Roger, and I slept in.

Now it's a Friday evening, so warm, and only the sound of one lawnmower. Robert descends his shaky stairs and sits with us in the easement. He has purchased a free-standing basketball hoop, and it stands before the little perennial bed, now endangered by balls and feet. Later, or tomorrow, he and Roger will shoot hoops, as they call it, Robert holding Roger up to the net for his turns. For now, Roger is kicking the basketball up and down our patch of sidewalk, with King Two getting in the way. Robert has a girlfriend these days, Sonia, whom Lucy and I don't like, but Robert has that glossy finish, so he's happy. Asa and I still see one another at the gym. We walk around the track, and our arms occasionally touch, and still the sparks bounce off, but we won't likely go on any road trips, likely.

Lucy is more famous than ever. I wonder if she wishes for someone who might be more of a sexual acrobat. She used to go to the ninety-ninth percentile rank with her videos and play acts with Roger, the things she did to make him laugh, but she has toned it down to the eighty-ninth percentile rank, and Roger has not had any more seizures. Not that I blamed her any more than I blamed me. One of the optometrists recently invited us all over for dinner. Next Christmas we will go to Lexington and stay with Howard. Events seem more lined up these days, on the rails, in the Tupperware. While Mom was here, she mentioned that Constance Tandy had died two days before she left to come west. Her nephew had arrived from Toronto to sort through *her stuff*, as Mom said it, in phonological quotes. I wondered if my box of coins would be found stored away, intact from 1962, amid a cache of impulsive, regrettable thefts. Although the moment seemed to call for it, Mom did not mention kleptomania, and neither did I.

ACKNOWLEDGMENTS

Many thanks to Naomi Lewis for her supportive input, editorial expertise, and sense of humour. Thanks also to my friendly readers and their advice — Linda Brown, Janie Dale, Jim Ellis, and Mary Polito. Thanks to Eric Savoy for all the Easement Talk. And a huge thank you to Kelsey Attard, Colby Stolson, Natalie Olsen, and everyone at Freehand for giving *The Game of Giants* a home.

MARION DOUGLAS grew up on a farm in southern Ontario, close to a very small place called Lakelet and its lake. She moved west in 1981, settling in Calgary in 1986 and that is where she stayed. At first she thought Alberta was short on trees, but now she loves the landscape. Her children grew up and moved to Montreal and Vancouver so she has good reasons to shuttle around the country, especially now that she has a very lovable grandson. This is her fifth novel.